Mending Hearts

W. Million

Stomill Books

Little Falls Series
Reading Order

Book 1 – Rival Hearts

Book 2 – Mending Hearts

Additional content: First Date Challenge by Wendy Million (novella about Kai and Mckenna who appear in Book 3)

Book 3 – Healing Hearts

Book 4 – Guarded Hearts

All books in this series have bonus content. You can check for that here: https://wendymillion.com/bonus-content/

To anyone who's ever felt like "too much" — there's a Tyler out there who's ready to love you just the way you are

Chapter One

Mia

I couldn't remember the last time I had been this nervous. It might have been when I was fourteen and executives from Shooting Star Records knocked on Mom's door to offer me a recording contract. Or it might have been when I was nominated for a Grammy Award at sixteen. That was the year I knew, without a doubt, that my life was no longer my own. Picking out clothes, styling my hair, choosing my meals—it was all controlled, examined. Every time I turned around, my mother was hiring someone else to make life easier. Was it working? Neither of us were capable of slowing down enough to be sure.

From the rental car, I stared at the well-kept secondhand shop on the edge of Little Falls, NY, and bit down on the tip of my nail. The acrylics I'd gotten at fifteen forced me to stop biting them. Even now, five years later, I hadn't broken the habit of putting my nail between my teeth, desperate for the rip and tear. I was so used to someone else making decisions that coming to this store without being instructed to, felt like anarchy.

No one knew I was here.

Out of the corner of my eye, my bodyguard, Pasha, stared ahead, expressionless. I didn't think he spoke much English, which was why I plucked him from the pack. He also seemed to be the only one my mother didn't have under her thumb. Laura Malone could never know what I was about to do.

"You'll wait here?" I asked.

"Yes."

A small smile played at the edges of my lips despite my nerves. Some nights I stared at the ceiling of the tour bus as it rumbled through another city and practiced speaking like him. Trying out his thick Russian accent was an opportunity to slip into another skin, another life.

God, that tour bus. I was so done with that bus.

Tomorrow afternoon I had to be in the right city at the right time to meet Mom and the tour. Only three more months. It was my mantra. Three more months on that bus. I didn't want to think about all the commitments flooding my calendar beyond the last tour date. People beyond me planned my life eighteen months to two years in advance.

Whenever I felt frustrated or despondent, I tried to remember I was lucky. Lots of people wished for this kind of success. My right to complain was voided.

"You sure person here, Ms. Malone?" He raised one pale eyebrow and scanned the sidewalk outside the shop. "Not busy."

"It's a secondhand shop and a costume place. Other than Halloween parties and being poor, why would anyone go in there?" I rolled my eyes and threw open the passenger door before I talked myself out of this.

My best friend, Sarah, was the only person who knew my secret. As one of the judges on the talent show *Center Stage*, it was Sarah who suggested Grady Castillo as a songwriter for my album. He'd been a winning contestant who produced a single hit album and settled into anonymity writing songs for other people. At first, I was wary. Men who avoided the spotlight usually had things to hide; behaviors, interests, habits that made a twenty-year-old girl like me a prime target. That sort of man gave me a vicious lesson at the start of my career, one that still echoed.

Grady turned out to be the opposite—funny, smart, creative as hell, and genuinely enjoyed the songwriting process, even when I called him a thousand times to discuss changes or ideas. I liked him. So, when he slipped in the clause to our songwriting contract about performing at a benefit of his choosing, I hadn't given the request a second glance. My mother and agent thought a benefit concert was good PR. What could go wrong?

They underestimated my ability to turn something so altruistic and mundane into a catastrophe. It was fine, though. I was handling the screw-up. Or I would as soon as I remembered this guy's name.

His store was the last one in the shopping plaza butted up against a pizza place. If there'd been more than one secondhand shop in Little Falls, I might have been in trouble. We exchanged very few details in my hotel room, but at least this one stuck. A costume designer confined to a costume shop seemed a little sad. Who'd choose this life?

The bell above the door tinkled when I entered. I kept my sunglasses on even though it was January, and the sun was hidden behind a swath of clouds. My black winter coat was from last season and the most discreet one I owned. Odd to be here on my own. Normally, I was surrounded by people—handlers, dancers, fans, bodyguards. Shedding that insulation was more disorienting than I'd expected.

From the back of the store, a deep male voice called out, "I'll be right there. Just helping another customer."

In the middle of the store, I stopped and took in the scene, a surge of panic running through rampant. Did he say he was helping someone else?

Shit.

There were other people here? We'd sat outside the building for fifteen minutes. What sort of service was he providing to whoever was back there? My Chucks were silent on the linoleum floor while I rushed to one of the clothing racks. My clothes were casual, non-designer on purpose. This was a secret mission. With feigned interest, I rifled through the racks, not seeing any of the clothes as they went by.

The bell above the door rang again, and I glanced up, half-afraid it would be another patron. I'd lose my nerve soon. Why did I come?

Another customer. A plethora of silent curse words reverberated in my head.

The owner, and I knew he was the owner because he'd told me that night, headed for the cash register. God, why couldn't I remember his name? '*Hey, you*' wasn't going to cut it in this situation. He retrieved a package from underneath the register and passed it to the woman who was getting out her wallet. His gaze skimmed over me and the rest of the store, not taking me in as he rang in the purchase.

"If there's anything I can help you with, let me know," he called out, his tone somewhat dismissive.

I liked the timbre of his voice just as much as I had that night, deep and calming. The measured way he spoke had been appealing, as though he was used to dealing with complaints or conflict in a rational, reasonable way. His blond hair was tinged with red—not quite brown—and that fascinated me too. The shade was unusual, pretty, even.

A few months ago, he'd been in better shape. Not that his physical appearance mattered now. He'd been tall and fit, and his voice turned my insides to liquid. He'd been enough. Unlike so many people in my life, he let me take complete control, lead the way. Being with him had been a vacation from being Mia Malone, superstar singer.

An escape.

Now, I was trapped. But I understood where the exit was.

I focused on the clothes whizzing past while I flicked through them. *Anything you can help me with? Oh, you know. Just a small thing. No big deal, really.* Sweat pooled on my lower back. This coat was too thick for the warm store.

Maybe I didn't need to tell him. Sarah had insisted he never needed to know. I'd be keeping the secret from everyone else—why not him? This was the first decision I could remember making in isolation. Not informing him was wrong. Wasn't it?

The bells on the door rang again, and I glanced up. The woman was gone, but I couldn't make myself look at him. This conversation would be easier if I pretended to be who everyone thought I was, the popstar who breezed through life without a care. When you're Mia Malone, all the world's a stage, and I was the most important player. Being here, talking to him, was just another role.

Pretend. Pretend. Pretend this conversation doesn't matter.

I relaxed my shoulders and strolled over to the counter. He glanced up from whatever note he was making by the register. His brown eyes reminded me of cognac. That night they looked almost golden when they caught the light in the dressing room. Smooth voice, cognac eyes—everything about him screamed addiction.

His look was puzzled, and he grabbed a lollipop out of an open container on the desk. While he sized me up, clearly trying to place my face, he twirled the lollipop round and round. "Can I help you?"

Wouldn't it be nice if you could?

"No." A small smile danced at the edges of my lips. "I doubt it." It was apparent he hadn't managed to place my face. I was still wearing my sunglasses, and maybe that was the problem. Or maybe he slept with a lot of random women. We hadn't discussed our sexual conquests that night. Once he'd come to my hotel room, there'd been little talking. A few shots of alcohol. Quick and hot had been what I'd been after. I'd ended up with a lot more.

"Okay," he said, drawing out the word.

I pushed the sunglasses onto the top of my head, my long dark hair swirling around my shoulders. When it was loose, my hair was a shield, part of my armor. The hair and makeup crew always pulled it off my face so people could see my eyes. Fans liked my vibrant blue-green eyes, the windows to the soul. The only protection I was allowed was whatever I could build inside. When my gaze met his, recognition dawned on his face like the rising sun.

"Mia Malone." He grinned, but it didn't unfurl properly. There was no joy or happiness in his expression. "Didn't expect to see you."

The words *ever again* hung between them unsaid. My stomach rocked as though I was at sea.

A garbage can. Where was a garbage can?

It had become second nature to look for a place to throw up when the rocking sensation hit. But I could weather this. Take a deep breath. Let my stomach even out, stabilize.

"What are you doing here?" He tore the wrapper off the lollipop, scrunched it up, and tossed it toward a can beside the desk. It hit the edge and tipped in.

At least I knew where to run now when the rocking sensation became more violent. Sighing, I tugged the sunglasses off my head and dangled them from my fingers. My insides were rioting, but I knew from watching myself on TV countless times what was happening inside wouldn't show on my face. I was an excellent poker player.

"Have you been watching the news?" I asked.

"Uh, not really? Are you—is this about you?" He frowned and rubbed his brow.

"Yeah. And you, unfortunately."

His furrow deepened.

"Class action suit against a condom manufacturer. 'Cocksure Condoms Cocked Up.' Ring any bells?"

"Do you have shares in that company? Are some of the people from the class action suit here in Little Falls?" With a shrug, he chuckled.

I gave him a bored look, so unimpressed I'd have to spell out the problem for him. In the back of my mind, I had a glimmer of hope he might make the leap without having to be pushed off the cliff. He was about to get a massive shove.

Right now, I wished I knew his first name, wished that had been the one detail stuck in my brain. I would have hinted at the gravity to come. *Oh, well.*

"I'm pregnant."

And then another wave hit my stomach so hard, I wasn't sure my sea legs would take me to the garbage can fast enough. By some miracle, I stared down at the lollipop wrapper as I lost the little bit of lunch I'd managed to eat.

Chapter Two
Tyler

Her glossy dark hair fell around her like a curtain over the tin I used for garbage next to my desk. I was fairly certain my brain was five steps behind where it needed to be in this moment. *Mia was pregnant?*

Gently, I swept her hair back from her face, securing it at her nape in my fist while she dry heaved into the can. I tried to avert my gaze, pretty sure she didn't want witnesses to this. Was this morning sickness? Emily, my sister, had been violently ill when she first got pregnant with Amir. She lost weight, a lot of weight, during the early part of her pregnancy. If our father hadn't been a doctor, we might have panicked. Mia was already thin—bordering on too thin. Had she looked this gaunt a couple of months ago?

When she stood up, I released her hair, grabbed a box of tissues, and passed them to her.

"Pregnant?" My mind scrambled trying to process the confession.

She wiped her mouth and threw the tissue into the can. Her lips twisted as if she was annoyed, and she pressed her fingers into her forehead. Stooping low, she picked up her glasses from where she'd let them fall on the floor. "Yep. Pregnant. Don't worry. I'm not keeping it. I *can't* keep it."

"Oh." The weight of her words settled faster than the initial revelation. "Um…" I searched for the right way to phrase my question. Was it possible to ask without offending her? Probably not. If the baby wasn't mine, her trip here made no sense. But a child was too important to let assumptions lead the way.

"Yes, this baby is yours. Whatever you've read, whatever you've heard, I don't sleep with random men all the time."

The night of the Magic Men concert, she'd invited me back to her hotel after I stitched up her dress. I'd said yes because I was between relationships, because she was pretty, because my dad's funeral was the next day, and anything that took my mind off that was exactly what I'd needed.

Afterward, I'd avoided searching for any information on her, on grilling Grady, on figuring out whether I *shouldn't* have slept with her. Once a decision was made, there was no going back. Now, there were consequences, and I needed to face those head-on too.

"How old are you, exactly?" Inside, I cringed. My sisters, Emily and Maggie, would beat me with their shoes for this question. I should have asked it that night.

"You don't know how old I am?" Her eyebrows went up in an almost comical look of disbelief.

"Do you know how old *I* am?" I countered, crossing my arms.

Her gaze traveled from my feet to meet my eyes. I remembered I'd liked her eyes. They were a strange blue-green, and they changed like a mood ring depending on how close she got to climaxing.

Jesus. Why did I let my mind wander there?

"No. But I'm famous. You should know my age." She gave me an assessing gaze. "No crow's feet, no gray hair. There's like a ten-year window here. I don't know. Like, thirty?"

"Like thirty-five. Just had my birthday not long ago. I'm Grady's age." I cracked a smile.

"Oh, Lord." Mia ran a hand down her face. "Another couple years and you could be my dad."

"What?" All the blood drained from my face. My heart kicked once in my chest. *Please don't be underage.* I should have asked. Or searched it up, or something. *Fuck.* So fucking dumb. She was famous. I should know her age. With all of the makeup and self-confidence, she'd seemed much older than she looked now, standing here with a bare face and a green tinge to her face. "How old *are* you?"

"I'm going to be twenty-one in a couple months. Too young to be a mother, that's for sure." She waved a hand around her head. "Also, my life is a circus. I can't bring a kid into that."

Relief coursed through me. Young, but legal. I could live with that. "So, you're just here to tell me..." I cleared my throat, the words getting stuck there unexpectedly. "You're having an abortion?"

"I thought you should know." She shrugged and grabbed a lollipop from my tin, read the flavor, clutched her stomach, and put it back.

I couldn't imagine she needed me to pay for the procedure. This whole conversation was surreal. Mia Malone was in my store, telling me she was pregnant. In one breath, she made me a dad, and in the next, she yanked it away.

A dad.

My father, who'd died at the end of October from a brain aneurysm, rose to my mind. Sadness swept over me at the realization that my father would never meet my future children, and would never know my wife. I'd had that thought before, but it had never punctured my heart quite so deeply. My father would never know this child or any other.

"Anyway," Mia said, drawing me out of my head. "I wanted you to know."

"Did you want me to go with you?" I took a step around the desk toward her. My mind felt full, stuffed with cotton batting. Thoughts jumbled together. Mia was here, pregnant, the baby was mine. If I woke up right now drenched in sweat, all of this a terrible dream, I'd be less surprised.

She shook her head, the layers of dark hair swaying against her shoulders. "No. I'm...I booked an appointment with someone. I'm here for the night and then I'm gone again." Her gaze strayed from the surface of the desk to my face, and her blasé expression shifted for the briefest moment. "Maybe I shouldn't have told you. The trash can is there." She pointed in the direction of my can. "If you're going to be sick, too."

Did I look sick? Shocked was more like it. Definitely shocked and not entirely sure what I should do or say. "Do you have someone to go with you?" She shouldn't be alone. Too young to be a mother, probably too young to do this without support, too. "A best friend, a parent..." The color drained from her face.

"Lord, no. No one knows. *No one knows*." Her hand landed on my forearm. "No one can know."

"No one?" I remembered the entourage she brought to Little Falls in October for the benefit. Dancers, backup singers, bodyguards. A blond woman who must have been her manager had hovered in the dressing room, eyeing me with suspicion until it was clear I could really sew.

"I'm taking care of it. No one needs to know." She met my gaze with an unexpected intensity.

I searched her face, trying to read her even though it was impossible. We'd slept together, but we were strangers. What could I hope to see in her eyes, in her face, other than a mirror of my panic and uncertainty?

"You're sure?"

"You don't know what my life is like. There's no room in it for a baby. I can't let all those people down."

"Having a baby would let people down?"

She slid her glasses onto her face, shielding her eyes. I didn't like the distance that simple motion put between us.

"Having the baby. Not having the baby. I can't win." She averted her face. "I don't even remember your name."

"You knew how to find me, but you couldn't remember my name?"

"I knew you owned this place. You told me that night. At least that detail stuck." She shrugged and looked toward the exit.

I furrowed my brow. Should I be offended that she couldn't remember my name or impressed that she remembered I owned a secondhand shop? There were several ways she could have discovered my name. She knew Grady. They'd written songs together, and my sister was semi-famous ever since Grady had declared his undying love for her on stage. Mia was here, but she'd made no attempt to find out more information. I couldn't get my head wrapped around what was really going on. Pregnant, but what else? "Tyler. Sullivan."

"Sullivan. Right. Your sister is Maggie. Lord, my head is not in the right place." She pressed her fingers into her temples. "Tyler. Tyler Sullivan." My name rolled around on her tongue, as though she was testing it out. "I like it."

"Thanks?" I chuckled.

"You look like a Tyler. I should have known." A real smile blossomed on her face.

For a moment, I eyed her, relishing the slightly lopsided beauty of her grin. "Probably should have known, yeah."

She made a *tsking* sound and wagged her finger. "No slut shaming, Tyler. I could have been fourteen for all you knew."

The blood drained from my face for a second time. "That's not—that's not funny. I don't normally do that sort of thing." I huffed in frustration. "I'm not a one-night-stand kind of guy." In fact, she was only the second one I'd ever had. Relationships were my thing. I liked the permanence, the connection, the intimacy.

Mia puckered her lips and ran her hand through her hair, tossing it over to her other shoulder. "I wish I could say the same. I don't do many repeats. Anything more is too much work, and I have enough of that already. And the breakup, the public spectacle of it..." She looked around the store as though suddenly remembering where she was. "I should go."

At the realization she would walk out the door and I'd likely never see her again, I took a deep breath and tossed my lollipop in the garbage. I followed her to the door. "I don't think you should do this by yourself." I tried to search her face, to figure out if she was set on having an abortion or if she'd come here hoping for another outcome. We hardly knew each other. What other outcome was possible given the life she led and the one I had?

"I'm not telling my mother." Mia pushed her sunglasses up her nose and fluffed her hair. "Anyone else is a liability. This *can't* get out."

"What about your dad?"

"My sperm donor?" She laughed and shook her head. "Uh, no. He's not around."

Was she serious or making a joke? "Your mom used a donor?"

"Might as well have. He's a total deadbeat. I never see him unless he wants money. Telling him about this would be like asking him to blackmail me. That's not happening."

"I'll come with you." I grimaced and put my hand on the door before she could push it open. "Tell me where, and I'll be there."

Mia sighed and tipped her glasses down, so she was looking at me over the top. "You don't owe me anything. It was a mistake. Faulty condoms. Not even our fault. I can handle this."

With a frown, I grabbed the back of my neck. I didn't want to piss her off, but I didn't understand why she'd come. We had no relationship. She wasn't planning on keeping the baby. Even if the abortion came out years from now, I'd never have suspected I was the father. Something had motivated her to come. Loneliness? While her relationship with her mother might be a mystery to me, her relationship with her father was clear. One last idea came to me.

"What about a sibling?" I'd depend on Emily and Maggie for anything, would trust them with my deepest secrets, with my life.

"Nope. My mom was eighteen when she had me. She's still searching for Mr. Right. If there's a loser within five hundred miles, she's on him like a dog on a bone, and what an expensive habit that is. Even losers don't come cheap."

"I'll come with you. Seriously, Mia. Give me the place and time, and I'll be there. I really don't think you should do this alone."

With an impatient sigh, she swept the bulk of her glossy black hair around, so it perched on her shoulder and cascaded down her arm. My fingers itched to tuck some stray strands behind her ear. She acted so cool and collected, I wasn't sure she'd appreciate the contact. I couldn't decide which version was the real one: the Mia I met the night of the concert or the one standing in front of me.

Pushing her sunglasses back onto the top of her head, she met my gaze for the longest time. I could see the indecision she was trying to hide. She might not want me there, but it was obvious she needed someone. Perhaps, like the night we slept together, I'd be good enough.

"New York City. Tomorrow morning before I fly out to meet the tour bus. I have the first appointment at seven-thirty. I don't know the address." She held out her hand. "Give me your phone."

Out of my back pocket, I produced my phone and watched her punch in her contact details.

"You don't have the clinic information on your phone?"

Mia glanced up from typing in her information to give me a wry smile. "Too many people have access to my calendar. I can't do shit in private. I booked the appointment from my friend, Sarah's, assistant's phone."

If I didn't know better, I'd think Mia was imprisoned in her own life. She didn't seem to have control over very much. "Are you happy, Mia?"

"Sure. Why wouldn't I be?" She passed me my phone without meeting my eyes. "All this money. All this fame. Pretty clothes. Pretty boys. Pretty songs." A smirk rose to her lips. "I've got it all."

With my phone clasped in my hand, I examined her. She was a mystery. Out the window, a familiar vehicle pulled into the lot. Danai from Zen Yoga climbed out of her car and approached the door. We'd been dating for the last three weeks, and I was supposed to meet her young kids tonight. *Shit.* I'd forgotten all about her in the chaos of the last hour with Mia.

Mia slipped her sunglasses back onto her face and followed my gaze out the window. "You know her?"

"Yeah." I gave a curt nod. Tension radiated off me at a rate I knew would be noticeable. "You'll text me the information for tomorrow. I'm serious. I want to be there."

"Sure." Mia's gaze was glued to Danai as she approached the shop. "She doesn't look much like me. I guess you don't have a type."

I had a type. But not a physical one. The differences between Mia, pale and slight, and Danai, brown and athletic, meant little. Uncomplicated, down-to-earth women who enjoyed long-term, committed relationships were my type. Danai had proven to be drama-free so far, and she'd said on our first date she was looking for something meaningful, not casual. So far, we were a good fit.

While Mia watched Danai, I studied Mia's profile. Whatever else she might be, I was sure uncomplicated wasn't it.

"Will she recognize me?" Mia ripped her gaze from Danai to stare at me.

"I don't know." We'd never discussed musical tastes. I'd seen and heard the crowd

the night of the benefit concert. People loved Mia. She'd been a tiny dynamo on stage. Did Danai worship her too? Possible, though unlikely.

"I should go," she said, her voice rising in panic. "No one knows I'm here."

"She'd never say anything if I asked her not to."

"That's not how fame works." Mia laughed, but it was a bitter sound. "She'll tell a friend, or her mom, or some other random person. They'll tell someone else—friend, foe, whatever—and so on. Everyone sworn to secrecy, no one being secret. That's how fame works. That's how I get fucked over. So, no. I'm going. I'll text you."

She ducked out the door, her head down. Just before she slid into the car, our gazes locked as Danai rose on her toes and pressed a kiss to my lips. The frown on Mia's face made me feel like I was doing something wrong. Guilt pinched, but I brushed it aside and smiled at Danai as she slipped past me into the store. I had no reason to feel guilty.

Mia's car sped off out of the plaza, and I let the door click shut. Before turning to face Danai, I gathered my thoughts. I couldn't meet her kids tonight if I was going to keep that appointment with Mia tomorrow.

"I'm going to have to cancel tonight," I said when I turned around.

"Oh." Danai's expression was full of concern. "An emergency?"

"Yeah, family. I'm really sorry."

"No, no. You gotta take care of your family first. Your mom, or Maggie, or Emily?"

I wandered behind the store's counter, hoping something other than a lie would pop into my mind. I couldn't tell her about Mia for more reasons than Mia's privacy. Already, I was second-guessing going along with her plan without asking more questions.

Pregnant. With my child.

Of course, I'd been in enough long-term relationships to think about having kids. With at least one of those women, I would have been happy if she'd come to me pregnant from a birth control malfunction. But Mia being pregnant? So young, so different from the women I normally dated? This pregnancy didn't feel like a happy accident, but instead a dreadful consequence of thinking with my dick instead of my brain.

"Emily," I said when I realized she was still waiting for a response. "It's just a lot, you know, with Omar and now my dad." Inside, I cringed.

She'd kill me for using her to lie to Danai, especially when I refused to tell her why I lied. I couldn't have them meeting in passing and risk this conversation being replayed.

"I can't even imagine." She rubbed my shoulder. "We can do it another night. Don't even give it a second thought. I hadn't told my kids anyway."

I nodded, but couldn't meet her concerned gaze.

"I just stopped by to say 'hi' and to say I was looking forward to tonight." She laughed and checked her watch. "I have a class in half an hour. Maybe we can get together tomorrow night instead? The kids are with their dad."

"Yeah," I agreed. I wasn't sure how I'd feel tomorrow. Right now, my mind was *buffering* and *failed to load,* and I didn't expect to reboot in such a short period of time.

My phone buzzed in my hand; with a frown, I read Mia's message. Jesus. Already it was a fucking dramafest.

Don't come. You seem happy. I'll be fine. You're not getting the clinic info.

I shoved my phone into my back pocket, and my jaw clenched. Why didn't I ask what hotel she was staying at? If she was still in Little Falls, the list was pretty short. But if she was on her way to New York City, there was no way I'd find her.

"Everything okay?" Danai asked.

"I need to get going." I grabbed my coat off the rack behind the counter. "I'll walk you out."

"You look stressed. Bad news for Emily?"

I shook my head, unwilling to drag my sister further into this web of lies. "No, that was a message from a supplier. Bit frustrated with them at the moment." Understatement. There were few things I hated more than people deciding things for me. It was bad enough that Mia was having the abortion without discussing the choice in any detail. I'd been present at enough dinner conversations with my family as a kid to know it was her body and her decision. My father had been adamant and vocal about being pro-choice. But to cut me out of supporting her when she clearly needed someone? That wasn't going to fly.

We walked out together, and Danai kissed me before sliding into her compact car. I climbed into my truck and drummed my fingers on the steering wheel while Danai drove out of the plaza. There was only one person I knew who could help. I hoped I didn't screw this up.

I opened the glass door to Maggie's pharmacy. Some days, she had a crowd of people getting prescriptions or asking questions. Thankfully, I'd hit a quiet moment. She grinned from behind the high counter, her long auburn hair tucked behind her ears.

"What's up, big bro?" Maggie scribbled a note to herself and then stepped down from the high counter where she filled prescriptions to the cash counter closer to the front door.

"Grady's still in L.A., right?" I grabbed the tin of lollipops Maggie kept for the kids of Little Falls or our nephew, Amir. Ripping the plastic off, I popped one into my cheek and stared at her.

"What's going on? You only do that when you want a cigarette. And that only happens when you're stressed."

"Can Grady get in touch with Mia Malone and find out where she's staying tonight?" I swirled the lollipop around my mouth. I'd called the local hotels on my way to see Maggie. I'd tried the alias she'd given last time she'd been in town. No luck.

"Mia Malone?" Maggie frowned, her dark-brown eyes full of curiosity. "Why would you want to talk to her? I thought you were dating Danai?"

I controlled my spike of irritation. Wherever Mia was, she wasn't going to the clinic until tomorrow. There was no reason to get pissed off with Maggie, especially when I needed her help. "You know how this fame thing works, right? Secrets don't stay secret. Is Grady good at keeping his mouth shut? I know you can keep a secret."

"He understands how damaging gossip can be to a career, yeah. What's going on? Is something wrong with Mia?"

I took a deep breath. "She's pregnant. The baby's mine. She's getting an abortion tomorrow. I want to go with her, but she won't let me."

All the color drained from Maggie's face and then rushed back in a blaze of red. "You and Mia Malone? When? Oh, my God. You slept with her? Tyler, she's *really* young."

I held up a hand to stave off her tirade. Thankfully, her shoes were still on her feet, so she didn't intend to smack me for my behavior. Not that I didn't deserve it.

"And you didn't use protection? What if she has some kind of disease? Tyler!"

When she went to open her mouth again, I jumped in. "Cocksure Condoms fucked up. Faulty product. It wasn't—we weren't careless. It was the night of the benefit in October."

"Oh." Maggie stared at her laced hands, lost in thought for a moment. That night had been a big one for both of us. "A baby."

"Yeah." The word banged around my head, not landing anywhere logical.

"You're a dad."

"For the next," I checked my phone, "fifteen hours or so."

"Are you okay?"

"The hell if I know." I pulled the lollipop out of my mouth and stared at it before popping it back into my cheek. A cigarette would be so much better. But I promised Dad a few years ago that I was done smoking. No way I'd break my promise now. "She doesn't want to keep the baby. I can't blame her. We don't know each other. She's got an incredible career. It doesn't feel like something I can ask."

"Do you want to?"

"I don't know." I leaned against the counter and gazed out the big pharmacy windows to the street. "I'm thirty-five. I've always wanted to be a dad."

"You're at an age where having a baby makes sense for you. You've got stability, maturity, financial independence. You live in a town where you'd have a good support system."

"Yeah, if only I could." I mimed taking a baby from someone. "Here, Mia. Let me carry the baby for you."

"Sure. Just ask Mia to have the baby and give it to you to raise." She wagged her finger. "That was a dumb suggestion. Sorry. My brain goes to some weird places sometimes." From under the counter, she produced her phone.

I turned back to the windows and let Maggie's words turn in my brain. Even if Mia went for that suggestion, as crazy as it sounded, how would we keep something like a pregnancy a secret? And if we managed that feat, how would we keep a baby secret once he or she was born?

"Tyler? Did you hear me?" Maggie tapped me on the shoulder.

"Sorry." I made a whirling motion with my finger on the side of my head as I rotated to face her. "My brain is working overtime trying to sort out my feelings."

"Grady got her on the phone under some songwriting pretense." She handed over her phone with a text message on the screen. "Hotel name and alias."

The hotel was a famous chain down the street from my secondhand shop. I frowned. When I'd called, I'd used the wrong alias. At least she was close.

"Are you going to talk to her?" Maggie plucked her phone from my hand.

"Yeah, at some point tonight. I need to get my head straight first."

"Whatever you two decide," Maggie said, "it's a permanent decision. There's no going back from it. You'll be tied together through that child for the rest of your lives."

I nodded and pushed off the counter to an upright position. *Forever.* I took the lollipop out and leaned over Maggie's counter, dropping it into the trash.

"I hear you, Maggie. I hear you."

I wasn't sure if Mia would hear me out, but a plan was beginning to take shape.

Chapter Three
Mia

I bit into the greasiest cheeseburger I'd ever eaten and moaned. Meat. Meat tasted so good. And cheese. The meat and cheese together were heaven. The inventor of the cheeseburger was a genius. Pasha was a genius for bringing this glorious creation to the hotel. He merely raised his eyebrows at my request. Not a single accented syllable in protest or rebuke. Then he'd said he knew "best place," and he hadn't been lying.

Denying this pleasure for so long was insanity. I took another bite, chewing slowly, savoring the chargrilled taste. In the summer, barbequed burgers were one of my favorite smells. They reminded me of childhood, of normalcy, of being at a friend's house in a better neighborhood for a pool party. Of life before the knock on my mother's door. Why had I given up red meat?

My mother. The answer was always Laura Malone.

And the fucking dietician she hired when she thought I had an eating disorder. I hadn't been sick. Not really. Had I been developing *something*? Probably. Looking back, my relationship to food hadn't been right. But what teenager could take the constant, unrelenting scrutiny of their body and survive? I'd burst onto the music scene as a plump-faced fifteen-year-old. Ripe for trolls and internet memes and all kinds of other nasty shit. Thinking about those magazine covers made my stomach dip.

The criticism still happened, but the jokes were rarely about my weight. Instead, they critiqued a facial expression or a bad camera angle or, in the rare picture, some cellulite.

It became second nature to examine myself in the mirror or to ask my mother whether I looked like a fat girl in skinny girl's clothes. The proof of my plumpness was splashed across countless magazines, on the internet, on the TV, radio, everywhere. The attention had been so extra. Too much. So, I'd lost the only thing I could—the weight.

I polished off the last bite, wishing I'd asked him to bring two, when a knock sounded on the door. Pasha was the only person who knew I was here. At the door, I checked the peephole. Sure enough, it was him.

"Did you need something?" I kept the open door propped against my shoulder.

"Man from shop here see you." Pasha threw a thumb over his shoulder. "I tell him wait down hall."

Around his wide shoulder, I could make out Tyler's frame in the corridor. I'd used a good chunk of cash to rent out the whole floor. Not that Little Falls was a tourist hub in January, but I'd learned early and often I could never be too careful. One social media post could light a fuse, blow up my life.

I bit down on my acrylic nail and narrowed my eyes. How'd he know where I was staying? Had I told him earlier? I didn't think so. "What's he want?"

"Talk to you."

Hadn't the text message been enough? At the shop, the woman who kissed him was clearly a girlfriend. If he cheated on her, I'd officially inherited my mother's poor taste in men.

From down the hall, Tyler held up a paper bag. I frowned. "What's he got?"

"Cheeseburger."

"For me?" I turned in surprise toward Pasha.

"Yes. Same place. Same burger. Can't have just one."

"All right. I'll talk to him." I grinned.

Pasha waved him over, and as soon as Tyler got close enough, I snatched the paper bag from his hand and ushered him into my corner suite. I opened the bag and breathed deeply.

"Huh. He wasn't lying." Tyler leaned against the wall after he'd closed the door.

"Who? About what?"

"Your man out there said I needed to get you a cheeseburger as a peace offering."

With a frown, I unwrapped the burger and took a bite. All my worries melted away, and I closed my eyes with a soft moan. "Red meat is my sin and salvation. Do you think I can turn that into a song?" I hummed a little tune as I took another bite. "What else could be my sin and salvation? I don't think anyone will buy a song about a burger." I turned it around in my hands, taking another bite. It was a pretty fucking amazing burger.

"I'm not sure I've ever seen anyone that happy for a cheeseburger. Though, I gotta admit, the burgers from that place are better than any of the others."

"I haven't eaten red meat in five years. Five years." I splayed out the fingers of one hand for emphasis.

"Got a craving?"

I cocked my head and thought about it. That was possible. Could the baby be the one who liked cheeseburgers this much? "Control freak for a mother. Gotta eat them while I can."

He continued to stand by the wall while I polished off the second burger. I patted my belly and threw the wrapper in the garbage. Across the king-size bed, along the bar area, across the other furniture, and on the desk, I had clothes spread out, trying to decide what to wear tomorrow. Thinking about the procedure made my brain hurt, made me wish I'd never met the man on the other side of the room, never found his voice soothing, his cognac eyes addictive. If not him, the father would have been someone else. At least he hadn't been an asshole when I'd told him. With faulty condoms, I was lucky I hadn't become pregnant sooner with someone worse.

"Why are you here? I told you I don't need your help."

"I know." He pushed off the wall and pulled out the desk chair, moving a small pile of clothes. His gaze traveled around.

I wondered if he was a neat person. The store had been well-organized and clean. Didn't mean *he* did that.

"So, why are you here?" I asked.

From his pocket, he pulled out a lollipop. Between his fingers, he twirled it, lost in thought before yanking off the wrapper and sticking it in his mouth.

"And what's with the lollipops?" He sucked on one the night of the benefit while he sewed my outfit back together. I'd assumed it was something they were handing out backstage, not a frequent occurrence.

He twisted the stick in his fingers. "I used to smoke. A lot."

"And now you eat lollipops like they're meals."

"I rarely finish one." With a shrug, he took it out of his mouth and dropped it into the bin under the table. "Helps me focus."

A smile played at the edges of my lips. I'd seen a lot of weird habits in the music industry, but a fixation with lollipops was a new one. If he'd been smoking at the benefit, I never would have gone near him. The stench of cigarettes stuck to everything, including someone's breath, lingered deep in their throat. Kissing a smoker was like licking an ashtray. Gross.

"I'm going to preface this by saying that if you reject my idea, I'm still coming with you tomorrow. I won't be an asshole about it."

"I can't raise this baby." I narrowed my eyes.

"You wouldn't have to." Tyler rose when I opened my mouth to speak. "Hear me out."

I closed my mouth and crossed my arms. Where was he going with this?

"I've been thinking about this since you came to my shop this morning. I would never have chosen to be a dad like this. It's not how I thought my life would go. But the baby is here, and if you'd consider it, I'd like a chance to raise him or her."

"I—"

"Alone."

I laughed, incredulous. "What? Honestly, how does that work? People would know, Tyler. People would know I was pregnant. I'll get fat, if nothing else. Whether it's the right thing or the wrong thing, the media, my fans, everyone would judge the shit out of me. They already annihilate me when I wear an outfit that makes me *look* fat. Abandoning my kid? Having an abortion? Either of those is career suicide. None of this can get out." These ideas had consumed my thoughts for the last few weeks, so much so I'd flubbed a few of my songs on stage. Mom had suggested that eighteen months of touring might have been a mistake. But I didn't want to cancel shows because that would set off an even bigger shit storm. "I still have three months left of my tour."

"It's your first baby, so you might not show right away. I did some research on the internet, and—"

"Oh, some internet research? That's *amazing*. Did you buy a degree while you were there? Cause I hear they're worth—oh—I don't know—absolutely nothing." I threw up my hands and leaned forward. "No, Tyler. I'm not having this fucking baby and giving it to you. No."

Both of his hands ran down his face which was pinched with frustration. I tensed, ready for a battle. An argument was brewing.

He clenched his jaw and gave a curt nod. "Okay. I had to ask."

"That's it?" I stared. I'd been geared up for a fight. Why wasn't he fighting? I wanted to fight. "That's all you've got?"

"You said no. I respect that. I understand it. I don't like it. I wish you'd change your mind or even consider what I've said. But I didn't come here to piss you off." He wandered closer. His gaze trailed over me, thoughtful rather than angry. "I thought maybe there was a chance you wanted to keep the baby, but didn't know how. I thought maybe that's why you told me."

I reared back and turned away. Had that been why I'd come? My mind spun, caught up in the notion he was right. Not telling him would have been the logical choice. Without meeting his gaze, I said, "How would it work? No one could know. I don't see how we could keep it a secret."

"I can't promise you we can. But I can promise I'll never ask for anything else from you. Not money. Not time. Nothing."

"On the tour alone, not thinking about anything else, too many people would find out."

"How?"

"Well," I said, thinking through the logistics. "For starters, when I put on weight, all my outfits will need to be changed or altered. Wardrobe will know. My managers would know. Then my mom would find out."

His head bent, focused on his long, lean fingers as they tapped the edge of the oversized desk. "I know how to make and alter clothes. It's what I do. It's what I went to college to do."

"And you live in Little Falls."

Tyler chuckled and our gazes met. "And I have a passport."

"You want to join the tour?"

"Want is a strong word. *Willing* would be a more accurate one. I want to raise our baby. I'm willing to do whatever needs to be done to make it happen."

I sank onto the king-size bed and put my head in my hands. "Tyler, this is insanity. Literally the dumbest idea on the face of the planet." He could solve the clothing problem. So, what? It was one of about five thousand issues. "You have a girlfriend." When I glanced up, I saw him swallow. "I saw you with her. She looked happy. You're probably happy. This would—I mean—you'd have to tell her."

He pulled another lollipop out of his jacket pocket and twirled it around. "We've only been dating a few weeks. It's not serious. We'll break up. I won't tell her. I'll have to tell my family, but they can keep a real secret. I know what you think. But quite genuinely, they won't tell anyone."

My mind churned worse than when I first discovered I was pregnant. There'd been no question what I needed to do. What I *had* to do. How could I keep the baby? Was Tyler's idea possible or was I fooling myself? "I'm like two-and-a-half months pregnant right now. At the end of my tour, I'll be five months pregnant. Almost six months!"

"What are you supposed to do when the tour is done?"

"No idea. I haven't asked. I can't think about it, or I'll go insane." I looked at him, weary over the thought of what else was probably booked—talk shows, social media events, private concerts, and who knew what else. There were no brakes on the money train, just me, sliding along the rails.

"Name a reason you'd scale back, cancel everything."

"Death. Death would be the only reason."

"I'm being serious."

"Me too. I don't cancel. I don't check into the hospital for exhaustion. I'm on so many immune boosters I rarely get sick. I'm the product. I'm the brand. I can't afford to go down." I shook my head. "I can't do it. I just...I can't. It wouldn't work. I'd never get these years back."

Tyler didn't say anything. He eased down on the bed beside me and passed me a lollipop.

I read the label. "You have the weirdest flavors. Blueberry jasmine?"

"It's calming."

With a laugh, I eyed him. "Do you really think it's possible to hide this baby? Really?"

"I'm not going to lie to you. It'd be easier if I said 'yes, it's possible.' Easy, even. You're half-convinced, aren't you? One big lie from me and I think you're all in." His gaze met mine, and I was reminded again how pretty his eyes were up close. A little piece of me thought I could get used to this view, these eyes, this man.

"Lie to me."

He chuckled and broke our eye contact to stare down at the lollipop he twirled between his fingers. "It'll be easy. We'll lie to everyone else, but never to each other."

"Could that be true?" My voice was hushed, wistful in the quiet of the hotel room.

"Say 'yes,' and we'll make it true."

Tears filled my eyes as I searched his face. He had a nice face, so open and sure of himself. I could see why he had a girlfriend now, why I'd been so drawn to him the night of the concert. There was so much kindness, and it had been so long since a man I wasn't paying had made me feel important, like my ideas and opinions were important.

"What if I say no?"

"I won't think any less of you. The risks for you, your career—I get it. I'll do whatever I can to protect you. But I might not be able to. I can't guarantee anything." His lips quirked up in an almost smile. "But I'll do my best."

I shifted my gaze to the ceiling and focused on the decorative swirls above. Did I want an abortion? No. But I didn't want to be pregnant either, wasn't sure I could handle the storm that would roll in if my mother found out, if the press got hold of the secret. Either way, I would carry this decision for the rest of my life. Another truth I'd bury. But which secret did I want to keep?

"You'll raise the baby?"

"I will."

"And if I don't want to be involved? 'Cause right now I don't. I can't. It's not in me to be a mom."

"I'll understand."

"What if I do? What if I change my mind and I do?"

He held my gaze for a beat. "I'd never cut you out. Never. No matter what."

I searched his face, trying to decide how honest he was. In his hands, I'd be putting my career, my life. The lives and careers of so many people who worked for me would be balanced there too. In my gut, I realized either decision would divide my fan base, probably outright destroy most of it. My career would be in shambles. Could I trust him? Sincerity was written across his face. He meant it—at least in this moment, he meant it. His conviction would have to be enough.

He was close to his family, Grady approved of him, and kindness oozed out of him. If I'd had to pick someone for this baby to live with, I couldn't have done any better on such short notice. All of those things made him better than the woman who raised me.

Taking a deep breath, I tapped my lollipop to his. Yanking off the wrapper, I popped it into my mouth. "I guess we're doing this, then. I don't know what the hell will happen," I gave him a sideways glance, "but we're in it together."

Chapter Four
Tyler

A surge of triumph followed by barely disguised panic welled up. I was going to be a dad. For better or worse, I just agreed to become a single parent in seven short months. I also agreed to tour around the world with Mia for three months, altering her outfits and helping her conceal our baby.

Jesus.

It was an idiotic plan. The worst plan.

I couldn't pull this off. How could I pull off this insanity?

What was I going to do about my store? Would I tell my family right away? Maggie already knew. I rubbed my face.

"Oh, for God's sake. Are you already having regrets?" Mia popped the lollipop out of her mouth and pointed it at me. "You talked me into this."

I wanted to say I never really expected her to say yes, but then she'd probably keep the appointment in the morning. Beyond all reason, I'd talked myself into wanting this baby, into thinking it was some sort of sign from Dad that it was time to invest in another person more than I had in a long time—more than I ever had before. I was going to put everything I had into this baby, into Mia.

"No. No." I met her gaze. "I need to go so I can prepare to come with you."

"You can't go anywhere until we've got an actual plan. We need ground rules and shit." Mia flopped back onto the bed.

"Ground rules?"

"You have a girlfriend."

"You keep coming back to that."

"It's a big deal."

"Yeah, if I'd been dating her longer than a couple weeks. I wasn't with her when I slept with you, if that's what you're worried about."

She eyed me for a moment, lips pursed.

I took in the skepticism on her face. Interesting. She thought I cheated on my girlfriend. Maybe she still thought that. She wasn't giving me much credit. Not a great starting place.

"Okay, but you and I aren't together. We're not going to be together. I don't do relationships. They're too much work."

"Yeah, I heard you the first time you said that."

We sat in silence for a few minutes. I didn't know where to start with building the lies. Cover stories. We would need those.

"My mother is going to be very suspicious that I've hired you. I never hire anyone."

"So, what are we telling her?"

"You know Sarah Telling?"

"The singer? Doesn't she judge *Center Stage*?"

"Yep. I'll tell my mom you worked with Sarah, and she recommended you."

I wanted to ask who I'd replace, but knew that wouldn't make my job easier. Better to pretend the position was new, that someone wouldn't be fired. "Three months on the road should be fine. We gotta figure out how to get you the time off from everything else once that's done."

"Have you ever toured before? Musicians? Theater? Anything?" Mia sat up, the lollipop still lodged in her cheek.

"Once. It didn't work out." I had no desire to get into that story.

"That's it? Why didn't you ever do something with your costume design degree?"

"I *am* doing something with it." I rubbed my cheeks. Frustration stirred. "Local theater. My shop."

"Don't you want more?" Doubt clouded her expression. "Didn't you go to school thinking you'd do more? I mean, you only live a few hours from New York City."

"Just an FYI, but these are the kinds of questions relationships are built on. Exchanges of personal information. You know, in case you wanted to avoid that." Mostly, I wanted to avoid talking about the choices that had led me back to Little Falls and to owning the shop. I didn't regret it anymore, but she was right. The life I was leading hadn't been the one I dreamed about when I went to college, when I graduated.

"Hmm." Curiosity coated her. Would she push? I didn't know her well enough yet.

"We need your schedule cleared long enough for you to have the baby and recover. Ideas? I don't know your life, so they all have to come from you."

She flopped down again. "Can I call Grady?"

"Grady?"

"Yeah. You told your sister, right? That's how you found out I was here. Grady will know. She'll have told him."

"Maggie is good at keeping secrets."

"He'll know." She sighed. "Can I call him or not? I trust his opinion, and he knows my life. He gets it."

If we were together, her comment would have stung. I liked being the one who got it, the one who understood. "Whatever it takes to figure this out."

Mia grabbed her phone from the nightstand and disappeared before I could think to ask why she was leaving the room to call Grady. I unwrapped the lollipop in my hand and stuck it into my cheek. Taking out my phone, I made a list of all the people I had to contact. As the list grew, I stared out the window. What excuse would I use? Little Falls stretched out through the top floor window. I'd grown up here, but I'd never expected to live here forever.

Seven months.

Seven months and I'd be a dad.

My phone buzzed. A text from Danai about making plans for tomorrow night. I didn't even know what city I'd be in. Not Little Falls, that was for sure.

Just then, the lock beeped on the door, and Mia stormed back in. "Grady is a genius. I swear to God, if he wasn't so desperately in love with your sister—" She stopped when she caught the look on my face.

Seven months of this.

With a sigh, I said, "What'd Grady tell you?"

"He knew about the baby. He tried to pretend he didn't, but he knew."

"And?" It took a lot for my temper to bubble over, but I didn't want another lecture about how people couldn't be trusted. Grady and Maggie might not be married, but given the way they looked at each other, they were in it for the long-term. They were family.

"And nothing." She gave me a wary look and tapped the keycard on the top of the desk. "I just thought I should mention that he knew."

"What'd he tell you?"

"I should let my tiredness show. Which isn't hard, because I'm fucking exhausted. All the time. He also gave me the only excuse my mom might believe for canceling stuff after the tour. Time off to write. I haven't written in forever. I miss it. It's a good excuse. She'll buy it. She knows how much I used to love writing."

"Have you been to a doctor?"

"No." A flush rose to her cheeks. "I just took fifty-six pregnancy tests when I was at Sarah's place for the night."

"Fifty-six?"

"Yeah, well, maybe not that many, but a lot. I couldn't fucking believe it." She rubbed her forehead. "My regular doctor is friends with my mom. I couldn't go to her."

"I know someone. My dad used to be a doctor in Little Falls. One of his friends scaled back his practice. I can probably talk him into helping us out." I snuffed out the pang of longing that always accompanied any mention of my father.

"Sure, let's bring more people into this." Her fingers pressed into her forehead in a circular motion.

"He's a family friend."

"You have all this faith in people. I've got none and about a thousand awful stories. What have you got?"

"A desire to make this work." My voice was tighter than I wanted. She probably did have a thousand stories of betrayal. But it didn't mean everyone I knew was suddenly going to turn evil. "We have to trust some people. Picking them carefully is all we've got. Okay? I trust David Rigilotto. He was my dad's best friend. There won't be a leak from him."

Mia shook her head, but didn't contradict me. It was possible we'd never see eye-to-eye about this. Did I have too much faith? I'd never had a secret this big with consequences this widespread.

"What time are we leaving tomorrow?"

"You can't come with me."

"Mia." I stared at her.

She examined her nails and avoided looking at me. "I need a couple days to fire Bonita and then pretend Sarah suggested you. My mom, Laura, will probably be the one to call you. She loves Sarah, so her word should be good enough."

"If I can arrange it, do you have time to see David before you leave? Make sure everything is okay?"

Her jaw tightened. "I guess I do since my other doctor's appointment will be canceled." With a sigh, she met my gaze, shoulders slumped. "Can you leave?"

"Yeah." I picked up my phone from beside me on the bed. "Are you okay?"

"No." She laughed. "I hate that I'm in this situation. That being careful still fucked me over. I'm just so angry and sad and frustrated and so, so tired."

I watched her for a minute, torn between respecting her wishes and trying to help her navigate all those feelings I was struggling to grasp, too. Not that I'd admit any of that to her. I'd asked for her to take this path, and it was up to me to carry all three of us if I had to. "I can stay."

"That's not going to help. I kinda never want to see you again." She ran a frustrated hand through her hair, piling it over one shoulder. "Instead, I've agreed to be tied to you forever. One stupid decision after another."

On my way to the door, I took a lollipop out of my pocket and slid it onto the dresser. "I'll just leave this here in case you need a reminder."

"A reminder of what?"

"That I'm here. That I give a shit. That you're not in this alone."

Her features softened, and she flipped her hair around again. "What flavor?"

"Lemon ginger, which my degree assures me is good for morning sickness. Stumbled across a doctor's degree on the internet while I was researching. Surprisingly easy to get that MD certificate. I don't know why it takes other people so long."

She laughed and crossed her arms. "I'll let you know tomorrow if your degree is legit."

"Has to be. The internet doesn't lie." We grinned at each other for a beat before Mia broke eye contact.

"Text me when you know what's happening with Doctor David. The guy who didn't get his degree off the internet."

"I will." I opened the door and glanced over my shoulder. She looked so tiny standing in the middle of the oversized room. A surge of protectiveness rushed through me. She and the baby growing inside of her were my priorities now. I would do everything I could to keep them safe. "Get some sleep."

Chapter Five
Mia

I sat in the car at the back entrance to the hospital. At just after six in the morning, I rubbed my eyes and wished I'd slept worth a shit last night. At one point, I considered fleeing Little Falls and heading to New York City to make my appointment. Keeping this baby wasn't the right choice, and I knew that, had known it from the minute I found out I was pregnant. But the idea of doing what needed to be done to no longer be pregnant caused a surge of panic. I couldn't do that either.

Pasha glanced my way but said nothing, his hands flexing on the steering wheel.

"I know," I said. "I need to go in."

"I go too." Pasha unlocked the doors and popped his open.

"I'm putting a lot of trust in you." I slid my gaze to him, not in any rush to get out of the car.

He nodded, his hand on the door handle. "And him."

"And him," I whispered, and I slid the tip of my fingernail between my teeth. "Am I being dumb?"

Pasha scrunched up his face and shook his head. A string of Russian words left his mouth in a blur that meant nothing.

"Just a sec," I said, searching my phone for a translation app. Once it was downloaded, I turned on the record function and made a reeling motion to Pasha. "Say it again."

The briefest smile touched his square-jawed face. A stream of Russian came again, and I recognized a few of the words from the last time he spoke. When I hit the button on the app to have it translated, my stomach dropped to my feet.

"How do you know I'm pregnant?" I stared at my phone and then looked at him.

He made a puking gesture and then pointed to the hospital entrance. Oh, Lord. He added those two things together, and he came up with the right answer. Who else would get there? I had to be careful for the next three months.

"From now on, you only speak to me in Russian, okay?" I stared at him, trying to convey how serious this was. "And you never, ever again say the word baby around me. Okay? Deliveries or packages or something, but the B word doesn't exist."

"I tell no one. Big secret. I understand."

"The *biggest* secret. There's no way you can understand. No one understands. If this gets out, my life is over. My mother will murder me."

"No murder. No baby." He nodded and focused on his hands in his lap.

I threw open my door, his words echoing in my head. His exact meaning wasn't clear, but I didn't want to get into it. I'd made my choice. My skin prickled at the number of people who already knew I was pregnant. A disaster waiting to happen.

I texted Tyler as we climbed the flights of stairs to the fifth floor. Pasha followed, his footsteps echoing in the stairwell. When I pushed open the door to the right floor, Tyler was pacing on the other side.

Our gazes connected, and then his light-brown eyes swept over my face. I could tell by the way his body relaxed that he'd started to wonder whether I would turn up.

Part of me didn't want to go through with this appointment any more than I wanted to go through with the one in New York. The sheer number of pregnancy tests I took had to be enough.

"I don't want to do this," I whispered, eyes pleading.

With only the briefest hesitation, Tyler gathered me into his chest, his arms circling around me. His biceps toned and firm, flexed, holding me close at just the right intensity. My mother claimed there was a sweet spot with hugs, a right number. I never hit it. There were always too many. Fan after fan after fan. Or too few. Days and nights on the bus. Sometimes, like right now, I wondered if it wasn't a number, but a feeling that a hug could give, when I could sink into it, let my worries melt into someone else.

"You change your mind?"

When his breath drifted down, a warped version of jasmine lingered. How many lollipops had he chain sucked this morning? Oddly comforting to realize he was also nervous, unsure. "Every five minutes."

"I'm not going to keep talking you into having the baby. If you've changed your mind, now is the time to say it. We'll figure something else out."

"Do you want me to change my mind?" My cheek was pressed to his chest and I could hear the boom of his heart through his shirt. The elevated staccato made me feel safe.

"No."

"You smell like lollipops." I pulled back and glanced up.

"I've got addiction issues." His eyes lit with a hint of amusement. "I swear it's just to half-eating lollipops."

"But it means you're not sure."

His expression turned serious. "No, it means I'm nervous, too. We didn't plan this. We're in the middle of planning this. Our lives are going to change forever. It would be weird if I wasn't nervous."

I ran my hand through my midnight hair, pulling it down my shoulder and along my arm so I could play with the ends. "Okay. Let's go see what Doctor David has to say."

He laced his fingers with mine, and I knew I should pull away, keep my distance. But having Pasha trailing behind us toward the examination room wasn't enough to make me feel safe. Physical safety wasn't the kind I was craving, but it was the type I'd gotten used to needing when this hint of panic flickered. When I glanced up at Tyler, he was looking down.

"Want me to lie to you?"

"Yes." A quasi smile touched my lips.

"Everything's going to be fine. We've got nothing to worry about."

Just before we entered the examination room, Tyler dropped my hand. I laced my fingers together in front, already missing the contact, the support. If I asked, would he take my hand again? Did I want that?

No. No. I couldn't want that. This baby was a contract between us, an agreement.

Doctor David had a jolly round face and a wide frame. He hugged Tyler and then stuck out his hand to me. "Tyler tells me you're expecting. Congratulations."

"It's uh—I mean—we're keeping this *very* private." I gave him a tight smile.

"Don't worry. I won't say a word. We'll need a nurse, but I have absolute faith in the one I asked. I was surprised when Tyler said you'd agreed to be his surrogate, but he has always loved kids, even as a kid. He was always offering to hold babies, doting on his younger sisters."

I cocked my head at Tyler but didn't contradict the doctor's version of events. "Yeah, surrogacy. Who knew? Such a rewarding experience for both of us." I batted my eyes at Tyler in mock sweetness.

He ran a hand through his hair and shot me a warning glance. I wasn't going to mess up his cover story, but I wished he mentioned it in the hallway.

We should be marking this occasion with something, a toast maybe. To the first lie. A shitty surrogacy lie is how we started.

"I'm surprised your regular doctor wouldn't have continued your care," David said as he gestured to get onto the examination table.

I used the stool to slide over the crunchy papered surface. "A few information leaks were traced back to her." I gave Dr. David a pointed look. "That's unacceptable."

Tyler's shoulders relaxed, and he winked. A ghost of a smile threatened, and I was tempted to roll my eyes. Who'd believe that a famous popstar was opting to be a surrogate? And yet, I guess, it wasn't too terribly far from the truth of our arrangement.

"I'll just grab my nurse to draw some blood. If you can fill out this form while I'm gone so we can get a sense of timing, that would be great." When I tensed, David patted my hand. "Don't worry. The nurse is my daughter. There won't be any problems there."

Why did everyone in this town believe everyone else was trustworthy? In my experience, family was the least trustworthy of all. Across the room, Tyler straightened at the mention of David's daughter. As soon as the doctor was out of the room to fetch his nurse-daughter, I narrowed my eyes at his change in demeanor.

"If she's not trustworthy, we're outta here. I'm not having this fall apart before we even start."

He shook his head but pulled a lollipop out of his pocket, twirling it between his fingers. I was starting to realize that motion was as much a nervous habit as sticking the lollipop in his mouth was a substitute for smoking. "You can trust her."

"Then why'd you get all weird?"

"It's a small town. People know each other."

"That's bullshit. What happened to the guy who sat beside me yesterday and said we'd lie to everyone else but never to each other?" I raised my eyebrows in challenge.

"We dated in high school. Satisfied?" He flushed.

A swell of something I couldn't quite pinpoint ran through me. Envy? Jealousy? I took out my phone to check dates and scribbled the answers to the questionnaire about my last period and all the other relevant health details. Anything to avoid analyzing whatever feeling had zipped through. He was roughly fourteen years older. Of course he had a history, and probably most of it existed in this town.

When I finished, I leaned back on my hands and let my gaze roam over him. There was definitely something about him that drew me in, even now when I should be angry that he hadn't given the truth right away. Honesty was going to be vital between us, at least on his part. I needed to know what was coming and how to navigate it. "I'm intrigued." What sort of woman had Tyler been attracted to in high school? "You only dated in high school?"

"College, too."

"So, long term."

His left shoulder rose and fell. With a chuckle, he wandered closer, his hands shoved into the pockets of his trendy jeans. The clothing he wore was another thing that threw me off when I first met him. He didn't dress like a thirty-something man with no sense of style.

"News flash for you, Mia. All my ex-girlfriends were long-term."

I frowned. How did that fit? Long-term relationships everywhere, no wife anywhere. He'd said he'd only been dating the other woman for a few weeks. "I don't get it."

The door popped open, and Doctor David strolled in with a petite brunette woman behind him. Unlike Tyler, she looked like she was in her thirties. I wasn't sure if I'd gotten used to seeing women with too many face fillers, but the lines at the edges of her eyes were oddly satisfying. Someday, I wanted to be like that—let the cracks show through, not give a shit if I looked my age. My mother hated any sign of aging, and her constant criticism of what she saw in the mirror drove me insane. Despite the lines, this nurse was pretty, but she only had eyes for Tyler.

When he didn't greet her or return her longing gaze, I cocked my head and stuck out my hand. "Mia. And you are?"

"Katie," she said, shaking my hand with the briefest motion. "I'll just grab some blood for the lab."

While Katie's head was bent over my arm, I examined her, trying to figure out what it was about this woman that made Tyler so uncomfortable, made the air thick with tension that the good doctor seemed oblivious to but was written all over them both. He was more relaxed about his current girlfriend meeting me than this encounter. My curiosity lit. A smile tugged at the edges of my lips, and when I looked up from the blood being drawn, Tyler's gaze was intent on me, ignoring Katie's presence completely. *What?* I mouthed to him, but he shook his head in response.

Katie withdrew the needle and disposed of it. The vial of blood was clutched in her gloved hand. "I'll let the doctor know as soon as we have the results. It won't take long."

"Is it a family affair? Your mom the one in the lab?" My lips twitched in amusement.

"No." Katie's cheeks turned pink. "It's—it's very confidential. The laws for the lab are very strict."

At least someone seemed to understand the gravity of the situation. This weird tension between Katie and Tyler was pricking at my sixth sense for gossip. People with grudges or wounds weren't good secret keepers. I'd moved out of my old neighborhood a couple years ago, but every Tom, Dick, and Harry had tried to sell a story before I left. No loyalty in those people to either me or my mother. Whenever one of the trashy tabloids ran a story, I rarely even remembered the person with the tall tale. None of my neighbors had much money. I knew *why* they did it, but it didn't stop me from experiencing a range of feelings from annoyance to outright anger at whoever was spinning lies and half-truths.

When David brought the ultrasound machine close to the bedside and had me lie back, he gestured for Tyler to come closer. I adjusted my clothes and closed my eyes, the gel cold against my skin. This was the part I dreaded.

When the *thump thump* of the baby's heartbeat filled the room, I squeezed my eyes closed and tried to block it out. Two large hands sandwiched one of mine, and I opened my eyes to see Tyler, his gaze intent on the screen, a look of awe on his face.

"We can't know the sex yet, right?" he said.

"No. Around twenty weeks, if we can get a good picture, we'll be able to figure out the sex." Dr. David glanced down, and I tried to ignore him, kept focused on Tyler. "You're doing a good thing."

Tyler tore his gaze from the monitor to peer down at me too. His face softened at the look of panic that must be evident. I felt the emotion rising, threatening to push me off the exam table and out the door. He leaned down so our foreheads were almost touching. In a voice barely above a whisper, he said, "To everyone else, never to each other." Then he pulled back far enough for our gazes to connect, and his thumb brushed my cheek. "I'll protect you with everything I've got."

All the tension flowed out as we maintained eye contact, and through all Dr. David's notes on due date, nutrition, next appointments, and everything else I now had to consider, Tyler held my hand and nodded along. When Katie came back with the test results, Tyler's frame tightened, but he kept my hand in his, as though he knew the contact kept me stable.

I didn't know how I was going to face my mother knowing what I knew and not crack or bend, or in some way, offer the truth. But if I told her now, while there was still time for a different outcome, I'd break my promise to Tyler. And to the baby. After hearing the heartbeat, I couldn't deny someone else was living inside of me now. For me, there was no going back.

At the rear entrance to the hospital, I stood outside the car facing Tyler while Pasha waited patiently behind the wheel as the engine hummed. "Two days," I said. "Will that be enough?"

"If you told me I needed to come with you today, I'd make it work. Two days is fine. If anything happens and you need me earlier, or if you're having second thoughts or anything, call me. Doesn't matter what time. Don't even look at the time. Just call."

I slid into the car, and Tyler shut my door. As we pulled out of the parking lot, he waved, and I waved back, feeling like he held a piece of me, one too important to leave behind. Already, I needed him. Panic swirled in my stomach, and I shook my head at the ridiculous thought. I needed his help; I didn't need *him*.

Laura Malone was on a rampage. The venue organizers hadn't left a single package of orange-flavored gum taped to my dressing room door as stated in the rider, so she was threatening to cancel the show. To be fair, my mother had stolen the trick from Van Halen. She always buried something loopy in the setup section of the venue instructions—for safety reasons, of course. Though, sometimes I wondered if Laura got off on the power trip more than the safety aspect. Nothing ignited her more than the missing item, whatever it happened to be.

The mistake meant I hadn't had to worry about my mother's focused attention when I got back from Little Falls. Most of the crew were standing outside the tour buses, waiting for further instructions. From the back parking lot, Mom's voice boomed out, each word a detonated bomb. Laura assured me that I should be proud to have someone who cared so much.

Sometimes, I did feel that way. But most of the time, Laura's behavior was embarrassing. Was it the manager or the mother at work? The two were so intertwined I never knew whether to call her Mother, Mom, or Laura around the crew. She was all that and none of it.

Laura's curvy frame strode toward all of us waiting with my stage manager, Rebecca, trailing behind her. Liposuction and a boob job had created her artificial curves. Unlike me, my mother had no patience for diets.

"Mia, you can get back on the bus. Until I'm sure the safety specs are up to snuff, you're not stepping foot on this stage for a sound check. No one else does anything until they have the all clear from me, Rebecca, or Taryn. Understood?"

No one dared to grumble, though I suspected a few people were covertly rolling their eyes. This wasn't the first time this had happened, and with almost three months left in the tour, it wouldn't be the last.

With a sigh, I climbed onto the bus. Rebecca followed, and Taryn, my road manager, was close on her heels. Two managers, one purpose. Keep me on the track, sliding along the money rails. Plopping down onto the closest couch, I removed one of the lollipops from my pocket and stared at it, twisting it between my fingertips.

Tyler.

The lemon-ginger flavor quelled the tropical storm in my stomach before it became a full-blown hurricane. A miracle. Divine intervention. Never knowing when I might feel the urge to puke on stage had been the worst part of this nightmare so far. When I'd stopped by Tyler's store on my way to the airport to see if he had more, he'd given me his whole stash. Then, he'd promised to order more to bring with him. Laura would freak out about the sugar content, but at least I wouldn't be losing my dinner on stage every night.

"Am I really going to sit here until she's satisfied? I haven't looked at my schedule." I slotted the reminder of Tyler into my jacket pocket. I was still wearing the bulky winter coat, and sweat pooled under my arms. We were in Miami, and while it wasn't exactly hot today, I didn't need the parka.

Taryn and Rebecca exchanged a glance that only couples could pull off. Silent communication. Who needed words when you knew each other so well you were practically telepathic? Technically, Rebecca was the stage manager and Taryn was the road manager, but they swapped duties all the time depending on who had more patience for me or my mother.

"Radio interview in about an hour." Taryn checked her watch and pushed her glasses closer to her angular face while Rebecca slipped out the door.

I let my head loll back on the couch cushions and focused on the recessed lights in the ceiling. If I opened more of the curtains on the bus, they wouldn't need to be on. The windows were heavily tinted, but I didn't like feeling as though I were in a fishbowl. The curtains were pretty. The windows were a reminder I was on display. Someone was out there watching and waiting for me to screw up.

"You all right? Have a good visit with Sarah?"

"The best." Most of the time, I didn't pretend with Taryn or Rebecca. Other people? All of the time. But the two of them had seen through the bullshit too fast to keep it up. Besides, it was exhausting to pretend perfection or indifference or any of the thousands of masks I wore depending on who was at the window looking in. "Does it matter if I fire

Bonita?" I eyed Taryn, who was leaning against the opposite wall of the bus.

"Fire Bonita?" Taryn frowned and peered at her phone. She shoved her glasses onto the top of her head as she read an incoming message. "Why are we firing Bonita? I thought you liked her."

"I found someone else. Fresh blood."

"Did you run this past Laura?"

"Of course not. I'm running it past you so you can get my mom to follow through. Tonight is Bonita's last. I want her replacement here and up to speed before the next stop." I ruffled my hair and sat forward. Tiredness blanketed my shoulders, and I wasn't sure how I was going to fake my way through this radio interview. Every interviewer wanted perky, full of interesting anecdotes, as though I held the world by the tail.

"Okay." Taryn's brow puckered. "And who are we bringing on? Feels a bit late for this change."

"Sarah suggested Tyler Sullivan. Grady Castillo knows him, too. They've both worked with him. He fixed one of my costumes at that benefit a few months ago."

"You want to bring a guy on tour?"

"Yeah."

"I can see why you're routing this through me. Laura would lose her fucking mind if she thought you were trying to bring a distraction on the road."

"It's not like that." It was both better and worse than Taryn thought. Once Tyler was here, it would be easy enough to prove I hadn't brought him on board as a boy-toy. We hardly knew each other. What did I care what he did in his spare time? As long as my costumes fit and no one discovered I was pregnant, he could look after himself. "He's supposed to be good. References from two of my favorite people. All I need is for you to make it happen."

"It's really not like that?" Taryn pulled a clipboard out of a slot by the door and readjusted her glasses.

"No. I need a change. I'm bored. Sarah said he was amazing." I might be overselling. Was he amazing? He'd fixed my costume at the fundraiser easily enough. And apparently, his ability to procreate was above average. That counted for something, didn't it? Fixing costumes and having sex—there were probably worse resumes out there.

"You sure it was his costume designs she was talking about? I've heard she and her husband have a very loose arrangement."

"Not that it's any of your business, but it was Phillipe who started that loose arrangement. If Sarah wants to screw around, I'm not judging." I shrugged, but inside darkness swirled. Stupid, irrational jealousy. Sarah hadn't slept with Tyler; she'd never met him. But the idea of them together was a scab: rough, hard to ignore. Other than being the father of whoever was growing inside of me, Tyler meant nothing. A warm body on a cool October night, that's all he should have been.

The door to the bus hissed, and Mom's heavy footsteps trudged up the stairs. I braced myself. Would this performance be the doting mother or the irate manager? Even in my head, I could never figure out if I should call her Mom or Laura. I knew what I wished for, but I was also aware of the person she'd become.

When she rounded the corner of the entrance, Laura smiled, her gaze raking over me. Our blue-green eyes and our smiles—the only two physical traits that labeled us mother and daughter. "You look tired. Long trip?"

Looks like doting mother today. I grabbed one of the silver throw pillows and traced the circular design with my finger. "You know Sarah. Always a party."

"We leave in twenty?" Laura eyed the clipboard in Taryn's hand.

"At least I don't have to get dressed." I flipped my long hair to the opposite shoulder.

"Yeah, you do." Laura moved to the closet near the back. "There might be paparazzi or fans. Leaving this bus is a commitment to those people to be your best."

"Is it? Or is it just a commitment to go talk on some radio show?" Doting mother was quickly morphing into irate manager.

"Do you want to go back to being poor?" Laura turned on her heel, her eyes blazing. "'Cause when you treat your fans like shit, they stop buying your shit."

"I could be poor. I wouldn't mind." I crossed my arms and sank deeper into the couch.

"Spoken like someone whose mother protected her from feeling *too* poor." Laura yanked a patterned dress off one of the hangers and laid it over a chair. "If you remembered what it was like, you wouldn't go back there. No one wants to decide between eating and buying medicine for their kid."

Without thinking, my hand strayed to my flat stomach. I'd heard the baby's heartbeat, which made him or her more real than they'd been before, but the burning desire to put the baby above myself didn't exist. Had my mother been like that five years ago, before this all started? Had she put my happiness above her own? I couldn't remember, and I couldn't imagine it was true. Once the money train had started to chug along the tracks, Laura had become desperate to keep it going. At any cost.

Bitterness sat on my tongue as I watched her pull out underwear, a strapless bra, and some accessories for the dress she'd selected. My mother might have sacrificed a lot when she was poor, but I wondered sometimes if she'd sacrificed more once she'd gotten rich. I had, still was. But I loved the music, the stage, lived for it or at least lived this life for those two things.

"I'm old enough to dress myself."

"Tell that to Bonita." Laura rummaged around in a jewelry box that housed most of the inexpensive things. Anyone on the bus with light fingers wouldn't get much. The good stuff was locked away.

My gaze slid to Taryn, who had been silent during our exchange. Taryn raised her eyebrows, prompting me to spill the Tyler beans. *Good fucking luck.* Even if Laura was in the right frame of mind to hear it, I wasn't in the mood to beg or make my case. There'd be no pleading. Taryn and Rebecca were masters at building stories to win over Laura Malone. They could be the architects of this one, too. To make sure my lie to Taryn stuck, I couldn't seem too invested in Tyler. No one could put the pieces together like Pasha had done in the car that morning.

"I need to chat with Rebecca about a couple of things. I'll be back in fifteen to round you two up." Taryn slid the clipboard into its spot by the door and gave me one last encouraging look before slipping out.

Laura flipped through a set of necklaces before selecting one and draping it over the dress. "How is Sarah?"

"Same as always." I tossed the pillow onto the opposite side of the couch and wandered over to where the stack of clothes and accessories lay.

"You really do look exhausted. Are you going to fix your face, or should I text Gina to get her ass over here?"

"I'm exhausted." I stared at her while she was focused on a box filled with bracelets. "When we're done with the tour, I think I need a break."

"We can chat about that when we're closer to finishing." Laura plucked a silver bangle out of the box. "We have financial commitments."

"We're not going to be poor if I take a break."

"How long? A few weeks?"

I laughed. "No, more like a few months. For God's sake. I've been working flat out for five years. Albums. Tours. TV shows. Talk shows. Fan appearances. Private concerts. That doesn't include the diet, hair-care, body treatments, and whatever else you've piled on."

"Someday, you'll look back on these years as the best of your life."

That was always her defense for this frantic pace, as though cramming so much into a short time would make me nostalgic one day. I knew what would come next from her arsenal of guilt trips. It was the most effective one, though lately, I had developed some resistance.

"You know, there are lots of young girls out there—hell, not even young girls, but grown women—who would literally murder someone to be you. The success you have, the audience, your fan base. It's almost unparalleled."

Off the top of my head, I could name several artists who'd had a similar record of success. The only difference? I hadn't yet shaved my head or chopped off my hair and bleached it blond or even written albums full of breakup anthems. Nope. So far, my image was squeaky-clean, even if my day-to-day vocabulary landed in the gutter.

But I had also met enough wannabe singers and performers to know Laura was right about the feverish desire. Did I want this life? I wanted the writing, singing, and performing. The rest of it wore me out, wore me down, made me feel as though I was someone to everyone and nothing like myself. Who was Mia Malone? My value came from what other people saw, and that realization kept me up at night, staring at the ceiling, practicing my Russian accent, pretending to be someone else. Most of the time, I weighed the truth down, sank it deep, and acted like it didn't exist. I was Mia Malone, too famous for an existential crisis, whatever that would look like.

"Sure, until I do something that pisses them off, and then I'm fucked."

"I really wish you'd stop using that word. Someday, you're going to slip up and say it in an interview, and then we *really* will be fucked."

"You've trained me well, Mother." I grabbed the hem of my shirt and tugged it over my head. "Just like a seal. I clap my flippers and bark on command."

"Yeah, right." Laura put a hand on her hip and scoffed. "You think I'm doing all this for my benefit? Traveling around the world for me? Ensuring the safety guidelines are followed for me? Sitting up at night making charts and following trends to further *my* career?"

I snatched the dress from the back of the chair and stepped into it. "You're right. What possible benefit is there for you?" I stared at her, waiting. "What was the price of the last house you bought with your share of my money?"

"You've come back from seeing Sarah in a foul mood." Laura rolled her eyes and huffed out a breath. "Lord, give me patience."

"Yes, Lord." I looked up at the ceiling of the bus and put my hands together in a praying motion. "Please, please give my mother more patience for her overachieving daughter." I was riling her up on purpose, which I loved and hated doing in equal measure.

"Look at me." My mother's features were taut. "There is no one in the world I love more than you. Your happiness is the most important thing in the world."

I swallowed down my retort. I could only push so far before a layer of ice solidified between us, sometimes lasting for days. With Taryn and Rebecca working behind the scenes to get Tyler on the tour, I didn't want her to have a reason to say no. Whether she loved me or not, Laura would thwart Tyler's appointment here if it meant winning one of the silent battles we sometimes waged.

"I know you love me." I slipped my fingers under the straps of the dress and tugged them onto my shoulders. I was likely the *person* Laura loved most in the world. The problem, as far as I could tell, was that Laura loved money more. I offered her a small smile, a peace offering. More than the fame, more than the money, I wanted my mother's love. And sometimes that meant I backed down, gave in, rolled over and took whatever she dished out. After all, a little bit of love, even love attached to purse strings, was better than no love at all. "I love you, too."

Chapter Six
Tyler

I toggled the mouse to wake up the computer as I continued talking to Vanessa about running the store. She'd been a part-time employee for the last few years, and by some miracle had agreed to take on a full-time role for the next three months while I was gone. Everything was falling into place to exit Little Falls and follow the whims of Mia Malone. Almost like fate.

The bells above the door jingled, signaling another customer. I was busier than usual this morning. When I glanced up from showing Vanessa another ordering spreadsheet, my gaze connected with Emily's. She was two years younger than me and had inherited the same reddish tinge to her hair that I possessed. The only one who'd been blessed with a true red was Maggie, and hers was a deep, rich auburn that Katie had coveted. I shook my head. Weird to have my ex-girlfriend creep into my thoughts again. I hadn't thought of her in any concrete way in years. I wasn't sure when and why she moved back to Little Falls. Not that it mattered. Seeing her must have triggered a memory or two. That was all.

While Vanessa scribbled more notes in the three-ringed store bible we were putting together, I rounded the counter and hugged Emily. Our father had insisted hugs were good for mental health, and as a result, I hugged freely and often. Emily clung on for longer than normal.

"Is there somewhere we can talk?" Her brown eyes were piercing.

"Yeah. Back office? I take it you talked to Maggie."

"Uh, yeah. And Mom. I gotta say, we're all freaking out."

"You're freaking out?" I closed the office door tight and sighed before taking a seat.

"I know how hard it is to be a single parent. So, yeah, I'm freaking out. For you. For her. For the baby on the way."

She sank into a chair across from me while I leaned back into my swiveling high-backed leather desk chair, waiting.

"Have you thought this through?"

"Enough to know I want to do it."

She unbound her ponytail, gathered her hair up, and redid it tighter. A hint of a smile played on my lips. Emily was getting her game face on—the one she used to talk me or anyone into or out of something. I supposed it was what made her successful in her real estate business. She knew how to work an angle. Wouldn't matter. We'd each been dealt an ample amount of stubbornness, and I would dig in on this one. A decision made was a decision followed.

"You never wanted to be a single parent, Em. It wasn't in your game plan. I get that."

"And you want to be a single parent? It's in *your* game plan?" Her expression filled with disbelief. "Really?"

I picked up a pen from my desk and twirled it between my fingers. I should have grabbed one of the lollipops off the front desk before coming back here. *A cigarette.* God, I wanted a cigarette. "That's not what I'm saying. But I'm approaching this situation differently than you. My frame of mind isn't the same."

"You have no idea what you're getting into."

"I'm well aware."

"Are you? The endless nights? All the worry on your shoulders? The cost—emotional, physical, and financial? When you don't have someone to share those things, sometimes it feels like you're going to drown under the weight. I just...I wouldn't wish that feeling on anyone."

"I'll figure it out. Will it be hard? Probably—"

"Not probably. A certainty. There isn't enough help in the world to reduce your parental guilt the first time you have to pick putting food on the table over going somewhere to support your kid." Emily swallowed and stared at her hands folded in her lap. "Maggie said Mia doesn't want anything to do with the baby once it's born."

"That's what she thinks, yeah." I didn't plan to dwell on her initial reaction to the pregnancy. As long as no one found out, she'd have time to decide how she felt about the baby over the next few months. I was sure she'd come looking more for help with the baby than for an agreement to have the abortion. Was I reading her right? I didn't have a clue. Wishful thinking, maybe. But I wasn't planning to close any doors.

"You don't believe her?" She glanced up and tilted her head.

"What do either of us know for sure until the baby arrives? All we know is it's coming." I drew open a couple of desk drawers, looking for a stray lollipop. Earlier, I'd cleared them out. Having either Mom or Emily show up at some point today had been inevitable. Though, I was a little surprised it was Emily first.

"That's a very simplistic view of a complex problem."

"I'm a simple man." At the back of the middle drawer, a lone lollipop rolled around. I plucked it out and ripped off the wrapper. Blueberry jasmine. A hint of a smile threatened to materialize before I popped it into my cheek and met Emily's gaze.

"There's simple, and then there's idiotic." Emily sighed. "We've crossed the line here. If she wanted the baby, that would be one thing. But I don't understand why she's agreed to this for you."

"Honestly?" I raised my eyebrows. "Me neither. But I've always wanted to be a dad, and now with our dad gone, it's important for me to do this. Let's face it, none of my other relationships have gotten me there, and I'm thirty-five. I don't want to be a first-time dad in my forties, and most of the women I'm meeting now have kids already." I spread my hands wide. "Hard is not impossible. I'm going to be a dad."

"I can't decide if that explanation is a shitty reason or a really good one."

"Go with a good one. It'll make you feel better." I grinned and pointed my lollipop in her direction.

"Mom is not going to be comforted by this conversation."

"She sent you?"

"Uh, yeah. Of course. She thought I might be able to talk some sense into you." Emily released a deep breath. "*I* didn't think that. We're all the same. Too stubborn."

"This is going to be good for me. I can feel it."

"That's because you have no idea what's coming. You're like the lobster in the pot, unaware the boil will happen." Emily rose from her chair and threw her purse over her shoulder. "But don't worry—Maggie, Mom, and I will be there."

"You'll yank me out before I get boiled alive?"

"Hopefully before the third-degree burns set in." Emily smiled. "No promises. That stubbornness, you know?"

As we exited the office, the bells above the door jingled again. Grady, tall, lean, and perpetually tanned, stood framed in the entryway.

"Jesus," I said, twisting the stick to the lollipop still lodged in my cheek. "Maggie's called in the big guns."

"We want to make sure you've heard all sides of this—even if you don't change your mind."

"I'm not changing my mind." I'd made a promise to Mia. She was putting her career on the line to carry this baby. Her reputation was at stake, and while a reputation was changeable, sometimes easily earned and lost, hers mattered to her. And so now, it mattered to me. There was no greater priority than Mia and the baby she carried.

"Hey, Tyler," Grady said with a wave from the door. "Got a minute? Maggie asked me to swing by before you hit the road."

"Yeah, why not? Join the parade through my office. I'm planning on turning my front door into a game. Who will appear next in a desperate bid to talk some sense into me?"

Vanessa's head swiveled between the two of us as she pretended to busy herself on the computer. She knew I was going on tour with Mia, but I hadn't revealed what motivated this sudden flip.

"I promised Maggie." A smirk rose to Grady's lips.

"Yeah, I get it, man. No worries. Come on back." I gave Emily a quick hug before following Grady into the office and closing the door once again. "So, you're here to warn me off Mia or being a single parent?"

"I have to pick one? Aww, shit. I came unprepared for that." He grinned.

I rocked back in my chair as Grady assumed Emily's seat. "Nah, have at 'er. What is it that Maggie wants to make sure I understand?"

Grady pressed his fingertips into his forehead and then crossed one foot over his knee. "Mia's life—"

"Is a circus. She told me."

He took a moment and glanced up at the ceiling. "I like her. We get along. But she's fucking all over the map with what she wants. It's part of the reason her mom keeps her on such a tight leash, I think. She's just...impulsive. Or maybe it's just that she's young. I don't know. But I can guarantee there are things going on with her you've got no idea about. None."

"Isn't that part of the fun of getting to know someone?"

"Maybe." Grady rubbed his face. "Seems like the frustrating part to me." He chuckled. "Then, you know, the whole single parenting thing. I watched my mom struggle after my dad died. It's not an easy life you're choosing."

"Why do you think Mia came to me? Why tell me if what she wanted was an abortion?" I took the lollipop out of my mouth and dropped it into the trash can.

"Part of the mystery of Mia. I'm not sure there's an answer to that question." Grady's phone buzzed, and he took it out of his pocket and set it on the desk without looking at the display.

"Maggie?"

"Probably. She really wanted me to come. I really didn't want to."

"She's worried about me." I crossed my arms.

"We've gone beyond worried." Grady made a step-by-step motion with this hand. "We're about five years past worried to where you're living off of government assistance and Mia has somehow forced you into paying her child support for a baby she doesn't possess."

I laughed and ran a hand down my face. "Jesus."

"Exactly. Overthinking is her full-time job." Grady pressed his hands into the arms of his chair. "Stupid question, maybe. But did your dad help keep her overthinking in check a little? I mean, it's..."

"Yeah. They were very close, and saw each other a lot with the pharmacy work. Dad was the calm in all of our storms. Nothing he wouldn't do for us." I ran a fingertip over the smooth wood of my desk. "We miss him. I think we're looking for him in different places. Figuring it out in different ways."

"Is that what this is about?" Grady stared at me intently.

"There are worse ways to pay tribute to my dad. Becoming a father myself. Doing the best I can for Mia and the baby."

"She doesn't want to be in the equation. She was very specific about that when I talked to her." Grady picked up his phone and glanced at the message before setting it face down again. "I've offered to build an apartment in the old train station I bought when I first moved back home. I've already built a recording studio there, so Mia would be able to use both to work on her next album either before the baby comes or once it's here. Since I'm producing the album, it might be the best fit. Think about it. Mia already knows. Have you two talked about timing? She was vague on the phone."

"No, not really." I needed another lollipop. God, why did I give Mia all the ones out of my office drawers? When she'd said they made her feel better, I'd rounded up all but the ones on the front counter. A rush order was supposed to arrive tonight by the close of business so I could take them with me. Her appearance at the shop to get more had been amusing after she mocked my use of them and my internet research. Sometimes Google knew things, even medical things.

"I think my job is done." Grady stood. "Single parenting: hard. Mia: hard. Be careful."

"Your campaign slogan for mayor is starting to make more sense now. I thought you were good with words?"

"Only when I sing them." He extended his hand to shake. "Maggie is freaking the fuck out right now. I was supposed to remind you that family looks after each other."

During Maggie's first campaign for mayor, I ran for town council so I could back her decisions or offer a reasonable second opinion. I'd looked out for Maggie the night she stayed at Grady's and slept in, missing the pharmacy opening, worrying everyone. When Omar was dying, I spent many nights watching Amir while Emily clutched her husband's hand. When Dad died, I slept at my parents' house for almost a month, so Mom didn't have to be alone, even though every morning without Dad in that house put another dent in my heart. I understood what it meant to be part of a family, to look after each other, and I was grateful that my sisters and parents had never neglected the bond either. Sometimes, I found their concern frustrating. I certainly had eight years ago when Katie and I split, but most of the time, I was grateful for their love, knew I only had to ask, and they'd step up. Families that didn't function like that were baffling. Why wouldn't you want the best for the people you love? When the worst came, you loved them harder.

I took Grady's hand and shook it. "Are you a hugger?"

"Ah, the famous Sullivan goodbye." Grady grinned. "I'm learning to appreciate the art of the hug. Joanna explained Jim's philosophy. Made sense to me. Maggie's always given the best hugs."

Standing beside Grady made me feel short, and at six feet tall, I knew I wasn't. We embraced, patting each other on the back with mutual affection.

Like his brother, Trent, Grady had a naturally fit frame. As far as I knew, Grady walked his dogs obsessively, but did little else in the way of exercise. While I was no longer on the strict diet and exercise routine

Maggie's best friend, Lila, had put me on before the Magic Men show, I hadn't completely let myself go. Last time I'd been on tour with the theater company, I'd had hours of idle time, so perhaps I'd be able to get back into a fitness routine.

As Grady and I reached the front door, my phone rang. When I took it out of my back pocket, a blocked number flashed on the display. As soon as I answered it, there was a long pause. I waved to Grady as he climbed into his truck.

"Hello?" I said again.

"Tyler Sullivan?"

"That's me." I leaned against the cold windows. Where would Mia be tomorrow night? Tonight, it was Miami, but I hadn't checked the concert schedule online beyond that.

"My name is Laura Malone. I got your name from Sarah Telling, who speaks very highly of you. We're in need of a costume designer-slash-wardrobe person to join Mia Malone's concert tour for the last three months. Normally, I'd ask for references and an interview, but I've already spoken to Sarah, and I understand you've worked for Grady Castillo before too." She cleared her throat. "We may have met in passing at the benefit in Utica. I was in the dressing room when you first started fixing Mia's costume."

Realization dawned. I remembered the blonde who'd kept such a watchful eye before disappearing on some errand. *She hardly looked older than me.* Which made sense since Mia said her mother had been eighteen when she'd gotten pregnant. I closed my eyes. "Right, yes." I managed to get out. "I remember."

"I realize this is very last minute, but we need someone to join the tour starting tomorrow night. Is there any chance you'd be willing to jump on board? I can email you a contract to look over."

"Send me the contract. I'll take a look and let you know within the hour." I was glad Mia had told me not to accept right away. According to Mia, nothing made her mother more suspicious than eagerness. "I have a lot on my plate, but for the right incentive, I might be able to shift some things for a few months." Those words felt sleazy coming out, but Mia had told me to work the money angle. They'd pay me whatever I asked, and Laura needed to believe that she won me.

"Of course. You'll be more than fairly compensated for taking the job on such short notice." I could hear the clack of the keyboard over the phone. "I adjusted the numbers and sent the contract. Call me when you've reviewed it."

"Will do." Without a goodbye, the connection went dead in my ear. I stared at my phone for a minute. So, that was her mother.

The vibration from the email coming in pulled me back to the task at hand. Now, I needed to negotiate like I didn't care if I got the job while my insides screamed to just say "yes."

Chapter Seven
Mia

Already, I was doing a terrible job of pretending I didn't give a shit about Tyler Sullivan. He'd driven a hard bargain in negotiations with my mother, which made her practically swoon when she got off the phone. Since he'd arrived, Laura had taken the lead, showing him around backstage and through various buses. Each time Mom put her hand on his arm, or flicked her hair, or stared up at him like he was the second coming of Tom Ford, I wanted to vomit. This time, the rolling stomach had nothing to do with morning sickness.

"Not like that with him, huh?" Taryn chided in my ear. "You're launching daggers at him and your mother from across the stage. Do your sound check before she notices."

Tearing my gaze away, I glared at Taryn. "She's all over him like a dog in heat. It's fucking distracting."

"Distracting? Why's that? You have a thing for dogs in heat?"

"No, I have a thing for my manager not sexually harassing my employees. It's illegal."

Taryn threw her head back and laughed, drawing Rebecca's attention from a stagehand she'd been talking to at the bottom of the stairs. She took the steps two at a time to join them.

"What's so funny?" Rebecca asked.

"Mia's upset that her mother finds the newest addition attractive."

Rebecca glanced over her shoulder at Laura, cozied up to Tyler as they flipped through some costumes on a rack. "Not my type, but I'm not blind. Objectively, he's attractive. You know your mother."

All too well. Other than his age, Tyler didn't fit the sort of men my mother favored. Wild men who didn't give a shit about anyone but themselves was her addiction. If there was a bad choice within a mile, Laura Malone would be dry humping him by the end of the night. I crossed my arms and rocked back on a heel, forcing myself not to look at Tyler again. He wasn't a bad choice, so I had no reason to worry about Mom.

"Sometimes, I think Laura doesn't want men on the crew because it distracts her more than it's a danger to you," Rebecca said.

A danger? I supposed they were, although I wouldn't have used that word, exactly. Not about these guys on tour. Men were great until they weren't, and I'd had more than my fair share of them who went after pieces of me or other women as though they were entitled. A hand grazing my ass. A murmured comment about a private show. A low whistle as I wandered past. There were men like that who worked the venues, but they didn't keep their job long. My mother and I had a reputation. I didn't need men like them on tour buses, at the gym, at the afterparties in my bus, and as soon as they showed their true colors, they were fired. In my experience, less men meant less hassle, less chance of something going wrong, less chance of a *misunderstanding*.

In those first heady days and weeks after I'd signed my contract at fourteen, I'd learned about men, especially men who held a hint of power or authority. At the time, someone like me didn't dare cross them. Usually, they were the ones hitting the emergency stop on an elevator, locking their office doors, cornering me at a party, causing me to look over my shoulder for my mother, clutch her hand tightly, make her promise never to leave me alone with any of them ever again. Once I worked up the guts to tell her, Laura hadn't left me, not without seeing our secret signal, a sign I was confident whatever man was involved wouldn't corner me, try to steal something. I gave her the signal the night I asked Tyler to my hotel. With all my heart, I wished I hadn't.

I finished my sound check and realized Mom had disappeared some-where, leaving Tyler in the wings of the stage, watching me with his arms crossed, a hint of a smile. A flutter in the pit of my stomach made me want to erect barriers, pretend his presence didn't matter.

"My mother showed you around?" I breezed past him, barely glancing in his direction.

"She did." His hands sank into the pockets of his black denim jeans, and he turned on his heel to follow. "Can you run me through your routine with Bonita for costume changes? Laura said a few of them are quick."

Pasha, my constant shadow, joined me at the end of the stairs, and I didn't turn to look at Tyler when I called over my shoulder, "Ask your assistant, Verity. She looks after merchandise too, which you'll oversee. I have things to do. If she's useless, talk to Taryn or Rebecca. They can run you through or schedule you a couple minutes with me before the show." My stride never faltered as I headed to the bus.

The next thing on the agenda was a surprise appearance at some superfan's birthday party. Those events were press generators, and they did one every few months to show how connected I was to my MiaMites. They'd named themselves, obviously.

"Yeah, sure." Tyler's heavy footfall paused behind me. "If you're too busy, Laura offered to give me a breakdown."

I stopped and half-turned, tilting my head at Tyler. "No. Talk to Verity. If she's useless, talk to me. For the record, I fucking *hate* repeating myself." My words were sharp. I didn't want him spending more time with my clingy mother. Instead of apologizing, I stared him down. So, I was a bitch. Better he learned now. There was no room for softness on tour. He listened, or he left.

Or at least that was how I'd always worked things in the past with the few men I'd struck up an arrangement with, but Tyler wasn't like them. Sending him away, especially after a certain point, wasn't an option.

"Does anyone like repeating themselves?" Tyler's tone was mild. "I don't want to fuck up. If you're too busy, you don't get to dictate who *isn't* too busy to help."

I stepped toward him, even though he towered over me. "I do get to dictate. This is my show. My job. Consider me your dictator."

"Can I call you that?" He raised his eyebrows, a hint of a grin threatening at the edges. "Mini-dictator?"

My expression clouded, and I frowned. He never bit back; instead, he sifted through my blows as though they were mere puffs of smoke. "No, you can't call me that."

"You want to dictate things, but you don't want anyone to acknowledge that you're acting like a dictator." His eyes darkened a fraction. "You'd rather dominate in private?"

I met his gaze, and a memory jumped between us. A hotel room. Dim lights. His tongue pressing against my core, licking and sucking, making me feel like I couldn't get enough. My hands tangled in his hair. *Faster. Harder. More. Don't stop. Don't ever fucking stop.*

Tearing my gaze away, I turned my back on him, burying the memory. "Call me whatever you want. Just don't fuck up or else I'll have to fire you."

"Noted," Tyler called. "No fucking...up."

The urge to turn back, give him another piece of my mind surged through me. Would it work? Already, he was meeting my annoyance with mild reason. Why fight when the other person wouldn't fight with you? Luckily, I knew someone who met a fight head-on, just like me.

I found Mom in the office portion of her private bus, which was her second-favorite place to be after she was done in the center of the stage, screaming at random workers about any and all injustices she could find.

"Ah." Laura turned in her swivel chair after I drew the door tight. "My gorgeous daughter. You want me to fire him yet? Personally, I think he's lovely."

I suppressed an eye roll at her fake British accent that she loved to put on as a bit between the two of us. Sometimes the gesture made me laugh. Today, I wasn't in the mood to be amused. "I saw how lovely you found him. Lovely while you riffled through my costumes. Lovely while you dragged him from bus to bus. Probably lovely as you shoved your tongue down his throat." I ran a finger along the windowsill and didn't look at her, as though her response meant nothing. Tyler was nobody, after all.

"Now, now." Laura made a tsking sound. "I'll save that for the end of the tour." She winked and turned around again. "Never mix business and pleasure."

"Except, you do it all the time."

"Sure, with local stagehands or whoever I want who doesn't travel with us." She cast a glance over her shoulder and then scribbled a note to herself before turning around. "Name the last time I fraternized with a roadie."

"You used the wrong F word there." I sank into the couch and stared at her. Technically, the rotating opening acts didn't count as people on the road with us, but her sexual conquests weren't as fleeting as she made them seem either. Had she slept with someone in a role like Tyler's before? No way to be sure.

"I was surprised you were okay with him joining the crew. I know we'd met him before, and he had the okay from Sarah…"

"And that was enough." I bit the tip of my pinky finger. The hard plastic didn't offer the same comfort as my brittle nails. Other than going to see Tyler, I couldn't remember the last time I lied to my mother. We didn't always get along, but a couple of years into this madness, we agreed that the only way to survive was to be honest with each other, even if we weren't with other people. Tyler had said something similar in his bid to convince me to keep this thing growing inside me. *Never to each other.*

"Well, he's delicious and old enough to be your father, which suits me just fine."

"He's only old enough because you and my sperm donor had me when you were twelve." I ran my finger along the arm of the couch. "Did he look thirty-five to you? I didn't think he looked that old."

"Your father was twenty, and I was eighteen when we had you." Laura flushed and flipped her hair. "And thirty-five is not old." She narrowed her eyes. "How'd you know his age? Why would you ask him?"

Already I was messing up and piling lies on top of lies. Everyone knew you didn't compound lies—remembering them became too hard. My list of who had been told what when was only going to grow in the coming months, hopefully not in direct proportion to my uterus.

"Thirty-five is old." He just wasn't *too* old. Or at least, not too old to find him attractive.

Once.

I found him attractive once.

"Kenny Connors is meeting us in Nashville when we stop there."

"Why?" Kenny was a producer I'd been forced to work with by my label when I first broke out. He'd gotten me alone under some guise of helping me. Instead, he'd helped himself. Unease slithered down my spine.

Laura rotated her chair and leaned back. "Word on the street is that he wants to take the lead on your next album."

"No chance. None. Not happening." Pinpricks burst across my skin, and I rose to my feet, pointing my finger. "You know what he did."

"Do you want to go after him?" Our gazes connected for a beat.

My shoulders slumped, and I ran my hands down my face. Back then I wanted to ruin him, rip him apart with my bare hands. Laura wouldn't let me. That had been before I understood how the industry functioned, how much women were expected to bury for the sake of their career. "I don't want to work with him again. I'll quit before I work with him again."

"We have contractual obligations."

At this moment, I longed for my mom instead of my manager. The contract, whatever money was at stake, was nothing compared to the anxiety brushing against my chest cavity, wiggling up my throat. "I won't work with him again. We can meet with him, but it's only to tell him 'no.' I don't care how high we have to go, how much shit we gotta stir. The answer is no. Pasha comes to the meeting. You come to the meeting." Kenny was a door locker. And that fucking office was soundproof. Sometimes, I wondered if he videotaped the shit he pulled in there. "The answer is no."

Chapter Eight
Tyler

I unpacked the last of my things into the drawer closest to my bunk. I shared the space with a rotation of bus drivers who might need a break or a place to sleep, and Pasha, the preferred bodyguard. Men and women didn't share buses on Mia's tour, and he and a few other bodyguards were the only male crew members. When I'd raised my eyebrows and opened my mouth to question the gender balance, Laura had said it was merely a coincidence they hired so many women to work the jobs. Those women just happened to be the most qualified.

I'd nodded, as though her reasoning made complete sense. In Little Falls, smart, capable women surrounded and abounded. There was no doubt the women on the crew *could* be the most qualified. But I wasn't convinced that was the reason women were hired in such large numbers. The imbalance didn't bother me. I liked women; I liked puzzles. At some point, I'd figure out their reasoning.

The ring of the doorbell made me jump, and then I grinned. The last tour I'd been on hadn't been anywhere near this level. *A doorbell on a bus.* Already the things I didn't know or understand were piling up. I wasn't sure I would be able to pretend I'd done this job before for Sarah Telling. Her shows were just as huge. I wandered through the small sitting room to the front entrance and pressed the button to release the doors.

Mia was at the bottom of the stairs, dark glasses concealing half her face. She climbed the stairs, and I stepped back so she could pass. Surprise flickered. When we crossed paths at the stadium after her sound check, I'd teased her. Or maybe I was flirting, even if it wasn't wise. Whatever it had been, it pissed her off. Her reaction had reminded me why I found her so attractive the night we slept together. The fire raging inside of her ignited an answering flame in me.

"I asked Taryn to get me some time with you before the show tonight. She said she would." Her fingers touched the arm of her sunglasses, but she didn't remove them. When her hand lowered, it shook.

With a frown, I searched her face. The confidence she'd shown at the stadium was gone, replaced by a girl folding in, closing up.

"You okay?" I couldn't tell if she was meeting my gaze behind the dark glasses or averting it.

"Sure." She touched the edge of her glasses again without taking them off. "Fine. Great, even."

"Hey." I closed the distance and gently removed her glasses. She turned her face away, but she didn't stop me from taking her shield. "Never to each other."

"*You* can't lie. I can do whatever I want." Her blue-green eyes hardened when our gazes met.

For a moment, I let her stare me down, but I didn't back away or break eye contact. Just like when she came to Little Falls, I didn't think she wanted to lie to me. Her anger, like the sunglasses, was armor. After sound check, she'd been annoyed, whether it was my presence or my reliance on her mother, I wasn't sure. The sharpness in her tone wasn't the same right now. Something had brought her here. "You're upset. You didn't come to tell me Taryn would give me time with you later. What happened?"

"I should go." She snatched her sunglasses out of my hand, but I gripped her bicep, holding her in place when she tried to flee. "Coming here was stupid."

My lips were close to her ear when I said, "Talk to me, Mia. I want to help." I couldn't get the sight of her trembling hand off my mind. "If someone hurt you—" Each time she breathed out, I caught a whiff of lemon and ginger. Those scents shouldn't turn me on, and yet they were. Another thread of protectiveness stitched between us. Whether she liked it or not, we were a unit; and if someone hurt her, I'd find a way to make them regret it.

A shudder rocked her tiny frame, and she closed her eyes. "You can't help. I don't know why I came." She tugged her bicep out of my grasp and moved toward the door. "I'll walk you through the costume changes in a couple hours when I get back. Don't ask anyone else." Slipping her glasses back on her face, she pressed the button to open the doors and clomped down the stairs.

I watched her descent with a mixture of frustration and heartache. Had I pushed too hard? Maybe the trick was to say less, hold back, let her take the lead. The way her hand had shaken, the tiniest wobble of her chin, as though she was on the verge of a breakdown, had made me want to pull the information out of her and tear apart whoever had shifted her sense of self so completely. A few hours ago, she'd been my mini dictator. I didn't know who'd shown up in my bus just now, but Mia felt like a woman split in two. She was a real-life mimosa pudica: a confident flower in bloom one minute, and closed-up, protecting herself from predators the next.

Grady had warned me she was, if not unstable, then unpredictable. Maybe this seesaw behavior was normal. Was her life full of high highs and low lows? I couldn't imagine anything worse.

I tugged the sparkly outfit up Mia's slight body, and when our gazes met, she grinned. "Pretty great, right?"

"You're killing it, Mini." I returned her grin. Would she get the reference? I'd worked it in a few times tonight during my first concert backstage, but she'd ignored it.

"I'm starting to think you've forgotten my name." Mia's eyes danced with amusement while the stylist rapidly worked Mia's locks into a complicated braid. All of this was happening on the fly while the applause from the crowd roared around us.

"I remember." The look in her eyes when our gazes met again made me wish I could subtly readjust my pants. No chance of that with the crew hovering. Someone would notice. Even this exchange was dangerous. "Mini suits you better."

"I'll let my mother know she got my name wrong," Mia drawled over her shoulder just before a technician led her away.

The night had flown by in a blur of costume changes for her and her dancers. Backstage had been nonstop action, and I hoped I hadn't screwed up. True to her word, she'd taken me through the whole routine in a dull and professional session when she'd gotten back from wherever she'd gone. I didn't know if her monotone approach had been for the benefit of her mother who'd overseen it or for me. God forbid anyone suspect she gave a shit about something or someone.

I'd gone back to my bus and written out each change based on the set list she gave and then I cross-referenced it with the costumes' racks. There'd been one literal snag when one of Mia's sequins caught on my watch during a rapid change. We'd had to rip it off. I wouldn't make that mistake a second time, and I was already trying to recall where I'd seen the spare sequins. This outfit was the last of the night. Encore number two called for her to drop from the ceiling in a silver sequined one-piece. She started the show descending from the rafters, so my heart shouldn't be pounding so hard in my chest. Laura's tirade about safety while she led me around the tour earlier made more sense after seeing the show from start to finish. Mia did some dangerous shit.

Mia's heels clacked along the stage floor in a rapid staccato that matched my heart. The technician who'd led her away clipped her into a harness and yanked on all the connections. That was it? A couple rough tugs and those ropes were supposed to hold her? My heart kicked. I'd been so busy at the start of the show I missed this part.

From the side of the stage, the lights blazed on Mia, suspended, the attachments for the harness making her look like a butterfly. The crowd exploded with screams and clapping before all the lights went out. Then, as the beat to her most famous song started, the crowd lit up, their LED bracelets and crowns synched to the music. Each flash of the stage lights showed Mia closer to the ground. A spectacle of the best kind.

I crossed my arms and absorbed the energy from the crowd, the stage, the night itself. There was no way this feeling could ever become routine. Did Mia feed off this the same way I was? After almost two hours, I couldn't believe the amount of energy she was still exuding on stage.

Every dance step was precise. She adjusted the notes to the songs higher or lower based on her breath control, which she'd told me the night I fixed her costume. She'd been unbelievable that night, too, but on a much smaller, more intimate, scale.

"Incredible, right?" Laura's lips were a hair's breadth from my ear.

"That's one word." I didn't turn my head, content to watch Mia dazzle the crowd, dazzle me.

"Was Sarah Telling's show this good?"

"She was great. Not like this. But great." The lie sprang out with no conscious thought. Vague. Complimentary. If Laura brought out details of Sarah's tour, whichever one I supposedly worked on, I'd be screwed. There was only so much I could fake.

The lights went out, and the crowd burst into applause and whistles. I made out Mia's shape as she appeared beside me. On her toes, her lips brushed my ear.

"A bucket or a lollipop. My stomach is fucking rioting."

Out of my pocket, I produced the lemon-ginger one she favored and ripped off the wrapper in one quick motion. Her sigh was audible as she popped it into her mouth.

"Is that a lollipop?" Laura's frown was clear in her voice.

"Yep! Sugar, Mom. Can you believe it?" Mia drew a finger down her cheek. "I can feel a line forming on my face already from the toxic effects."

"Empty calories."

"I got news for you, Mom. I'm going to be consuming more empty calories at the bar later. You know, the appearance you arranged for me? Gotta decompress somehow."

"A bar?" I frowned and scanned Mia's face. That sounded like the last place she needed to be.

"Sure. After about—" She grabbed my wrist to check the time. "Two or three hours of meet and greets. They paid out the ass for a photo and a few minutes of my time. Right, Mom?"

Through clenched teeth, Laura pushed out, "You told me yesterday you wanted a break. I'm not a magician. When you cancel, you disappoint. Let's just get through the tour as it is, and we'll go from there."

I rocked back on my heels, surprised Mia had already broached the break with Laura. I opened my mouth to say something, to support Mia, but I couldn't. We weren't supposed to know each other. Truthfully, we didn't know each other, despite our deal.

"Clasp all that money a little tighter. A dollar might slip out." Mia mocked.

"Take care of the dollars, and the millions take care of themselves." Laura's reply was breezy.

Not quite how that phrase went. But I supposed they were beyond counting pennies. They'd have lots of money, wouldn't they? I couldn't understand why her mother would be so worried.

Laura turned to me. "I know you need to sort out everything here and repair that snagged costume. Though, I think we have like six of them somewhere for when this happens. Anyway, when you're organized, did you want to grab a coffee?" Her voice went up at the end, full of hope, the opposite of the bold bitterness running between her and Mia.

"He can't." Mia took the lollipop out of her cheek, went pale, and stuck it back in. "He's coming with me."

"Excuse me?" Laura frowned and crossed her arms.

"It's his first night on the tour. I'm going to take him out, show him the sites. He's thirty-five, not thirty-nine. He's not going to want to go on a coffee date at midnight when he can mingle with hot dancers and do body shots in the VIP area."

Her mother flushed. "He doesn't exactly seem like the body shot type." She gestured toward me, flustered.

Mia raised one eyebrow. "Which means he's not likely to be your type." She shifted her weight in my direction. We both knew I had no problem with body shots. I'd done some off of her the night we'd slept together. "Did you want to fuck my mother, Tyler? Cause that's where we're heading here."

I rubbed my hand down my face, trying to decide if I was angry, annoyed, or amused by this pissing contest. I'd never seen a mother-daughter relationship like this.

"Mia, don't be rude." Laura grabbed her daughter's upper arm and practically dragged her along with her toward the dressing rooms. "We need to get started on the meet and greets."

"Two hours, Pretty Boy," Mia called over her shoulder.

As soon as Mia was at the top of the stairs dressed in a sparkly blue mini dress, her exhaustion was palpable. It was almost two o'clock in the morning, and I'd had to have coffee at midnight by myself to keep from falling asleep. The last thing I wanted to do was go to a club for body shots.

"You got your good underwear on? I'm pretty sure I can get you laid." She crossed her arms and cocked out a hip, another lollipop lodged in her cheek.

"You're obviously not feeling well. Why are you going out?" I shook my head, ignoring her comment.

"Because I'm paid to appear. Thousands of dollars to show up. They'll have advertised it. Some of those people who took photos and shook my hand at the VIP already mentioned they were going because I'd be there. Everyone wants a piece of me. The bigger Mia Malone gets, the more pieces they want to take." With her hands, she mocked chipping away at some unknown shape. She took the fake fragment from the block and rubbed it all over her. "They want to figure out how to get some of this shine on them."

"Seems logical." My voice oozed sarcasm.

"Does it? Most of the time, I think it's pathetic, sad. My mother would say it's because I didn't spend enough time wanting what I have to be able to appreciate it."

"And what do you think?"

"She's probably right, but I'd never, ever say it to her face."

"Why not?"

"Doesn't matter." Mia shifted her gaze toward the windows and shrugged her shoulders. "Are you ready? I want to get this over with so I can come home and either collapse or puke my guts out. I'm barely holding it together."

I rubbed my index finger along my forehead. For the last few hours, I'd been debating whether the potential conflict was worth saying anything. Better if I spoke up. The comment she'd made earlier to her mother about consuming more empty calories to unwind was stuck in my head. I couldn't let it slide. "You know you can't drink, right? Or do any other drugs?"

"Are you fucking kidding me right now?" Her eyes bulged out of their sockets, and she puffed out her cheeks. "You're not my boyfriend. You're not my dad. You're going to lecture me?"

Pasha's head popped over the edge of the bus stairs, and he frowned. Hopefully, her voice wasn't drifting outside to other people.

"That wasn't a lecture. It was two questions. And you're right, I'm not your boyfriend or your dad. But I am someone's dad, and my job is to look out for that someone." I pointed to her stomach, annoyance zipping through me.

"On second thought, you're not coming with me." Mia whirled around, her dark hair flying. "I don't need another person looking over my shoulder telling me what I can and can't do." She turned back, her blue-green eyes blazing. "You want to stay on this tour? Know your place. I'm not an idiot, okay? Don't be a dick." She clomped down the stairs and exited the bus before I could get my thoughts together.

God, she was so flipping frustrating. The worst part was my inability to decide which version of her I liked best. Most of them were infuriating. Made me clench my teeth to keep from losing my temper. But my blood pumped, hot and thick in my veins. Whether I liked it or not, being around her was the most alive I'd felt in years.

Chapter Nine
Mia

I straightened my posture in the plush brown leather chair on the other side of Kenny's steel desk. Behind me, Pasha stood at the back of the large concrete and glass office that looked out over Nashville. In the five years since I shot to stardom with the label, Kenny rode my coattails all the way to the top floor. He was credited with launching my career. On days when the thought of him didn't make my skin crawl, I could admit he understood music and had taught me a few things at fifteen that I still took into consideration when I put together an album. Remembering what he taught me always left a bitter taste in my mouth.

The price for his lessons had been more than I wanted to pay. Had I said no to him? Any time I played the sessions back, I couldn't remember. But I hadn't said "yes." Not once had that word crossed my lips.

As if sensing my mood, Mom took my hand, sandwiching it between her own. Mom knew, of course. Not all of what had happened. A shiver ran through me. Not all of it.

"I don't understand the problem." He steepled his fingers and leaned across his desk. His dark hair was styled with too much gel. I bet he dyed it jet-black to hide the gray. His midnight eyes were hard. "The label wants this."

"And I don't." I stared at him, trying to pretend the sight of him didn't cause the queasiness in my stomach to swell, a cold sweat to break out across my skin.

"You either let this go, or we go to the label about what happened last time you worked with Mia." Laura's voice was steely. "The age of consent in Tennessee is eighteen."

"Did she tell you we slept together?" Kenny chuckled and shook his head. "Mia. Mia. Mia. Why would you lie to your mother?"

"I didn't *lie*." Rage swirled in me. The rest of the words wouldn't go past my lips. What he'd done was a violation.

"Is that the problem? You wiggled your ass last time, and I didn't take the bait?" He stared at me. "Now you're bitter. You pranced around here *begging* for it. But I never gave it to you."

Had I flirted with him? Maybe. A little. Thinking of how naïve I'd been made my chest hurt. I'd been fifteen, new to the business, and he'd seemed attractive for an older man. Charming, even. Harmless. I thought he would be harmless. Now when I looked at him, all I saw was a monster, a man who took advantage of a girl who was too afraid to speak up.

"You gave her something." Laura snorted. "You can pretend you didn't do what you did, but we have proof. Documented proof. So, you back the fuck off or we'll be coming after you and the label in the court of public opinion. We've chosen not to ruin you so far, but if you don't step back, this train will run you over."

I froze in my seat, afraid to look at her. What had happened to contractual obligations? Was Laura really going to rescue me from this nightmare? I squeezed her hand and swallowed the tears threatening to spill. Neither of them would get to see me cry.

"Proof?" He raised his eyebrows. "Whatever proof you have will do as much damage to her as to me. Her fans would never approve of a fifteen-year-old girl seducing a man my age in my position."

"Seducing?" I almost choked on the word. "I was fifteen."

"I didn't ask you here to fight." Kenny held up his hands. "We need to hammer out some dates to get this next album laid down." He toggled the mouse on his desk and brought up a calendar on his computer, turning the monitor toward us.

"We're not working with you." Laura let go of my hand and opened her oversized purse. Out came an envelope, and she tossed it across the desk.

"It's cute you think you have a choice." He smirked while he fingered the opening of the long manila envelope. "Fucking women." He slid out the stapled pages and scanned them, his smirk fading. Each page caused his smirk to slip into a frown. "You couldn't have obtained any of this legally."

"Fucking women, right?" Laura laughed. "Turns out if you burn enough of us, we band together and start an inferno of our own." She shifted closer to his desk as though letting him in on a secret. "Five years ago, I didn't know how to handle you. What could we do? Who'd believe us? A mother-daughter duo from a trailer park in butt-fuck nowhere. I had no connections. No money, except what the label had given us as an advance." She eyed him. "Now, you're the one on your knees sucking *my* dick."

"This information would ruin Mia, too." He'd gone pale under his spray tan. "The public isn't that forgiving."

"Oh, Kenny. I've learned a thing or two in five years." Laura smirked and leaned back in her chair. "You think I can't spin what's in there? I don't play cards until I'm sure they're winners. One of the benefits of that dog-eat-dog upbringing. I learned when to go for the jugular. Right now, I've got my teeth around yours. It's up to you if I bite down or release...for now."

"How am I supposed to explain this to the label?" Kenny eased the papers back into the envelope.

"That's not my problem."

I sat beside her in stunned silence. I'd seen Laura in action before, but it had usually been against me, not fighting for me. My world was tipping, and I was careening toward the edge, in danger of toppling over. What had gotten into my mother?

"I do this, and none of this information goes public," Kenny said.

"Agreed." Laura rose and offered her hand across the desk. "It's been a pleasure." Kenny made no move to take her hand. "I'm sure that's the first time you've heard those words out of a woman's mouth. That feeling welling up in your chest? It's called shock."

That was definitely what was welling up in my chest while I followed her out of Kenny's office. Once we were on the street, Pasha on one side, Laura on the other, a realization hit like a punch to the chest.

"Mom?"

Laura's heels clicked along the concrete sidewalk toward the waiting car. "What's wrong?"

"It wasn't just me?" My steps faltered. "He did those things to other women? Not just me?"

"Of course." With a sigh, Laura glanced my way and pushed her sunglasses onto her head. "Men like him never do it just once. He wasn't going to have the opportunity to do it to you twice. Not when I knew."

I grabbed my hair in my fist, letting it trail over one shoulder, and I absorbed her words. "Is he still doing it?"

"The last singer I tracked down was from three years ago. Men like him don't stop, Mia. They just get better at hiding it."

Others were at risk. Some fifteen-year-old girl could be bent over his desk tomorrow, his lips making shushing noises in her ear as he pushed up her skirt, his hand clamped over her mouth. "We have to do something."

"No."

"Mom," I pleaded.

"The only person I need to protect is you. You're it." Laura yanked open the back door to their waiting car. "Coming forward would ruin your career."

"What he's doing is wrong." I couldn't make my brain formulate the words I wanted to say, the ones I thought might convince her to do something more.

"Someday, someone will do something." Laura wouldn't meet my gaze. "It doesn't have to be us. You're safe now."

I didn't know exactly what Laura had revealed to Kenny. Safe wasn't what I'd call giving him the information in the envelope.

"What if he calls your bluff? What if he tries to get ahead of this and releases whatever was in there?"

"You don't need to worry." Laura patted her hand. "The damage to him is too widespread."

I rubbed my face and ran my hands through my hair. How many? How old? How often? I knew what had happened to me, how it stuck, how it coated any interactions that came afterward.

"You're famous," Laura said.

Wasn't that why we should do something? How many of those other girls accomplished my level of fame? How many of them paid the price he demanded and bankrupted themselves?

"I don't think that should matter." Those weren't the right words.

"Your safety is the only thing that matters. We've got the freedom you wanted. Be grateful. We're out from under his thumb."

From my pocket, I produced a lollipop and tore the wrapper off. The rising tide in my stomach wasn't morning sickness though. It was something much more sinister. I hoped I could swallow down her truth long enough to stop thinking about whoever else was out there hurting, wishing someone would stitch them back together.

I stood at the bottom of the stairs to Tyler's bus, indecisive. As soon as I'd gotten out of the car with Laura, he was my first thought. My mind kept spinning, circling the right thing to do. Go after Kenny, make his life difficult, even if I couldn't bring him down, put so much pressure on him he wouldn't dare do what he'd done to another girl. My gut told me I couldn't sit by, silent.

But I was pregnant with a baby I wanted to keep secret.

I had a colorful past with men. My relationships weren't neat and tidy. My image. My career. What had happened with Kenny was messy and could bury me just as easily.

Simpler to ignore that six-month window of my life. Except... I'd thought I was the only one. He'd called me special, irresistible, and made me question my view of what he did. Had I wanted it? Given some signal it was okay for him to treat me that way? If what happened was wrong, if I didn't want it, why did I let it happen?

My hand strayed to my still-flat stomach, and I took a deep breath. I hoped this baby was a boy. Tyler would raise him to treat women better. The things little girls faced in the world? I hated thinking about it.

I'd been kind of awful to Tyler for the last few weeks since he arrived on the tour. One minute, I wanted to sleep with him again. The next, I worried he might sleep with my mom. Wouldn't that be something? Me pregnant and him fucking the grandmother.

He wouldn't.

At least, I didn't think he would. No matter what I threw at him, he shrugged off my words or actions. Sometimes, he even seemed amused by them, by me. In another life, I might have rooted for him to become involved with my mom, weather those storms and stick around.

The only storms I wanted him to weather now were mine, and then I wanted him to get the hell out of my life. Far enough away that I never needed to worry about changing my mind, about considering a life that could never make me happy.

The doors to the bus opened, and I jumped back, the costume in my hand swinging beside me. My free hand flew to my chest, pressing against my heart. From the top of the stairs, Tyler looked down, amused. His expression made my stomach flutter. There was something comforting about his face. Not just his eyes or his voice. *Him.* His presence was the same as slipping under the covers of my childhood bed after being on tour for months.

"You going to stand out here all night, or did you want to climb aboard?"

"I'm not sure."

"I believe that." He chuckled. "Get up here. I'll give you a lollipop."

I gripped the handrail and then followed him onto the bus. At the top of the stairs, I tossed the ripped costume at him. He caught it easily, examining it with a slight frown.

"I didn't know this was ripped." His frown deepened.

He could probably tell I sliced the seam. I'd wanted to see him, but showing up without a reason felt stupid.

With a shrug, I shoved my hands into the pockets of my skirt and strolled around the main room.

"Something bothering you?" He passed me a lemon-ginger lollipop and flopped onto one of the leather couches while I let my attention dance across his personal things.

"Nothing is bothering me."

"Come on, Mia. You've ignored me for the last couple of weeks, except during your shows. It's fine. I get it. But last time you showed up here, you were upset. You're here again. That costume didn't rip. Someone cut it." He raised his eyebrows, a hint of accusation crossing his face. "And there's a weird aura around you." He made a circling motion toward my body with his hand.

"You read people's auras? Does this mean I need to give you a raise?" I turned and crossed my arms, leaning against his closet. "You some sort of mystic or psychic or some shit like that?"

"Now you're deflecting." A grin played at the edges of his mouth. He stretched his arms across the back of the couch. "Laura said you had a meeting with a producer today. How'd that go?"

"Why would my mother tell you that?" Annoyance rose up like a volcanic eruption.

"We were just chatting."

"When?" I narrowed my eyes.

Tyler sighed. "I finally let her take me to coffee."

"You gotta be fucking kidding me." I pointed to my belly. "You cannot sleep with the grandmother of your child. That's a hard 'no,' Tyler. Gross. Just...don't, okay?"

"We chatted over a caffeinated beverage, not body shots at a strip club." He eyed me for a beat. "Strip club is tomorrow night. No decent ones in Nashville."

I gaped at him. "You—"

"I'm kidding. I'm kidding." He held up his hands.

"I don't find it funny."

"Clearly."

"Don't try to make me feel like I don't have a sense of humor." Anger sparked in my gut. "I can take a joke, and I get them, too. You know what else I get? Men. Most of them don't look for an invitation before trying to stick their dick in. My mother doesn't have a problem sending out the invites to the party in *her* pants."

The smile died on Tyler's lips, and he sat forward, all amusement gone. "That's been your experience? That men don't want or need an invitation?"

For a long time, I believed there was only one kind of man. A man who took what he wanted, no matter what. But I learned to recognize those men and could avoid most of them now.

"If that surprises you, you haven't been paying attention to the world." I scoffed.

"That happened to you?" He rubbed his face and stared at his hands. "Someone treated you like that?" When he looked up, his eyes were hard with suppressed anger.

"Not anymore." But even that wasn't true. Last week, at the end of a talk show performance, the male host had squeezed my ass as the cameras rolled and he joked with the live studio audience. My options had been to make a scene on camera or let him get away with it. Afterwards, I'd fumed to Taryn and Rebecca, and told Laura I wouldn't be going on his talk show again anytime soon.

"So, it has happened to you," Tyler said.

"My mom says it happens to every woman, but not every woman talks about it." I'd forgotten that conversation. We had it after I told her about Kenny. Laura had said those words as though my situation was something to be accepted instead of fought against. She had fought today, but only for me, for my safety, not for anyone else. My mind kept swinging back to the others.

"As far as I know, it's never happened to my sisters." His hands dangled between his knees.

"So, what? You think there's some kind of neon sign over my head? Over the heads of women like me telling assholes to take a chance? We won't mind." I stared at him. The truth was that I wondered the same thing. Was there something about me that made men realize they could get away with it? Did I somehow offer encouragement? Were the other girls like me in some way? "But your sisters have some sort of invisible...*aura* of protection?"

"That's not what I said." He shook his head. "Not what I meant, either. You and Laura have a strained relationship or—I don't know—a complicated one. But I don't get why she'd accept that kind of treatment for herself, and I *really* don't understand why she'd let it happen to you. You're both worth more."

I didn't let his words digest before latching onto a few of them. "So, you think some women *should* be treated that way?"

"No. No woman should be treated that way." He huffed out a breath.

"But you just said my mom and I are worth more. Worth more than who?"

"Not who." A ghost of a smile drifted across his face. "Worth, in this sense, isn't a competition. I mean self-worth, realizing *you* are worthy of better treatment."

"Yeah, well, my mom says I'm hard work. Not easy to be around. Maybe I'm too much work. Maybe this is the best it gets."

A beat of silence sat between us. "People don't have to be easy to be worth investing in. Sometimes, the people you have to work for, the relationships you earn, are more important than whether the journey was easy. I don't believe that whatever you've had before is the best you can do. Not even close."

My heart swelled at his words. Men called me all sorts of things: a tease, a slut, too open, not open enough, frigid. None of them ever turned the negative into a positive, made me feel like I could be myself, my real self, that I might be worthy of more. Men had always sought what I could give them, never considered what they could give me. A confession rose, and I let it float to the top of my consciousness.

"The first time it happened, I was thirteen." I couldn't look at him. The words tumbled out before I had a chance to stop them. "I was drinking at a friend's house. When I came home, my mom's boyfriend was in the living room, waiting up. Not my mom. Just her boyfriend." Tyler's feet appeared mere inches from mine, and I glanced up. When did he leave the couch?

"Did he hurt you?" His voice was rough, and his breath teased the tendrils of my hair loosened from my braid.

"Don't they all?" My heart hammered in my chest. "Everybody always wants a piece of me." Tyler did, too. He wanted the cluster of cells multiplying inside me.

"Did the producer you went to see hurt you?" His fingers were gentle as they skimmed my cheek, tucking the stray strands behind my ear.

"Yes," I whispered. I'd never admitted the truth to anyone except my mom. Even then, I'd been high on drugs when I finally spilled that secret. "Not today. Years ago. He can't hurt me anymore." His eyes were filled with so much concern that I wanted to melt into him. I inched forward and slid my arms around his middle, and he drew me tight against him, sighing into my hair. "Can we be friends, Tyler? Real friends?" His heart thumped against my ear.

He cleared his throat. "That's what you want?"

"I like the way you treat me, even when I don't deserve it."

"Aww, Mia." He made slow circles on my back. "You deserve kindness. You didn't deserve what happened to you at thirteen; you didn't deserve whatever happened to you with that producer, and you didn't deserve any other time some dirtbag laid his hands on you and you didn't want it." He drew back to stare into my eyes. "None of that is your fault."

"I should have done more to stop them." I closed my eyes, blocking out the thickness of the envelope Laura had thrown across Kenny's desk. There were other things I should be stopping now. But with the baby and my career, the risks were too great. "I think I might be a terrible person."

He crouched down and cupped my face in his hands. "You're not a terrible person. Their choices aren't yours."

I was still choosing to keep quiet, to hide the ugliness. So much better if my past didn't exist. "I should go. I'm sorry." A small laugh escaped as I broke away. "God, why am I such a mess right now?" I wiped a few stray tears that slid down my cheeks. "It's not like anyone is dying. I'm famous. I shouldn't be fucking complaining about shit that doesn't matter. Do you know how many people would kill to be in my shoes?" I twisted my ankle to show him my fancy stilettos. "Even these ones." I slid one hand down my face, slipping the invisible mask back in place. "I shouldn't have told you all that. I'm sorry. That was stupid. I should go." A smile flashed. "I'm glad we're friends, though. That'll be nice, right?"

"Mia—"

From the top of the bus stairs, I called, "When you get that costume fixed, just return it to wardrobe, okay?" My laugh sounded fake even to my ears. "Shitty seamstress, I guess. Came apart in my hand." *After I cut it with scissors.*

"You don't have to go."

"Things to do," I yelled back as the doors swished open. When I caught the first taste of fresh air, the tightness in my chest eased. I almost told him all of it. Then what? He'd realize I was weak, that I cared more about myself than other people. All true. But I didn't want him to see me that way.

My mother's words played again—we were safe now, and safety was all that mattered.

Chapter Ten

Tyler

With six weeks on tour under my belt, I knew the show forward and backward. Each night as Mia shimmied into her final outfit, glowing with sweat and joy, she exuded a contagious lightness. Those moments before the second encore were my favorite. No one could match her, and she knew it. We always exchanged playful banter, and then she gave me a look over her shoulder just before she hurried to her harness. The heat in her gaze made me want to drop to my knees and thank God women like her existed.

But as soon as the stage lights went out for the night, a flip switched inside of Mia too. Night after night I saw it. I'd heard of singers and performers who crashed after the big production, but Mia deflated, as though someone popped her internal balloon. Her behavior didn't seem to worry Laura, but the change from glowing and magnetic to sullen and quiet was unsettling. Her panic over losing her career made more sense after seeing the shift. How could she give up the one thing protecting her from whatever storms brewed inside her?

Eighteen months around the world and these high highs and low lows had to take a toll. It was a wonder she was still sane. I wanted to give Mia something, anything that inspired the joy I saw on stage or at least let her keep some buoyancy. Maybe the crowd, the lights, the sweeping emotion couldn't be replicated, but I sought something. I'd heard the performers who chased the high offstage turned to drugs. Made sense, but it wasn't an option I'd ever suggest—pregnant or not.

So, what? What could I do?

The only other thing that functioned like addiction was love, at least first love. The sweeping, all-consuming feeling had taken hold once. If I was generous, I'd come close to experiencing the high a few other times. Infatuated, perhaps on the brink of more, but never quite reaching those heights a second time.

Love gone wrong was its own kind of insanity; and in my experience, it was impossible to make someone fall in love or return the love you offered.

The click-clack of heels on the concrete floor directed my attention toward the door. All the costumes were in the backstage area at this arena because we had three concert dates in the heart of Kansas. An odd choice, but Laura had explained the hometown crowd was strong here. Mia was supposed to be a Kansas girl, and they played up her roots with multiple concerts.

"You busy?" Mia was framed in the doorway, a dress clutched in her hand.

"I'm making myself busy. Gotta earn my money." I smiled and leaned against the sewing table I used in my free time to make costume alterations for the backup dancers. "What's up?"

"This dress doesn't fit, and I need to wear it today." Tears pooled in her eyes, and she shook the black sequined dress in her hand.

With a frown, I took the dress from her outstretched hand. I checked it over and tested the fabric. There was no give. "We can make it fit." I caught her eye. "This is why I'm here, right?" Her costumes on stage were always built from material meant to stretch and flex. While Mia worried about showing early or putting on weight, her petite frame was almost exactly the same as a few months ago.

Perhaps not exactly. I wasn't blind. Her breasts would fill my whole hand now instead of only my palm.

"I can let a seam out. I'll need you to put it on to see if that'll be enough." I glanced up from the dress to meet her gaze. "Across the chest?"

A tear fell, and she scooped it up with a finger. "Yeah." She closed the door and flicked the lock into place. "This fucking sucks. I thought about getting implants a couple years ago." She put her hands under her breasts and bounced them. "But now I'm terrified someone's going to figure this out because I'll have these honking things and then I'll be flat as a board again."

Watching her play with her breasts made me want to adjust my pants. God, she was gorgeous. Sometimes, it stunned me that she was carrying my child. I gave a strained chuckle. "It's not that noticeable."

"Did you see the change?" She raised her eyebrows and crossed her arms. "'Cause you know all the pervs on the internet screenshotting interviews and appearances are going to spot my hooters if you did."

I grabbed a lollipop from the table and tucked it into my cheek. I wasn't a saint. She'd had nice breasts before, and it was the body part I noticed first on a woman. The expansion in the last week *was* obvious.

"That's a 'yes,'" Mia said. "You see them. You might as well attach a flashing sign to your lollipop addiction that says, 'Trying to hide my emotions and not succeeding.' I've got your number."

"You want the truth?" I took the lollipop out of my mouth and waited.

"Sure. Why not? Never to each other, right? Isn't that the mantra?"

"You had nice breasts before, and you have nice breasts now. Whatever some perv is screenshotting in his basement hasn't changed. Same breasts. Same spank bank." I shrugged. "Not much you can do about that."

Mia cocked her head and wandered over, her heels clicking on the floor. She favored dresses and skirts, and today was no exception. The candy pink skirt swayed with her as she sidled closer. My fingers itched to slide up her thigh and under her skirt. After the things she'd told me, I was determined I wasn't going to make a move. I wasn't the kind of man who took something a woman didn't willingly, enthusiastically give, no matter how tight my pants got.

"Do you have a bank?" Our fingers connected as she took the dress.

"Every man has one. If they tell you they don't, they're lying." My voice was rough, and our gazes met. She did this sometimes, tested, teased, seemed to be considering whether she wanted more from our arrangement. Whenever she heard I was out for coffee with her mother, she ramped up the sexual tension between us the next time we saw each other. I hadn't been out for a drink with Laura in a week, so I didn't know what was happening right now. I wasn't going to complain. This version of Mia was one of my favorites.

She braced her hand on my bicep, and she rose on her toes, so her lips grazed my ear. "What's in yours?"

I held very still while everything in me hollered to grab her, lift her onto the table, and show her all the things I'd been thinking about these last few weeks. When she drew back, I searched her face, trying to decide how honest I should be. Was this a test?

"Never to each other," Mia whispered, reading my mind.

"I get new material for mine every day," I said, her lips a distraction.

A sly smile slid onto her face. "Why's—"

A loud knock on the door startled us, causing the dress to fall. It hit the floor between us with a soft thud.

I cleared my throat and swooped down to pick it up. I passed it to her and went to the door. "Who is it? I'm in the middle of a repair."

"Time for coffee?" Laura called from the other side of the door. "I need to pick your brain."

Over my shoulder, I caught Mia's scowl while she tugged up the straps of the black dress.

"Give me thirty minutes." I pressed my forehead against the cool, steel door. The temperature in the room was already ten degrees cooler. When I turned around, Mia was wearing the dress, hands on her hips, breasts spilling out the top. Despite the pissed-off look on her face, it was an image I was storing for later.

"Don't mind me." Mia threw out her hands. "Don't let the mother of your child get in the way of your coffee *date*."

I walked a slow circle around her, assessing the dress and giving us both a moment to get collected. Two inches short of zipping closed at the back. Saying something I didn't mean would push us further apart. The baby we were bringing into the world deserved two parents.

"If our situation comes out, we're going to need your mother on our side, right? She needs to like me, Mia."

"You sleep with her, and I'm putting this child up for adoption." She pointed to her stomach.

Pursing my lips, I suppressed a sigh. From her experience, men made poor choices all the time, let her down, took advantage of her. Even though I knew where these thoughts came from, they made our age difference jarring. Jealousy wasn't reasonable, rational, especially since we weren't together.

"I'm going to say this to you one more time, no jokes, straight-up serious. I have zero interest in sleeping with your mother. Zero. Next time you toss out that claim, I'm ignoring it. I get that it's hard for you to trust what I say, but I won't lie to you. I promised you that much, and I want to be a man of my word."

Her dark hair fell around her face while she looked at the floor. I swept back one side of her hair and tucked it behind her ear, hoping to catch a glimpse of her expression. Her attitude often turned on a dime.

"I can let out the seam, and it'll fit." I kept my voice gentle. "What time do you need it?"

"Lunch." She tucked the other side of her hair and faced me. "I don't like you spending time with her."

"Why?" I pushed one hand into the pocket of my jeans and readjusted the lollipop in my mouth with the other. "It's just coffee and not even that often." But our meetings were regular, consistent. She usually asked once a week. I was careful never to initiate, but turning her down produced other complications. After all, as far as everyone knew, she was my boss.

"I like how you treat me. How you see me." Tears pooled in her eyes. "What if she tells you something to change that?"

Protectiveness gripped me so hard it stole my breath. As much as I enjoyed the flirtatious Mia, this version of her wiggled into my heart. The naked vulnerability made me understand how people committed homicides. I wanted to murder every person who ever made her think respect and kindness could disappear in a puff of smoke. "I've seen pretty much every side of you. Nothing is going to change how I view you, or how I treat you."

"How can you know that?" She wiped at her tears and stared at them on her fingers. "I never cry. Lately, I'm always crying. Why am I always fucking crying?" Her voice caught on a sob.

I slid my hand into her hair and tugged her into my chest. She clung on, pressing her face against me. "We'll check with David later today when we see him for your checkup. The tears are probably hormones, but we can ask, okay? Your schedule is insane, and you're riding the onstage and offstage emotional roller coaster."

"I used to even myself out with drugs," Mia whispered. "But I haven't taken anything since I took the tests."

Did Laura realize Mia used drugs to level her moods? Was that why her mother wasn't worried about her? She thought Mia was medicated?

"For depression...or...?" My heart hammered in my chest. She should have told me or David at one of the appointments. Maybe she needed to be on the meds.

A husky chuckle reverberated across my chest, warming my heart. "Self-medicating. Recreational. Nothing doctor prescribed."

I wasn't sure her revelation was more comforting. *Jesus.* Laura dropped the ball on a lot of shit with Mia.

Against my chest, she said, "I'll be okay." She rose on her toes and wrapped her arms around my neck, pressing her lips against the hollow. "Thank you for caring."

I spanned her back with my hand, and I drew her a little closer, our bodies slotting together. The caring came easy, which was starting to be scary. I wasn't sure I was going to be able to let her go when she was ready to leave, and the baby wasn't even here yet, not even visible on her body. How would I feel once she'd given birth, once we'd spent more time together? A baby was a bond, a profound one.

"I'll always care," I whispered in her ear and squeezed her tight.

Laura sipped her coffee and placed it back in the saucer on the table. We decided on this coffee chain because it was close to the stadium. I thought everything was overpriced and the food was not particularly good, but Laura liked the familiarity. Wherever she went, at least this place never changed.

"Mia's been going on about how much she liked Little Falls when we were in the area for the benefit. She wants to go there and work with Grady on her album. What do you know about him?"

"He's dating my sister, and while I don't know much about the music business, he seems to have written a lot of really popular songs." I stirred more cream into my coffee. "He's a good guy. Mia wouldn't have any worries with him."

"I don't doubt his talent. I just—I wanted to make sure she'll be safe going there." She fiddled with the arm of her coffee cup. "Of course, she'll still need a bodyguard. There're a lot of crazed fans out there. We're almost constantly in touch with law enforcement about one thing or another."

"People threaten her?" Political figures or controversial performers, sure. But Mia was America's sweetheart.

"Men, mostly. Delusional in one way or another. Some want to marry her, some want to have sex with her...some want to kill her." She shook her head. "It's the scary part of fame."

"She's got protection all the time, right?" A cold sweat broke out across my back. I don't know why the darker side of her fame hadn't sunk in yet. The last few weeks, I'd had a front row seat to how invested people were in her.

"Yeah. We take every threat very seriously. She's—we've had a few instances of people taking advantage of her, of people not treating her well. I was surprised she let you on the tour. But she seems to like you." She watched me over the rim of her cup for a beat. "I've seen the banter between the two of you."

"I have two sisters." I was unwilling to give her more than that. "Lots of practice." Lengthy explanations made people look guilty. Not that I had a reason to feel guilty. Nothing had happened between us since I joined the tour.

"Maybe that's it," Laura said. "Fourteen years is quite a gap. Her father is only a few years older than you."

Ah, so her observations were what I'd thought. She was warning me off. *Too late, Laura.* I sipped my coffee. "So, what's your feeling on Little Falls? I grew up there. So, of course, I think it's a nice town."

"I don't know. She wants six months." She eyed me. "Are you going back to Little Falls after the tour?"

"Sadly, no." I shook my head. "I have a job with a theater company. It was why it took me a while to get back to you about this job. I had to check some dates and juggle a couple commitments." I took another, longer drink. The lie came easily. I'd expected this question at some point with Mia pushing to work with Grady.

"Don't you think six months is too long? Mia loves touring and singing. I don't want her career to run cold."

"Like I said, I don't know too much about the music business. Kesha took off five years or something, didn't she? And Shania Twain was gone for years. Beyoncé spent nine months going around the world, right? Taylor Swift largely disappeared for a year. When there's an appetite for what you're producing, the length of time between products doesn't seem to matter as much. It's not like she won't be working. She'll be building an album."

Laura tapped her cup with her fingernail. "He says he doesn't know much about music, but comes up with a nice list of names and dates." She chuckled. "I'd say my daughter has gotten to you."

A slow smile spread across my face. I'd give her this one. She caught me. "She can be very persuasive when she wants something. She was running a few of her arguments past me. I paid attention." Or we were brainstorming together one night about other singers who went on hiatus and come back just as strong or stronger. Mia knew her mother's priorities.

"She's worked hard to get to this level, sacrificed a lot. I don't want to see her lose it."

"She seems tired. I'd be worried about burnout," I said.

"Has she said something to you about that? Taryn and Rebecca used the same argument on me."

"Hasn't said a word. It's written all over her every night as soon as the last song finishes. I don't have a stake in this beyond the tour. But she seems worn out." The lies were coming fast, and I drank my coffee to keep from meeting her gaze. She wouldn't see anything on my face. I could sell this line of thought because I actually believed it. But if Laura dug too deep, she might see my anger and annoyance at some of the choices she'd made when it came to Mia. A parent should protect their child above all else.

"She could just as easily work with Grady in L.A. or New York. I don't understand why she's pushing for the middle of nowhere."

"She's been doing this scene since she was fourteen. Maybe she wants some normalcy." I shrugged and drained my cup.

"Ah, well. Perhaps I should let her have it then? She'll be bored to tears in five minutes. My daughter craves the spotlight. Lives for it." Laura laughed.

That wasn't quite the Mia I knew, but it wasn't so far off from the truth for me to argue. Did she seem to enjoy it? Definitely. Did she crave the adulation because of what she was missing in her off-stage life? That was the question I was trying to answer.

"I'll have to keep thinking about it. I've already cleared her schedule for the first few months after the tour. Perhaps if I give her what she wants, she'll take less than six months."

I gave her a strained smile. I couldn't weigh in more. I'd have to trust Taryn, Rebecca, and Mia to stay the course and come up with better arguments. At least I'd be able to tell Mia about what Laura had said. Not that Mia would like knowing how I'd gotten the information.

I paced the top floor of the small hospital we were using just outside the city. The staff we were working with had been given an NDA. My mother, a lawyer, had written it up to be used for anything related to Mia's pregnancy. Hospitals and hospital workers were under pretty heavy privacy rules, but Mia had wanted an extra layer of protection. I got it. Understood it more every day.

"Tyler," a woman murmured my name off to my right.

I spun, recognizing her voice. "Katie. I didn't realize you were coming with your dad this time."

Her brown hair was in a ponytail, and she was wearing pink scrubs. It had always been a color that suited her, making her round face glow.

A small, familiar smile surfaced. For years, I'd lived for all her smiles, but I never liked this one, full of uncertainty. She gave me this one the day she broke up with me, as though I should somehow understand what was really going on. I never had then, and I had no interest in figuring it out now.

"Blood work."

"Someone here could have done that."

"Maybe." She shoved her purse higher onto her shoulder. She ambled closer. "I wanted to see you."

"Why?"

"I was hoping we could go talk somewhere. Maybe grab a drink after the exam?" Another tentative smile.

"Mia's on stage tonight. Time is limited." I held myself rigid. There was a reason I'd avoided her since we'd split. Not just one reason, reasons—plural.

"When I moved back, I heard you were dating Danai. So, I was surprised when you showed up at the hospital with Mia Malone." She scanned me, searching for something. "As your surrogate."

The truth sat poised on my lips. Danai had texted me a few times when I'd first gone on tour, and then those texts had stopped when I'd called her to make it known we wouldn't be picking up where we'd left off when I got back. I'd thought I'd made it clear before I left. But endings weren't my specialty.

"What are you after, Katie?" She didn't believe the cover story. It was a ridiculous one. Why would a world-famous pop star agree to be my surrogate? I spent ten years with Katie; she knew me better than almost anyone.

"You're going to raise the baby by yourself?"

I clenched my jaw and looked away. She was close enough for me to catch a whiff of her familiar apple blossom perfume. If I closed my eyes, I could go back to all the times I'd smelled it before, all the moments when I'd soaked her in, lived for this smell. Getting over her had been the hardest thing I'd ever done. A small piece of me still strained toward her in the corridor, wanted to hear what she had to say.

But loyalty was important, and mine didn't lie with Katie anymore.

"I've been thinking a lot about whether I did the right thing. With you and me."

When I said nothing in response and time stretched between us, she continued, "Are you and Mia together?"

Swallowing down the residual feelings creeping up my throat, I met her curious gaze. "You can't ask me that. We broke up. Eight years ago. *Eight years.*"

"I'm not...maybe we shouldn't have," Katie whispered. "I really want to talk to you. Talk about what happened back then. Ever since I saw you a few weeks ago, I can't stop thinking about you."

She'd crossed my mind, too. More than once. I'd blamed the memories on the shock of seeing her. Knowing she was back in Little Falls had screwed with my head.

"Well," Mia drawled, her heels clicking along the corridor. "This looks tense. You okay, Pretty Boy?" Her sunglasses dangled from her fingers, and she was eyeing Katie with distaste. "I'm going to have to call a janitor. I think there's a puddle of drool at your feet, Katie. Or did that wetness come from some other part of you?" She cocked her head, her eyes wide with false innocence.

I sucked in a breath at the sight of her and crossed the distance between us. Without thinking, I hugged her and pressed my lips to her temple. I kept my back to Katie, even though Mia's comments were rude at best. Earlier, I tried to tell her the jealousy she felt was misplaced. The difference between this situation and the other was my history with Katie and the hope sparking in my gut.

After she broke up with me, I spent many a drunken night rambling to friends and family about how Katie would regret it. We'd been perfect for each other. Someday, she'd see it.

Hearing her admit she might have made a mistake was a vindication. My instincts about her, about us, hadn't been as wrong as I'd thought. At the time, her justification for our split hadn't rung true.

Too late for explanations. Wasn't it?

It had altered the pattern of my life. Once the seam between two hearts had been ripped, it wasn't always possible to mend it. Sometimes, the two pieces would never again fit together.

Mia pressed her cheek into my chest, and I breathed her in. "I'm glad you're here," I whispered in her ear. At least I knew that much for sure.

When I heard the soft retreat of Katie's sneakers, I tried really hard not to care.

Chapter Eleven

Mia

Floating at the edge of my consciousness was the image of Tyler standing in the middle of the hospital corridor, too close to his ex-girlfriend. I'd gone through the concert motions, but the performance wasn't my best effort. Being on stage was my escape from all the other shit. But every tune, every lyric reminded me of Tyler tonight, and it was driving me insane. The urge to punch him or kiss him was overwhelming.

Perhaps punch him, and then kiss him.

Jealousy was eating its way through my gut, and it was different from how I felt about his relationship with Mom. Too different. Because when he'd turned in the hall, there'd been an expression on his face I'd never seen before.

Guilt.

Whatever he and Katie were talking about had made him feel guilty. Had he betrayed my secrets? Made promises to his ex about a future once the baby was born and I was out of the way?

From Katie's body language and how she'd looked at Tyler, her regrets over their breakup were obvious. And his face, God, the expression on his face before he realized I was there. Round two between them didn't seem out of the question.

My gut clenched.

"You tired?" Tyler's brow puckered before he helped squeeze me into the final outfit of the night. The second encore was usually my favorite because I could make the crowd wait for a minute or two while we flirted. Not tonight. I wasn't in the mood.

"Sure. Yeah. Tired." I'd held my tongue at the appointment and responded to the doctor's questions with short, truthful answers. I even spoke to Katie a second time without being completely rude. Other than the sickness, the crying, and the expanding breasts, I could almost forget I was pregnant. Wouldn't that be nice?

He studied me for a moment, and then we stared at each other, mute.

"You gonna talk to me?" he asked.

Since I'd come off the stage for my last change, I'd barely spoken to him. Normally, we were energized, almost frantic in our playful exchanges. The best kind of foreplay...as though we'd rip each other's clothes off later.

"I'm talking to you right now." I tipped my head at the stagehand who usually strapped me into the harness, and then we walked off together, leaving Tyler behind. Other nights, our playful banter left him watching me when I walked away, and I always threw him one last glance. Tonight, when I looked back, it wasn't with my usual sassiness; and his eyes weren't glued to me either. He was deep in conversation with Taryn and didn't notice me at all.

I ground my teeth and flung out my arms, letting the stagehand buckle me into the butterfly harness. Whatever this feeling was building in my chest needed to go away. Jealousy. I had no time for jealousy. Tyler needed to be exterminated from my thoughts.

He wasn't a knight in shining armor sent to save me. Even if he was this bright, saintly example of manhood, I didn't need saving.

The harness yanked tight, and I was propelled toward the ceiling, arms out, wings flapping in the breeze from the arena's cooling system.

I was Mia Malone, at the pinnacle of my career. Fans buzzed around in the darkened arena, filling up the space with an energy I'd kept at bay all night. When the lights flashed and the crowd burst with their frantic screams, I breathed a sigh of relief and let their enthusiasm flood me.

This. This feeling.

Who wouldn't want my life?

Taryn eyed me in the mirror while the makeup artist removed my stage makeup and applied another coat for the club appearance. I had an hour to get there. Rebecca stood behind Taryn consulting a list of commitments scheduled for the next week.

"You're exhausted."

"I'm fine." I held still in the chair and tried to keep my features neutral. If I went with Grady's suggestion, I would agree with Taryn, admitting this life was all becoming too much. It was. But the work wasn't doing me in or even the pregnancy. The baby daddy was the real problem. I'd never wanted to yank someone closer while also pushing them far, far away. Whatever feelings were sprouting, I needed to find some weed killer.

Then he could make eyes at his ex in the hospital hallway, and I wouldn't care at all.

"You're not fine. Tonight's concert was lackluster at best. Social media is abuzz with how off you were." Rebecca didn't look up from her calendar, passing the clipboard to Taryn. "We're going to cut some things. We don't need you spiraling and being hospitalized."

"One lackluster concert is hardly spiraling." I rolled my eyes. "Give me some freaking credit. Almost eighteen months of this and I have one bad night? Sound the alarm!" I threw up my hands. "Mia's on a downward spiral."

"This have anything to do with Tyler?" Taryn crossed her arms and leaned against the wall, the clipboard back in Rebecca's hands.

"Tyler? Please." I shifted in the chair to catch a better angle of my makeup. Lighter for the club atmosphere, softer.

"I got frostbite from your conversation between the first and second encore. You know what I normally get?" Taryn gave her a pointed look. "Burnt from the heat between you two. Something is going on there, and whatever happened today threw you off. That's my developing theory."

"A lover's spat can do that," Rebecca said.

"We'd know." Taryn laughed.

I had rarely seen them fight, but when they did, their animosity was obvious. Neither of them could focus on anything and were hard to be around. Was that me right now? Tyler and I weren't fighting. And we weren't lovers, not anymore. I frowned.

"You could do worse than him." Rebecca's voice was soft.

"Oh, I know." I fluffed my hair and pretended indifference. "But there's nothing happening. Just a bad night. Nothing to do with him. He's too old for me, anyway." The way he'd looked at Katie was burned into my retinas. I wanted to scrub my memory clean, give my brain something else to focus on. Usually, performing gave my mind the break I craved. Hadn't worked tonight.

"We're going to chat with Laura about your schedule. Okay with you?" Taryn rubbed her hands together and then slid them along the small of her back.

"Whatever. I'm fine. If you can convince my mother to slow down this madness, I'm not going to say no." I couldn't decide if I should be welcoming or fighting this suggestion. What would I do if I wasn't pregnant?

The two of them filed out of her dressing room, and the makeup artist put on the finishing touches. I turned my face, watching how the lights hollowed me out and plumped me up. A roundness was starting that reminded me too much of my chubby past.

A knock on the door dragged me back to the present. "You can go." I waved off the makeup artist. "Come in!"

In the mirror, my gaze connected with Tyler's when he entered the dressing room. He was carrying one of my costumes, but I knew it didn't need any work. The games we played. A hint of a smile touched my lips, and I swiveled the chair around, tilting my head.

"What's up, Pretty Boy?"

"I came to ask you the same thing." He shook his head and squinted.

"I'm living my best life." I tipped my chin. "How about you?" I splayed out my hands and shrugged.

For a moment, he studied me in silence. "I'm working on it." He glanced down at the costume and then back at me. "It occurred to me you might have misinterpreted what you saw between me and Katie in the hall."

"Misinterpreted?" I raised my eyebrows and rotated my chair back toward the mirror. "There was something to interpret there? Can't say I noticed." I smoothed my eyebrows and grabbed a cotton swab off the makeup counter, dabbing random places on my face. If he knew anything about makeup, he'd realize I was avoiding him. "I can't remember why you two broke up. Why was that again?"

He twisted the scrap of fabric in his hands and didn't meet my gaze in the mirror. With a deep breath, he made eye contact. "There's nothing between us anymore. We've been apart for eight years, almost longer than we were together."

"You didn't answer my question." The muscles in my face tightened in annoyance.

"I know."

"I want you to answer my question."

"I realize that."

"Don't be a dick. It's a simple question. Why did you break up?"

"Maybe the answer isn't simple. Maybe it's not something I want to share. Maybe...you don't need to know."

"Fuck you. Never to each other, right?" My voice dripped with contempt.

"I'm not *lying* to you. Refusing to tell you something that has no bearing on our arrangement is not lying to you. I'm guarding my privacy. I'm maintaining the line *you* said you wanted between us."

"I'm giving you a baby," I hissed, swinging the chair around. "The least you can do is give me an answer."

"Why are you asking?" He came closer, so close I caught a whiff of the jasmine lollipop he favored.

"Is she the reason you've been hiding out in Little Falls?" I narrowed my gaze. His attachment to that place made no sense. He was good at costume design, and he'd taken to the show without any blips. Why had he only done one tour with some second-rate theater company? There'd been a single entry, ten pages into a Google search. He quit the show early and needed to be replaced. One tour, cut short. A thrift store in Little Falls. Nothing added up, and I'd tried to count it so many ways.

"You have nothing to worry about with Katie. If that's what this is about, you don't need to worry."

"Why would I worry?" I threw out my hands. "She's like thirty-some-thing. A nurse in a tiny town in the middle of nowhere New York. I'm the opposite." I slid off the chair and sashayed over. The dress I'd changed into swayed against my thighs. "I'm young and rich." With my finger, I drew a line down his chest. "Why would I worry about someone like her?"

He gave a sharp shake of his head, and when our gazes connected, I stepped back, surprised at the anger splashed across his face instead of the desire I expected. "Sometimes," he said, "you really show your age."

"You can leave." Heat rose to my cheeks. "Don't let the door hit your ass on the way out." I spun on my heel and yanked open the dressing room door. When Tyler shifted past, not even bothering to argue, I caught sight of a familiar head of dark hair.

Cade Brewer. Finally, a stroke of luck.

"Cade!" I waved, a grin splitting my face. When Tyler half-turned back, surprise flickering on his face at my sudden change in mood, my grin widened. "Long time. Come on in."

Pasha frowned and moved toward the entrance with Cade.

"It's okay." I motioned to Cade. "We're old friends." Friends wasn't the right term, but I wasn't going to broadcast he was a conquest in the hallway. We'd pretended to date for a few months almost a year ago, and I'd test driven him in bed. He was a reliable econocar, nothing too exciting, but not terrible either. Two celebrities passing in the night and occasionally posing for red carpet photos. My mother's idea, of course. The public, the fans, needed to see me as well rounded. Too many had commented about my long work hours.

"I can't believe you didn't call me to say you were coming this way," Cade said as soon as the door clicked shut.

"We always come this way. I'm from here, remember? What are you doing in Missouri?"

"Shooting a movie." He lit a cigarette and turned to offer me a drag. "Thought you might have heard."

"Cigarettes are bad for my voice."

"Never stopped you before." His gaze traveled over my body in a way I hated. Predatory, almost. The look reminded me of too many other men, too many other rooms. Cade hadn't been like them though. Econocar. Reliably bland.

He dropped the partially smoked cigarette on the concrete floor and stubbed it out with his heel. His hand roved down my side, settling on my waist.

If Tyler saw this, he'd realize what I said was true. Men wanted me, valued me. Was Katie holed up in a dressing room with an international movie star? Nope.

With a tug, he yanked me flush against him. "You've put on a bit of weight in all the right places." He cupped my breast. "As soon as I heard you were here for a few days, I figured you'd be up for another round. Last time we ran into each other, you were begging for it."

I couldn't help the laugh that burst out. That's how Cade remembered it? He was still self-obsessed, but there was an edge to him tonight that I didn't like. Cocky. Someone must have told him he was better than an econocar. He was never sharp before. I didn't play with sharp men. They cut too deep.

"Begging for it?" There'd only ever been one person I begged because he'd brought me so close to the edge over and over, and it wasn't Cade Brewer. Last time I met Cade in a hotel room, I hadn't even climaxed. Of course, *he* had no problem reaching the finish line. Thank God my faulty condoms arrived *after* that encounter.

When I tried to wiggle away, he gripped me tighter and chuckled in my ear. "Feeling feisty tonight, are you? That's all right. I'll have you bent over the chair and crying out my name in no time."

Bent over anything wasn't my style, not that I'd ever told him why. I'd made it clear that item wasn't on the menu.

"We're not happening." With all my strength, I pushed on his chest. A surge of panic rose in me when he didn't move. "Let go of me." His bulging muscles were new. Whatever role he was playing had to be one that required him to bulk up. Another strike of fear, almost terror-pierced me. Why had I told Pasha to stay outside the room?

He shifted his grip, pressing his hand into the small of my back, making me arch against him so I could feel how turned on our exchange made him.

"Don't be a cock tease. God, Mia. It's not like we haven't fucked before. A quickie to release some tension. That's all I want."

We'd never had sex like he just described. Hotel rooms. Beds. A hint of romance. Not a quick fuck in my dressing room.

"No, Cade. Okay? I'm not fucking you here."

"I'll make it good for you." He licked a line from my collarbone up to my neck and bit my earlobe. "You'll be screaming *yes* by the time I'm slipping into you."

"No." I pushed against his chest. "Pasha!" I heard the hint of panic in my voice, and the handle rattled. "Pasha!" I hadn't locked the door. I never locked my dressing room.

"Who the hell is Pasha?" Cade breathed into my ear. His free hand tried to slide between my legs. "Come on, Mia. I know you're wet. Don't try to deny it."

"Did you lock the door?" Definitely panic in my voice.

A sly grin slid across his face when he pulled back to look at me. "Of course. No interruptions." He tried to kiss me, and I turned my head. His slobbery lips gobbled my cheek.

"Pasha!" I screamed his name in Cade's ear, and he released me when the door burst open. Pasha had his forearm across Cade's throat, and he was pressed against the wall before I could get another word out.

"I said no," I whispered, and Pasha unleashed a string of Russian in Cade's face. Was it cold in here? I looked around, dazed. There had to be a window open. But there weren't any. My arms shook as I hugged myself, and I stared at them, stunned.

Tyler's hand slipped into my hair, and he drew me to him. I clutched his biceps and closed my eyes.

"I said no." Where had he appeared from? He'd been angry or frustrated or something. My nails dug into his arm.

"You said no," he murmured in my ear. "He should have listened when you said no."

When Cade had come on to me, I'd felt vindicated at first. But the truth was, I didn't want other men.

Tyler's lips grazed my forehead, and his palm smoothed down my loose strands. His fingers toyed with the collar of my dress. "I can mend this for you."

I met his fingers on my shoulder, and I was surprised by the tremble when I touched the jagged edge of my dress.

"Mia," Laura popped her head in the door. "I just spoke to Taryn and Rebecca." She looked around the room, surveying the overturned chair and table before landing on me and Tyler with narrowed eyes. "What happened in here?"

I shrugged, letting Tyler fall away, let the incident drop from my mind, and I hurried to the makeup table to grab my clutch. "Nothing. Cade Brewer thought he'd try his luck. Pasha put him in his place. He must have escorted him out of the building."

I hadn't seen them leave, but the minute Tyler's fingers slid into my hair, I hadn't cared about anything or anyone else. My heart beat erratically in my chest, not quite back to normal, not quite believing what had almost happened. How many times would I be pinned into a corner before I learned to fight back instead of freezing?

"Cade Brewer," Laura murmured and frowned. "Shame. He's good PR, normally. Heard he's become a crackhead, though."

Out of the corner of my eye, I saw Tyler tense. I wanted to run my palm down his arm, tell him to let it go, shrug it off. That's what I would do. What I always did. In my hand, my purse shook, subtle, but there.

"Anyway," Laura said. "Appearance tonight at Club Zeal, then we'll chat about scaling back. You weren't great tonight. I don't want people complaining on social media. It's bad for future ticket sales."

Ticket sales, right. Of course. Briefly, I closed my eyes, trying to find my way out of the lingering panic.

"Mia." Tyler tried to catch my gaze as I breezed past him, my heels clicking on the concrete.

"I'm fine." Under my lashes, I gave him a small smile. "It's not the first time. I'll be fine."

His shoulders slumped, and the hand he had raised toward me fell to his side. My mother's eyebrows raised, but she didn't say anything.

I found the rip at my shoulder, and I glanced at Laura. "I need to change before we go."

"What's wrong with that dress?" Laura frowned.

"It's dirty." But the dress wasn't dirty, and I wasn't sure changing would wipe the sensation away.

Pasha fell into step beside me as we headed to my bus, and I whispered "thank you" in Russian. It was the only phrase I'd learned the last few weeks. I didn't understand what he said in response, but his tone was kind and gentle. Tears pooled in my eyes, and I kept my head down while they slid down my cheeks.

Chapter Twelve

Tyler

I slid the metal clip into another stack of weights and pulled down on the lateral bar. Another set to be counted out. I'd likely increase the weights again. Ten miles on the treadmill hadn't been enough, and now I was working my muscles to exhaustion. My mind might be in a million different pieces, but at least my body would benefit from the internal chaos. Besides, as far as I could tell, I was one of the few people who used the exercise equipment stored at the back of one of the buses. It was expensive stuff. Someone might as well use it. I yanked the bar down again, muscles burning.

As soon as Mia left for the club last night, I called Grady in L.A. to find out how I could stick a figurative knife in Cade Brewer's back. Instead, my sister, Maggie, had been visiting him and talked me off the ledge. Or at least talked me down far enough that I stopped trying to search Google Earth for Cade's movie location so I could exact some revenge.

For the first time in my life, I understood why people snapped, committed murder. If Pasha hadn't already had the guy by the throat when I got there, I wasn't sure what I would have done. Seeing Mia standing there shaking, tears pooled in her unfocused eyes, had ripped right through my gut and pierced my heart. What kind of life was this? What kind of man did that to a woman? No wonder she didn't want to raise a kid in this environment. Her life was a viper pit. Every day, another one punctured her.

She was so young. How many more wounds could she take?

Across the gym, my phone vibrated on the table. There were very few people who'd call me at two a.m. *Maggie*? Had to be. Trying to make sure I hadn't stolen a car and driven around Kansas City on a mission. With a sigh, I let the weights rest and wandered over to grab my phone before it went to voicemail. My sister would probably send out a search party if I didn't answer.

I understood the unreasonable worry. Every night, I stayed awake until I heard Mia come back from whatever club appearance she went to after the shows. She'd never asked me to go with her after the first failed attempt, when she'd stormed off my bus without me. But I forced myself to be awake, no matter how late she appeared. Tonight, it wouldn't be an issue. Adrenaline hummed despite the run and the weights.

When I got close enough to see the name on the display, my heart thumped. She never called.

"Mia?" Her name was out before I'd even gotten the phone to my ear.

For a second, the line seemed dead. Then, a sniffle.

"Mia? Are you okay?"

"No." Her voice was thick, almost garbled. A sob burst from her, hitting me in the chest.

"Where are you?" I swiped my bus keys off the table and hesitated at the top of the stairs. A ride. I didn't have a vehicle. "What happened?"

"I'm bleeding."

Her words were so mangled, I wasn't sure I heard her correctly. "You're bleeding? Is Pasha there? Are you hurt? Do you need to call an ambulance?" My mind was on a tilt-a-whirl. Had someone hurt her? Was she cut? Or, God help me, I hope she didn't hurt herself. I knew people who'd used cutting on the outside to ease their turmoil inside, but I'd never seen any evidence on Mia.

Her voice caught on another sob.

"I'm coming. I'm on my way. Club—" God, what had the place been called? I'd heard so many club names over the last few weeks. Zen? Zilch? Zeal. "Zeal, right? I'll be there as soon as I can. Call an ambulance."

"I'm bleeding." She was almost hyperventilating.

Outside the bus, I looked around, the phone pressed to my ear. A car. Across the parking lot, a guy was smoking a cigarette beside a Civic. Punch him and steal his car or beg for a ride? At this point, I'd steal the cigarettes, too.

I took quick strides in the guy's direction, patting my pockets for a lollipop while Mia took a few shaky breaths.

"Pasha called you an Uber."

The guy across the lot dropped his cigarette, grinding it into the ground with his heel. "You Pretty Boy?"

"That's you," Mia whispered.

"That's me," I agreed with a grimace. "My girl's got a sense of humor."

Mia's sharp intake of breath made my gut clench. What had happened to her? With an audience now, I wasn't sure how much more I should say or ask.

"Apparently." The driver opened the door to his car and slid in.

I held the phone to my ear, listening to Mia breathe while the car zoomed toward Club Zeal. I could hear her shuffling around in a place with an echo, but I was afraid to ask. She was still at the club, so whatever had happened couldn't be that bad.

When the car pulled up in front of a packed nightclub, I climbed out and approached the bouncer on the door. "I'm—"

"Pretty Boy." The bouncer checked me over from head to toe. "You look like the picture her bodyguard showed me." He moved the velvet rope aside and pointed to the back of the club. "VIP is at the back on the right. She's there somewhere."

The bouncer wasn't panicked, and when I moved through the packed crowd, it became clear no one else was injured. Across the phone line, her breathing was steady, and she hadn't cried again in a while. But she said she was bleeding. *Bleeding.* Would she call about a simple cut? No, she'd have to be bleeding out before she'd admit she needed me.

I shook my head. *Bleeding out.* Then it clicked.

The baby. Oh, God. The baby.

The words were on the tip of my tongue, but I caught them just in time. Even with the loud music, there were too many people around. "I should call David," I said into the phone.

I tried to drag up fragments of my conversation with David and Katie at the hospital. Did they fly back tonight, or were they somewhere in the city? I weaved through the dancers, my heart tap dancing to the rhythm of the song.

"I'm in the bathroom at the back." Her voice was almost too quiet to hear. "I think it's stopped, though. I think—I think it might be okay."

When I saw Pasha guarding a door near the back of the VIP section, relief swept over me. "I'm here," I said. "She's in there? You in there, Mia?" I tipped my head at the door behind Pasha's wide shoulders.

Pasha nodded and shifted sideways to let me squeeze past into the bathroom with several stalls, only one occupied. "Mia?"

"Tyler?" Her voice caught on another sob and the stall door swung back. Mia sat perched on the edge of the seat, black streaks of makeup ran down her face, and her phone was pressed to her ear. "I don't want to move."

I dropped my phone into my pocket, then crouched in front of her, and smoothed her hair from her face. I leaned forward and kissed her forehead and then her temple. "I'll carry you out. We'll call David from the car and decide if we're going to the hospital or back to the bus."

Her fingers played with the damp strands of hair on the top of my head, our foreheads pressed together. I'd forgotten how sweaty I was.

"I knew you'd know what to do."

"Just give me a second," I backed away from her and stuck my head out the bathroom door. "Back exit?" I asked Pasha.

"Ready to go." He nodded and pointed down the deserted hallway.

In the stall, I helped Mia rearrange her clothing and then I swept her into my arms. Immediately, I wished I hadn't done that last heavy set of weights. The burn didn't feel quite so good when I was in danger of dropping her. I clenched my jaw and followed Pasha down the narrow hallway to the back exit. Mia's face was buried in my neck.

"Even your sweat smells like jasmine," she murmured.

With a chuckle, I settled her tighter against me. "Oh, yeah?"

"It's nice. I've never liked the way a guy's sweat smelled before. You were working out again?"

"Yeah." I gave a curt nod as I slid her into the back of the car.

"You do that a lot."

"Yeah."

"But you didn't always work out this much."

I gave her a sideways look as I settled beside her. "No, I didn't." Before she could prod any further, I flashed my phone. "I should call David. You don't think you're bleeding anymore?"

"No. But it seemed like a lot." Her chin wobbled. "It was a lot."

For a moment, I examined her, tried to decide if I should prod, and then I dialed David. "You were scared?"

Instead of answering, she shifted closer, and I wrapped my arm around her shoulders, drawing her into my side. From the front seat, Pasha stared at us in the rearview mirror, waiting for instructions. On the fourth ring, David picked up the phone.

After a lot of back and forth and a conversation with Mia that had her in tears again, David said he'd come in the morning to check on her before leaving Missouri, but if the bleeding had stopped, rest and avoiding stress was the prescription for tonight. It was the first time we'd had to strike a balance between the need for privacy and secrecy and the potential need for care.

When we got back to the bus, Pasha offered to carry Mia, but she clung to me, and truthfully, I didn't want Pasha to take her. I liked that she'd called, that I'd been the one she turned to for help. Once the bus was swept for any security issues, I carried Mia up the stairs and back to her bathroom.

"Did you want to shower?"

She nodded, and when I turned to leave, she grabbed my hand. "Will you stay?"

"In here?" I cleared my throat and glanced around the bathroom. Watching her shower and then walking out of here would test every bit of my willpower.

"In my room, tonight. I don't want to be alone. What if I wake up later and it's started again? I can't handle it. I don't *want* to handle it." Tears pooled in her eyes again, and I slid my hand into her hair and pulled her against my chest. That surge of protectiveness I was coming to expect around her consumed me. I'd battle wild animals for her, cross a desert, walk through fire. Whether the intensity was the baby or something else building between us, I'd never felt protective like this for anyone other than family.

Maybe Katie. Maybe. The situations were so different I couldn't compare them. I hated that she'd come to mind, almost against my will.

"Yeah," I murmured against her temple. "I'll stay."

She eased the sliding door closed between us, and I went to her bed and sat on the edge. My mind wandered to thoughts of her, slick with water from the shower, back arched, and I jumped up, guilt like a lightning strike. I rubbed my face, annoyed with myself. She'd thought she was having a miscarriage, and not even an hour later, my brain was going to places it shouldn't. When the water shut off, I breathed a sigh of relief.

In the closet to the left, I dug out some sheets. Couch or floor? The couch was outside her bedroom. Would that be better or worse?

The bathroom door slid open, and Mia stood in the entrance, a towel wrapped around her slight figure.

I was screwed. Between the vulnerable look on her face and the dewy dampness of her pale skin, this version of Mia would be seared like a tattoo in my mind. Permanent. Unforgettable. God, I wanted her, and I hated myself for feeling that way right now with the night she'd had.

"You okay?"

She tucked her wet hair behind her ears with her free hand, the other keeping the towel secure around her. "Yeah, I—I probably overreacted." She looked down at herself. "I saw all the blood, and I knew... I thought..."

I didn't know what to say. When I asked earlier if she'd been afraid, she avoided the question. Fear would mean she cared, and I didn't want to push her harder to admit her feelings if she wasn't ready. She had to be ready.

When she glanced up, she cocked her head, her gaze full of almost playful curiosity. "Are you changing my sheets? I have someone who'll do that, you know."

I'd forgotten I was holding them, and I chuckled. "I was trying to figure out if I should sleep on the floor or the couch out there." I jerked my thumb toward the front of the bus. "I wasn't sure which you'd prefer."

She sashayed into the bedroom over to a chest of drawers and let her towel drop to the floor. "Neither."

All my good intentions burst through every closed window of the bus. I'd seen her naked before, and then there were glimpses of her during every show. But that was different—we were working, surrounded by other people. This was the opposite of that, and every part of me strained at the seams. I moved the sheets in my hand a little lower to conceal what had sprung to attention.

Over her shoulder, she cast a long gaze at me before opening one of the drawers and pulling out a wisp of fabric, tugging it over her head. The pale-pink silk slid along her body. I'd never seen anything sexier. Normally, lingerie looked best on the floor, but this was definitely vying for first place in my memory. That tilt-a-whirl feeling was back but for a very different reason.

"Neither?" My voice was rough with need.

Her palms slid down her body, smoothing out the negligee, drawing it tight against her.

Sweet Jesus. I was in trouble.

She dragged her hair around to rest on her shoulder and flexed her hands. Strange to witness the insecurity creep in as soon as she had clothes on. The thought grounded me, re-centered my desire. However beautiful the outside package was, she needed more from a man than lust, even if she didn't know it.

"I can go back to my own bus, if you've changed your mind." I was sure that hadn't been her intention when she'd said she didn't want me on the floor or the couch, but would she admit it? Would she let herself need me more tonight?

With a fluff of her long hair, she went over to the bed and threw back the covers, crawling in. "The bed is big—a king. You don't even have to touch me if you don't want to." She turned on her side, her back to me. "Up to you."

Being around her was like being showered with heat and then having someone suddenly turn on the cold water. Burnt or frozen. There didn't seem to be anything in between. "Maybe I should shower." I'd been so sweaty when she called, and now that we were back here and things were calmer, I worried I stank.

"I already told you. You smell like jasmine. Those lollipops are lodged in your pores." She glanced over her shoulder. "There are worse smells."

Not the most enthusiastic invitation I'd ever gotten, but I knew Mia well enough to understand it was the best I'd get from her tonight. Crossing to the closet, I put the sheets back and gave her one last considering look. Then, I dropped my pants, shed my shirt, and flicked off the light. Darkness descended so completely I was disoriented for a moment.

"You take this whole lights-out thing seriously," I muttered.

"Weird hours. Weird sleep patterns. I like total darkness."

I heard her shift in the bed while I fumbled for the edge and slid in behind her. Once I was settled, I listened to her breathing. She'd had a hell of a day. "You okay?"

"No, but I'll survive. I'm a survivor."

"What can I do?" Even though it was pitch-black, I turned my head, wishing I could see her face, gauge whether she was telling the truth.

"Would you—" She turned in the bed, and I caught a whiff of lemon and ginger. The sickness had mostly passed for her, but she still stole lollipops whenever she saw the lemon-and-ginger ones. "Will you hold me?"

Her breath brushed against my cheek, and I wrapped my arm around her, drawing her into my chest. Her cheek rested against my bare skin and her fingernail traced slow circles around my nipple. After she'd circled it three or four times, I was so hard I was considering a shower for a different reason. I gathered her hand in mine, stopping the slow madness.

"I thought you liked that. You did last time."

My chuckle was strained. "Things were a bit different between us then."

"'Cause I seemed glamorous and not like damaged goods." She drew her hand back and tried to turn away, but I tightened my grip.

"That's not what I said. Not what I meant. If we go down this road, sex means more now. There's more at stake."

"Sure, cause the stakes ended up being so low last time."

"You know what I mean."

She resettled against me, her small hand resting over my heart, and she was quiet for so long I wondered if she had given in to sleep.

"Should I quit the tour?" she whispered.

It took a moment to follow her logic. "Because of what happened tonight? With the bleeding?"

"Do you think he'll tell me I need to quit?"

"I don't know. If he does, are you okay with that?"

She let out a long breath. "I had a really bad day." Her voice was thick with tears. "Maybe it's a sign to take a break. Cade was never like that before. I don't know—why would he act like that?"

"You two used to date?"

"A PR stunt, mostly. But yeah. I mean...we've slept together before. Today wouldn't have been the first time. Which he so kindly pointed out while trying to slide his hand between my thighs."

Tension shot through me, causing all my muscles to tighten. "I'm not a violent guy, Mia. But seeing you like that, knowing what he tried to do? I wanted to beat him, maybe even kill him. I've never felt that," I searched for the right word, "intensity before."

"You hid it very well." There was an edge to her voice.

"I didn't want to scare you." I huffed out a breath. "He'd just attacked you, and then *I* get violent?" I rubbed her arm. "But Laura coming in with the useless comments about PR and the nightclub was the pinnacle of stupidity. I know she's your mom, but...like, what the hell was that?"

"I didn't tell her what happened."

"Doesn't matter. You were clearly upset. The room looked like there'd been a fight. Pasha had to escort him out. Making the leap isn't rocket science." I bit off the next comment I wanted to say about how terrible Laura was as a mother. Maybe these things made her a good manager for Mia's career, but they made her a nightmare as a parent. But I had friends with bad parents, and I learned family lines couldn't be crossed, even if the family member was awful.

"That's just my mom."

Talking about Laura more might cause a rift, and I liked having her tucked into my side, her breath drifting across my chest. I'd have to let it go. "I'm glad you called me."

She rose onto her elbow, and I could sense more than see her looking down. Her hand slid up my chest and cupped my cheek. Her hair fell around my face as her lips brushed my cheek. "Thank you for coming."

"Pretty Boy didn't have much choice once you called me an Uber." A grin spread across my face, and I pushed her hair back gently. "We need to chat about that nickname."

"You don't like it?" Her voice was breathy in the darkness. "You call me Mini sometimes instead of Mia."

"That's because you said you were my dictator."

She muffled her laugh in my neck, and goose bumps rose across my arms. Barely clothed, in bed, in a pitch-black room with one of the sexiest women I'd ever met who happened to be carrying my child, and I was determined I wasn't going to make any moves. I wasn't going to be an assertive asshole who read too much into her affection.

"I remember. I can be such a bitch."

"I'd never call you that."

"You don't know me that well yet." Her lips grazed my ear.

Tonight, I was going to die in this bed and God would make me a saint. St. Tyler, patron saint of sexual frustration.

Nope. Not even that was working as a suitable distraction.

"Do you want me to know you?" My voice was rough with desire, but I couldn't conceal it any longer. "You can't seem to decide."

"Are you calling me a tease?" She pulled back as though I'd sloshed cold water over her.

"No." I reached for her when she tried to move away. "I'm saying you seem confused sometimes. Or unsure. Or indecisive. That doesn't make you a tease. Do you know what you want? I know you thought you did. But is that still what you want?"

Silence stretched in the dark, my hand on her stomach, keeping her within arm's reach, as it rose and fell with her breathing.

"Not really, no," she said. "But I don't think you'll give me what I want."

"Try me." My heart kicked in my chest, and I had to remember not to drive her away. Baby steps.

"I want us to be friends."

"I think we are."

"Better friends. Friends who have sex."

Warmth spread across my body like a wildfire. She'd definitely lassoed the attention of several body parts. "Friends who have sex?"

"Forget it. I knew you'd think it was a dumb idea."

"No." My voice was strangled. Her idea wasn't dumb, just unrealistic. Friends who had sex were in a relationship. Any way you sliced the connection, what she described was exactly what all my long-term relationships had been. "If that's what you want, what you've been thinking about, it's not dumb." God knows sex with her crossed my mind about five hundred times a day.

"But you're not interested."

I tugged her back against me so her ass connected with my erection, and she could feel just how interested I was. "It's not that. But it's a slippery slope. What about after the baby comes?"

"There is no after. We break ties. We're just for now." Her voice had the breathy tone I remembered from our one night together.

"Friendship and sex."

"Might as well, right?" She turned in my arms and cupped my cheek. "The worst that could happen already did."

My gut clenched at how naïve her statement was. Heartbreak. Mine. Hers. Maybe both of us. She'd never experienced it, not the romantic kind, anyway. Foolish to believe our hearts wouldn't get involved. "You think that arrangement would work?"

"Sure. Why not?" She shifted closer, her hand dancing along my shoulder. "A few months of us getting what we need from each other. Doesn't have to be more than that. No feelings. Friendship. Sex."

Should I try to warn her of how devastating heartbreak could be? "After the baby arrives..."

"Once I lose the baby weight, I'm gone. You keep the baby, and I come back..." She took a deep breath, "to this."

I wanted to say "no," but my reaction wasn't related to the sex or to the friendship, but rather to her coming back to this lifestyle, to this environment—alone. Months stretched between now and then. She'd already gone from zero involvement to friends with benefits. Could I get her all in? Is that even what I wanted? Did I want to be all in with her?

"That's what you want?" A part of me resisted because we'd be making an already messy situation an absolute tornado of emotional madness. She might not feel the chaos coming, but I could sense the changing winds between us.

"I feel safe with you. I just want to feel safe for a while."

Like an avalanche, any objections I'd had were swept away. I couldn't deny her something so simple, something everyone should feel.

"Yeah, Mia. If that's what you need, we can do that." I located her face, and I brushed my thumb across her cheekbone. "Friendship tonight, though. We gotta make sure you're okay."

"Is it really me you're worried about?" She toyed with the short strands of hair on top of my head.

"Both of you. I worry about both of you."

Another lengthy silence lay between us while her fingers whittled away the tips of my hair. Should I ask what she was thinking? I could only nudge her so far. If there was even a sliver of light, I'd be able to see her expression. I wasn't sure she'd have asked if the room wasn't this dark, if the risk wasn't minimized by her *not* being able to see my face.

"We should probably seal the deal with a kiss, don't you think?" she murmured.

Given how hard I was, that was probably the worst idea in the history of bad ideas. But she nailed me to the cross when she implied she only felt safe with me. A saint, a martyr, I'd do it all.

I drew her toward me, and somehow our lips found each other in the dark, gentle at first, testing. When she angled her head, deepening the kiss, and her tongue slipped into my mouth, I suppressed a groan. I couldn't stop myself from tightening my grip on her, from meeting her tongue. The kiss went on, coming up for air, and then diving back in for more. When we finally broke apart, we were panting, and my muscles strained with the effort to hold back. Was it possible to die from a hard-on?

Mia touched her forehead to mine and whispered, "I forgot how good you were, how good this was. This is gonna be fun, Pretty Boy." With a satisfied sigh, she nestled into my side, and it wasn't long before her breathing evened out.

For a long time, I stared into the darkness and wondered if I was really keeping her safe with this new deal. A hell of a big risk. I told her I'd protect her, and I was a man of my word.

But if I'd been honest with her, I'd have warned her, tried to talk her out of this arrangement. Our new game was more dangerous than the last one, the risks equally volatile for us both.

Feelings didn't play by anyone's rules.

Chapter Thirteen
Mia

M^{ia} I heard him fumbling for his clothes in the dark room, and I almost asked him to stay longer. Almost. Then he slipped out my bedroom door back into the main living room, and the moment passed.

Alone in the darkness, I stared into the nothingness. Tyler had agreed to the friends-with-benefits plan, so I didn't understand why I felt so empty. Getting him to say yes was a triumph, a success, something to be celebrated. He hadn't seemed like the type for friends with benefits. Instead of elation, I felt robbed, as though I won the lottery only to be blindsided by having to give half of it to the government for taxes. Why was I so unsettled? I couldn't put my finger on what I was mourning.

My mother's voice rang through the living room, piercing the morning quiet. "So, you're the reason Pasha didn't want to let me in here? You've got to be kidding me!"

The hysterical edge in Laura's voice was a bad sign. I threw back the covers and sat on the edge of the bed. If I was going to quit the tour, I needed to make sure I looked awful. No matter how much I wanted to throw myself in the line of fire to spare Tyler her wrath, I had to be prepared for battle.

"You're fired." Laura's voice dripped with venom. "Pack up your stuff and leave."

Shit.

I scrambled off the bed and rushed into the bathroom. Quickly, I powdered my face with a shade I knew made me look sickly. I stared at myself in the mirror when the last puff settled, pleased with the result. As long as she didn't get too close, this would work. Carefully applied makeup had worked before.

At the door between the bedroom and the living room, I listened to my mother rage, trying to gauge whether Tyler had lost his temper. It would be surprising, but Mom could drag the worst out of anyone.

"Laura, it's not what you think. We aren't having sex."

Because he's a saint. I pressed my hand into the door and turned my ear to catch her response.

"Something is going on. I don't know what it is, but something isn't right between the two of you. If you're the real reason she's so insistent on going to Little Falls for her break, I'll never let her go. I will throw up every roadblock I can come up with."

"I told you I won't even be there. I have another job."

"It's funny. I can't find anyone who knows anything about that job. Who'd you say you were working for again?"

Okay, I'd heard enough. Sliding open the door, I took in Mom's combative stance and Tyler's relaxed pose on the couch. He hadn't even bothered to stand up. The calmness on his face when our gazes connected was immediately soothing, brought my heart rate back down to normal. He was the center of a hurricane, the place where everything went still.

"It's not about Tyler, Mother. I need a break. I was so sick last night. Tyler was looking after me."

"Sick?" Laura stepped toward me, concern falling over the anger she'd been directing at Tyler.

"I might be contagious." I held up a hand and turned my face away, putting my other hand over my mouth as though I might vomit.

"Should I call a doctor?"

"No. It's starting to pass." I shook my head and avoided looking at Tyler.

"Get to bed," Laura said, shooing me into my room and going to the kitchenette to pour a glass of water from the fridge. "You can leave." Laura eyed Tyler. "But this conversation isn't over."

"I want him to stay." I crossed my arms and considered digging in, even if I was supposed to be sick.

"You should have called me last night." Laura glanced at Tyler over her shoulder before ushering me back to my room and into the bed. The bathroom light was still on, giving the room a faint glow.

The low lights would make it hard for Laura to suss out the truth about my invented illness. Her wrist brushed against my forehead.

"You looked a little yellow in the living room. You're warm. Did you have a fever last night?"

"No, just a bad stomach. Maybe something I ate at the club."

"I'll call and tell them. That's ridiculous. They need better health and safety standards if they're giving you food poisoning." Laura slipped the full glass of water onto the nightstand and settled next to me on the bed. She tucked the covers around in a way she hadn't done since I was little. She scanned my face, thoughtful. "You know I love you, right?"

For a beat, I stared back at her and then nodded.

"Tyler's a lot older than you."

Every muscle in my body tightened. As though I hadn't been surrounded by men much older all my life, as though age had mattered so much to her when she'd left me alone with those men. Those terrible men. And there was nothing terrible about Tyler.

"Your point?"

"You need to be careful. You've worked hard to get this far in your career. Throwing it away for a man…"

"I never said that. When have I said that?"

"There has to be something behind this insistence on going to Little Falls. He owns a store there, doesn't he? Some sort of thrift shop?"

The disdain in her voice caused me to bristle for Tyler. "There's nothing wrong with owning a thrift shop."

"He's done a good job on the tour so far, but he can't stay. If he's a distraction for you, he can't stay. I'm sorry."

"You're not sorry. You live for this shit." I sat up and pulled my knees into my chest. "I tell you I'm sick and Tyler helped me, and your response is to fire him? You understand how crazy that is, right? Is this because he wouldn't sleep with you?"

"It's because I think he wants to sleep with you."

"As if you care." I glared at her. "You've made this," I gestured down my body, "literally and figuratively." I threw out my hands. "So what if he wants to sleep with me? That's what you created, Mother. Mia Malone—girls want to be me; guys want to be *with* me. Wasn't that what you all agreed in the marketing meeting when I was fourteen? I was fourteen and you were already talking about men wanting to fuck me."

"You're only twenty now—"

"I'll be twenty-one soon. I don't know why you think my age matters. I'm legally able to have sex in all fifty states." I met her gaze, every revelation and secret sitting between us. "We both know I'm no virgin."

Laura stretched to her full height while still staying perched on her bed. "It's not about sex. What have I always told you?"

I swallowed, and my hand strayed to the side of my stomach under the covers. "That love makes you do stupid things. That it's not worth the hassle."

"You've never let another man into your life like this."

I could feel her focused attention, but I wouldn't meet it. I didn't love Tyler, probably wasn't capable of love, anyway.

"Twenty or twenty-one is too young for forever, so he's a distraction. Possibly a mistake, a really costly one. I don't regret having you, Mia. You know that. But I don't want that life for you."

"I won't make the same mistakes as you." I met her stare head-on, my chin tilted in defiance. When my mind tried to slip toward thoughts of the baby, I slammed the mental door. The baby wasn't mine. It was Tyler's, so I wouldn't ever have my mother's life of regret. "I want a break from work. A break. I'm not quitting. I'm not running off to get married. I want to go write songs in Little Falls with Grady Castillo, who is a super talented writer." I took a deep breath and doubled down. "If you fire Tyler, I'll be taking a break from you, too."

In the half-light, Laura's eyebrows rose. "Don't be an idiot."

I quit.

I quit.

I quit.

The words sat on my tongue, but I didn't have the guts to say them, even though seeing the expression on her face would almost be worth it. Laura would talk me out of abandoning everything, convince me to tough it out. Deep down, I wanted this whole situation to go away, and it was easier to pretend the baby didn't exist. Not that I could do that for much longer.

No, I needed to get Taryn and Rebecca to deliver the blow about the tour.

As much as I wanted to avoid thinking about the baby growing inside me, last night had proven I wasn't willing to put myself first anymore. Seeing the blood should have been a relief. A miscarriage would solve everything. But that hadn't been how I'd felt. Tyler would have been really upset if I lost the baby; I didn't want to disappoint him.

Beyond all that, he didn't deserve to be painted as a villain in whatever narrative Mom was writing in her head.

"He's not like the others. He's not going to hurt me. I won't let you fire him. Don't make me choose."

"Whatever is going on between the two of you is a bad idea. As much as I'd like to believe it's possible, you can't control your feelings. None of us can."

"We're friends. *He's* my friend." The conviction in my voice wasn't fake. It felt true. In many ways, he was becoming my best friend, my most trusted person. "I'm not quitting. It's a break. I need a break. I'm sick, and I need a break."

Laura eased off the bed, stared at me and then shook her head. "Is the break his idea?"

In a way. "No, it's mine. I don't need you to understand it, but I need you to accept it."

"Getting involved with him is a mistake. If this is about your father—"

"Tyler is nothing like Dad." Bile rose in my throat. Laura thought I had a daddy complex. So gross. Tyler didn't even look his age. "That's disgusting. Like, really, really awful you'd suggest anything like that."

"Tell me what guy in the industry you're interested in, and I'll get you an introduction. Are you lonely? Is that it? Eighteen months on the road is a long time. Too long, maybe. I...the tour seemed like a good idea. You've always loved the live shows, the energy from the crowd..."

"I want to go to Little Falls and write songs. That's it." I sighed and stretched out under the covers turning my back on her. "I'm tired." And that was true, too. I was tired of talking about it, tired of living it, tired of feeling all of it.

A heavy silence filled the room. "I'll let you get some rest."

The soft whirl of the door sliding open was a relief. All the tension left my body in a rush, and I let out a deep breath.

"You're still here." Laura's disappointed tone was evident even from the head of the bed.

"I am." Tyler's voice was almost too quiet to catch. I strained toward the sound. "The only person who gets to dismiss me is your daughter, and she wants me to stay."

"She always has things she wants. You give in too much, and everyone loses."

I thought about getting out of bed to defend myself or Tyler or maybe the two of us. When was the last time I had asked for anything?

At the soft knock on my doorframe, I turned to see Tyler silhouetted against the dim light from the living room.

"Did my mother vanish in a cloud of eau de pissed off?"

"How'd you guess?" A small smile twisted his lips in the dim light.

"She thinks we're sleeping together." I rolled my eyes. "And it's not the sex part or the age gap that worries her."

"The age gap was certainly her focus with me." He came further into the room, his hands in his pants pockets.

"She's worried I'll give all this up for love." I thrust my hands wide into the air. Saying it aloud clarified the ridiculousness. Give up this sure thing, the job keeping me afloat on something risky like a feeling. I giggled. "Can you imagine?"

Tyler leaned a shoulder against the doorframe. "Yeah, I can imagine."

"You can imagine me doing that?" My laughter left in a rush.

"No, I can imagine love seeming more important than other things—material things."

"Sure, like maybe I give you the last bite of my ice cream cone or something. But give up millions of dollars? Uh, I don't think so." I threw back the covers and crossed to the bathroom, grabbing a washcloth from the linen closet. "And I like my job. Sometimes, I can't believe I get paid so much to do these fun things." I tilted my chin in the mirror, examining my makeup. "I just don't always like the extras." I ran the cloth under the warm water and wiped my face, the powder coming off easily.

Tyler's arms stretched across the doorway, his gaze traveling my face in the mirror as I washed the powder away. "Like how you have to manipulate your mother to get what you want?"

"She doesn't want me to throw away my life on something that won't last."

"Not all love ends. My dad died still in love with my mother."

"Well," I said, wiping my face one last time with the cloth before tossing it into the laundry, "he's the exception. From what I've seen, all love goes away eventually." I returned his gaze in the mirror and wondered whether my next question was wise. "Name one person you've loved in a romantic way." I turned and pressed my back into the counter, eyebrows raised.

"You want to go down this road?" His look was long and searching.

"Friends, right? This is what friends talk about. Things that matter."

"Katie. I loved Katie."

"But you stopped loving her?" A dangerous question.

The frustrated sigh he didn't bother to suppress was surprising. "It's not a switch, Mia. It doesn't just flick off one day. Love left untended withers. It's a living thing—you gotta water it and care for it and look after it. Neglect it? And it'll go away. What choice does it have?"

"So, who neglected it? You or Katie?"

He shifted in the doorway and crossed his arms. "Maybe we both did." His phone buzzed in his pocket, and he retrieved it. "David just texted. He can meet us at the hospital in an hour."

I grabbed my phone from the charging station in the bathroom and scrolled through my schedule for the day. Not that it mattered. As soon as I got back from meeting with David, I was canceling everything. With a deep breath, I sent a text to Taryn and Rebecca asking for a meeting.

"What are you thinking?" Tyler's voice was quiet.

I was tempted to lie, to brush him off. But he rarely did that to me, even when I might deserve it. Meeting his gaze, I shrugged. "That I'm about to blow up my life, and I'm not even that upset about it. Maybe I really do need a break."

"You work hard. I'm not sure I've ever seen anyone work harder than you."

He rested his hand against the bathroom counter, his body so close I caught another whiff of jasmine. I was starting to love that smell—wanted to bathe in it. When I glanced up, there was a tenderness in his gaze that tugged at my heartstrings. It was a look I could get used to, one that made me feel special, important. Other people looked at me like I mattered, but it always felt like it was my superstardom drawing them in. They had stars in their eyes. He was looking at *me*, seeing *me*, caring about *me*. The real Mia.

On my tiptoes, I pressed my lips to his, set down my phone, and slipped my hands into his hair, drawing him closer. He met my kiss with a hunger I hadn't expected. He lifted me easily onto the edge of the counter, our lips never breaking contact. He stepped between my legs, his hands sinking into my hair.

"I could kiss you all day," he murmured, deepening the kiss again.

I wrapped my legs around his waist, tugging him closer. "I like your thinking, Pretty Boy."

"Doctor first." His lips broke from mine. "Quit your job second." His lips found mine again in another searing kiss that made me wish we could stay on this bus all day uninterrupted. "Then more of this."

I withdrew from him, and we stared at each other, his gaze straying back to my lips, and I ran my thumb along them. "You make it sound so easy."

"I know it's not." He leaned in and brushed his lips against mine again.

"I need to get ready, or we'll be late." My phone buzzed beside me. Taryn and Rebecca had agreed to the meeting when I got back from my doctor's appointment. "One for the road," I said, giving him a quick kiss before hopping off the counter.

Doctor David liked to talk, and I was having trouble focusing. The baby was fine, so the rest of his words were noise. I understood what I had to do, even if Tyler was asking every question he could think of in support of staying on the tour. Sort of sweet for him to try so hard to give me options. Except I was fine with being done.

Against my will, my attention strayed to the fourth, largely silent, person in the room.

Katie.

Every time I glanced in her direction, the naked longing on the other woman's face was a neon flashing sign. Embarrassing. She should try to hide her emotions or at least hide them from the woman carrying Tyler's child, for God's sake.

The sadness in Katie's eyes wasn't for a love that had faded into something else like Tyler claimed, and his rigid posture meant he was keenly aware of her too. Fascinating and frustrating. This room was like being with Taryn and Rebecca when they were engaged in a silent feud over something. Why was there still so much weirdness between them? How did the doctor miss the tension?

I was about to burst from curiosity and something much darker, an emotion I wasn't keen to name, when one of Tyler's questions caught my attention.

"Can you summarize what you think she can and can't do physically? We want to be absolutely clear."

With a frown, I tilted my head at Tyler and then looked at the doctor. We'd been over this already. "No more aerial stuff, right? Lots of rest.

I heard all that. Obviously, I have to quit the tour." I met Tyler's soft gaze and basked in his caring for a moment. Then what he was dancing around clicked. "Tyler just wants to know whether we can have sex. Is that off the table or…?" In my peripheral vision, Katie straightened, and Tyler slid me an annoyed glance. Whatever. It was a valid question and what we wanted to know. Baby was fine. Great news for Tyler.

Tyler squeezed my hand, but I had no intention of meeting his gaze. I could tell from the rigid way he was holding himself that he wasn't happy right now. He'd get over it, especially if his three-step plan from earlier worked out like I hoped.

Doctor David's uneasy chuckle filled the room. "As far as intercourse goes, there is no medical reason you can't."

That was a strange way to phrase it. Perhaps the doctor *was* aware of his daughter's lingering feelings. "Good enough for me." I shifted my butt on the crackling paper until I could get down. Now, I just had to quit the tour. A chill slid down my spine at how awful the next few hours would be. "David, is it possible to get a medical note?"

"You want me to lay all this out on paper?" He raised his eyebrows.

"Not exactly." I winced. "I was sort of hoping for a diagnosis of exhaustion or depression or mono or something?" I put my hand up in a stopping motion. "Not pregnancy. I'm doing Tyler a favor. It's no one else's business."

David peered at me and seemed to consider the options. "I can write a note for exhaustion. There is a chance you'll eventually be on bed rest."

"Once I'm off the tour, I'll be in Little Falls for a while. So, bed rest won't be an issue." I waved him off. "Lots of rest, so no need to be stuck in my bed." I slid a sly glance toward Tyler. "Well, not one related to the baby, anyway."

Tyler's jaw clenched.

God, what was his problem?

"Right, well, I'll get that note for you. Katie," David turned to his daughter, "can you come type it up? You're faster than me."

She glanced at Tyler under her lashes, and then she followed her father out the door. A stony silence settled over the room.

"The baby is fine. I don't understand why you're in such a pissy mood." I crossed my arms.

Tyler produced a lollipop from his pocket and ripped the wrapper off in one swift movement. "If you put even one second of thought into it, you'd know why I'm annoyed with you."

"Clearly, it has something to do with your formerly precious Katie." I didn't even try to contain my own frustration. "The tension between the two of you is ridiculous and not in a hot way. All her feelings are lying on the floor at your feet."

He grunted and crossed his arms. I wanted to reach out and squeeze his bicep. I appreciated whatever was causing him to work out so much. God, he was gorgeous.

"You're deliberately rubbing our arrangement in her face."

"Please." I twisted my features into what I hoped was disbelief. Acting wasn't my strength. "My excitement at getting to have sex with you has nothing to do with her. Like zero." I formed a zero with my fingers. "If she doesn't think we're sleeping together when you look like that and I look like this and I'm carrying your baby, then she's not too bright."

"Mia." Tyler's lips barely moved when he said my name. He took the lollipop out of his mouth and pointed it at me.

"Why do you care what she thinks?"

"I don't care what she thinks. I care how she feels. You're making her feel bad on purpose." His eyes glittered with anger.

"Why do you care? Do *you* still have feelings for her?" When he opened his mouth and I sensed a lie coming, I jumped back in. "Never to each other, Pretty Boy. Don't you dare." My heart dipped low in my chest.

"That's not an easy question to answer."

"No, it is. It really is." I tried to ignore the rush of insecurity.

The door popped open, and Katie entered, her hand extended with a white envelope. Doctor David came behind her, medical file in hand.

"Thanks." I smiled and tried to make it genuine for the pissed-off Pretty Boy. Had I taken my comments too far? Maybe. But I hated the tension between them, that Tyler wouldn't just explain why the tension existed, that he still cared about Katie's feelings. What kind of guy cares about whether his ex-girlfriend's feelings get hurt? Ridiculous. Half the guys I knew wouldn't care if their *current* girlfriend's feelings were hurt.

"Your manager or whoever is welcome to call me with questions. I would prefer my note didn't make it into the press since it's skirting the truth."

"Sure, of course. It's not like I want all this public." I folded the note and slid it into my bulky purse. "Thanks for seeing us again today. I—I might have overreacted."

"Not to worry. Bleeding can be scary." He patted my shoulder. "You're under a lot of stress and physical obligations with your show. Bleeding isn't uncommon, but as I said earlier, it should always be checked if it's unusual or excessive or you just need to ease your mind."

"Thanks for your time." Tyler stretched out a hand and shook David's. He hesitated before offering Katie his hand. "I appreciate the help."

That last comment was too heartfelt and filled with hidden meaning. Katie's hand wrapped around his a little too quickly. My smile faltered. I took a deep, steadying breath before I lost my temper.

He could have feelings for Katie. I had no claim over him. None. We were having a baby, but not even together since he'd be raising it alone. In fact, it would be better if the baby never realized I was its mother. I rubbed my stomach, and Tyler slid his fingers down my arm until we were linked. Tears pooled in my eyes, and I had to pretend to look for something in my purse with my free hand to keep them from spilling over. Finally, my fingers hit on a forgotten token from Tyler, and I pulled out a lollipop in triumph, all thoughts of crying gone.

A hint of smile touched his lips when I twirled it in his direction. We slipped out the hospital door with Pasha leading the way to the car, fingers locked together.

"Are you still mad at me?" I whispered.

We slid into the car, and Tyler didn't respond. I snuck a glance at him, afraid I'd see anger there again. Jealousy burned inside at the thought of Katie and Tyler together. That wasn't something a friend felt—a friend would behave differently. But I'd never had a guy as a friend, so I wasn't sure what that looked like either. How was I supposed to feel about him and Katie? Surely not happy.

"I'm sorry."

His arm slid around my shoulders, and he tugged me into his side. His lips pressed against the top of my head, and he breathed me in. "You're so mature in so many ways, I forget that you're young. We need a code word for when you're feeling insecure and just need reassurance."

"I wasn't feeling insecure." I tried to pull away from him. *Insecure?* Please. Jealous, maybe.

"Having feelings isn't a weakness."

"I know that." I swallowed down more of a protest. "I don't *hate* the idea of a code word. It could be fun, I guess."

He laughed and kissed my temple. "We can go straight-up ridiculous, or something that could be inserted into a regular conversation?"

I curled into his side and slipped my legs onto his lap, and his free hand cupped my knees. Giving pieces of myself to him felt normal, easy. So different from anything I'd ever experienced before. With other men, they took and took and took. Lost in thought, I picked at his shirt until I said, "Puzzle. That's the code word. Puzzle. Puzzled. Puzzling."

"Goes both ways?"

"What do you mean?"

"What if I feel insecure?"

I gave him a light punch to the chest. "Sure, yeah. You're going to be insecure. About what?"

"We got a bit of road left to travel, Mia. You never know."

The thought of the road ending or coming to the fork I could see in the distance caused sadness to seep in. "I guess we do." My internal timer ticked. "Will you sit in on the conversation with Taryn and Rebecca?"

"Are you sure you want quitting to be so closely linked to me?"

I patted my purse. "I have a doctor's note."

"From a doctor connected to me and Little Falls."

"I want you there." I twisted my finger in his shirt and then released the material.

"Then I'll be there." He met my gaze, sincerity in his depths.

Taryn and Rebecca had passed the note back and forth between them several times before eyeing me and then Tyler and circling to Pasha, who I also insisted on having in the bus.

"Why didn't you go to our team doctor? We could have had her here at a moment's notice." Rebecca's eagle eyes scanned Tyler. "A doctor from Little Falls is declaring you exhausted, and you took yourself to the hospital today."

"I don't want this getting out. Or at least getting out uncontrolled." I'd applied some strategic makeup to make me appear washed out before the meeting. "I thought you'd be proud of me for handling it myself."

"We're paid to handle stuff like this." Taryn frowned. "The costume guy isn't."

"He helped me out of a jam last night." I refused to acknowledge Tyler, hadn't glanced in his direction since Taryn and Rebecca arrived. He was across the room, far enough not to be a distraction, but close enough to offer comfort. Whenever he was in a room, I felt grounded, safe. He'd never let anything bad happen to the baby, so he'd never let anything bad happen to me.

"It's not like we didn't see this coming, Mia." Rebecca sighed. "We just wish you'd been more up front about where your head was at. Now, we're going to be scrambling to reschedule."

"We're not rescheduling," I said. "We're canceling."

Both Taryn and Rebecca gasped, and the doctor's note fluttered to the floor between them. "Canceling?" Taryn squeaked out.

"I want to be done."

"Holy shit," Rebecca muttered and pressed her fingertips into her forehead. "Laura is going to eat us for breakfast." Her gaze connected with Taryn. "How do we spin this? The lost money alone will give her a coronary."

"Laura would be fine with rescheduling," Taryn said, swooping down to pick up the note. "But canceling outright? There's no way, Mia."

"This is why *I* pay you." I spread my hands wide and looked between the two women. "Get her to accept it. Get her on board with me spending the next few months in Little Falls."

"This your idea?" Rebecca eyed Tyler. "You know if the tour ends, you don't get paid either."

"It's my idea." I rose from my chair and blocked Rebecca's view of Tyler lounging on the couch. "I don't know why people find this so hard to believe."

"You're a workhorse," Taryn said. "There is no end to your hard work. You aren't a quitter. It's one of my favorite things about you. So, what's really going on?"

Over my shoulder, my gaze connected with Tyler. We hadn't talked about how far I might have to go to quit. With a deep breath, I studied Taryn and Rebecca. I rubbed my hands together and pressed them against my lips.

"I'm pregnant." I dropped my hands as the two women gasped again, and Rebecca fell backward into a chair.

"What?" All the color drained from Taryn's face. "Does Laura know?" She shook her head. "Of course, she doesn't know." Taryn glared at Tyler and then Pasha. "Which one of you is the baby daddy? It's gotta be one of you." She whirled on me. "You can't be very far along. We've got options."

"I'm not telling you because I need your help. I don't." I laughed, surprised at how light I felt now that I'd told them. "At least not with the baby part. I need you to manage my mother. Tyler is going to keep the baby. I'm not. I'm not having anything to do with the baby, okay? It's just—I'm the vessel."

"You got pregnant on purpose?" Rebecca cocked her head.

"No, no." I shot Tyler a pleading look.

"I agreed to keep and raise the baby instead of her getting an abortion." When both women stared at him, Tyler laid out the sequence of events in a way I was sure I couldn't have done.

"My God." Taryn rubbed her forehead. "Laura would drive you to a clinic. It wouldn't matter how far along you were. This is her worst nightmare. She's always been paranoid you'd get pregnant young like her."

"I know that," I said, unable to conceal the tension in my voice. "That's why she doesn't know."

"Are you ever coming back?" Rebecca put her head in her hands and sighed.

"Yes! God, I'm not quitting. Well, I'm quitting right now. But I love performing and singing, it's not...Tyler told you. I'm really going to make an album with Grady while I'm off with the baby. It'll be fine. No one needs to know."

"Why are you telling us?" Taryn took off her glasses and cleaned them.

"You both signed NDAs, and I needed you to understand there's no talking me into continuing the tour. So, you need to figure out a way to get my mother to agree to all of this."

"It's your mother. We need a hammer. If we can't use the pregnancy, what's the hammer?" Rebecca met her gaze. "If we absolutely can't win her around with some sort of deal, how do we get to her?"

I'd realized this question would come at some point. Sometimes a carrot worked, but other times we needed a stick. A heavy one. "She thinks Tyler and I are together. We're not. But use that idea. Tell her I've said if I have to make a choice, I'll choose Tyler and freeze her out. Make it clear she needs to let this thing with Tyler run its course. I promise you both I'm coming back. I'll come back better than ever. But I need out for now."

Taryn and Rebecca exchanged a long, exhausted look. "She won't want to lose you," Taryn admitted. "The threat would work. But you can only use it if you mean it. If you'll follow through." Taryn held up her hand. "Even if she agrees, Laura will want to see you at some point over the next few months."

"I'll deal with that when she finally decides to visit me. I'm counting on her being too pissed off at me to visit any time soon." I shrugged. "At some point, she'll be too late."

Taryn and Rebecca linked hands and squeezed. With deep breaths, they seemed to find comfort in each other. I glanced at Tyler, and I understood that feeling, finding strength in someone else. It happened all the time with him.

"All right," Rebecca agreed. "We'll figure it out. You three should leave tonight. Once she knows—"

"I know. If I'm still here, she'll steer every guilt trip she has in my direction." My chest grew tight at the thought. "I'd never leave."

Tyler's arm circled my waist, and our gazes met. He ducked his head and nuzzled my neck. My knees almost buckled at his stubble brushing against all the sensitive spots. Alone with him. That's all I wanted.

"Tonight," he agreed. "You pack. I'll book the flights."

My body lit up.

"Pasha, you're coming with us?" Tyler tipped his chin in Pasha's direction.

I hadn't asked him, but I knew he would. Like Tyler, he'd become someone I counted on.

"I come." Pasha nodded. "I pack light."

Taryn's hand slid along my back and drew me into a hug. In my ear, she whispered, "I love you, kid. We'll come visit instead of Laura if we can swing it."

Relief coursed through me. Maybe I should have told them weeks ago, but I'd thought I could handle everything.

"Thank you," I whispered.

"You deserve to have happiness. Let yourself be happy for a while." She squeezed me a little tighter before letting me go.

Chapter Fourteen
Tyler

From everyone's behavior, leaving the tour made me feel like we were fugitives fleeing the country instead of a pop star, her bodyguard, and whatever I was, running away from her mother while sitting on a private jet. As much as I wanted to spin our situation in a different direction, that was the reality. Mia wasn't quitting the tour so much as quitting Laura for the next six months or so. Exactly how long Mia would stay after the baby was born hadn't been concretely decided.

When her plane landed in New York, a single text from Rebecca had said, *It's done. You've got your time off.* Mia had turned to me in triumph while Pasha steered our rental toward Little Falls.

Too easy.

Laura could show up unexpectedly and uninvited at any time. Not a single text or phone call had arrived to either me or Mia from Laura. Was silence really the best sign?

"She'll be mad at me." Mia stood beside the car outside my house and oversaw Pasha trying to unpack the suitcases.

She had three oversized bags, and one of those was filled with accessories and makeup. I didn't have a problem with her excessive packing, but Pasha had grunted extra loud when he lifted that third bag into the trunk.

"But she'll come around, and when she does, she'll want to see me," Mia warned.

"You're sure you're okay with staying here while the train station renos finish up?" I grabbed a couple of the suitcases and walked toward the front door of my modest brick bungalow.

"This place is cute." Mia followed behind with her purse over her arm.

David instructed her not to lift anything heavy, not that she would have carried her own bags anyway. Her inability to do practical things for herself hadn't worried me until we pulled into the driveway. Cooks and maids and bodyguards made her life easier at every turn. Did she even know how to make a sandwich?

"I'll need to do some grocery shopping. There won't be much food in the house," he said.

Behind me, Mia's step faltered. "Oh, right. I guess you have to do those things yourself." Her heels clicked a little faster on the cement walkway. "Can I—would it be okay if I came with you? I haven't been to a grocery store in a while."

I opened the front door and slid the first bag across the entrance before pushing the second one behind it. "You'll have to decide whether you're okay with people knowing you're here, possibly posting you're here on social media. The grocery store is almost as popular as appearing in the town center."

"When I start to show, I'll hole up in your house or the train station or wherever I need to be. People will think I left town. But I don't want to start like that when I still look like this." She gestured down her body. "My boobs look amazing, and maybe I've put on a few pounds, but I don't look...you know, yet."

Her excitement was palpable, and I couldn't determine if it was because she'd escaped her mother, was enjoying the sense of normalcy, or was looking forward to playing a warped version of house. All of those things made me uneasy. Bringing her here had seemed like a great plan, but as she walked past me into the house and I caught a whiff of lemon and ginger, I wondered if I miscalculated.

Despite all of my long-term relationships, I'd only lived with one woman, and that hadn't lasted long. From experience, Mia's loss would sting so much more if I let her stay here when the train station was done. Getting her moved over there would be my best bet at surviving whatever was blossoming between us.

"Men don't usually have good taste." Her gaze zipped around the open concept living space decorated with a country chic vibe. The white décor with open beams and patches of brick were timeless. I'd missed this place.

"I'll take that as a compliment." I hoisted one bag and took it down the hall. "Pasha can have this spare room on the left. At the back here, there's a master suite," Tyler called. "Or there's one in the basement."

"Which one do you use?" Mia's bare feet slapped against the wooden floor behind me.

I tossed Pasha's light bag onto the queen bed and then passed Mia to get her first suitcase from the front hall. "I've been sleeping in the basement for the last few years." Since Katie had moved out, actually, but there wasn't much point in telling Mia that tidbit.

"Oh, well." She bit her lip and twisted her hands in front of her.

"Puzzled?" I raised my eyebrows, and I lifted her bag. Would she admit already to some form of insecurity?

"Well, kinda, I guess." A flush rose to her cheeks.

It was rare for her to be so genuinely unsettled. "What aren't you sure about?"

She fluffed her hair and drew her mane around to rest on her shoulder. "If I'm up here and you're down there, it makes it hard to do what I want to do." She leaned toward me, glancing over my shoulder in Pasha's direction.

"Oh?" A slow smile spread across my face. "What's that?" I scanned the house in mock confusion. "There's just you, me, and Pasha. We could probably do whatever you wanted."

"You think Pasha is into a bodyguard with benefits scenario?" Mia perked up and tilted her head. "I didn't take you for a threesome guy, but if that's what you want—" She turned toward the door, where Pasha was still struggling with her last bag.

I chuckled, but I didn't haul her back like I was tempted to do. I wanted to see how far she'd take this.

She took two steps in Pasha's direction and spun around. "You'd really let me ask him?"

"Would you? I thought it might be funny to watch you try."

"My suffering amuses you?" With a groan, she smacked me in the chest with her open hand.

"Aww, Mini." I set down her suitcase and smoothed her hair, drawing her into my chest. "This isn't suffering. Suffering will be when you figure out you have to cook and clean for yourself."

"I still have money, Pretty Boy. I'll be paying people to do those things." Mia laughed into my chest.

"What?" I held her away, feigning surprise. "You're telling me my fantasies of you in a maid outfit or wearing just an apron aren't going to happen?"

"They'll only happen if you take out my bodyguard first. Are you up for it?" Her fingers slid into my hair, and she tugged me down so her lips grazed my ear.

"Where do I have to take him?" I nuzzled her neck and flicked my tongue along her earlobe.

The chuckle that escaped her was deep with amusement and desire. "I think you should show me the basement."

"There's a second bedroom down there," I murmured before kissing her neck.

"There's another bedroom down there?" She trembled in my arms, clearly distracted, and then she gasped, smacking me in the chest again.

"Yeah, two up, two down." He winked. "You didn't ask how many bedrooms there were, just where I slept."

"You knew what I was asking."

With a wicked grin, I picked up her suitcase easily just as Pasha finally staggered in the door. "How these fit in plane?" A thin sheen of sweat glistened on his brow.

"We took my jet, so I can do what I want. For commercial airlines, if you throw enough money at a company, they'll let you do almost anything. I'm in the top tier of all the frequent flier programs, so that goes double for me." She grinned. "They're not too heavy for you, are they?"

I watched the exchange and couldn't help but smile. There was a lightness to Mia today, as though a tremendous weight had disappeared. Did she feel the difference? Every time she said or did something, she glowed. Maybe I had made the right decision by asking her here, by convincing her to do this. On the tour, I wasn't completely sure. She did love to entertain, or at least parts of the spectacle, and she was damn good at it.

Mia caught me staring at her. "What?"

"You look happy. It's a good look on you."

She grabbed her hair in a fist and seemed to consider my words before straightening to her full height. "I am happy." A soft laugh of disbelief filled the entryway. "Imagine that."

The best part was that I didn't need to. She shone, shone in the same way she did when she was on stage and the fans were belting out her songs back to her. Somehow, at least for today, she was finding that level of energy inside herself instead of having to absorb it from a crowd.

"I'll take your bags down," I said as Pasha disappeared out the door to grab anything else from the car. "Then we'll hit the grocery store. I don't want you getting hangry."

"I think I'm going to like it here." She twirled a strand of her hair around her finger and nodded.

Chapter Fifteen
Mia

Mia

While we wandered through the grocery store like an old, married couple, I tried to ignore the stares. For the most part, I was finding success. Wherever I went, I attracted attention, and I hadn't exactly gone incognito in my short skirt and glittery top. Got to flaunt it while I still got it.

"The whole town will think you're shacked up with a stripper." I popped my gum and tossed a bag of kale into the cart.

"You really think most of these people don't know who you are?"

I pointed to my head and face. "I'm wearing a hat and sunglasses inside at the beginning of April in New York State. Clearly, this is a disguise." At his sideways glance of amusement, I grinned. "I actually thought there might still be snow on the ground. That's why I packed so much stuff." Didn't explain why I had chosen to wear so little out of the house. Without a doubt, my nipples would try to leave my body in the frozen food aisle.

"That's why you packed so much stuff?" His voice was full of disbelief.

"Well." I laughed. "Maybe I just like clothes." With another glance around, I shrugged. "No one has asked me for an autograph or a selfie. Am I in an alternate universe where I'm not famous?"

"You actually want people to ask you for those things in the grocery store?" He stopped walking and squinted.

"If I don't want to be seen, I stay home." I flipped my hair onto my shoulder. "That's what my mom always says. Leaving the house is an agreement to be social, to be on, to be accessible."

"You mean, your manager." He picked up some apples and examined them before putting them back.

"Sure, my momager. I learned a long time ago the two roles aren't separate. She might try to separate them once in a while, but she can't." Short of firing her as my manager, I wasn't sure what I could do. Easier, and probably simpler, to fire Laura from being my mother.

"Hmm..." Tyler plucked an apple and dropped it in the clear plastic bag and then grabbed a few more.

"Tyler?"

We both looked up, startled at the interruption. When I saw who it was, I slid my hand across Tyler's back. Danai's gaze followed my hand, her lips tightening.

"I didn't realize you were back in town," Danai said.

Before he could speak, I jumped in. "Just got here last night. I don't think we've met." I extended the hand that wasn't perched on Tyler's broad shoulder. "I'm Mia Malone." Danai accepted my hand in a loose, brief shake.

"I know who you are. The grocery store was buzzing when I walked in the doors with the news you were wandering the aisles. I didn't realize you were with Tyler."

"Yep." That sounded better. People were talking about me at least. I smiled wide. "I'm with Tyler." When I turned to him, he was searching my expression.

"You're such a puzzle," he said.

"What can I say, I have an addiction to them." I flushed.

"That you do." He gave me one last sweeping glance before focusing on Danai. "It's nice to see you. Sorry, I haven't called. The tour was hectic, and we just got into town. You're doing well?"

"Very well," Danai said. "Things are great. The tour was good?"

"I survived. Happy to be home." A brief smile flashed across his face.

My heart sank, and I straightened, letting my hand fall off his shoulder. I grabbed an apple and slipped it into the bag dangling from Tyler's fingers. I'd been reduced to an experience he survived.

When Danai wandered away, he slid his arm around my shoulders and tugged me into his side, his lips brushing against my hat. "Don't read into what I said. I liked being on tour with you."

"So, why would you say that to her?"

"Because it's true. I survived the tour, and I *am* happy to be home. I survived the tour because of you, and I'm happy to be home, because you're here too. I wasn't going to give her some big, long story when her presence made you uncomfortable."

"Just, you know, ballpark figure. How many ex-girlfriends am I going to come face-to-face with in this town?" I tipped my hat and slid down my sunglasses to make eye contact.

"How far back are we going? 'Cause if we're going back to kindergarten, you're in trouble. Those were my player days."

"That was a serious question." I smacked him in the chest, and he chuckled.

"You've got nothing to worry about. While you're here, I've only got eyes for you, okay?" Our gazes locked, a fire smoldering. "You need your ego stroked, let me know, and I'll look after it."

A sly grin tipped the edges of my lips, and I polished the apple in my hand against my breasts. "I wouldn't mind stroking your ego, Pretty Boy." I gave him an exaggerated wink.

"If that isn't an incentive to forget the groceries and head straight home, I don't know what is." He laughed and tugged me against his side again.

"Sorry," I said with a grin. "You gotta feed us. Doctor's orders."

"Oh." Tyler brushed back the strands of my hair that had fallen forward away from my hat. "I'll feed you all right."

I was giddy. How had I missed that he was this much fun? "I'm going to need more than a cockmeat sandwich."

A laugh so loud it drew attention from everyone in the produce section burst out of him. Pride flooded me. I did that; I made him laugh so wholeheartedly. Another emotion I didn't recognize followed, swelling my chest. He was amazing. How had I managed to meet someone so amazing?

"All right," Tyler said when his laughter faded to a grin. "Tell me what's on your list since you already vetoed mine."

"You know what I'd really like?" I stared into the half-full grocery cart. None of it was appealing.

He stared at me expectantly.

"A burger from the same place as last time, the one Pasha recommended." At my insistence, Pasha had stayed outside the grocery store by the entrance. He hadn't been happy about it. Perhaps this would smooth over his grumpy attitude and satisfy my craving for red meat.

"Burgers, it is," he agreed. "Let's pay for this and give Pasha the good news."

I couldn't stop staring at him as he moved around the kitchen, eating one of his burgers and getting himself and Pasha beers. He'd already slid a glass of water across the island to me. Pasha was hunched over his bag of burgers, steadily working his way through them, each one making him grunt less and talk more.

When the bag was empty, he stood up, took the mountain of burger wrappers around him, and threw them into the garbage. "I walk house. Then bed. Long day."

"Thank you." I ran my hand down his arm and smiled at him.

He patted my head and slipped out the back door. Even though Pasha was only thirty, he often seemed so much wiser. A protective big brother.

"Do you have that sort of relationship with all your bodyguards?" Tyler tipped his beer and took a long swallow.

"No." I pressed my water glass between my palms. "He told me a few weeks ago that I remind him of his little sister back in Russia."

"Makes sense." He nodded and set his empty bottle in the sink. "He seems attached to you. Why do you like him?"

"I've never worried he'll betray me." I gave him a fleeting smile. "A quality I don't take for granted in anyone anymore." I swept up my burger wrapper and took it to the garbage next to Tyler. After I dropped it in, I glanced up at him. "Jealous?"

"I'm not sure." His lips quirked up into an almost smile. "Curious, definitely. Maybe it's jealousy of a sort. You rely on him. You trust him."

"Want to know what I like about you?"

"You mean besides my sweat smelling like jasmine?" His eyes brimmed with affection.

A soft laugh tumbled out, and I rose on my toes, wrapping my arms around his neck. "Besides that. Though, it is incredible anyone's sweat can smell so good. If I didn't know better, I'd think you were magic."

"So, what is it, then?" He nuzzled under my ear, and I sighed with contentment. I couldn't remember the last time I'd been this relaxed and at peace with my life.

"Your honesty. You'll tell me the truth, even if I don't like it."

"I'm trying." He took a deep breath and kissed my bare shoulder before meeting my gaze again. "I can't say I've ever been *this* honest with anyone else."

His admission was comforting and frustrating. He wouldn't tell me the one thing I really wanted to know. Why had he and Katie split up? Who'd broken up with whom? Asking him right now would destroy this mood, and I definitely didn't want to do that.

Pasha came back in through the sliding side door and waved without looking at us directly. "All okay. I go bed and read. Call you need me." He flipped the lock into place and moved the metal bar down to secure the doors. He ambled along the hallway without a backward glance.

"A reader." Tyler's voice was pitched low. "Never would have guessed."

"In Russian." I laughed and sprang onto my toes for a quick kiss. "He's tried to teach me a few words, but I'm useless. He's smarter than me."

"Necessity breeds some skills. You don't need Russian, or you'd learn it."

"One skill I have to relearn is how to write music. Or find my rhythm again. It's been forever."

"Your guitar and keyboard should be delivered to the train station tomorrow. We can go pick them up, or I can drop you off there to write on my way to the store."

I scanned the open kitchen and living room, and a pang of contentment hit me. This would be a good place to write. If I needed a break, there was a kitchen and a TV and the internet. The only thing I'd have at the train station was the studio. There was lots of time to be holed up there alone.

"Here, I think." I gazed up at him. "Is that okay?"

"Wherever you think you'll work best. Whatever will make you happiest."

Warmth spread across my chest at his words. He made me happy. For the moment, being here with him made me happy. Had I ever experienced this lightness, this freeness before? As though I could take on the world and win.

Lacing my fingers with his, I led him toward the basement stairs.

"You tired?" he asked as he trod down the stairs behind me.

"Nope." I glanced at him over my shoulder.

"You want my help with something?" He squeezed my hand, and his tone was teasing.

"I've got an itch only you can scratch." At the bottom of the stairs, I turned in his arms.

"Oh, yeah?" He dipped his head to rub his scruff along the most sensitive part of my neck. I clung to his arms, desire shooting from my neck to my toes. "Is it there or somewhere else?" His gruff voice made my legs tremble.

"Just," I whispered, sliding his hand along my thigh and up under my skirt to where I was already throbbing with need, "here."

Two of his fingers circled in a slow, leisurely movement. "Like this?"

I clung to his shoulders and then tugged his lips to mine, our mouths sliding over each other, tongues tangling. When he increased the pressure of his fingers, I gasped into his mouth and squeezed his biceps.

"Too much?"

"No, God, no. More." My lips collided with his, and I pressed closer.

His hands slid around my ass and lifted me, so my legs circled his waist. With a few quick strides, he had me against the doorframe of his bedroom, his tongue in my mouth, and my hands tangled in his hair.

I couldn't remember the last time I was this turned on by so little. Had our encounter been this good, this desperate last time?

"I want you so badly." I moaned when his tongue flicked along my earlobe and then returned to my mouth. His erection pressed against my core, and when he shifted his grip, he rubbed against me. "Oh, God," I breathed. "Do that again."

One of his hands secured our lower bodies together against the door while his other dug into my hair, kissing me deeply as he thrust against me. He broke the kiss, his breath heavy in my ear as he thrust against me again.

There were still too many pieces of clothing between us, but the friction was amazing. I wanted this tingling, breathtaking feeling to go on forever. Already, I was close to coming and could feel my climax building.

"I've been thinking about this all day, burying myself deep inside of you, feeling you come around my cock." His voice was gruff with need.

Weeks. I'd been thinking about being with him for weeks. Too long. I ran my fingers through his hair and brought his mouth back, our tongues tangling, and he pressed us tight together before walking us to his king-sized bed.

He laid me on the duvet, and when his fingertips skimmed my panties, he groaned. "You're so wet."

I tangled my fingers in the bottom of his shirt, tugging it over his head and tossing it onto the floor. I ran my hands along his chest before leaning up and flicking his nipple with my tongue. He groaned and pulled my shirt over my head, releasing my bra with a snap of his fingers. All of it he tossed aside, not caring where it landed.

"Gorgeous," he muttered, bending his head to take each breast into his mouth, sucking on each nipple before grazing them with his teeth.

My hands were buried in his hair, keeping him close, silently begging him for more. I couldn't get enough, didn't know if I'd ever get enough.

While he teased my breasts, his hands shimmied my skirt and panties to the floor. I reached for the button on his jeans, but he shook his head.

"Not yet." He skimmed my folds with his fingertips.

"Tyler," I moaned.

He spread my legs and then dipped down between them, his tongue lapping me up. "God, you're so wet, so sweet. I could eat you all day."

"We could arrange that," I murmured, arching my hips, squirming with need. I dug my fingers into his hair. All day in bed with him sounded like the best day ever. I ran my hand along his shoulders, feeling the muscles contract and release. There wasn't anything about him I didn't like. To think I hesitated to sleep with him again, had honestly believed we wouldn't fuck again. Being with him was so good; he was so good.

When his finger dipped inside and his thumb circled my clit while he continued licking, I gripped the sheets as my body wound tight. My breathing was labored. "Please. Tyler, please."

"What do you need, Mini?" His rough voice sent shivers down my spine. There was so much want in it, so much desire. "Tell me what you need."

"I need you inside me. I want to feel you inside me when I come." I gripped his hair, encouraging him up. His jeans were still on, and I fumbled with the button.

When he backed off, I tried to reach for him.

"No, come back."

He chuckled and unzipped his pants, letting them drop to the floor. Our gazes locked when he shed his boxers. I curled my finger in a come-hither gesture, and he smirked before crawling along my body, kissing every inch as he worked his way back to my mouth.

"Have I scratched the itch yet?" he muttered in my ear.

"Close. So close," I whimpered, reaching between us to stroke his silky length.

"Tell me how you want it."

"Inside me," I said.

"I got that part." He kissed the side of my lips.

"I want to be so close to you I don't know where you end, and I begin."

He drew back and our gazes connected. He slid one hand under my head, and his other slipped under my butt, tipping my hips. I felt him brush against my entrance. For a moment, he scanned my face, and the room came alive with something more complicated than sexual attraction. I didn't recognize the emotion, but I wanted to bask in the implied tenderness, wanted to cling to it. I'd never been with someone who so obviously cared about me. Intoxicating.

He opened his mouth as though to speak and then shook his head before pressing his forehead against mine. "As close as we can get." He angled his head and captured my lips as he drove into me, his hands adjusting our bodies until my clit brushed against him with each thrust.

When I arched my back, he met me, burying himself deeper, stroking longer. The rhythm was heaven, and the slow build inside made my toes tighten in anticipation.

"You feel so good." My fingernails dug into his ass. "Don't stop, okay? Just don't stop."

His pace was slow and glorious, each thrust propelling me closer to the edge. We were locked so tightly that we were slick with sweat, and the scent of jasmine filled my senses. I'd never smell it again and not think of him, of this.

"Tell me when you're close, Mini."

"Are you?" I spanned his back with my hands. The edge was there, just there.

"From the minute we came downstairs." Our gazes locked, and he whispered, "All I think about is you."

"Tyler," I moaned. "Holy—I'm coming. Don't stop. Don't stop."

He drew me tighter, his rhythm steady, our lips finding each other as he swallowed my cries. I'd never had an orgasm so intimate, so connected. Despite my history, I'd always liked sex. But sex had never been like this.

His cheek was pressed to mine, and his labored breath was in my ear. "You feel so good. I can't—"

"It's okay." My fingers wound into his hair. "I want you to come inside me."

And then he was kissing me again as a tremor rocked through him, and I felt him pulsing inside, spilling a seed that had already been planted.

If there was anything better than this feeling with him, I'd never experienced it before.

I traced figure eights on his chest and sighed with contentment. "So, if you're a relationship guy and you don't normally do the whole one-night stand thing, why did you sleep with me after the benefit concert?"

Ever since we'd cuddled up, the difference in all my sexual experiences kept playing in my mind. I understood sex could be this crazy connection between people, but I'd never felt it—until now, with him, and I wasn't sure I ever wanted to go back to what sex had been before. Why would Tyler settle for the disconnected, if pleasurable, sex we had in my hotel room? There was no way that was good enough after experiencing something like what we'd just done.

He sighed and slipped one hand behind his head while the other rested on my hip, keeping me snug. "My dad died a few days before the concert. I was staring down the path of my life, what it had become, and I wasn't sure I liked what I saw."

"Really?" I frowned and went onto my elbow to gaze down at him. "You weren't happy?"

"Not really, no." He wouldn't meet my gaze, keeping his trained on the ceiling. "So, when you asked me to your room, I didn't figure I had anything to lose."

I wove my fingers into the short strands of his hair. The reddish-brown-gold shade was so pretty. Would the baby have his hair color? Or would it end up dark like mine? Or some shade in between? "One decision set off a bomb in both our lives."

"That's how you see it?" A brief smile flickered across his face. "A bomb?" He turned onto his side, so we were face-to-face.

"Don't you? Everything's changed—complete change. None of us will ever be the same." Truthfully, our situation terrified me.

For a minute, he searched my face, his eyes brimming with kindness, and my heart squeezed. "I guess you could see the baby as a bomb. I don't. This is more like the seasons are changing. Yeah, everything is different, but you can find beauty in change too."

I love you.

The thought was so swift, so sudden, so all-consuming, I gasped and shifted away from him. "Holy shit."

"Mia, what's going on?" He chuckled and tried to pull me back, but I resisted.

"What? No, nothing. Nothing. I just—is that the time?" I pointed to the nightstand clock. "I didn't realize it was so late. Sleep sounds so good right now." My heart galloped in my chest, and the instinct to run, and run, and run was impossible to resist. Sleep was the last thing on my mind, but I couldn't tell Tyler my fleeting, ridiculous thought. He'd laugh. I should be laughing. *In love with him?* I hardly knew him.

Whatever just crossed my mind wasn't love.

I loved the way his mind worked.

And the way he always smelled like jasmine.

And how he treated me like an equal, never condescending, never like an object.

And how he could make me laugh one minute and kill me with his sincerity the next.

And how the muscles bulged in his arms when he tugged me close.

But I didn't love *him*.

"It's nine o'clock. You normally stay up until all hours of the morning."

"Sure, yeah, when I'm on *tour*. But when I'm *not* on tour, I always go to bed super early." I scrambled off the bed, gathering my scattered clothes, and I headed for the door. "That was fun. We should definitely do it again." With a quick wave, I tugged the bedroom door tight and tried to block out the bewildered expression on his face.

Outside of his door, I took a deep breath and then let out a soft chuckle.

Love.

Impossible. More like *hormones*. That was it. My shoulders eased down, all the tension leaving. Of course! The rush of love came from the baby.

That flood of emotion was just the baby.

Chapter Sixteen

Tyler

Two weeks. She'd been living here for two weeks, and it was going...well. Better than well, actually. We'd fallen into an easy routine of work and sex and sleep. I'd worried our lives might not fit together. But she'd slid as seamlessly into mine as I'd slid into hers.

My family had all met her, and while none of them were enthusiastic about the arrangement, they were polite and kind to Mia. When we left my mother's house after a big family dinner, Mia turned to me with a wistful smile and said it was no wonder I was such a good guy when I grew up surrounded by all of that.

The moment had been bittersweet. I hated to realize she didn't have anything remotely close. Her mother was her only family, and Laura wasn't fully present in their mother-daughter relationship. At least, not in the right way. It wasn't my place to say anything, but keeping quiet was getting harder and harder.

So, today, I was determined to make her feel special. After all, it was her birthday. Twenty-one.

I gazed toward the front counter of Kathy's Café, the small establishment in town that made the best caffeinated drinks. All of the pastel tones gave the place a calm, rustic vibe. Mia liked the sparkling mint-lime iced tea the café sold, and I'd made a bulk order for her surprise party. Twenty-one surprises for her twenty-first birthday.

Last night, I hid some of her favorite things around the house once she left my room. She never slept beside me. I tried not to let the arrangement bother me, tried to remember she was skittish. Tried to decide how far I wanted to nudge her to draw us closer together.

Since she wasn't really showing, other than looking as though she'd put on a few pounds, I hadn't been sure how big the surprise party should be. In the end, I decided on smaller instead of bigger, and only invited people Mia trusted. The baby news needed to be under wraps, and she was so much more relaxed around people who knew everything. So, I hadn't invited her mother, and I still wasn't sure if I'd made the right choice.

She rarely talked about Laura, but once or twice, I caught her scrolling through photos of the two of them on her phone. Maybe if I were a better man, I'd try to bridge that gap, but I preferred it to expand. Could Mia ever give up on her mother and the life they built together? Any time the topic came up, she said her time in Little Falls was a break from her mother, not a breakup. The distance was for the baby, no other reason.

At the counter, Sabrina Kim fumbled through ringing up my order and then disappeared into the back to get the industrial-sized containers I'd ordered.

"That's a lot of sparkling mint-lime iced tea," a wry female voice commented from behind.

I stiffened and then half-turned to see Katie. Of course, I'd known people were waiting in line, but I'd been so deep in thought about Mia and her party, I hadn't looked around since I'd arrived. "Who can resist that combination?"

She pushed her purse further onto her shoulder in a move that was both familiar and foreign. *Eight years.* She moved out of the house we shared and across the country to some lateral nursing position, as far as I could tell, on a whim. Poof. Bags packed. Gone.

"I've never tried it. You'd recommend it?" That hesitant smile tugged at her lips.

Out of my pocket, I produced a lollipop and carefully removed the wrapper, focusing on the crinkling plastic. "It's Mia's favorite. Today's her birthday."

"Oh." Katie rocked back. "Of course. Right."

"I—" I took a deep breath and glanced toward the counter, wishing Sabrina would be faster. "I'm sorry about some of the things Mia has said to you and your dad."

She avoided meeting my gaze and shrugged her shoulders. "She's young. Clearly, a bit insecure." After a beat she said, "Did you enjoy being on her tour? You always had big plans. I was sad to see you didn't follow through on those."

My jaw tightened involuntarily, and I slipped the lollipop into my cheek, hoping to ease the tension. "It was good, yeah. As for the other stuff, I've got my shop."

"Eight years ago, the shop was a compromise."

I shook my head and scanned the café to see who was watching and listening to our exchange. The last thing I wanted was for a chance meeting to get back to Mia on her birthday. "You know it was. And then, it became my life."

Sabrina banged back through the swinging doors, an enormous plastic container dangling from each arm. "Why are these so heavy?" She complained coming around the counter. "Be careful. They're so heavy, Tyler."

With my head low, I concealed my smile as I picked them up easily. Katie's eyes were on me as my muscles flexed with the weight.

"Can we—could we maybe get coffee sometime? Either while Mia's here or once she's gone?" Her expression was hopeful.

I suppressed a sigh as I stared into her light-brown eyes. They'd always tugged at something deep inside, and I wished this moment was different. But the vulnerability I saw in her made me want to agree to coffee at least.

As though sensing my weakness, she added, "To catch up. As friends."

"I'll let you know." Denying her outright was harsh, and maybe when Mia left, I'd need some kind of distraction from the fallout. Who knew? Rehashing the past might not be such a grenade in a few months. Maybe the conversation would be a balm.

"I hope she loves whatever you've got planned. You always arranged the best surprises." She averted her gaze and stepped up to the register before I could muster a response.

Emily and my mother, Joanna, were filling up balloons with the helium tank and trying to wrestle them into groups while Amir, Emily's son, sucked in gas from a stray balloon and sang to the playlist I'd created just for the party. Twenty-one of Mia's favorite artists and songs.

Her passion for music was one of the things I loved about her. Any time I could get her talking about what songs, songwriters, or musicians she loved, I was guaranteed an education. She lit up. Creating the playlist had been a no-brainer, and since I paid attention the last couple months about which songs and artists she never tired of hearing, the hardest part had been narrowing it down to twenty-one.

"You're quiet," Emily commented while she passed another balloon to our mother to tie.

"I'm mulling something over."

"Something Mia-related? You two seem like you've gotten close. The Pretty Boy nickname the other night got quite a laugh. Why do you call her Mini?"

"Long story." Some things I wanted to keep sacred, and those nicknames were meant for just us.

"I hate when you get like this," Emily said.

"Like what?" I'd been staring at the wooden island and lifted my gaze to meet hers.

"All broody and introspective. You're so much more fun when you're being a communicator."

"That's because you like gossip."

"That's true!" My mother chimed in. "I do, too. So, tell us what you're mulling over."

"I saw Katie at the café when I was getting the iced tea." I pressed my fingers into the smooth surface of the island.

"She's basically your personal nurse for the baby, right? You've seen her a few times. Why would seeing her at the café make you introspective?"

"She wants to have coffee. It's not the first time she mentioned meeting, but I didn't outright turn her down this time."

"That ship sailed, Tyler." My mother *tsked* and tied another balloon.

"Yes, Mother. I'm aware the ship sailed across the country eight years ago. I just can't figure out why she's back and why she's so keen to reconnect."

"Regret," Emily said in a sing-song voice. "Romantic regret is the worst. It feels like you've totally screwed up your life."

"How would you know that?" I raised my eyebrows.

"Don't you remember how crazy she was about Terrence?" Mom tipped her head in Emily's direction.

"High school Terrence?"

"First love, worst love." Emily shrugged. "Until I met Omar and fell in love with him, I thought breaking up with Terrence might have been the dumbest thing I'd ever done. I broke up with him because I didn't want to do long distance. Looking back, though, our breakup was probably because I didn't love him enough. I don't know. Feelings are complicated." She passed our mother another balloon. "But that ache for him lasted until I met Omar. If Katie's had that ache for that long, I get why she'd want to talk to you."

"We can't go back." I glanced at the clock. I needed to be home in half an hour or Mia would realize something was up.

"What about going forward? Would you be willing to give Katie another shot?" Emily turned off the helium machine and surveyed our handiwork. All the balloons had the number twenty-one on them. "Twenty-one. God, she's young."

"Truth?" I rubbed my face with both hands.

"Uh, of course. I'm your sister. I'll stand behind you even if you love one woman and you got another one pregnant...who we're throwing a surprise party for tonight. That's sweet, by the way. To do all this."

"That's not the problem. I don't love Katie anymore. I'm sure of that. Seeing her today in the café without having to worry about concealing anything from Mia, I realized that I *don't* love her anymore. I care about her. Could I love her again? I don't know. I don't know. Could I ever trust her?" I held up my hands in a helpless gesture.

"What about Mia?" Mom raised her eyebrows. "How do you feel about her?"

"If it's possible, that's even more complicated." I sighed. "She's so determined to get the hell out of here once the baby is born that I'm letting distance sit between us."

"Letting distance sit between you?" Emily frowned. "What does that mean?"

I grabbed one of the presents sitting on the island. Even though I'd told them not to get Mia anything, they'd all bought small presents. With my fingers, I twirled the wrapped box while I tried to figure out how to phrase it, whether I even wanted to vocalize it.

"She's asked about Katie a few times, and I've resisted giving her the story."

"Why?" Emily's frown deepened.

"Partly because I don't talk about Katie with anyone, ever. What do I say about all that? It's...I can't imagine an explanation would make someone I'm with feel secure. But the other side of it," I took a deep breath, "is that being honest with her, telling her, closes some distance between us." I placed the box back in the pile. "And then what do I do when she leaves? 'Cause she's not gonna stay. She's made that very clear."

"She might," My mom said from across the room as she took the helium balloon from Amir. "Having a baby is a profound experience. You can't understand those feelings until you've experienced them. Walking away might not be as easy as she thinks."

"That's true," Emily said, love for her son pouring out of her as she gazed at him. "It's a whole other level of love." Amir ran across the large open living room to plow into his mother's side, wrapping his arms around her and burying his face in her stomach. "I love you, kid." She leaned down and kissed the side of his head.

"But I can't count on that." I pursed my lips, unsure of how to even explain all the complications I could see. "And even if I could, that just means she loves the baby, right?"

"Yeah, but how do you want to look back on this experience?" Emily hugged her son close to her side and seemed deep in thought.

"What do you mean?"

"Well, in five years or ten years when you look back at the months you spent with her, do you want to wonder what might have happened if you'd put yourself out there, or do you want to know you gave it your all? I mean, do you think you *could* love her?"

I stared at the clouds of balloons in the living room, thought of all the things I'd left at the house for her, at the iced tea in the fridge, at the way my room felt cold once she'd left it each night. "I think I'm half in love with her already."

"What's that saying?" Mom called over. "In the end, we only regret the chances we didn't take? Put your heart out there, Tyler. We'll help you pick up the pieces if it comes to that."

"Easy for everyone to say when it's not their heart, their sanity. Once she leaves, I'll still see her everywhere. As long as she's famous, I'll have to see her all the time—sometimes in places I'll expect to, and other times, it'll be like a punch to the gut. How do I...I barely survived Katie leaving me." I grabbed the back of my neck. "I barely survived, and I *never* had to see her."

It was the most honest I'd been with Emily or my mother about that period of my life. When Katie left, I spent months drowning in alcohol, half-heartedly building the thrift shop, and praying she realized she'd made a mistake and come running back.

Lately, I was seeing that I broke off most of my long-term, committed relationships when they didn't seem to measure up, when the buzz I'd felt with Katie didn't appear. But maybe I'd also been a bit afraid to risk my heart with the same intensity I'd done with Katie. Maybe there'd always been a part of me I'd held back, meaning I could never experience the same emotional heights. I knew how far that fall was, how much it hurt.

"I guess I need to figure out what regrets I'm okay with having." I grabbed my keys off the counter and headed for the door.

"I vote none," Emily called. "For the record, I vote for no regrets."

Chapter Seventeen
Mia

Mia The day had been overwhelming. Every time I opened a cupboard or reached for something familiar, I stumbled across a token from Tyler. The gifts started this morning when I opened my bedroom door and found a gorgeous dress hanging in the basement from the ceiling. It was the prettiest shade of blue-green I'd ever seen. So rich, it made my teeth ache. Of course I tried it on, and no surprise, it fit like someone had made it just for me. I was pretty sure Tyler had sewn it in the back room at his shop. Last week when I stopped by to visit, he'd thrown a drop cloth over something this color on his sewing table.

In ten minutes, he was picking me up for dinner.

What would it be like to have him for more than just this birthday? Would he do something like this every year?

The amount of thought and work he put into these little surprises caused tears to pool. I didn't even know when his birthday was, and he did all of this for me.

Beside me, my phone pinged with a new email. They'd been arriving all day from people all over the world with birthday wishes. When I opened my device, I was only a little surprised to see Laura Malone's name. The frosty silence was broken for my birthday.

Happy Birthday, my darling daughter. I hope you're enjoying your time off. Two things—the VISION Gala is coming up, and last we spoke, you didn't have a designer pegged. Use some common sense and make some calls. We don't want this opportunity to slide, or you won't get an invite next year.

There's an up-and-comer from the label sniffing around trying to get some face-to-face time with you. Avoid her at all costs. She's a fame seeker. You know the type.

When you remember I'm your mother and I love you, call me. I really do hope you're having a good birthday. I'll spend the next few hours reliving my labor pains and wondering what I've done to deserve being cut out of your life (however temporary).

At the bottom was a photo of a beaming Laura in the hospital holding me, with my father cropped from the scene.

I rolled my eyes at the last few lines and threw my phone toward the couch. Leave it to my mother to burst my lovely Tyler bubble. That photo only made an appearance when we were having a particularly vicious fight. Still, that was probably the first family photo ever taken. Crossing the room, I picked up my phone and clicked on the photo again, enlarging it. This time, I studied it.

Had my mother really been as happy as she looked in the photo? I never trusted pictures anymore since I was forced to smile in all kinds of situations, sometimes when I really wanted to be screaming or crying at some injustice. Laura probably understood the value of a false narrative even back then. She'd been the one to teach it to me.

Most people believed what you showed them. Very few bothered to lift the veil, to ask the tough questions, to really know the person behind the mask.

When I took in all of the trinkets Tyler had left strewn around the house, I had to admit, he really knew me.

And the dress.

I gazed at it on the hanger. The lace overlay was something called a lavender pattern. I'd looked it up. Wearing it felt like letting him claim me, and I loved the notion while also feeling terrified of it. The halter top hugged my body and slid away. Sometimes, that's the way I felt about Tyler, too. He was so close, and yet, oddly far away.

Pasha opened the front door and nodded toward the dress. "Get dressed."

"I'm admiring it," I said, straightening while my fingers trailed along the fabric.

"He think you no like. Get dressed." He threw his chin in the direction of the small two-piece bathroom.

A valid point. I should get it on before he arrived. My mother's email had distracted me, and then my scattered feelings were also hard to pin down. All of these baby hormones were playing with my head.

And my heart.

But it was just the baby. Once I had the baby, all these feelings would disappear in a puff of placenta. Wouldn't that be nice? No more clouds of emotional confusion. Absolute clarity awaited me on the other side of intense physical pain.

I swallowed. Best not to think about the giving birth portion of this whole thing. One meeting with the midwife and a couple YouTube videos had been more than enough.

When the front door opened again, I said, "I'm getting dressed." Annoyance tinged my voice. Pasha was such a mother hen sometimes.

"If you don't like the dress, it's okay. You can wear whatever you want."

I closed my eyes for a beat, silently cursing. When I turned toward Tyler, my smile was genuine. "I love it. I've loved all the things I've discovered today." With a few quick strides, I was at the island, and I threw out a hand like one of those pretty girls showing off items from a game show. "I had no idea you knew me so well."

A slow smile spread across Tyler's face, and he leaned against the doorframe. Pasha's disapproving head shake was at the edge of my vision. *Yeah, yeah, Pasha, you told me.*

That smile stretching across Tyler's face catapulted my heart rate and made the whole lower half of my body long to drag him downstairs instead of out to dinner. I'd never wanted someone this consistently, constantly. He was an addiction.

Hormones. So many hormones.

"Maybe we can just order in?" I wandered over and slid my arms around his neck. "Wanna sing me happy birthday in the basement? I'm sure we can find a nice, tight spot for you to slide into."

"I have plans for you." He gave my butt a light slap. "That's one plan, but it comes after the other plan. Give me a few hours out of the house, and I'll sing happy birthday to you as many times as you want."

"As many times as I want?" I closed my teeth gently around his earlobe. "I like the sound of that."

His fingers dug into my waist, and he tugged me flush against him. "Need me to help you get dressed?"

"Just undressed," I breathed into his ear.

"Careful, I could get used to this kind of greeting. Might insist on it every day."

"I've had a good day. When you're a good boy, it makes me want to be a very bad girl." Under my lashes I took in the desire smoldering in his gaze. Sex had always been about power, or at least in my experience. When I could, I'd chosen men with less power than me—dancers, singers from opening acts, a waiter, an up-and-coming actor. Technically, Tyler fit the mold, too. It was why I'd asked him to my hotel in the first place. But the dynamic had changed. I didn't know who held the power, and I wasn't sure I cared.

"You gonna get out the whips and chains later, Mini?" His hands slid into my hair.

"You into that, Pretty Boy?" I laughed and rose onto my toes to press my lips to his. "Can't say I saw that coming."

"I'll try anything once."

"Somewhat comforting to hear this would be a first. I was worried I didn't really know you." I gave him a flirty glance, and I stepped back to snatch the dress off the hanger. "Back in a sec."

"If you need any help in there," Tyler called, "let me know."

When we pulled up outside his mother's house, I frowned. "We're eating *here*?"

"You'll see," he said, climbing out of the car and coming around to open my door. He linked our fingers and led me toward the front entrance.

"It's pretty dark, Tyler. Does your mom know we're coming?" I frowned, uneasiness stirring in my gut. Pasha trailed behind us, but something about the house felt off.

Without punching in the code, he turned the handle and pushed the door wide. When the door swung open, he turned, and our gazes connected. The sincerity in his depths stopped my breath for a beat.

"Happy Birthday, Mini."

All of the lights in the living room came on, flooding the front entrance, and a chorus of *"Surprise!"* burst out along the crowd of familiar faces. An enthusiastic and off-key round of "Happy Birthday" followed.

I squeezed Tyler's hand, and I scanned all the people he'd gathered. My heart dipped into my stomach, because my mother wasn't among them. Of course, she wasn't. Why would she be? We were fighting.

But it was my birthday.

Grady appeared in front of them and swept me into a warm hug. He'd taken on the Sullivan habit of hugging, and I had to admit, he gave good ones. They were almost as good as Tyler's.

"Happy Birthday, Mia." He kissed my brow.

Behind him, Maggie stepped forward, embraced me, and wished me a happy birthday. A blur of familiar faces from around town or on my tour followed until I got to Taryn and Rebecca. Up to them, I'd held my emotions together, but seeing them and realizing my mother really wasn't coming caused tears to spring to my eyes.

"I thought maybe she might come," I said in Taryn's ear while we hugged.

"She's a stubborn one," Taryn said. "When Tyler said you still weren't showing, we did tell her. I don't know if he wanted us to, but I knew no matter what was going on, you'd want her here."

"How's the writing going?" Rebecca sipped her drink and smoothly changed the topic.

"Is that sparkling mint-lime iced tea?" I peered into Rebecca's cup.

"Yeah, I think that's what the sign said. It's good." She held the cup away from her face and examined it.

"Oh, my God. He's like..." I couldn't even finish the sentence while I looked for him in the sea of familiar faces. He was over by the punch bowl talking to Emily and ruffling Amir's hair.

"The best thing that's ever happened to you?" Taryn finished softly.

"Let's not get carried away." A smile tugged at the edge of my lips. "But that's my new favorite drink." I pointed to Rebecca's cup. "I love it. It's just—I've never known anyone else who noticed these things about me." I shook my head. "My mother doesn't even notice these little things."

Taryn and Rebecca exchanged a loaded gaze before they sipped their drinks. "It is delicious," Rebecca agreed.

"So," I rubbed my hands together, "tell me what I've been missing. Give me all the gossip. I've been so busy writing. I've been trying to stay off the internet unless I'm looking something up for a lyric."

"It's going well then?" Taryn asked.

"Sure, yeah. I mean, it took me a minute to remember how I like to work. But I'm in the zone now. I should be able to get enough songs for an album before...you know."

"You give birth?" Rebecca eyed my rounded stomach that hadn't popped so much as expanded. Bloated, not pregnant.

"I try not to think about that part. It freaks me out. I'm not good with pain."

"So, you don't want me to tell you all the birthing horror stories I know?" Taryn chuckled.

"God, no. I'll probably get enough of those when I start to show." I frowned. "Not that I'll be allowed out of the house once that happens. Not really looking forward to that part either. It's been nice to feel average or normal or whatever this is the last couple of weeks."

"Your dress is gorgeous." Rebecca ran her fingers down the edge of the material. "Nothing normal about this."

"Thank you. Tyler made it. He's so freaking talented." I sought him out in the crowd again.

"Strange he's never done more with it." Taryn followed my gaze across the room.

"Maybe he didn't want to do more," Rebecca said. "Not everyone has a desire to conquer the world."

"Did you hear from your mother?" Taryn's voice was gentle.

"She emailed me. Reminded me that I needed a designer for the gala. I can't go, though. I mean, I'll be showing for sure in another month. I'll have to cancel. And then she gave me a heads-up about some label stuff."

"Oh," Rebecca said. "About Kenny Connors? Jesus. What a mess."

"What about him?" My heart dipped.

"Rumor has it there's a huge lawsuit coming down the pipe. One of the girls he worked with a couple years ago is claiming he's a notorious and serial statutory rapist." Taryn shook her head and sipped her drink. "A witch hunt, maybe. Hard to say. Can you imagine no one saying anything? He works with young girls all the time. All. The. Time."

"Oh, really?" A cold sweat broke out under my armpits. I wished I could drink. Something really strong right about now would ease the tightness in my chest. Or Tyler. Tyler would make this awful feeling fade. "You don't believe her?"

"Well, you worked with him, didn't you? I can't imagine you or Laura putting up with shit like that." Taryn laughed. "Laura would rip him a new asshole."

Except she hadn't. Not back then. At fifteen, I hadn't understood what had happened, not really. When he pushed me up against the desk, I giggled. *Giggled.* But then when he started pawing at me, I tried to slow him down, stop him, but no words had left my mouth. Not one. Afterward, he told me I was so sexy, he just couldn't control himself, like his abuse was a compliment, like I should've been flattered.

Even now, when I understood what really happened, we let him off, allowed him to stay loose to prowl after others, to hunt more girls. Bile rose into my throat.

"Right," I said, feeling lightheaded. "I should go mingle."

Across the room, the front door swung open, and Sarah Telling, tall, willowy, and blond, entered flanked by two burly bodyguards. I let out a squeal, the sick feeling in the pit of my stomach disappearing, and I raced across the room, practically attacking my best friend.

Sarah laughed and yelled, "Happy Birthday!"

"I can't believe you came." I squeezed her tighter, reluctant to let her go. At least she came. I didn't know how Tyler managed it, since Sarah's schedule was worse than mine.

"I can only stay for an hour. Sorry. I know that's shit, but it was the best I could do." She passed me a tiny box. "Where did you get that dress? I want one."

"Tyler made it." A flash of pride struck my chest.

"Boyfriend made the dress. Impressive." Sarah's fingers trailed down it while I lifted the top off the tiny box. Inside was a delicate silver bracelet.

"He's not my boyfriend." I lifted the bracelet to catch the light. "This is gorgeous."

"It spoke to me. Seemed like something you'd like." Her gaze traveled around the room. "So, where is your boyfriend? I've seen him blasted across social media as you paraded around this town with him. You look happy."

"Social media?" I frowned and dropped the bracelet back into the box.

"Yeah, you know that thing you've been neglecting for the last couple weeks. News flash—the town has been filling in the gaps for you. You're lucky it's all been super boring stuff, or the paparazzi would have been on Tyler's doorstep." Sarah smoothed my hair. "It's cute how he holds your hand everywhere."

I'd never noticed, but the thought brought the shape and feel of his hand back to me in a rush. Perhaps we did hold hands a lot. I scanned the room for him and found him watching me. A grin emerged, and an answering one lit his face when our gazes connected.

"This must be pissing your mother off something fierce. Quit the tour, shack up with an older man, get pregnant."

"She doesn't know about the baby." My smile faded, and I turned to face Sarah.

"What?" Sarah's blue eyes went big and round. "You haven't told her?"

"She'd have drugged me and driven me to the clinic."

"You don't still think—"

"Maybe. Probably. I don't know. It was a long time ago." I never let those thoughts settle.

"Have you been following the Kenny Connors drama?"

I shook my head and grabbed Sarah's hand. "You should come meet Tyler before you have to leave."

"That girl's legal team will come for you, Mia. Everyone knows what he's like, even if no one ever confronted him."

"No comment, right? Wear them down with bullshit." I glanced at Sarah over my shoulder while I weaved through the crowd.

"They're talking subpoenas. Just watch yourself. The timing is awful for you."

Tyler's arm slid around my waist as soon as I got close enough, and he passed me a glass of tea. "You're looking pale," he whispered in my ear. "Need a lollipop?"

"I've got what I need." I looked up into his cognac eyes and drank him in.

He tugged me into his side, and I wrapped my arms around his waist.

"Sarah, this is Tyler. Tyler, Sarah." They shook hands and enthusiastic comments about how good it was to meet flew between them.

As they struck up a conversation, I listened in silence, my mind ticking through Taryn's and Sarah's comments. How many girls had Kenny manipulated? Raped? It was terrifying and comforting to think they might not even need my testimony. How many accusers were enough to bring him down? Had this been what my mother had been alluding to in her email? A fame seeker? More like a truth seeker.

When Sarah had to leave, we hugged, and we squeezed each other extra tight. She was one of the few people who knew everything that had happened with Kenny. Some of that should never see the light of day.

"You okay?" Tyler whispered in my ear. "You've been really quiet."

"I'm okay." I glanced up at him. "Thanks for my party. And you got me my favorite drink." For the first time, I became conscious of the music playing in the background, and my stomach swooped low. "And all my favorite songs."

"Twenty-one surprises for your twenty-first." He kissed the top of my head.

A familiar welling up of love coursed through me. When the feeling came now, it wasn't shocking; it was soothing. Hormones. The baby. "You're going to be a fantastic dad."

"I'm going to try my hardest." He squeezed my hip.

I didn't doubt his intention for a second. He'd done all this for me, someone he didn't love, so I could only imagine what he'd do for a child, someone he would love more than anyone else.

When I looked around the room again, my smile faded a little at who wasn't there, who hadn't bothered to show up.

Our baby had won the daddy lottery. I wished I'd been a winner, too.

Chapter Eighteen
Tyler

Mia's lips were so soft. She had an addiction to lip gloss, so the suppleness of her lips shouldn't be a surprise, but every time we kissed like this, long and deep, there was an extra jolt of pleasure that I got to experience her lips. I could kiss her forever.

The regrets might come, but I didn't intend to take any of these moments for granted. I sank my hands deeper into her hair, drawing her closer. She scooted her butt along the kitchen island, wrapping her legs around me.

Pasha went to bed while the two of us were doing shots. Well, Mia's glass was filled with sparkling water, but she couldn't close out her twenty-first without some sort of liquid in a shot glass. So, I drank vodka while she poured herself some of the fancy sparkling water I gave her as part of her twenty-one gifts. After each shot, she pretended to get progressively drunker while I actually got a bit drunk. Our laughter was probably keeping Pasha awake.

When she perched on the island for her last shot and arched one eyebrow before tipping it back, I knew I didn't want any more vodka. Her twenty-first needed to go out with a bang, not a fizzle. I still owed her a song...or two.

With ease, I lifted her off the island and cupped her ass in both hands. At the stairs, I shifted my grip, so I could grab the railing to navigate down. She laughed against my lips.

"This doesn't feel safe." She wrapped her arms around my neck and nibbled on my earlobe.

"It felt safe until you started doing that."

She laughed against my neck, and when we got to the bottom of the stairs, I slid her along my body.

"I owe you a song," I murmured.

"You're going to sing to me?" Her blue-green eyes sparkled when she stared up.

"I am. I'm going to sing," I kissed her, "until you climax," I kissed her again, "while crying out my name." There was nothing better than hearing my name in her strangled cry when she tipped over the edge. I heard it every day, sometimes more than once a day since we started this friends-with-benefits arrangement, and I had every intention of hearing it more than once tonight. I scooped up her lips for a deeper, longer kiss, and I gathered her dress around her waist, bunched in my hands.

"Are you a good singer? Is this a promise or a threat?" Her voice brimmed with amusement.

I tugged her dress over her head, and then our lips met again, my thumb circling her exposed nipple. "I promise something will be explosive, but I doubt my singing is all that great."

"Well," Mia said, drawing me closer. "This should be interesting." Her fingers undid my jeans and pushed them down my hips, so they pooled around my ankles.

I gazed at her for a moment, an ache spreading across my chest at how beautiful she was, how lucky I was. Then I started a low, uneven tune,

"*Happy Birthday to you.*" I nibbled her neck in between words, and I slid my hand along her ass, savoring her soft, smooth skin.

"So far, so good." She gasped when I eased my hand between her legs.

"*Happy Birthday to you.*" I grazed her breast with my teeth, and then I picked her up again, her legs locked around my waist.

At the bed, I laid her down, and she clutched the sheets when I parted her legs. I loved that she knew what was coming, already bracing herself for the pleasure. Along her inner thigh, I trailed kisses, teasing her. "*Happy Birthday, dear Mini.*" I flicked my tongue along her center before pressing a little more firmly, the way she liked. "Happy Birthday to you," I mumbled against her, feeling her tense with the pleasure.

"Tyler, please," she moaned.

"Sing it again?" I asked, my tongue circling her clit.

A stifled laugh escaped her. "No, I want you. Inside me. God, I want to feel all of you."

"Who am I to deny you on your birthday?" I crawled up her body and shed the rest of my clothes as I went. When we were face-to-face, I stared into her eyes for a moment. Those perfect, perfect eyes. Who knew one night all those months ago would lead to this? "Happy Birthday, Mia."

She stroked my face, and another piece of our connection solidified, unspoken, lacing us tighter than any words could. Then she pulled me down for a kiss, and I slipped inside of her, my favorite place in the world, and we started to move in sync.

She was sprawled across my chest when she let out a sigh of contentment. "I don't think I've ever had a birthday this good. Actually, I know I haven't."

"I aim to please." I linked our hands and kissed her fingertips. Celebrations and surprises came easily. Pay attention, and the rest fell into place.

"I'm going to take advantage of your post-sex bliss and ask for a favor." She shifted onto her side, flipping her hair around to lie against her shoulder. "And just because it's my birthday, you don't have to say yes."

"What do you need, Mini?" I stroked the side of her face. Denying her seemed unlikely.

"A dress." She grinned.

"Another one?"

"Yeah, but this one is for the gala run by the editor of VISION. You know what I'm talking about?"

"The biggest fashion event of the year." I rubbed a hand down my face. With a sideways look at her, I shook my head. "I can't make your dress for that. It's in what—" In my head, I went through the time between now and then. "Four weeks?"

"I sort of forgot about it until my mother reminded me today."

"You heard from her?" I frowned and turned to my side, so we were face-to-face.

"Sure, yeah. I mean, she's not heartless."

I wasn't going to get into that debate, and I didn't want to admit I hadn't invited her to the surprise party. Maybe Mia had figured out the omission. "They're not going to let some nobody design your dress." For a designer, dressing someone for the VISION Gala meant you'd made it.

"I can ask whoever I want. People think you're assigned a designer, and some people are. But I'm not big enough for that, not trendy enough yet. I want you to make it."

"What's the theme?"

"Space exploration." Mia covered her face and peeked through her fingers.

"Space exploration?" Shouldn't be surprising. The themes were never something you could anticipate, which is what created such a buzz in the industry. The gala was a melding of fashion and art. "You're almost definitely going to look pregnant a month from now. If you don't, you're some sort of freak of nature."

"Gee, thanks."

"I'm just saying," I ran my hand through my hair, "it's a massive risk for you if I don't get the dress right to conceal your bump."

"That's what you're worried about?" She raised her eyebrows. "Not the international attention or designing to some wacky theme, but that my pregnancy might show?"

I stared at her for a beat and was tempted to laugh. She really didn't understand me at all. "You and the baby are my priorities. So, of course exposing the two of you is my biggest concern. To spend months hiding your pregnancy to have the truth crash down around us over a dress at a fashion expo is ridiculous."

She collapsed onto her back and stared at the ceiling. I watched her in silence, my mind already drawing sketches, considering materials, the best way to conceal her bump within the parameters of the theme.

"I might be able to do it," I admitted.

"I *know* you can. The dress will be incredible. My dress today, Tyler, was one of the prettiest, most *me* things I've ever owned. Do that again, but on a bigger scale."

"So, your expectations are pretty low then. Perfect." I chuckled and picked up a strand of her hair, twirling it around my finger.

Mia opened her mouth and then closed it again. "Okay, don't take this the wrong way. I'm not trying to be a dick, for once. You're really talented. Why are you wasting your vision in a thrift shop in a tiny town in New York?"

I blew out a breath and eased onto my back beside her, lacing my fingers across my middle. Another opening to be honest, to draw us closer emotionally. She was probably expecting me to blow her off as I'd done every other time she asked anything about the shop or Katie. She had no idea how closely linked the two were.

"I worked on a small theater tour when I finished college, which you know. I networked my ass off to get a spot on that crew. Months of shitty jobs in Little Falls while I tried to build a portfolio and make some connections in the industry. Katie and I were living together, and I caught a break. I was so sure that's all I needed—a foot in the door."

"But you didn't stay."

"No, I didn't stay. Four or five months into the tour, Katie came to visit, which she'd done a few times when the tour was relatively close. We didn't have a lot of money. She showed up and broke up with me. Just...out of the blue. Ten years together, gone. So, I quit the tour and followed her home, here. She was packed, and had already taken a job on the other side of the country. Somehow, the relationship slipped through my fingers, and I didn't even feel it going."

"Why didn't you just go back on that tour or *any* tour?" Mia's voice was quiet in the dark room. I wanted to look at her, but I wasn't sure I'd like what I saw.

"I dropped out, left them in the lurch, so getting a reference from them was tricky. My parents bought me the thrift shop as soon as I got back, before it was clear Katie wouldn't change her mind and wouldn't stay. For months, I thought she'd return, or admit she made a mistake. I was afraid to leave."

"In case she came back?"

"Yeah."

"She didn't?" Puzzlement was clear in her tone.

"Never heard from her. Not once. Seeing her at the hospital a few months ago was the first time I'd seen her in eight years."

"Wow," Mia breathed out the word. "You don't know why?"

I shook my head and realized she probably couldn't see that in the dimly lit room. "No. At the time, she said we'd grown apart. But it was a bullshit reason. A total fabrication. I don't know what happened, but the problem wasn't that."

She was quiet for a long time, and I wondered if I should admit Katie wanted to talk, maybe reconnect.

"That must have been really hard," she whispered.

"It was, yeah."

"And now, she's back."

"And now, she's back." I let a beat sit before wading in. "I ran into her today at the café when I was getting the iced tea." I took a deep breath, sure she wasn't going to like the next part. Mia might not want me beyond the next few months, but she was territorial right now. "She wants to get coffee and talk."

"I don't want you to." Her response was almost instant, a hint of panic in her voice. "You can do whatever you want when I'm gone. But when I'm here, I don't want you to see her. Other than our appointments, I don't want you to see her. Okay? Can you promise me?"

I turned onto my side and stared down, brushing her hair back. "Whatever was between Katie and me ended eight years ago."

"It's fine." She shook her head and bit her lip. "You can do whatever you like when I'm gone." She met my gaze, her blue-green eyes glittering. "But you don't go near her while I'm still here, okay?"

"Mia—"

She wrapped her hand around the back of my neck and pulled me down for a kiss. "My birthday ends in ten minutes, and I don't want this conversation to be what I remember about it." She shifted so she was under me. "Sing to me."

I searched her face for a minute, at the naked vulnerability shining back. God, I hated hurting her. I'd told her the truth, and I was already regretting it. "I'm sorry, Mia."

"Don't." She shook her head and pressed a fingertip to my lips. "In five or six months, you can do whatever you want. I will be. But right now, you're mine. You're mine."

Five or six months.

I wanted to protest, to somehow convince her she didn't need to go anywhere in a few months, that I'd take whatever this was with her over anything I'd ever had with anyone else.

But she didn't want forever; she wanted just for now.

I touched my forehead to hers, our gazes locked. "Okay, Mini. Whatever you want."

Then we were kissing, and I was singing a muffled "Happy Birthday," but there was a desperate edge to everything that hadn't been there earlier in the night.

Between us, a clock ticked.

Chapter Nineteen

Mia

I'd been avoiding this place, secretly hoping the train station renovations would be delayed so I could stay at Tyler's house. If I asked him, he'd let me. While Grady showed off all the modifications he completed so people like me could come here, dropped into a songwriting oasis, I had to admit he'd thought of everything. Given that he was also a very talented songwriter, his attention to detail made sense.

I eyed Grady while we took in the studio space. He was taller and leaner than Tyler. Since Tyler had gone on tour, he'd bulked up, and in places his muscles had muscles. I'd never complain.

When I first met and worked with Grady, I worried he'd be like many of the other men in the business. Instead, he was creative and driven and understanding of my songwriting quirks. I liked him—a lot—too much. Now, looking at him, he felt like a big brother. The crush that had threatened to blossom before had wilted.

"When are you back here full-time?" I asked, thinking of how close he and Maggie had been at my surprise party a few weeks ago. The way they looked at each other had caused my chest to ache.

He grabbed a handful of his almost too-long brown hair before shrugging. "Who knows? I gotta prove myself."

"I can't imagine anyone not wanting to work with you and not being happy to work here in this space. You've done an amazing job."

"I tried to make it high level, elite. I want good people. I want this to be my job, my life, here in this town. The recording studio was already top-notch, but I needed the apartment to be the same."

"You want this life with Maggie?" I remembered his performance at the benefit, how the song he'd written for Maggie had gone viral. Half the internet had been in love with him after that, me included. To be loved like that...

"With Maggie." He grinned. "And hopefully, some little girls and boys who take after their mother."

"I want this baby to be a boy. I want him to be like Tyler."

"Really?" He frowned. "Why? Women seem to want a little mini-me running around. You're due at the end of July, right? You don't know what you're having yet?"

I crossed my arms over the bump that had popped out a little over a week ago. Two hours of staring at it in the mirror hadn't managed to make my stomach go back to reasonably flat. So, now I was slathering oil on it, praying I didn't end up with stretch marks I'd have to explain to people. "Tyler has an envelope with the baby's sex in it."

"So, he knows?"

"No, I asked him not to look."

"And he listened?" Grady raised his eyebrows.

"You know Tyler. He's a good guy." The best guy. "You wouldn't look if Maggie asked, I know it."

"It's a bit different."

"A baby is a baby." I scrunched up my face.

"Yeah, but Maggie and I would be doing the whole thing together. Unless something has changed, he's on his own once the baby is born, right?"

I gritted my teeth and recrossed my arms. My leaving sounded so cold when he put it like that. Tyler and the baby were better off. "So, is this place ready to move into? You're right. Tyler probably needs to get his house ready for this baby. Only a couple more months."

"That's not what I meant."

"You know, the label might owe me a favor soon. I'll make a few calls and see if I can get you back here permanently or at least working out of New York. It's bullshit they pushed you into L.A." I gazed up at him. "You'd like that, right? Being back on the East Coast?"

"That's the goal. I'd appreciate anything you can do. I don't have that kind of clout—yet."

"I do. I should. They owe me. They definitely owe me." Despite the growing storm around Kenny, I hadn't said a peep.

Grady was quiet for a minute, and then he went to the stocked bar fridge and pulled out one of my favorite sparkling waters and passed it to me.

"They owe you because of Kenny Connors?" Grady cracked his can and gulped it back.

I stiffened. Annoying, maybe even enraging, that people seemed to know what had happened. Or at least, thought they knew. Not a single person stepped in, stopped him, and people obviously knew.

"I don't know what you're talking about." I opened the can and took a sip, wandering around the room. "I just meant I've made them a lot of money."

While I trusted Grady, once a topic became hot, it was easy for people in dark rooms or recording studios to let something slip, a harmless tidbit. All it would take was one, *Oh yeah, Mia Malone mentioned something to me about that,* and the fuse would be lit.

He took the hint and tossed his empty can into the recycling bin by the door. "Did you want to move in here, or are you going to stick it out with Tyler?"

The question was loaded with meaning both obvious and barely disguised. He tipped his head at my protruding belly. "Going back and forth is risky."

It was May, so my bulky coats wouldn't be inconspicuous much longer, and I would only get bigger now that my stomach had given up the fight. Once I moved into the train station, I wouldn't have to leave again until I lost the baby weight. Grady even installed a small dance studio and a tiny gym with a treadmill and elliptical to help drop the pounds afterward.

Moving in here would be one step removed from Tyler. No more nightly orgasms. No more lazy evenings in bed, his ear pressed to my belly while I toyed with his hair. The truth was, the hurricane swirled around me, waiting to suck me back in, spin me around. The eye was the dangerous place, where it was easy to forget the vicious winds awaiting.

Maybe it was better if those comforts stopped now, before I got too secure, lulled into believing the chaos wouldn't come for me.

The idea of moving in here alone made my stomach roll, even though I was long past needing lollipops to appease it.

"He can stay here, too." Grady tried to catch my gaze.

"I don't know. I guess I need to make a decision soonish. After the gala." I had to wade through the VISION Gala minefield in a few days.

"You and Tyler driving to New York for that?"

"We leave tomorrow," I confirmed. "When we get back, I'll let you know whether I'm moving in here. It's the most logical choice."

"Like I said, if you want Tyler to shack up here with you, I could care less. We're all family, right?"

Family.

I nodded but didn't meet his gaze. "Do you think you'll marry Maggie?"

"If she'll have me."

"How did you know, you know, that she was it? The one. Your person?"

He took a deep breath and leaned against the wall. "She's been the woman for me for so long, I can't really remember a time when she wasn't." With a finger, he traced the light switch. "You're wondering about Tyler?"

"No," I said. "No, I just—I can't imagine feeling that way about someone. *Forever.* People aren't built for that."

"Hmm." He searched my face, his brown eyes seeing more than I wanted. "I don't know what's actually going on between you and Tyler. It's none of my business. But since you asked and my answer doesn't fit, I'll tell you this. When you love someone, when you *really* love someone, the idea of going through life without them is equivalent to having an organ removed. There's this gaping hole." He touched his chest. "The only person who can fill it is the one you love. That's when you know."

"Are we in *Jerry McGuire* right now? You complete me?" I gave him a wry smile. "Is that what you're saying?"

"You know that movie? Sometimes that shit isn't wrong, Mia. But, nah, it's not really about someone completing you. I was a complete person before I managed to convince Maggie I wasn't a total asshole." He looked up at the ceiling and seemed to be searching for the right words. "She gets me. We're very different, Maggie and I, but when we're together, the world makes more sense."

The train station door opened, and Pasha dipped his head in, pointing to his watch. I had a fitting with Tyler at the shop in fifteen minutes. This was the first but also hopefully the final one before the gala in a couple of days.

"Well, thanks, Grady. I'll let you know if I'm moving in anytime soon." I should move in. If I were smart, I'd go home and pack right now. The longer I stayed with Tyler, the harder it would be to leave.

Pasha popped open the alley door which led right into Tyler's workroom at the back of the shop. Slipping out of the car, I squeezed past him into the room. I hadn't seen the dress since Tyler showed me his sketches a couple of weeks ago.

Against the wall, the dress dangled from a hanger, and I sucked in a sharp breath at its beauty. The dress was art. Of course, I'd known Tyler was talented. Based on what I saw on tour, what he did with the dress he made for me, his own clothes which I discovered he often tailor-made from thrift store finds, all pointed to his gift for design. Sketchbooks littered his house, brimming with ideas. Every piece of creativity scattered around his life was how I knew he could design something fit for the gala.

The dress hanging against the wall exceeded all of my expectations. People were going to freak out when I showed up in it. I traced the galaxy he'd created on the dress. So much of the material was handstitched in vibrant colors which popped off the rich, black velvet.

When the door opened behind me, I didn't turn to look, too busy peering at the tiny, intricate details in the dress. "This dress—"

"Isn't quite finished." His shoulder brushed against mine. "Creating a fictional world in space is more time-consuming than I anticipated."

"It's gorgeous…"

"But."

"It looks too long?" The dress was poised above my head, but I knew my height, my dimensions from countless fittings. I wasn't this tall.

He tipped his head toward the corner. "The way it is now, it would also show off your gorgeous curves. But that contraption," he pointed to the round metal piece, "slipped underneath will give you some breathing room and make the dress just the right length."

I ventured to the corner, my hand running along the series of hoops. "A hoopskirt?"

"Also called a farthingale during Elizabeth I's reign. I had to custom build it since we'll be putting it just under your bust and I need to be sure you'll be protected from speculation." He collapsed it down with his hands and looked at me. "Strip."

I threw him a teasing smile before I removed everything except my bra and underwear. Once I stepped inside, he let his hands go, and it sprung up around me. I laughed, delighted. "God, that's so smart. Look at you, all clever."

He grinned and took a lollipop out of his pocket to twirl between his fingers. Without opening it, he tucked it back in his pocket and carefully removed the dress, slipping it over my head so it slid over the boning of the hoop. When I looked down, it grazed the floor, perfect. At my back, he used clips to tighten the dress.

As soon as he finished, I swished over to the full-length mirror. With my hair spilling around my shoulders, I looked like a giant, wild solar system. I twisted my hand into my hair and secured the bulk of it on top of my head. Turning from side to side, I marveled at the detail.

"People will go wild about this."

"I don't know. It's a bit on the nose with the theme. But the solar system is all invented—none of it is real. I have reasons to explain my choices if anyone bothers to ask." He chuckled. "I was worried it would feel too... I don't know...something. But you wear it exceptionally well."

"You're going to be more famous than me after this." My comment wasn't flattery. I couldn't imagine anyone else arriving in something so gorgeous and perfect. How had I managed to hook up with someone this amazing? After all the terrible men I'd known, he was a gift—one I'd have to return, but a gift, nonetheless.

"I doubt that," he said, his tone wry.

While I stared at myself in the mirror, I realized I'd probably never get another moment like this, one where Tyler had dressed me, where we were a team, where I was protected and cherished. Tears pooled in my eyes and slipped down my cheeks.

I didn't want this to be the last time, the only time this moment happened. But I wasn't capable of long-term commitment, didn't want to be a mother, couldn't be responsible for other people's happiness.

For the first time since I'd hit it big, I had the headspace to figure out what made *me* happy. Being around him made me happy. Being on stage surrounded by thousands of fans made me happy. Writing songs made me happy.

Having a baby did not make me happy.

"What's going on in that head of yours?" He stepped in front and brushed away my tears.

"The train station is done."

"Okay," he drew out the word. "I knew you were meeting Grady today." He ducked down so our gazes connected.

"And you need to get things ready for this baby—like a room and some clothes and, I don't know, lots of other things."

Out of his pocket, he produced the lollipop and ripped off the wrapper. He stared at it for a minute and then focused on me. "I was hoping you might want to do some of the planning and organizing with me."

I shook my head and wiped my cheeks where tears continued to fall. God, why was I always crying? It was annoying. There was no reason to be crying. I had a good life before Tyler and this baby. I'd have a good life once this baby was born, and I was on my own again. "I don't want to do any of that."

He stuck the lollipop into his cheek, and I caught the scent of jasmine. Did he even order any of the other kinds anymore? Sometimes, I still found a stray lemon-and-ginger one lying around the house, as though he left me a token, a reminder. Maybe he did. There was no end to his thoughtfulness, his kindness.

"Okay." Tyler turned his back and busied himself at his worktable. "Are you telling me you want to move your stuff over to the train station?"

My heart sank, dipped low into my stomach. It was the middle of May. The baby was due at the end of July. I could still have...eight, maybe ten weeks with Tyler before I had to give him up.

"Move into the train station with me." The words left in a rush, not thought through, not planned. But Grady had planted the seed, and now it was sprouting.

"Move out of my house into the train station?" With a frown, he turned to face me.

"Temporarily. Think about it." I held up my hand to stop his objections. This was an excellent plan, actually. "Pasha and I will be gone from your house, and with you gone too, you can get someone to decorate the bedroom, fill it with all the stuff you'll need. You won't have to smell the paint or whatever."

He rubbed his face, and I could sense another objection coming. Logic had no place here. I wanted him, wanted him more than I'd ever wanted anything or anyone.

"Please." Tears rolled down my cheeks. The distance between us already felt too great. I crossed the room and squeezed between his legs, the dress surprisingly flexible. "Please, Tyler." Once we separated, I'd never have another relationship like this again; I knew it. Much worse, I'd never get to be with *him* like this again.

He cupped my cheek, and he brushed away my tears with his thumb, tenderness in his gaze. "Are you sure?"

I nodded my head and didn't bother to acknowledge the tears blurring my vision. Moving him to the train station was a terrible idea and would only make what came later harder. But I wanted him so badly.

"If you're suggesting this because you think it's what I want, you don't have to. I want to be with you, but you like your space, and I get that."

I gaped at him. He thought I was considering what he wanted? With a laugh, I wiped my face, wetness on my fingertips. What he wanted had never occurred to me. I was too much in *my* feelings.

"You'd want to move to the train station?" I asked.

"Mostly, I just want to be with you, wherever that is." His lips quirked up in a partial smile. "I like being with you."

Did he love me? Was that a question you could ask someone? What if he didn't? What if he just liked having sex, and I was reading too much into this?

Did I love him? No. I didn't. The *baby* loved him. The baby loved him so much. All these feelings I'd never felt for anyone else were because of the baby. I was riding those hormones for all they were worth, that was all.

He peered down, his eyes narrowing. "What's going on in there?" He tapped my temple gently.

The reality was he loved the baby and *enjoyed* being with me. That was all. Expecting anything else was ridiculous. Once the baby was born, I'd feel like myself again. I just had to get to that point without becoming a complete fool.

"Nothing," I said with a headshake. "Just hormones."

Chapter Twenty
Tyler

Being on Mia's arm at the gala was like jumping into a churning sea after having spent hours floating on my back, staring at the clouds. Each flashbulb, each shout trying to get her attention, blurred together like waves on top of waves. Beside me, she glowed. Every time our gazes connected, it became more and more obvious how much she'd missed this, how much she was sacrificing by being in Little Falls, by having this baby, by settling for any life with me.

Even while I answered questions about the dress and posed for photos with her all over the red carpet, part of my mind was consumed with second-guessing the connection I'd been feeling between us. Maybe being in our bubble in Little Falls was what had made us so close.

No. No. We'd gotten close while we were on tour together too. I'd just always been backstage, never in the swirling storm of fans, paparazzi, and press outlets. Everywhere we turned, someone wanted a piece of Mia, wanted to talk about her cutting the tour short, wanted to know who I was. Her responses came easily, the lies spilling out. It had been months since she slipped on a mask, *this* mask, and it made me question whether I really knew her.

But I did. I understood her.

I went through the motions, talked about the dress, smiled at the right times, gave Mia my hand when she reached for it.

She had been right, though. Whether for show or if people were being authentic, everyone we encountered loved the dress, were surprised at my talent, couldn't believe they hadn't heard of me before. Their flattery reminded me of what I'd wanted ten years ago. Fame. Recognition. I'd wanted what I was experiencing right now.

But I'd also wanted a wife, kids. Back then, my whole dream had felt within my grasp. My first tour of what I hoped would be many, my home with Katie. I'd been on the cusp of greatness.

Then, my life fell apart, and I spent years thinking I'd never get what I truly desired, never reach anything close. I wondered if long-term, comfortable relationships and my shop might be the best I could do.

Mia talked to one of the reporters, and I scanned her lovely face, marveled that I was here, with her. Again, I was so close to having everything. If only it was possible to make someone love you *enough*. That was the key, at least with her. She felt something. Some sort of intense emotion flowed between us like a current when we were alone—moving, changing—but constant.

"Just one last question before you go inside," the reporter in front of us begged Mia. As far as I could tell, she was selective about who she talked to, and this reporter earned a wary glance before she slowed her stride. She gave the reporter an expectant glare, the cue to let him know she was listening.

"Can you comment on the Kenny Connors lawsuit that's pending? He produced your first album."

"Yes, he produced my first album." Mia's tone was pleasant and straightforward, but I could sense the strain.

"Maybe you haven't heard with your illness, but he's accused of rape, of committing statutory rape. Of raping the girls he produced."

"I don't have anything to do with that lawsuit, so how could I possibly comment?" She gave him a sweet smile, one I knew was fake. She squeezed my hand once we were linked again, while we moved toward the entrance to the art gallery.

"But *could* you be part of that lawsuit? *Should* you be?" the reporter called out after us.

Mia kept her focus on the entrance to the art gallery, but I had been following the story, remembered how Mia told me once that Kenny hurt her. The tension zinging through her was unmistakable. This dickhead reporter thought he already had something on her, thought he had a right to these details at an event like this.

Letting go of her hand, I walked back to the reporter and leaned in. "Are you really trying to ask her on the red carpet of a fashion gala whether or not she was raped? Are you fucking kidding me right now?" I pointed my finger into the camera. "This guy needs to be fired."

From behind me, Mia tugged on my arm. "He's not worth it, Tyler. Reporters ask stupid questions all the time. Small minds, small questions. You just gotta let them go."

"I won't let this idiocy go." Inside, I was fuming. "He doesn't have the right to ask you that question—not here, not anywhere. The entitlement. It's unbelievable."

She laughed, but there was sadness in it while she gripped my hand tighter and led him away. "Welcome to my life—the ugly bits."

I saw some of the other ugly bits—the social media comments, the magazine articles, the people who didn't know her ranting about things they didn't understand, couldn't comprehend. A few times, I was tempted to respond, but I always understood my interference wouldn't make the hate better. Tonight, I didn't care. The reporter's comment had hurt her, and while I might not know all the details, I understood enough. I had no patience for cruelty, especially when anyone directed it at her.

When we entered the art museum, I was still fuming, so caught up in my anger, I didn't notice the woman approaching us until she was there, too close to avoid.

"Mia!" Laura snatched her daughter from me and enveloped her into a loose hug. "I was so happy to hear from you."

Happy to hear from you? She'd been in touch with her mother? Laura ignored me while she rattled off things she'd been doing and oohed and awed about Mia's dress.

"Who'd you pick in the end?" Laura asked.

"Tyler designed it, actually." Mia tipped her head in my direction, at my spot just behind them where Laura had not so subtly pulled her away.

Her lips pursed, and she glanced in my direction. After making such a fuss over the dress, backpedaling now would make her look petty, and we all knew it.

"You did a nice job." Her lips barely moved.

"Thanks." I pushed my hands into my suit pockets. My outfit was the other half of her solar system. The two pieces didn't make sense separately, but flowed seamlessly together. Had Laura bothered to look at me for even an instant before tugging Mia away, she would have seen it herself.

A giant TV in the entryway was tuned to one of the more reputable celebrity-gossip shows covering the event. There, almost life-size, was my rant at that reporter.

Laura coughed and raised her eyebrows at Mia. "He needs better training. That's not going to help you or the situation."

"I asked you here so we could work things out, and *that's* what you say? He's not a dog, Mother. He's my boyfriend, my partner tonight." Tears pooled in her eyes, and she shot me a helpless look.

She was crying again, angry tears, but tears, nonetheless. The last week or so, as soon as her emotions overloaded, she cried. Last night, she cried over the last slice of cheese in the fridge. Right now, it was obvious she didn't want to be in tears. She wanted to be pissed off.

"I said what I said. No one gets to speak to her like that when I'm around." My pointed comment was probably lost on Laura—that should have been the rule when she was with her daughter, too.

Laura's eyes flickered with annoyance, as though I was a pest she needed to tolerate for now. When she focused on Mia again, a frown marred her face. "Are you...crying?" Laura stepped closer and stared into her daughter's eyes. "Our fight has been that hard on you?"

Mia slid a bewildered glance to me before dipping her head. When she made eye contact with her mother, she said, "Yeah, Mom. Of course. We've never gone this long without talking."

"Oh, honey." Laura gripped her daughter's hand and smiled. "I thought it was just me who was miserable. Look, I can set up some things for you. Nothing big. Just a few appearances. Honestly, with all this Kenny drama, it's probably good you've been lying low."

Very slowly, Mia took her hand out of Laura's grasp and reached for me behind her. "I'm not ready to go back. I need some more time. You're right, with everything hitting the fan with Kenny, it's better if I keep a low profile. Stay out of the spotlight."

"I have people calling me all the time, so whenever you're ready. Whenever you're ready." Laura's attention drifted to me and then away.

She hadn't asked about her birthday, about her songwriting, about her life in Little Falls, about anything that meant something to Mia. Instead, she shifted into business mode, pushing her daughter to sink into their uneasy alliance. My temper had flared with the reporter, and it simmered now. I couldn't believe Mia had contacted Laura without discussing it or at the very least telling me she'd done it. Laura's complete obliviousness to her daughter's needs made the meeting even worse.

"There are some people we need to talk to." Mia tipped her head in the direction of a small crowd gathered around a large art piece at the end of the spacious room. "I'll be in touch."

"Yes." Laura nodded. "I'm glad you called."

That was it? No lingering hugs or offers to visit? Not that either of those would be good for our secret. When we wandered away, Mia leaned toward me, eyes cast down, her hands wrapped around my bicep. "I feel so different since I left the tour, you know? I just—I wanted her to be different, too."

I brought her hand up to my lips, and most of my anger dissipated. At her core, she was a daughter who wanted her mother's love. How could Laura not see that, not want to fill the void, not wish for Mia's happiness above everything else?

"Why didn't you tell me you were talking to her?"

With a shrug, she focused on the people wandering past, offering smiles and saying hello. In front was another art piece, but I didn't know if she was taking it in; I wasn't.

"Calling her seemed like the easiest way to keep our secret. I contact her first. She sees me here." She touched a hand to her hair, to the complicated pattern I helped her do in our bedroom instead of trusting a stylist. With a deep breath, she said, "That's not really why. It's just that if I asked her to come, and I told you and she didn't show up, what would that mean?" Her voice cracked.

Laura would be a shitty mom. No surprise there. Turning up today didn't change my mind. She was Mia's manager first when what Mia really needed, had probably needed for a few years now, was a mother.

I wrapped my arm around her shoulders and leaned into her ear. "It says nothing about you and *everything* about her. You deserve to be loved."

When she looked up with her big, gorgeous eyes, glassy with tears, I was a goner. There wasn't anything I wouldn't do for her. In that moment, we were back in our Little Falls bubble, and I couldn't imagine wanting to be anywhere else. With her, always with her, that was where I wanted to be. Our connection pulsed, alive, electrifying.

"I don't care about all this art. Let's go home." Her voice was soft, and she rose on her toes to kiss my cheek.

What would my life be like in a few months when she disappeared? When I watched events like tonight and longed for her? An ache that would never go away, that would be magnified each time I looked at our child.

"Let's go home," I agreed, drawing her close and kissing her temple. Even if I was going to lose her, I still had her now.

Chapter Twenty-One
Mia

One of the things I loved about Tyler was the space he gave. He never tried to crowd or force me to tell him things I didn't want to deal with. Sometimes, I wished I was more like that.

"I need you to tell me again." I lay in our bed at the train station, staring at the ceiling and cupping my stomach. Now that we slept together, curled around each other like cats, Sunday was my favorite day. He never went to the shop, and I rarely bothered to write unless inspiration struck like lightning. "But you need to mean it this time."

Tyler laughed, and then he peered down at me. "I meant it the last time." His eyes danced.

"Yeah, but you were laughing, so it didn't *sound* like you meant it."

"You asked me if you looked like a manatee. I don't even know how you'd come up with a comparison like that."

"It was either that, or like... I don't know...a hippo? Except, I don't have a tail that shotguns shit, so that comparison is unrealistic."

"That's why the comparison is unrealistic? You look nothing like a manatee or a hippo. You're not that big. You might feel that big, but you're not."

"It's like someone blew up a beach ball in my uterus."

"Maybe a basketball, not a beach ball."

"When you imagined your life, did it look like this?" With a sigh, I turned my head to look at him.

"Are you still joking, or is that a serious question?" The smile slipped from his face.

"Serious." I tangled my fingers with his. "When you were my age, what'd you think your life would be like at your age now?"

"Well..." He glanced up at the ceiling and released a long breath. Propping his head up with his hand, he rubbed my bare belly in slow circles. "In my head, it looked a lot like the other week at the gala."

"What?" I cupped his cheek, forcing him to meet my gaze. He'd hinted at his former dreams the night we talked about Katie, but I hadn't realized he wanted *that* level of fame.

"I wanted to design kick-ass clothing that people loved, or that transformed people on stage."

"What else?" There was an *and*; I could feel it.

He stared down at me for a long time, and the air began to hum. The baby was taking over, dominating me body and soul. When he looked like this, I loved him, loved him so much. The emotion caused my chest to ache, caused my heart to beat unevenly with the fear and excitement of speaking those words. But saying them would be a lie, so I pressed my lips together, willing them to stay in. This sweeping, soul-deep feeling made me glad it was the baby and not me. I'd never survive loving someone this much, this intensely. *This* couldn't be regular romantic love, the kind everyone experienced.

"What's your best childhood memory?" He traced the side of my face with his finger.

"Hmm." I tapped my lips with a manicured nail. Tyler had learned how to put on and take off gel nails once I couldn't leave the house.

"Learning to play the piano with my grandmother. My dad's mom. Singing with her, too. She's the reason I know how to do anything. I spent every day after school with her until I was twelve."

"What happened when you were twelve?"

Tears pricked at my eyes, and I blinked them back. There had been no weird cravings, no ferocious mood swings, just this liquid seeping from my eyes all the time. Like the tears I refused to shed for years were leaking out, one random conversation at a time. "She died. Heart attack."

"What was her name?" He brushed his lips against my temple, my forehead, and then my mouth.

"Victoria." I ran my fingers along the tips of his hair. "She's the reason I love music so much, the reason I started writing songs. I had all this grief and nowhere to put it. My mom was too busy working, and since I was twelve, I was old enough to look after myself. My dad, well, he's never been much good and only got worse after my grandma died."

With a tenderness that made my stomach swoop low, he wiped away my tears. "I know you can't control it, but, God, it twists my gut in knots to see you crying."

"You might need an antacid or two for that." With a soft laugh, I cupped his neck and pulled him down for a kiss.

"Or a whole bottle." He left my mouth and trailed kisses down to my beach ball before putting his ear against my stomach, his hands on either side of my bump.

If we were really having this baby together, it would be cute, adorable even. There were a few moments where his excitement for the baby was almost contagious. Almost. But this baby wasn't mine. It was his.

"I think it's a girl." He glanced up. "My money is on a girl."

"Nope. It's a boy. Has to be."

"Why do you always say it has to be?" Tyler laughed and came back to lie beside me.

"Because it's my body, and I'm telling that thing in there to grow a penis already. It's not a place for girls to grow."

He tried to catch my gaze, but I pretended to examine my nails. Since I'd arrived in Little Falls, I wasn't as tempted to bite them. Actually, since I turned up at Tyler's shop, I hadn't felt the same desperate need to devour them. *Strange.*

"Is this because of everything that's happened to you?" His voice was quiet, and he picked at the blanket between us.

"I don't want a girl for a lot of reasons. Stuff you know nothing about." I hadn't thrown up walls between us in a long time. He got the most authentic version of me. Some topics were off-limits, and I liked that he didn't pry. I'd never had to tell him to leave a subject alone.

"Will you tell me?"

"You want me to relive my traumas with you? No, thanks. I think I'd rather slit my wrists."

"Mia—"

"I should go get some writing done." I threw back the covers from my legs and struggled to get up. More tears formed a stream down my cheeks when I realized I couldn't get up. He put a gentle hand on my arm and helped me sit up. "I can't even storm out of here."

"Do you want me to help you slam the door?" A touch of amusement lit his face.

"That's not funny. You're not funny." With my fist, I punched his arm lightly.

"Come on," he said. "It was a little bit funny."

Maybe it was, but I was rattled about my reaction to him asking for this piece of my past. Every time I asked him to do something for me, he did it.

Don't talk to Katie. Done. Don't look at the baby's sex even though you really want to know. Done. Make me a dress and attend this really fancy party. Done. Move all your shit to the train station to shack up with me. Done.

When I thought about his sacrifices, I knew I was really fucking selfish. Yet another reason why I'd be a terrible parent.

With a headshake, I pushed myself off the bed and grabbed a robe from the walk-in closet. "Someday, I'll tell you, okay? Not today. But I promise I'll tell you someday." If I gave birth to a girl, I'd tell him everything, every terrible detail so he'd know how bad the world could be, how dangerous it was to be a woman. There was no doubt in my mind he'd protect the baby; he'd already done everything to keep me safe.

But the baby was a boy. It had to be.

"I didn't mean to push, Mia."

"Yeah, you did. But I didn't need to be a bitch about it. It's fine." I opened the door to our master suite, which led to the kitchen. Pasha was already sitting at the island, drinking his coffee, eating his breakfast, and reading the weekend paper.

It was almost July. The countdown was on. From now until the baby was born, I'd be seeing Dr. David and possibly Katie every week. There was still tension between Tyler and Katie, but all of it flowed out of Katie now, as though Tyler had somehow made peace with whatever was or wasn't between them. A few times, I considered requesting a different nurse. But more people meant more risk, and Katie was competent. I just hated their complicated history and unfinished business, at least whatever that was in Katie's mind.

Often, I worried Tyler and Katie would reconnect when I left. The thought whirled around whenever I let it in. The idea made my stomach drop out, as though I was free-falling out of a plane. The idea I'd be so easy for Tyler to replace was deeply depressing.

From the bedroom, Tyler appeared fully dressed as I spooned some granola and yogurt into a bowl and added fresh berries.

"Em just texted and asked me to pick up Amir from a friend's place."

"Oh, yeah?" I slid the yogurt tub back into the fridge. "Are you bringing him here?"

"Just for the morning. She's got stuff going on."

Around my spoon, I smiled. He was always doing stuff for his family—taking a meeting for Maggie, walking Grady's dogs, picking up Amir from one thing or another, getting quotes to fix his mom's driveway. His commitment to all the important people in his life was unwavering. Katie had been an idiot to leave him.

From the shelf by the door, he grabbed his keys and was gone.

"You two fight?" Pasha cut into his egg and deposited the piece onto his toast.

With a frown, I turned to face him. "Not exactly. Why?"

"Weird feeling." He made a circular motion in the air with his knife.

"Yeah, well, he asked me to talk about something I didn't want to talk about."

"He do things for you all time."

"So what?" I shot him an irritated glare. "I'm just supposed to lay myself bare to him?"

"I think you do already." He chuckled and sipped his coffee.

"Uh, not emotionally." I made a back-and-forth motion with my hand. "He and I have an agreement. Whatever is going on isn't emotional."

Pasha rolled his eyes, actually rolled his eyes. "He love you. You love him. Have baby. Be happy."

I shook my head and shoveled a spoonful of granola and yogurt into my mouth, chewing slowly. Once I swallowed, I said, "I don't love him. The baby loves him."

The coffee cup was at his lips when I spoke, and he sputtered, spilling coffee on the island. A string of Russian flew out of his mouth, and the look on his face was full of disbelief.

"I mean," I conceded, "sometimes, I think *I* might love him a little bit too. That maybe it's not *all* baby hormones." I stared into my bowl and then glanced at Pasha. "I'm going to tell you something, but you're not allowed to think I'm a bad person."

He frowned while he wiped the counter with a cloth. "Okay."

I took a deep breath and wondered if I could really speak the thought aloud. It was a new one, a crazy one. The only other person I'd told was Sarah. "I wish it was possible to keep Tyler, you know, as my boyfriend, without having to be a mother to this thing." I pointed to my enormous belly.

Pasha reached for my phone and turned on my translating app. I always knew we were getting into a serious discussion when broken English wasn't enough. Sometimes, I got a lecture, and sometimes, I got understanding. He spent more time with me and Tyler than anyone else. I trusted his judgment.

"You don't like kids?" The robotic voice was the newest app we'd discovered that did close to real-time translations. Pasha had said the only

thing better would be hooking up something directly to his brain. The visual had been disturbing, and I'd told him never to mention it again.

"I like kids. Other people's kids, mostly." I stirred my granola, swirling it around the berries. Not that I'd been around a lot of kids. "I'm only twenty-one. What do I know about being a mom?"

"Lots of women are mothers at twenty-one."

"Maybe they had a better role model to start with." I shrugged, avoiding eye contact. "I don't think I could protect a child."

"Why?"

I recognized the Russian word before the app translated. A good question, one I wasn't sure I knew how to answer. No one protected me, and I suspected I would be just as terrible with a child.

"In all seriousness, if you think Tyler loves me, do you think I could ask him to put the baby up for adoption and keep me instead?" My heart hammered in my chest. I couldn't believe I voiced the thought out loud. I'd danced around the idea with Sarah, who fluffed me off as being a romantic instead of a realist. If allowing a husband to cheat constantly was being a realist, I didn't want her version of real life. I would rather live in the land of romantic notions.

Pasha shot me an annoyed look and shook his head. He stuck his fork into his egg and sliced through it with the knife, driving the piece into his mouth. When he'd finished chewing, he stared at me until I started to squirm.

"It was a dumb question, I guess."

"It's an impossible choice." He sighed and rubbed his face. *"Don't ask him to do that. It's not fair."*

The sight of the food in my bowl turned my stomach. With my spoon, I scraped it into the garbage and rinsed it out before depositing it in the dishwasher. "So, I guess I just have to hope all these feelings really are the baby, huh?" When I turned to look at Pasha, his eyes were filled with sympathy.

"You need to talk to someone about all the things that have happened to you, the reasons you think you can't do this."

I frowned at the translation app on my phone and shook my head. The only good thing about waiting for my phone to spit out his words in English was the chance to avoid eye contact. "Like therapy or some shit? Uh, no. That sounds like a terrible idea. Let's take every bad thing that's ever happened to me and hold it up to a microscope to dissect. No. Nope. Not gonna happen."

"You like being unhappy?"

With my index finger, I pressed *end* on the translation app and glared at Pasha. "For the record, I wasn't *unhappy* before I met Tyler. I was fine. I'll be fine after this baby is born and I leave this nowhere town. You know when I wasn't fine? When I was stuck in a nowhere town dirt poor in an area that barely passed for livable." That was my mother's narrative, not mine. Deep down, I didn't remember my life as being terrible before I became famous. My mother always insisted it was awful, the worst, nothing worse than being poor. I'd never been sure that was true, but I didn't need my bodyguard taking me to task about being *happy*. My jaw clenched in defiance. "What would you know about being happy anyway? All you do is work for me. No life beyond this." I threw out my arms.

"I happy once. Long time ago." He stared into his coffee cup. "She die. I leave Russia."

"Oh." All the anger rushed out as I breathed the word. "Oh, I...God, I'm an asshole. I'm sorry."

"When you happy, you—" He clenched his fingers around the cup. "Hold on."

"I can't love this baby. I don't feel anything." With both hands, I rubbed my face and sighed. "It's just a thing growing inside me. I...I'd be a terrible mom." Tears sprung to my eyes. "I know what it's like to have a terrible mom. I don't ever want to do that to someone else."

"Maybe—"

"No." I shook my head and met his sympathetic gaze. "You're right. I made a deal with Tyler, a promise. I can't go back on it just because I think I might have feelings. When the baby is born, maybe I'll realize all the things I think I feel aren't real. Hormones. Just lots of hormones. Then what? I'll have asked him to do the unthinkable, and it'll turn out I didn't really mean it."

He pursed his lips, but didn't say anything as he rose and took his plate and cup to the sink. As he wandered past, he patted my shoulder.

Whether he believed me or not didn't matter. Even if I could go the distance with Tyler, I could never love this baby. That kind of love just wasn't in me.

Chapter Twenty-Two

Tyler

From across the gym, Katie's gaze drilled into me. Seeing her wasn't a shock. There were only so many gyms in a small town, and she liked places with fitness classes.

Maggie's best friend, Lila, picked this gym a little less than a year ago when she talked me into bulking up for the charity Magic Men show. After the tour, I came back out of habit and because the exercise helped clear my head from thoughts of Mia.

My preoccupation with her was bad on tour, but it was almost unbearable now that we lived together, slept together every night, since she started to feel like a life partner rather than just a partner in this strange deal.

As I eased down the weights, Katie approached out of my peripheral vision. Since I slipped the note in her mailbox, we'd avoided speaking except at the hospital. While I didn't think my prior feelings for Katie could overshadow what was developing with Mia, I'd clung to my residual love for so long, I couldn't be sure what would happen once Katie sliced open those wounds.

"You're lifting heavy nowadays." Katie's smile was hesitant. "I didn't know you were this into fitness."

"There are probably things you've done in the last eight years I'd be surprised about, too." The biggest one was that she left at all. I plucked the disinfectant spray from beside the machine and wiped down the equipment, avoiding eye contact.

One social media post from anyone in the gym, and Mia would know I talked to Katie. For some reason, Mia began monitoring all her mentions on every platform after her birthday party. Occasionally, she read them out, laughing or raging about whatever was written. Being stuck in the train station didn't help with her boredom scrolling.

"I'm sorry, Katie. I really can't talk to you."

"She's got you so far under her thrall you can't have a casual conversation with me in public?"

Suppressing my anger at her tone, I set the spray in its holder and made eye contact. "Honestly, it's none of your business what arrangement Mia and I have about anything." I grabbed my towel from beside the weights and wiped my forehead. "I made a promise. I honor those."

"I was so sorry to hear about your dad. He was such a kind man." Katie didn't miss a beat, as though I hadn't said anything at all.

Being around Katie raised my hackles, made me question too many things. My defenses were up before she even approached. The desire to lash out, to be rude, to hurt her lay just under the surface. With every interaction, the impulse rose a little closer to the surface. *Eight years.* The bitter tang was surprising. I'd genuinely thought I was over the abandonment.

Shit happened. She left. Move on, Tyler. That had been my motto. Lately, I was praying I didn't need that motto a second time.

"I appreciate your concern." I couldn't help my frosty tone. Katie hadn't come to the funeral, sent a card, or even emailed. Maybe she was sorry, but she hadn't been sorry enough when it mattered, when my heart had been ripped out of my chest at my father's loss.

"If *you* need anything, you can call me."

"I can't do that." I rubbed my forehead.

"Right, yeah, it's just—I was part of the family for ten years."

She followed behind while I made my way toward the locker rooms. I wasn't done with my workout, but if she couldn't honor what I asked for in my note, I couldn't stay here. Mia didn't deserve to have some speculative bullshit splashed across social media. Already, a few people had their phones out. Whether that was for selfies or to post something, I couldn't be sure.

People in town had latched onto the Pretty Boy hashtag Mia started months ago, and it wasn't uncommon for her to be tagged in random photos of me from around town. The whole social media barrage was strange. Why did anyone care that I bought some milk in workout clothes? But there was no doubt if *that* was news, then this conversation with Katie would be a golden nugget to anyone who knew our history. Making a scene would only make it worse.

"I said we could talk when things settled down. That's not right now, and it's definitely not here."

"It's just—" She twisted her hands together, and there was a desperate tinge to her voice. I hated noticing the differences in her, seeing things in her behavior that other people might not. My heart contracted at the hurt oozing out of her. "I thought I knew what was going on with you two, but now I'm not sure. And—and I'm worried I might never get to talk to you."

My curiosity flickered. I'd assumed she knew the cover story was bull-shit. Why would a world-famous pop star agree to be my surrogate? Our arrangement was ludicrous. "When she's gone, okay? We can talk when she's gone."

"So, she *is* going? I thought—well, looking at you two during the appointments, I thought maybe her intentions might have changed."

Everything had changed, at least for me. I wanted Mia to stay, wanted a life with her so badly, it was a constant ache underpinning everything. "Nothing has changed." Leaning into the door with my shoulder, I gave her one last glance. "When she's gone, I promise."

While I stripped to shower, my mind kept returning to the desperation in Katie's voice. Why now?

As soon as I was in the shower, my phone buzzed on the bench outside the door. My head was still too caught up in Katie's plea to answer. The water streaming down was a good reason to avoid whoever was calling.

When my phone buzzed again, I frowned. My family and Mia were the only ones persistent enough to hang up and immediately call again.

Opening the door, I checked the display.

Mia.

Any time she called repeatedly like this, my heart raced with anxiety. Now that we were so close to the baby's birth, my heart leapt into my throat. Under protest, she packed a hospital bag the other day. Labor terrified her. With my online MD, I'd read many first pregnancies go past the due date, sometimes by weeks. She'd thrown all my research at me like confetti when I suggested a few things in a bag might not be a bad idea.

Without turning off the water, I stepped out of the shower and grabbed my phone before it could go to voicemail again.

"Mia?"

"Oh, thank God, Tyler." Her voice was a hushed whisper.

"Are you okay?" I frowned and tried to towel off with one hand while grasping the phone with the other.

"I'm hiding in the bathroom."

"Hiding from what or who?" My heart kicked in my chest. "Should you be calling the police? Where's Pasha?" I tugged my shirt over my head.

"My mom just pulled up outside the train station. She's here, Tyler." Her voice cracked. "I look like this, and she's here. I can't see her. I can't talk to her. I can't show her this. She'll never forgive me."

I held my breath, trying to decide whether Laura's sudden appearance was better or worse than Mia going into premature labor. "Where's Pasha?"

"Out there talking to her. Grady's here too. They've told her I'm not here."

A sniffle. She had to be crying. It took so little to set her off. My heart lodged in my throat.

"She said she'd wait for me to get home."

I released my breath in a whoosh and ran a hand through my wet hair. "You're in the bathroom? The en suite?"

"No. I panicked."

I closed my eyes. That meant she was in the two-piece bathroom inside the studio. As soon as Laura needed to pee, Mia would be caught. Grady and Pasha would have to pee in the bushes to keep her hiding spot a secret. My next suggestion was the last thing I wanted. "You could just tell her?"

"Just tell her?" Mia squeaked out. "Just tell her? Really? After all these months, that's your advice? She can't know. She can't."

Deep down, I didn't want Laura involved. There was a chance Mia might pick me and the baby, but if Laura was in Mia's ear whispering another narrative, I didn't think I stood a chance. She craved her mother's love, and Laura lorded that craving over her like a drug dealer.

Getting her out of the bathroom without being seen was going to be tricky. "I'll be home in ten. Sit tight."

A frustrated, stifled laugh rang through the phone. "Sure, 'cause I have so many other options. I'll sit tight, don't you worry."

I love you.

The feeling hit me in the chest. It wasn't the first time. But I was finding it harder and harder to hold back the words. Right now, over the phone, wasn't the time. Telling her I loved her seemed like a betrayal of what I promised. No strings, just the baby.

We'd become so much more than that. I still didn't know if it was enough to get her to stay or at least consider staying. We needed to talk, but if I couldn't get Laura out of the train station and out of town, I might not get the chance.

As soon as I got close enough to the front entrance of the train station, it was clear Laura's visit was worse than Mia knew. A camera crew circled the station, filming.

Fan-fucking-tastic.

I parked my truck and slipped in the side entrance closest to the parking lot, the one they often used to enter the apartment portion of the station. At the heavy door that led to the studio, I rubbed my face and took a deep breath. *Protect Mia.* That was all I needed to do. Keep her hidden.

"Grady!" I called while I wandered in. "You still here?"

"In the sitting area!" Grady's voice was pitched higher than normal. "Laura came for a visit."

I leaned against the doorframe of the sitting room, my gaze averted from the bathroom door almost directly behind everyone else. Mia could not have picked a worse place to hide. There wasn't a place to sneak her off to.

"This is an unexpected surprise." I stared at Laura. "Did Mia know you were coming? She's not here."

"So, I've heard." She returned my glare. "I called Grady and asked if they were recording today. He said they would be. So, here I am. We need some bonus material and some promo stuff for the new album. Studio stuff is always well received by her fans. I've tried texting her, but she's not answering."

"To be clear," Grady looked between me and Laura, "you didn't tell me you wanted to bring a camera crew," he held up a finger, "or that *you* were coming *here*."

"Yes, well, my job is to manage Mia's career. Whether she likes it or not, getting a bit of footage of her in the studio will be good in a few months when she's done with her temper tantrum. None of you would understand this, but a manager's job is to look beyond the immediate problem to what's ahead. She's not going to quit. She loves performing too much. So, I need to make sure we're prepared when she's ready to hit the throttle again."

"Are you staying in town today?" I asked. A reminder she was also Mia's mother sat at the back of my throat, threatening to burst forth.

Truthfully, we didn't need either version of Laura here. "I can call you when she's back."

"Where is she? Neither one of these two seemed to know. Since she left her bodyguard here, she can't be far. I wouldn't put it past her to be hiding somewhere in the building to avoid me."

"Spa. All this writing has been hard on her." My lips tipped up in a partial smile at the lie. A bathroom was like a spa, right?

"At the spa? Without a bodyguard. That's irresponsible. You don't know the type of mail we receive, the crazy people obsessed with her." Laura rose from her seat and gestured toward Pasha. "I should fire you."

Pasha frowned and glanced at me, unwilling or unable to defend himself.

"We hired a private firm to handle a few hours a week of security to give Pasha a break." I frowned. "You're aware of the employment laws, right?" I chuckled. "It's not like Mia could work him twenty-four hours a day, seven days a week." We had used a firm a few times when Pasha had wanted to go somewhere or do something. He rarely asked for any time to himself, but we tried to provide it.

Laura shook her head and narrowed her eyes. "I don't know what you think you're doing, but I can assure you, you're temporary, Tyler. You're not her manager, her father, or her husband. You're her hashtag Pretty Boy, right?" With her fingers, she air quoted the hashtag. "Isn't that what she calls you?"

"What's between us is none of your business, Laura." I crossed my arms and returned her look. "She's healthy. She's happy. She's making music. You don't need to be here right now. She asked for space...from you." That wasn't completely true. Mia had asked for space from the business end of things, and Laura had interpreted it as space from her, too. The break could have been an opportunity for them to reconnect, or finally connect. I couldn't be sure what their relationship had been like before Mia got famous.

"And you've latched onto her, hitched yourself to her star power. All your social media accounts are on the rise, right? Your Instagram followers alone went from a couple hundred to almost half a million. I don't know how you convinced her to shun all those other designers for the VISION Gala, but it certainly turned out well for you."

That reminded me that I needed to get Mia to block Laura from all my social accounts. I'd forgotten we followed each other months ago.

Since the gala, Mia had been running all my handles. At her suggestion, she'd been filming while I sketched designs, talked about materials, cutting and sewing, essentially our own little Project Runway. I agreed because the videos made her happy, and half the time, she ended up giggling over something I said or did. There wasn't a better sound in all the world than her laugh.

As soon as she turned off the live feed, I'd sweep her into my arms, and she'd whisper all kinds of dirty things in my ear. The memories, so many of them, made me smile, and I ran my hand down my face to conceal it.

Laura was right. People were following me because of Mia, not because of anything I was doing. The posts were a glimpse into her life, and people ate it up like candy.

Once, she'd read out messages from my fans like I was actually famous. When she'd pretended to write back to them, I'd panicked and tried to take my phone back. But when I checked my messages later, she'd been kind and polite, even to the women proposing marriage. When I questioned her, she said, *Yeah, well, I'm not being me, am I? I'm being you. You're nice to people even when you shouldn't be.*

Maybe Mia would be proud of me because I was done being nice. "Accusing me of using her is a rich statement coming from you. The only things I've offered Mia are love and security. You did your job as her manager. She's got lots of money. Maybe it's time you focused on your other one? The mother part? The role where you give a shit if your kid is happy and healthy and not just whether she's willing to work herself into the ground."

"Like you know anything about the things I've done for Mia, the ways I've protected her."

"Protected her?" I growled. "Like how you protected her from Kenny Connors? Or how you protected her from the stream of your boyfriends who wanted a piece of her? You barely batted an eye when Cade Brewer tried to force himself on her in her dressing room. You've stood by and let people use her. You're little better than a pimp." The last line slipped out before I could reel it in.

"I love my daughter. You can't protect what you don't know about. You think she came running to me about any of that? No. She didn't. When I knew, I helped her."

I shook my head, anger spewing out. Grady and Pasha shifted uncomfortably in their seats. "You never thought to ask yourself why she didn't tell you, Laura? If Mia had so much faith in you as a mother, why would she keep those things from you?"

The bathroom door creaked open, and my heart dropped into my feet. I'd gone too far. The pimp thing was too much. Mia was so pissed she opted to reveal herself.

Laura's back was to the bathroom, but when she turned, she gasped.

Mia wasn't looking at Laura, she was focused on me. "Tyler, I think the baby is coming."

She was so pale. A cold sweat broke out across my back. Her bright-pink leggings were dark until halfway down her thighs. My brain couldn't process her showing herself to Laura, to the sight of her looking so pale and scared, to the darkness of her thighs. Was she bleeding again?

"Holy shit," Grady breathed. "Your water broke."

"Yeah," Mia said. "My water broke."

"You're pregnant?!" Laura screeched.

Chapter Twenty-Three
Mia

I closed my eyes, the activity swirling around me. My mother was freaking out, following Tyler around the house, railing over his betrayal. Pasha was rushing to the bedroom to get the hospital bag. Grady was hovering somewhere, paralyzed.

Join the club, Grady.

"I don't want this." I shook my head. Once the baby was out, there'd be no reason to stay. My old life echoed around me in my mother's rage, incoherent, impossible to ignore.

"Mother, stop! Stop!" I screamed the last word, but I kept my eyes closed until there was silence. When I opened them, I stared at her. "You're not helping, and if you can't help, you need to leave."

"I don't understand how this happened." Laura groaned, scanning my figure from across the room.

"Please, Mom. You had me. You know exactly how this happens." Gingerly, I moved toward Tyler, avoiding her.

"Either the baby is really early, or I'm missing something. The timeline doesn't work." Laura shook her head. "Why would you—why would you *want* a baby? You've got your whole life ahead of you."

Laura's tone was surprising, not accusing but mystified. I couldn't answer her because I *didn't* want the baby, had never wanted the baby, but Tyler did. And I wanted Tyler, *so badly*. Saying the truth felt like betraying him, bursting the bubble we'd built together in this town. He didn't deserve to be hurt.

"Why did you keep me, Mom?" I'd never asked the question. Deep down, I'd been sure I wouldn't like the answer. There hadn't been a lot of love in our house. The words had been there, but I'd never felt them, never known what it felt like to have someone look at you and to know, beyond a doubt, they loved you. Now beside Tyler, I linked my fingers with his. Anytime my hand could slide into his, I drew on his silent strength.

Laura's mouth opened and closed like a fish, and then she sighed. "Your father and your grandma Victoria said they'd help me raise you. They said I wouldn't have to do it alone." With her palms turned toward the ceiling, Laura's face was filled with regret. "I did the best I could. I realize you don't believe me. But I've been doing the best I can. I...I didn't have a good relationship with my mom. Maybe part of me kept you out of spite, too. I don't know. I was young. A bit of a romantic. And I loved your dad. But love is rarely enough." She tucked stray strands of her hair behind her ears and stared at my hand linked with Tyler's. "You can't live off love."

"I have bag!" Pasha declared, bursting back into the studio. "We hurry, hurry?" He made an ushering motion with his arms.

"There's a camera crew out there," Laura said, her voice quiet. "I don't know why you haven't told people you're pregnant, but that would be one way for it to get out."

I turned and buried my face in Tyler's side. He wrapped his arm around me without a word and stroked my hair. "Side door," I mumbled.

"We'll take the exit toward the parking lot. Grady," Tyler said, focusing on him, "can you look after the crew?"

"Yeah, I'll go regale them with stories of my recording glory in here with Mia. I can bring them in and play them a track or two. Don't worry." He glanced at Laura. "They'll earn their money and stay out of your way."

"Pasha, let's go."

I kept my face buried and let Tyler lead me to the side exit of the apartment. I didn't know if my mother was following us, but there was a heaviness directly behind me, like the air was weighed down. "Is she coming?"

"She is," Tyler whispered into my hair. "Want me to get rid of her?"

I shook my head. I couldn't explain the push-pull I felt when it came to her. He squeezed me to his side and kissed the top of my head.

"I got your back, Mini. You tell me what you want or what you need, and I'll get it done."

In the parking lot, Pasha opened the back door for me and Tyler. Pasha glared at Laura and gestured toward her rental car. "You follow."

Laura reared back. "There's room for me in the front." She peered down at me. "Why do these men think they're in charge of anything? Have you been letting them railroad you?"

From inside the car, I sighed. Although my water had broken, there was only a mild cramping so far. The worst was yet to come. Annoyance at my mother bloomed. I didn't need to manage her on top of what was coming. "Mom, take your rental. Follow us."

"Oh, fine." She threw up her hands and stomped to her car.

All things considered, she was taking the surprise pregnancy well so far. I had half-expected her to call the police...or the paparazzi.

"That could have been worse," Tyler said, easing into the seat. "How are you feeling?"

"Terrified. Abso-fucking-lutely terrified. I wish they could just pull the baby out."

"They can—it's called a C-section."

"Oh, there you go with your fancy online medical degree. Watch any YouTube videos on how to do that? Want me to pass you an X-Acto knife?"

"Careful now. I'm quite good with an X-Acto knife. Normally, I'm cutting fabric, but how hard can flesh be, really?"

"You two," Pasha said from up front, "are too weird."

"Come on." I shifted in the seat, trying to find a position that didn't make my back ache. Should I have changed my pants? I looked like I pissed myself. What a weird feeling that uncontrollable gush of water had been. Too late now to worry about it. "Embrace the X-Acto knife madness, Pasha."

"Can't." Pasha shook his head, but when he met my gaze in the mirror, his blue eyes were full of laughter. "Too sharp."

"Yes, very clever." I grinned at him. "You made a funny."

"Very funny," Pasha said, wagging his finger.

Tyler chuckled beside me, and my whole chest filled, felt like it was overflowing. I snuggled in beside him, relishing the closeness, the hint of jasmine that seemed to cling to his skin. Why hadn't he taken a lollipop out of his pocket? Was he that sure everything would work out?

When we pulled up to the hospital, Pasha jumped out to grab my bag. As Tyler helped me exit the car, I said, "You really want this baby?"

Tyler's brow creased, and then he leaned forward to kiss my forehead. "I really want this baby. You okay, Mini?"

"There's nothing you want more?" I couldn't help the hope in my voice. Pasha's eyes were on me. His disapproval felt like a gardener spotting a weed in a garden of flowers, who believed they could pluck it with the intensity of their thoughts alone.

Tyler drew me into his chest, and his breath stirred the top of my hair. I'd wanted to see his face when he answered, to know for sure I shouldn't ask him, suggest it, hint at it. Weed or not, the question had grown taller than the flowers, impossible to ignore. He couldn't have me and the baby.

"I want this baby more than anything."

I pressed my face into his shirt and clutched his arms, letting his shirt absorb the tears that were leaking. "Okay," I whispered. "Okay."

It turned out labor was kind of boring when it wasn't painful. The lulls between contractions were both my favorite and least favorite. No one would willingly choose pain, but at least it gave me a focus. Otherwise, I was stuck in this private hospital suite sitting in silence with my mother or wishing desperately I could plead my case to Tyler.

Surely if he knew he couldn't have both me and the baby, he'd choose me. He knew me. I was pretty sure he loved me, whatever that meant. He hadn't said it, but no one had ever taken such good care of me. I'd been *managed* before by lots of people, but I'd never been cared for. Even if he didn't love me, maybe I loved him enough to satisfy both of us.

My mother sat stiff and silent in the chair beside the hospital bed. Tyler was getting a coffee, and Pasha and a team of bodyguards were outside the door and in the corridors keeping everyone but David and Katie from entering the room.

In hindsight, I should have done some more research into different ways to give birth. Wasn't this supposed to feel like an event? If I'd told people, I could be live streaming this right now. I still could—that would make it an event. *Surprise! I've been hiding this for nine months. Aren't I clever?*

"So, you must have gotten pregnant at that stupid fundraiser? The one Grady insisted on." Laura bit out the words as though it pained her.

"If the shoe fits." I reached for an ice chip from the bucket and popped it into my mouth.

"I thought I taught you to be more careful than that."

She had. If there was one thing Laura Malone had been adamant about, it had been safe sex. Not that Laura always had control over who I slept with. Her safe sex advice had started after the episode in Kenny's office. A shudder washed over me at the thought.

When Cocksure Condoms had sent a boatload of samples, I'd never questioned the wisdom of using them. I got lots of free things all the time. None of them had ever gone this wrong.

"You know that lawsuit against Cocksure Condoms?"

"The huge class action suit?"

"Yep. I could have been part of that. What'd they get? A hundred bucks each in the end. Like that'll cover a baby or whatever else people got from their defective condoms. Maybe I should offer to pay for other people's baby expenses?" Grabbing my phone off the side table, I started an internet search about people from the lawsuit. Any excuse to avoid my mother. Helping them out would be good publicity. Win-win.

"Why didn't you tell me? I would have helped you."

The door opened, and Tyler strolled in with his steaming coffee clutched in his hand. Just the sight of him made my insides melt.

"Helped me? Helped me, how?" I wasn't listening, the words an automatic reply. Instead, I was watching the way the muscles in Tyler's arm flexed each time he raised his cup to his mouth. When the pain got really bad, there was a chance I might never want to have sex again. This wasn't that moment. This desperate ache for someone could not be normal.

"Helped you get rid of it, obviously. The last thing I wanted for you was this version of your life. I would never have let you choose this. You're twenty-one. You should be out with friends, making mistakes, kissing guys on dance floors, traveling the world, not changing diapers and tying yourself to one man for the rest of your life."

Tyler straightened and stared into his cup.

I could tell her the arrangement, that I wasn't raising the baby. Soon enough, she'd find out. Right now, she didn't deserve to know. "Your mistakes aren't mine."

"Sure, they are—you're making the same ones right now."

"So, I was a mistake."

"I didn't mean to get pregnant with you, but you aren't a regret. There is a difference."

"Sounds like I'm a regret." I sucked in a deep breath. "If we were still dirt poor in the middle of nowhere, would I be?" When we'd first hit it big, I hadn't wondered, had never thought to wonder. But every time my mother had put the business ahead of my wishes, my well-being, I'd wondered.

Tyler laced his fingers with my closest hand.

"I do not regret you."

I wanted to feel rage. That wasn't an answer, not to the question I'd asked. Instead, a deep sadness settled. Telling the truth might stop the money train, might push us even further apart. "You haven't been a very good mother."

"Maybe it's genetic. I didn't have a very good one either."

Genetic. Was that why I didn't feel anything for this baby? Why the idea of being a mother was terrifying? Laura had always been able to tap into my greatest fears.

I'd be a bad mother, just like her.

Tears pricked, and I closed my eyes, willing myself not to cry. Tyler would be an excellent father. This baby would be loved. I hadn't made a mistake. There would be no regret.

Opening my eyes, I hardened to my mother's manipulation. "Did you really come to Little Falls to film my recording session?"

"Why? What did you hear?" Laura stiffened.

Tyler squeezed my hand, but I stayed focused on Laura. "What should I be hearing?" I'd been checking all my social media and Tyler's for any sign of trouble. In the bathroom, before my water broke, I'd seen a photo of Tyler and Katie talking in the gym splashed across my feed. Of course, the asshole who posted it had tagged all three of us as though we were locked in some salacious triangle. All these randos bringing the drama, and none of them even knew about the baby.

They all thought we were holed up together. #LoveCave had trended. I'd spent that day screenshotting people's ridiculous ideas and sending them to Tyler.

At least I wouldn't have to turn over my memories of the last few months. I'd keep them close, never let anyone have them.

Laura narrowed her eyes, and she drummed her fingers on the arm of the chair, yanking me out of my thoughts. "This probably isn't the right time to get into it."

"I've got nothing better to do." I pointed to my belly. A distraction from all these thoughts of Tyler might be a good idea. "The stubborn kid in here isn't moving too fast. Entertain me, Mother."

"It's about Kenny Connors." She arched her eyebrows. "Still want to be entertained?"

"Nope." I popped another ice chip into my mouth and bit down hard. I was supposed to suck them or something, but I found the crunch far more satisfying. "That subject is not entertaining."

"What about Kenny Connors?" Tyler asked. Idly, without looking at me, he stroked my arm.

"It's private," Laura sniffed.

"I hear the court case will be quite public, actually," Tyler said.

His unimpressed tone was amusing. Being dragged into court would not be. A vise tightened around my middle, and I hissed in pain, squeezing Tyler's hand.

Laura rose from her chair and peered over the bed. "You need to breathe. You gotta breathe through them."

"Tyler...get her out of this room before I scream." I gritted my teeth and tried to ride the wave or whatever mumbo jumbo David had spewed during our last appointment. Riding a wave sounded pleasant.

"I was in labor for thirty hours with you," Laura said as Tyler called for Pasha.

Pasha's grip on Laura's arm was rough as he led her out of the room, her advice running over me without sticking.

"I don't want to ask you if you're okay, but I don't know what else to say," Tyler said.

"Say nothing," I grunted out, releasing his hand to grip his forearm.

"Want me to read you random advice from some of my best doctor sites? They're all the ones I used to get my online degree."

The pain was easing, and my laugh was half pain, half amusement. "Sounds awful." I gave him a sideways look. "And kinda fun. Only the funniest ones, okay?"

"Of course. I know the rules of this game." Tyler drew a chair to the side of the bed and started searching his phone. "Ah, got one. You're going to love it." He took a deep breath. "According to this person, jumping can cause the baby to just," he made a whooshing gesture with his hands, "fall out. How about that?"

I giggled. It was funny, but it wasn't as funny as I was finding it. The more I thought about the ridiculousness of that advice, the harder I laughed. "Fall out? God, I wish that was possible. Jump. Done. How awesome would that be? What planet is that person on?"

"Oh, they aren't the only one saying it. It's stated more than once."

"More than once?"

He turned the phone to show the list of advice for pregnant women.

My laughter rang through the room, and when our gazes connected, I loved the way his cognac eyes softened. "Tell me another one."

"Give me a sec."

While his head lowered to search his phone, I gazed at him, overwhelmed with love. How had I gotten so lucky?

How had I been so stupid? I should have used five condoms that night. Layered them like T-shirts. Another streak of pain shot through, and I screamed.

"Watch your voice," Laura chided. "You don't want to strain your vocal cords."

"Why is she back in here? Get her out! Get her out!" I could barely gasp out the words. The urge to push was overwhelming.

Tyler called for Pasha to remove Laura again as he stroked my hair.

"Stop touching me," I panted, pushing Tyler's hand away. "I need to push."

"Almost," David said from between my legs. "Almost."

"I hate that fucking word," I cried. "Use the vacuum. Just pull it out. Okay? Get it out. I want the drugs. Give me the drugs!"

"It's too late for that," Katie said from beside her dad at the foot of the bed.

I really wanted to tell her she could follow my mother out the door. We had a doctor. Did we really need a nurse? The one who, even in the middle of this, kept shooting Tyler those glances that set my teeth on edge, and they were already grinding pretty hard.

"Okay, we're going to push," David said.

"Oh, thank God," I whimpered.

Once the intervals between resting and pushing started, I couldn't think about anything except getting the baby out. I didn't care how it happened anymore.

"One more good push, Mia. We're almost there."

"Again with that word."

Tyler chuckled, and I glared at him.

He leaned down. "You're doing great, Mini."

"Sure. This whole thing has been great. So glad I agreed to do this."

"And push. Come on. Come on. Keep going."

I wanted to tape Dr. David's mouth shut. Maybe staple it. Yes. A staple. Several staples.

A cry rang out in the delivery room. *The baby.* David passed the squirming, wailing ball to Katie, and she took it to the next room.

David had told them the baby would be cleaned and weighed in an adjoining space before being returned to them. Privately, I'd told David I didn't want to hold the baby right away.

I lay back, afraid to ask what I'd had. I could sense Tyler's anticipation. He leaned down and kissed my head.

"You were amazing, Mini. Just...wow."

I closed my eyes and rested my head against the pillow. If the baby was a boy, it was a sign I should stay.

If the baby was a girl, it was a sign to go, to leave. I couldn't stay, couldn't take the chance I'd ruin her childhood the way my mother had ruined mine.

Katie came back carrying a bundle wrapped in pink.

My heart sank.

She stopped beside Tyler and gazed into the blanket. The longing spewing out of Katie was magnified by the baby. Tyler looked down at the parcel cradled in her arms, excitement lighting his face. Seeing them shoulder to shoulder, both of them happy and excited, it was like they were the family unit. Katie, Tyler, and their baby.

If it was possible for a heart to shrivel into nothing, that's what mine was doing. Curling up and dying.

With exaggerated care, Katie passed the baby to Tyler. His arms flexed as though expecting a heavier weight.

"She's so tiny," he whispered.

"Seven pounds." Katie smiled. "Two weeks early, and she's still seven pounds."

I stared at him holding the baby. Our baby. I should be happy, but all I felt was this strange mixture of love for him and grief over what had passed. We'd never be the same again. I couldn't process it.

"A girl," he murmured before looking at me. He searched my face, tenderness in his gaze. With his thumb, he wiped the tears falling down my cheeks. "You did it. You did it."

No, I hadn't. My body had betrayed me. The baby should have been a boy.

"There's some paperwork to fill out," Katie said, her fingers grazing the edge of the blanket to catch another glimpse. "Whenever you're ready, Tyler."

"Give us a minute, will you?" He glanced at Katie and then nodded toward David, who was puttering around the room.

She took a last look at the baby before following her father out the door.

"You okay?" Tyler used one arm to pull a chair forward. "You look like someone just shot your dog."

"I don't have a dog."

"Do you want to see her?"

I shook my head. The tears wouldn't stop falling, but I didn't care.

With the baby secured like a football in his arm, he leaned forward and touched his forehead to mine, our gazes locked. "I want to know what's going on in there."

"Nothing. Nothing."

"*Never* to each other."

Neither of us had brandished that phrase like a weapon in months. There'd been no need for it.

"I...I—"

"Knock, knock." Laura stuck her head in the door and then wandered closer. "I saw the nurse walk past with a pink blanket. So, the cycle continues, huh?"

"Get out." Tyler rose and pointed toward the exit. "Get out of the room. Get out of the hospital. Get out of our town."

Laura's gaze flicked over Tyler as though she could care less what he had to say. "Only if my daughter asks. My daughter and I have things to discuss before I'll leave town."

I rubbed my forehead. "Mother—"

"All ready to do that paperwork?" Katie asked from the door.

With a sigh, Tyler passed me the baby. I drew the bundle toward me but kept my face turned upward, toward Tyler's departing figure as he ushered my mother out of the room, his shoulders filled with tension.

In my arms, the baby squirmed. I pursed my lips and focused on the door. *Come back, Tyler. Come back. I can't do this. Come back!*

When the baby made a noise, my gaze dropped to the blanket. The sight of her tiny features tore at my heart, left it in tatters. Her eyes were open, and even though I knew she couldn't see me, I felt more seen than I'd ever been in my life.

A baby. My baby. My baby with Tyler. She was...she wa—

"I'm your mom," I whispered. Tears spilled down my cheeks. "I'm your mom." A sob escaped, and I clutched the baby tighter. "I didn't want to love you. I tried so hard not to love you." That same feeling I had whenever I saw Tyler had filled my chest when my baby stared back. How was it possible to feel this way?

Maybe it didn't matter how. I loved this baby. I loved Tyler.

Now what?

Chapter Twenty-Four
Tyler

As soon as I was out of the hospital room, I turned on Laura. "You can't even be supportive for one minute. She just had a baby. *A baby.*" I couldn't remember the last time I'd been this angry with someone. The gala, that reporter. Anyone who was attacking Mia was attacking me, too. "You come waltzing in talking about some bullshit parenting cycle?"

"She's twenty-one. You're temporary. I don't need to answer to you for anything." She shoved her finger into my chest. "To think I thought you were a decent guy."

"Yeah, 'cause raising my daughter is so indecent."

"Letting Mia keep the baby is indecent. That's the indecent part." Laura shook, meeting my rage with her own anger. "You're ruining her life. You've trapped her."

"Cut the shit, Laura. The only thing you're worried about is the gravy train coming to a halt."

"You think all I care about is money? I had her at eighteen. I know how hard it is to be a young parent, to see your friends out partying, to want to go places and do things and realize there's this impossible weight bearing down on you. Sure, at thirty-something parenting seems great to you. You've done all those things I just named. She hasn't, not really." She rolled her eyes. "What the fuck do you know about babies and breastfeeding and sleep deprivation? Talk to me in two months, three months, when you're so out of your mind from lack of sleep you can barely string together a sentence. Then you'll know what you've done, how you've saddled her with impossible choices."

What Laura didn't know was that Mia had already made her choice, months ago. I pressed my fingers into my forehead, and then felt around in my pocket for a lollipop.

I needed a cigarette. Maybe a whole pack. Parts of today had become such a fucking disaster.

"If you want to come back here," Katie said from the other side of the nurses' station, "I can show you what we need filled out."

Ignoring Laura, I circled the counter to stand shoulder to shoulder with Katie. I stared at the papers, but I wasn't focused. Back in the room, I'd been so close to asking Mia to reconsider, telling her she didn't have to go, asking her to stay.

I couldn't decide if Laura was right and asking her would be selfish. Would that make me just as bad as her? Only willing to consider what *I* wanted?

"Tyler?" Katie stroked my arm. "You okay? I don't think you heard a word I just said."

"I didn't. Sorry. It's...I...does Mia need to fill out any of this?"

"Well, yes, at least some of it. Your circumstance is unusual. Did you two talk about that?"

I shook my head. Any time I'd brought up details about the baby, she'd stonewalled me. A lot of things hadn't been decided, including the baby's name. Although, I had an idea, if she'd let me use it.

At least the baby's room was ready, but even that was in my house, not the train station. Since I'd started preparing for the baby, she'd refused to go there.

Maybe she'd come home with me, and maybe she'd return to the train station without us. I'd loved the little bubble we'd built so much I hadn't wanted to ask or imply anything that would burst it.

From the counter, I gathered up the papers and snatched a pen. Ignoring Katie, I stormed past Laura to the entrance of Mia's room. We should be happy—this should be a happy day. Instead, it felt like my life was falling apart in front of my eyes. From the moment Mia had turned up at the shop to announce she was pregnant, my life had been chaotic and strange; but at every turn, it had been better because of her. Life had been better, and I feared my world was about to become wonderful with the baby and awful without Mia at the same time. I couldn't reconcile how both realities could be true.

Taking a deep breath, I opened the door, but I didn't make it past the doorway. In the bed, Mia was hunched over the baby, tears dotting her cheeks as she tenderly traced our daughter's features.

The door clicked shut behind me, and Mia glanced up, wiping her face with her free hand.

"Do you need me to sign something?"

I stared at her, trying to decide the right thing to do. *Stay with us. Don't go. We can make it work.*

Laura's biting words clung on. Was it selfish to ask her to choose me when she was still so young? Twenty-one. At her age, none of this would have been on my radar. I rubbed my face with my free hand and wandered over to the bed.

"How are you doing?" I locked eyes with Mia.

"I'm a fucking mess." She laughed softly and tucked some of her hair behind her ears. "She looks like you."

"Does she?" I peered into the blanket and ran my fingers along her puckered forehead. My daughter. *Our* daughter. "It's funny. All I see is you." I leaned down and kissed Mia's forehead. "Maybe we look for the traits we want to see."

A beat of silence filled the room, heavy with things unsaid.

"What have you got there?" Mia tipped her chin at the papers and sniffed.

I passed her a tissue from the box, and she gave me a small smile. "We need a name." I dragged the chair close to the edge of the bed. "Can we talk about it?"

"Yes." Her bottom lip trembled.

"I think we should name her Victoria Anne. Victoria for your grandma and Anne for mine. But if you've got something you want—"

"It's perfect." Mia's words were garbled around a sob. "I'm sorry. I'm so sorry."

"What? Hey. Hey. What's going on?"

"I'm sorry," she choked out. "I probably ruined all this for you. All the excitement. All the planning." She covered her face with her free hand. "You wanted to be a dad. You deserve someone who wants to be a mom."

"No, hey, no. Mia..." Where had all this come from? The last few months would have definitely been different if we'd both been excited and looking forward to the delivery, but she hadn't ruined anything. "I wouldn't have wanted to do this with anyone else. I can't...the last few months have been the best of my life." I swallowed and stared at the papers clutched in my hand. The words were on the tip of my tongue, but I couldn't decide if they were the right ones, the fair ones. Words could be weapons, and I never wanted Mia to feel I backed her into a corner. If she even hinted she might stay, I'd go for it, say something, lay myself bare.

"I've been sitting here thinking. Thinking. Thinking. Thinking. You know?" Mia sniffed and grabbed another tissue from the box I passed her.

"What have you been thinking about?"

"Knock, knock!" David said as he wheeled in a bassinet. "Things have been a little crazy. Sorry to interrupt. I need to get you stitched up, and then we'll have someone in here to talk about feeding and other care essentials. If everything is good, we'll have you on your way in two days."

"On our way?" Mia paled. "On our way?"

"Home." David grinned. "We don't keep you hanging around too long if there are no complications. Everyone is healthy and doing well. Katie will be checking in with you both once you go home."

Inside, I cringed. The reminder of Katie hovering wasn't what we needed. A few minutes alone together, to sort all this out before we didn't have a chance anymore, that's what we needed.

"Katie, huh?" Mia slid me a look. "Will she really be checking in with us at home...or somewhere else?"

So, she'd seen a photo of us at the gym. Great. Fantastic. Let's wedge another problem in there. Hopefully, she knew me well enough to realize I wouldn't have approached Katie.

Without missing a beat, David said, "At home. I know how important privacy is for you. Though your mother yelling at some lawyer on the phone outside isn't particularly private."

"I'll talk to Laura." I set the papers on the nightstand beside Mia. We'd gotten this far without the press catching wind of the baby. If Laura blew it all to hell in the hallway of the hospital, I'd never forgive her, even if Mia could.

"Lawyer?" she asked, cocking her head. Beside Mia, her phone buzzed.

On instinct, I accepted the baby when she shifted to grab her phone. The pieces surrounding Laura's visit were clicking together, and I wasn't sure I was keen on the picture forming. Her mother had something else she needed to talk to her about. She was arguing with a lawyer on the phone in the hall. The mention of Kenny Connors earlier...

"Who is it?" I didn't like the frown creasing Mia's brow.

"Taryn. I sent her a photo of the baby. She's congratulating me."

"I feel like there's an 'and' there."

"Yeah, there's an 'and' all right. I need to talk to my mother. Can you send her in? Alone. I need to talk to her alone."

"Luckily, not too many stitches," David said. "I'll send Katie in to get you fixed up with everything else you need."

"Sure, yeah. Can you give me a minute alone with my mother? Everyone. Just like...leave us alone for a minute."

"Mia, what's going on?" I asked.

Her eyes filled with tears, and she sniffed. "I was hoping I could stay for a while, maybe. But I think I might need to leave. I'll...I'll talk to you after my mother and I have a chat."

"You're not done with the album yet." Though we hadn't confirmed how long she'd stay, I'd never thought she'd leave this quickly.

"I know, but...I just need to talk to my mom."

"Can I stay in the room when you talk to her?" It had to be about Kenny. That was the only time she acted like this, shut down, shutting me out.

Mia shook her head, and my heart sank. If she'd been thinking about staying and I left her alone with Laura, I was sure her mother would win. I placed Victoria in the bassinet, hoping she might be enough of a reminder of me, of us, of what could be.

"I'll send her in." I took the birthing documents and pen off the nightstand and headed for the door.

"Tyler?"

"Yeah?" I half-turned, my gaze traveling over her, hoping this wasn't really the end.

"The last few months have been the best of my life, too. Okay? I just…I wanted you to know that." Her voice cracked, and she broke eye contact, looking away.

That sounded too much like a goodbye. We didn't end like this. We couldn't. I wasn't just going to accept it. "Stay." I stormed back to the bed. "Stay here, in Little Falls, with me. Don't go back." I searched her face, looking for any sign I should press on.

"Oh, Tyler," Mia breathed out the words. She switched her focus to the bassinet, and she shook her head. "I…I—"

"The doctor said you wanted to see me?" Laura stood in the entry to the room looking frazzled. "Did you name her yet?" she asked, nodding toward the baby.

"Victoria Anne," Mia whispered, shock and indecision coated her face.

Leaving this room felt like nailing our relationship shut. Whatever Mia wasn't telling me was pulling her away. The shift in her had been immediate.

"I meant what I said." I linked my fingers with hers.

"I know." She stared at our hands. "I just don't know if I can." She didn't look up when she said, "I need to talk to my mom."

Walking away felt like someone had put boulders in my feet as I shuffled to the door. Laura slid me a sly smile as I went past. I had to remind myself that strangling her would be wrong.

Chapter Twenty-Five
Mia

Laura stayed by the door until it had clicked shut and Tyler was completely gone. "If you want to leave here, I can have us out and on our way in twenty minutes. I can help you escape."

"Oh, yeah?" A bitter chuckle escaped. "And where would you be taking me? To some lawyers? For the Kenny Connors' trial, perhaps? 'Cause I hear I've been summoned for a command performance." I wasn't dragging Tyler and Victoria into the mess my mother was creating. Not a chance.

"The only person who knows—"

"Yep. Taryn." I shook with what I told myself was anger. "I am not testifying at the trial or anywhere else. Do you understand me? I need you to get me out of it."

"I've been trying to do that." Laura crossed her arms. "There are very few options since our primary residence is Nashville and the whole debacle is happening in Nashville."

"So, change our primary residence. We own more than one house."

"I would have needed to do that before they served the subpoena. It's too late now. Trust me, I don't want you there either," Laura muttered. "Flee the country. That's it. But you'd probably never be able to come back."

Never be able to come back? Tyler. The baby. I glanced toward the bassinet. Either price was high. On one hand, I'd have to admit to the world what had happened with Kenny and how we'd handled it; and on the other, I'd have no choice, no chance at a family with Tyler.

"What will people think of me?" I twisted my hands in my lap and wished I'd let Tyler stay.

"That you were a fifteen-year-old girl led astray by, at the time, a forty-something man." Laura sank into the nearest chair.

Led astray. She still didn't understand. I'd admitted I hadn't told Kenny no. At the time, that had felt like the most important part. The older I got, the more I realized what wasn't said mattered just as much, and I'd never said yes. Of course, his hand over my mouth had prevented me from saying much of anything.

"Why don't we go away for a few days, let the lawyers straighten things out? You've always wanted to go to Bali. Maybe now is the time. You're taking a break. Why not make it a vacation? We'll give them a chance to find a loophole."

"You want me to go to Bali?" The words were stiff, foreign.

"Tyler can look after the baby." Laura held my gaze. "You hid the pregnancy. Not just from me. As far as I can tell, you hid it from pretty much everyone. The Mia I know would have been shouting it from the rooftops if she was sure she wanted it, if she was sure she was making the right decision. You don't do things you love quietly."

I swallowed. It was eerily accurate. The baby made a noise, and I drew the bassinet closer. The right thing to do was impossible to know.

"I'm not going to Bali." No matter what, I couldn't take away the option of being with Victoria and Tyler, not until I was sure I didn't want it. Right now, I wasn't sure of much.

"Somewhere else, then? Maldives? Cape Verde? Name the place, and I'll book the tickets."

"I want to see the subpoena." If Laura really understood how difficult it would be to talk about what happened in Kenny's office, this push to escape would be loving and unexpected. Instead, it felt like she was trying to rip me from Tyler, from here, from the life I built without her.

If Tyler were in my shoes, I knew what he'd do. He wasn't a runner. Vanishing would be off the table. Leaving wouldn't be the right thing to do in any scenario. Of course, Tyler would have done more to stop Kenny in the first place. My mother's affirmation that at least *we* were safe wouldn't have been enough.

People would know I'd stood by and let more girls get hurt. I was party to other girls being manipulated, allowed them to feel worthless, less than. The realization caused my stomach to twist.

I imagined Tyler standing beside me, sliding his hand into mine. I wanted to bottle his strength and use it like an elixir for what was to come. Someone like him wanting to be with me was an inoculation against the rest of the world's vitriol. No one else knew me like he did. If he saw value in me beyond my voice, beyond my ability to entertain a crowd, maybe it was really there.

Victoria stirred, and I laid a gentle hand on the mound of blankets. Good mothers slew beasts. Threw open the closet doors and banished the things that went bump in the night. Letting the Kenny Connors of the world win meant I was leaving them for my daughter's generation. *These things just happen* wasn't good enough anymore, should never have been okay in the first place.

"The subpoena, Mother."

Laura rummaged around her purse and tugged a folded envelope from the depths. Lips pursed, she handed it over.

"I have to appear in four days." A cold sweat broke out across my body as I scanned the document. "Four days! When did you get this?"

"A little while ago." Laura shifted in her seat.

"How long ago?"

"Does it matter? I was working on getting you out of it. When it seemed like I might not be able to, I came here. I certainly wasn't expecting to find you barefoot and pregnant."

"I had shoes on, nice ones too." I tossed the subpoena on the bed and rubbed my cheeks. What a disaster. Today would never have been my favorite day, or I never expected it to be. But Laura's arrival, the subpoena, realizing I really, truly loved both Tyler and our baby, and now having to figure out where all the pieces went in the next three days was too much.

"Well, you'd better be wearing spectacular shoes when you waltz into that appointment," Laura nodded toward my expanded tummy, "'cause that belly won't be gone by then. People will be talking. We can only hope it's about your shoes."

Understanding dawned, and tears pooled in my eyes. I hated crying in front of her. I should have let Tyler stay. "The press will hound Tyler." All the months of hiding the pregnancy had come to this. Once again, Kenny would be a black mark stamped on my life.

"After all of your social media bragging about your Pretty Boy, there's little question about the father, is there?"

Bali was looking more appealing. If I went, I could stop the press from going after Tyler, from caring about Victoria's existence.

I stared at my hands in my lap and wished I could quiet all the churning thoughts. "I need to be alone while I figure out what I want to do, okay? Just give me a bit of time."

Tyler paused in the doorway, and my heart kicked at the sight of him. Love for him flooded me, and rather than fighting it, I let it rise and flow. I'd have plenty of time to fight that tide later. The papers were in his hand, and I wondered if Katie had helped him fill them out. How long would it take Katie to weasel into my place?

"Can you tell me what's going on now?" He ran his free hand through his hair, and then came to stare into the bassinet where Victoria lay sleeping.

"I've been subpoenaed for a deposition in the Kenny Connors case." Admitting that was the easy part. The rest of this was going to be hard. I'd talked to the lawyer we'd hired. The case wasn't in court yet. If I broke things off with Tyler now, I might be able to protect him from the onslaught, from the disaster of my life careening around the corner.

"I figured it had something to do with him." He took a deep breath. "When do you have to go?"

"I have to present myself in four days."

"Four days?" He pinched the bridge of his nose. "Four days."

"I'm going to...I'm going to head back to Nashville with my mom as soon as I'm out of the hospital. I can't fly, so we have to drive." My chin wobbled, and I prayed I could keep it together.

"As soon as you're out of the hospital?" He sank into the chair beside my bed, but his gaze was focused on Victoria, not on me. "And after...will you come back?"

This was the hard part, the words I dreaded saying. "I don't know."

His jaw clenched, and it took a moment for him to respond. "I want you to. Selfish or not, I want you. I want this life we've built together."

A sob slipped out, and he dropped the papers on the bed, his arms circling me, his lips in my hair.

"I don't know how to do this," I cried.

"Come back to us, Mia. We can figure the rest out."

"I'm a mess, and I don't just mean because I gave birth. I mean, like, seriously fucked up."

"You're not—"

"I am." I pulled back from him and took a shuddering breath. "You know how I know? 'Cause for the last, like, four months I have been convincing myself that the baby was in love with you. Not me. *The baby*. Because if I was the one in love with you, I didn't know how I would ever be able to leave." My voice cracked. "I don't want to leave, but I can't stay."

"Why can't you stay? Beyond the court case, why can't you?" His voice was rough, and he averted his gaze.

"I don't know how to be a mom. I don't. I don't even know if I *want* to be one. And...and I can't screw up her life or your life while I figure it out. I won't." When I looked up, he was staring down at me.

I could have hidden the truth behind my work. For almost nine months, I'd been telling Tyler I'd never stay, so he might have believed I wanted my old lifestyle more. But lying to him felt wrong. My love for Tyler was unequivocal, visceral, the realest thing I'd ever experienced, greater than any stage, any performance, any song I'd ever written or heard. When I looked at Victoria, thought of her, held her, I loved her, too. They deserved the best version of me, and that person wouldn't exist for months, possibly years. Kenny's case would detonate, shrapnel sinking into all of them, destroying everything.

"Will you stay with me one last night before you leave? I don't...I don't want this hospital room to be goodbye." His voice hitched. "I don't want this to be goodbye at all. I love you. I love you, Mia."

"I love you, too." Another sob almost consumed the words. "But I just don't know if I can be good for you, good for her."

"What did Laura say to you? What did she say?" His hand gripped mine. "Nobody's perfect. We all make mistakes. We're both going to make mistakes. You're good for both of us. You are."

"But I don't *feel* like I am." My voice was thick with tears, my throat burning from holding back the sobs. I wanted to stay with him, stitch together the pattern of our lives.

Victoria deserved a mother who wanted to be a mom, who knew how to be a parent. If only I hadn't spent nine months wishing for a different outcome, maybe I'd have some of these answers, or I'd at least have considered the questions. Figuring out what I wanted was too much, and I was out of time.

It turned out, sticking my head in the sand wasn't the answer at all to motherhood or to what had happened with Kenny.

"I wish I could say it enough times that you'd believe me, that I could make you believe me," he said.

"I wish it was that simple too."

He let go of my hand and went to my bag, rifling through it. At last, he pulled out a lollipop, ripped off the wrapper, and stared at it for a moment. "Some days, this is a poor substitute for a cigarette."

"Don't start smoking again." Through my tears, I smiled. "It's gross. I love the way you smell—like candy."

"I hate her for what she's done to you, the way she's manipulated you." He twirled the lollipop, not putting it into his mouth. "You're incredible, and the only time she lets you feel that way is when you're dancing to the tune she plays."

Maybe that was true. For the last few years, the one person I trusted and had turned to in a crisis had been my mother. "My relationship with her is all I've known." I drew my hair around to rest on my shoulder. "I don't think I'll be a good mom."

"You're not like her." He squeezed my hand.

I might not be like her, but I'd been raised by her. When I was cornered, I bit back like Laura, willing to say or do whatever I needed to get out of a jam, to come out on top. There was too much of my mom in me to be sure I wouldn't eventually slip into my mother's shoes. I didn't want to, but I couldn't imagine changing my mindset was as easy as Tyler made it seem. *Just don't be like her.* Simple. Impossible. Half the time when I was acting like Laura, I couldn't see it until afterward.

Even if I was sure I wanted to be a mother, sure I could overcome my upbringing to do better for Victoria, there was still Kenny's trial looming. I didn't want to drag Tyler and Victoria into this version of the spotlight. The press coverage would be dirty and ugly and filled with my most shameful moments.

"There's no version of you I don't love." He peered down, his cognac eyes intense. "I've seen every side of you in the last few months. I love all of them. I don't know if I'm being fair saying these things to you. You've been very clear from the start about where we were headed." He searched my expression. "But I've seen what regret looks like—desperate and ugly. I don't want that for you. I don't want it for me. So, I'm putting everything out there. Whatever is happening with you, I want to be part of it. I don't care how messy the situation is. I don't care how hard our life is."

When I met his sincere gaze, my resolve faltered. He'd stand beside me. Hell, he'd probably carry me on his back like an albatross for the rest of our lives if I asked. There was no question Tyler was the kind of man any woman would want in her life. Without Victoria, I'd stay with him, let the madness consume us. I loved our daughter too much to risk everyone's happiness and well-being.

"Can I think about it?" Tears were pooling in my eyes, slipping down my cheeks. There'd be no more thinking. I'd made my decision.

His shoulders sagged, and he nodded. "Yeah, of course."

"But when we're released, I want to go home with you. If that's okay?" *One last time.*

He'd been focused on the baby, and at the tremble in my voice, he smoothed down my hair. "You'll always have a home with me and Victoria. You'll always be welcome. You never have to ask." His voice cracked, and he bent to pick up the baby.

Chapter Twenty-Six

Tyler

We'd been dancing around each other since we got back to my house for our final night together. I'd slept at the hospital with her and Victoria the last two nights, trying to get a handle on some sort of routine, knowing that soon Mia wouldn't be part of it.

At the house, nothing felt quite right. The baby's room had made Mia cry. In trying to be gender neutral, I'd decorated in soft gray and yellow tones. Seeing her joyful surprise was a moment I would have treasured if Laura hadn't come up behind us and loudly declared it "too bland" for a little girl.

Then, Laura insisted on staying in the basement rather than the hotel she'd been at the last few days. Her stubbornness almost led to an all-out war between us with Mia as an exhausted Switzerland. Everything Mia had ever done somehow became Laura's successes and failures. Any chance she had to wind up her daughter, she took it.

I wanted to protect Mia from Laura's toxic influence, but I didn't know how and wouldn't have a chance once the morning came and she vanished from my life.

Night had fallen even though I wished time would slow down, let me savor these last few hours. Away from here, Laura would sink her claws deeper into Mia, convince her that life in the spotlight, life on the road, untethered to other human connections was the best thing for her. If you never loved anyone, you never got hurt by anyone either.

Victoria was in the bassinet next to the bed. Everything we needed to make bottles and change diapers was set up in the bedroom and en suite. Pasha was sleeping on the couch, so he'd be aware of any intruders, and we had two other bodyguards at the doors, just in case. In the hallway, Pasha had told Mia that Laura was the only intruder he needed to worry about. Never had a truer sentence been spoken.

Beside me, Mia eased into bed and hauled the covers up to her shoulders. We'd never slept in this room together before we'd moved to the train station. The basement had been our domain. When I'd been planning for the baby, I'd figured having everything on the main floor would be easier. Right now, I was regretting it. A heaviness rested between us. The feeling was compounded by the strangeness of the room, the newness of the baby, the realization that everything we'd been to each other up to this point was shifting, had already shifted, was, perhaps, drifting away.

There was a very strong chance Mia would never come back. We'd been so busy since leaving the hospital that I hadn't had a chance to dwell on that nugget of truth. Now, in the darkness of the room with her even breathing beside me, it was all I could think about.

In the morning, she would leave. Tomorrow night when I turned my head, there'd be an empty spot, in this bed, in my life, in my heart. I knew what was coming—the emptiness, the misery. Last time I'd had my family and a whole lot of alcohol to pull me from the depths. This time, I couldn't let myself fall apart. Victoria needed me. My sisters needed me. My mother needed me. Maybe later, miles from here, Mia might need me too, so I had to keep myself together, even if my heart was in tatters.

"Having a baby is weird," Mia said. "I got more instructions with the last lipstick I bought. They just, like, let us leave. What if we were terrible people? What if we didn't have enough money to look after the baby? What if we didn't have a house?"

I rolled onto my side and propped my head in my hand. "We were there for two days. David and Katie have known you for months now, and they've known me for years."

"That just means they know I'm a hot mess. That's what that means. They know I'm not fit to be a mother, and they let me leave with her anyway."

Mia's insecurity was my least favorite side. I loved every aspect of her, but this one made my heart ache. When she showed this part of herself, I understood these moments needed the most love, the most understanding, the biggest piece of my heart. My father had often scoffed at those who said self-love had to come first, as though it was a magic cure-all for finding any other kind of love. He'd told me, more than once, that people who didn't love themselves were as deserving of love as anyone else. In fact, they might even need it more.

"You've been incredible so far. We're figuring it out together. Babies don't come with a standard instruction manual because they're all different. What works for one kid might not work for another one. It's okay to mess up or not be sure. That's why we have the internet."

"You got your PhD in Parenting from Google University?" She laughed, and her finger trailed along the side of my face to my jaw.

"No one can ever accuse me of being a slacker."

Her expression softened, and she stared at me for a long time, impossible to read. "Do you think I'm a bad person?"

"No. Never." I took in the agony on her face. "Do *you* think you are?"

"I knew about Kenny Connors. He did it to me. I knew. And I didn't stop him. Didn't make him stop. All those other girls..." A tear slipped down her cheek. "How can people forgive me for that?"

A million responses ran through my head. Picking one that was clear and concise felt impossible. "Mia," I said in an even voice, "I don't want to ask, but I want to make sure I understand." I searched her face. "Did he rape you?"

"Yes," she whispered. "I think so. I didn't...when I was fifteen, I didn't know what to call it." Her bottom lip trembled. "I froze. When he trapped me against the desk, I froze."

"That's not your fault. Freezing out of fear isn't consent. You were fifteen. He would have been what? Old enough to know better, old enough to understand what he was doing was wrong."

"Sure, but...months ago..." She closed her eyes and pressed the heels of her hands into them.

"What happened months ago?" With a gentle tug on her wrists, I stared down at her.

"I knew there were others, that I wasn't the only one." She swallowed. "Nothing. I did nothing. All this fame, all this power, and I did nothing. I...I saved my own ass, that's it."

The right words were impossible to find. "You think people are going to criticize you for not coming forward sooner?"

"Of course. Yes. Haven't you ever read an article or watched the news? How often is the woman criticized? *What were you wearing? What'd you have to drink? Why didn't you say no? Why didn't you report it? Why didn't you help all those other defenseless girls who didn't have your power and influence?*" Her voice cracked at the end. "Why didn't I help them?"

"You can't go back, Mia." I hated how torn up she seemed, so conflicted over something that wasn't her fault. "He made a choice, and—"

"So did I," Mia cried.

"I don't have all the answers." I brushed my lips against her forehead and wiped her tears with my thumbs. "But I know you were young, so young, *too* young. You were scared, maybe you're still scared."

"Back then, I didn't know what to do."

"What are you going to do now?"

"I'm going to testify. I'm going to do everything I can to make sure he can't hurt another girl again." Her hand strayed to the bassinet. "Slay the monsters."

I wrapped my arm around her middle and tugged her closer to my side. "Sometimes, for whatever reason, we're not ready. If we're lucky, we get a second chance."

"When I show up at the deposition looking like this, the tabloids will come for you. They'll come for her." Tears pooled in her eyes again. "I still look pregnant, and the internet tells me that's not going to change for a while."

"I'll protect you. I'll protect our daughter." I kept my voice soft, soothing. "You don't need to worry about who comes looking."

"I don't want you to suffer for the choices I've made."

"While you're out slaying monsters, I'll gladly hold your shield."

Minutes passed between us, and Mia didn't say anything, her fingers gliding along the strands of my hair. Her thoughtful habit was one I'd miss. So many things I'd miss. Dwelling on them now wouldn't make them easier to bear tomorrow.

"I love you, Tyler. You know that, right? I'm not leaving because I don't love you."

My throat closed up, and it took a moment before I could speak. "Yeah, I know." I shifted closer, secured my arm a little tighter. If only my grip was enough to keep her here, attached to my side.

She'd spent the whole pregnancy convincing herself that a life with me, a life with a baby was the last thing she wanted. Was it still? Would it be once the trial was over? The only certainty was that when tomorrow came, I couldn't come apart at the seams. Too many people were depending on me.

Hold it together, Tyler. Hold it together.

Chapter Twenty-Seven
Mia

Across the conference table sat our family lawyer. His face was familiar, but I'd always let my mother deal with any problems. Legal things were a distraction, over my head. Or maybe that's what Laura had wanted me to think. He'd forced my mother to wait in the lobby of the law firm.

The conversation between the two of them had been tense, far more tense than any I'd seen between them before. In the end, he won. I wanted to know what dirt he had on her to make her fold. They'd been too far away for me to hear.

"There is no press here today because no one knows we're meeting." He flipped open his file.

"Right," I agreed in a bored voice. "Your point?" He was dancing around my appearance. I'd chosen my clothes carefully with Tyler's help before I left.

Is she fat? Is she pregnant? What's the right thing to say here? He must be wondering, but unable to find a polite way to phrase the questions.

I could ease his discomfort, but I had no intention of telling anyone anything. Everyone could speculate. Let them all run wild. Eventually, they'd run themselves out.

"There will be press tomorrow when you go for your deposition with the prosecution."

"Yep. I figured." I leaned my elbow onto the table and shifted. "But you wanted to see me before?"

"It's customary. Often, I'll meet a client just prior to a deposition, but I thought it would be beneficial for us to meet the day before."

"Why?" The chill between us was my doing. I wanted to be here, but I also really didn't want to be anywhere near Nashville right now. My heart started bleeding out when our car drove away from Tyler's house. If Laura hadn't been sitting beside me, I'd have collapsed onto the seat, sobbing. I'd have played all the heartbreak songs I could find and wallowed in self-pity.

For months, I'd been free to let my feelings explode. My emotions needed help when I was younger, and they got out of control: a tourniquet or an ice bath. Right now, I was trying ice. Later, I might need the tourniquet, a necessary evil. I'd tied off my emotions once before.

Cut out the heart to save the soul.

"The police have a search warrant for all the properties, offices, and spaces Mr. Connors has used in Nashville."

That sounded ominous. I'd only met him at the label in his office. Maybe he'd taken girls to other places. Promises. Hope. He would have fed them to the girls like Turkish Delight. My stomach clenched, and a wave of nausea swept over me. It had been so long since I'd felt like this that it was almost surreal.

"Okay," I said. "What does that mean?"

"They've obtained an envelope during those searches that appears to have originated with either you or your mother. She's also being deposed tomorrow."

"My mother?" Ice shot through my veins so quickly that the hairs on my arms rose in protest.

"She's not the only mother being deposed in this case."

He was staring at me, but I didn't know what he expected me to do or know. Nothing. I'd never seen the contents of the envelope. I had no idea what my mother knew.

The blank look on my face must have given him a clue because he muttered under his breath, "So *this* is why she wanted to be in here."

"I don't understand." The iciness was gone, and in its place was a taste of panic.

"In your own words, I want you to tell me what happened with Kenny Connors." He clicked his pen open and pushed the file to the side, grabbing the notebook from the other side of him. "We'll get into the types of questions the prosecution will be asking you. You're not the one on trial, but we have to prepare you as though you will be." When our gazes met, his eyes were full of sympathy. "This case isn't going to play out in the courtroom alone."

"Is there a chance it won't go to court at all?" There was still the ray of hope. I wanted him to go down, but if I didn't need to testify, that was even better.

"Never know. Deals might happen behind the scenes." He opened his mouth as though he was going to say more and then closed it again. Adjusting the grip on his pen, he said, "In your own words, please."

So, I told him. When and where and how often. The last part I'd never divulged to anyone else. Twice.

Fool me once, shame on you, fool me twice, shame on me.

After the first time, I'd tried to get out of meeting with him alone. But the whole experience had been so confusing that I didn't have the words to tell my mother or anyone else why I couldn't meet with him in private. I'd been ashamed that I'd allowed it to happen and confused about what it meant that I'd frozen stiff, hadn't fought him, hadn't said anything other than *I'm not sure* in a whispered voice.

When I finished telling him the whole tale, I raised my head. His was still bowed over the paper, frantically scribbling notes. At last, his pen stilled, and he twirled it without looking up. "Anything else?"

"Should there be?" The ice was back. The question undermined my experience. What else did he want? Blood? Gore? The damage had never been physical. Kenny Connors had ripped me open in his office, torn so deep I'd never looked at myself the same way again. At thirteen, I'd fought off my mother's boyfriend, defended myself, hadn't allowed him to do more than squeeze a few parts. Why hadn't I done the same with Kenny? The question haunted me.

"His defense will dredge up anything they can find to discredit you, so I want to make sure we know everything."

"One of my mom's boyfriends tried to attack me when I was thirteen. I fought him off. Is that what you mean?" I cocked my head. "I told you all the Kenny stuff—that's it. Twice. Just like I told you."

"Were you on birth control? Did he use any form of birth control?"

"They'll ask me that?" I straightened in my chair.

"Yes, I believe they will." He fiddled with the edge of the folder.

"I was fifteen, and I wasn't sexually active. So, no, I wasn't on the pill. Did he use a condom? Doubtful given how quickly it all happened both times. One hand over my mouth, the other pinning me in place—I can't see how he could have."

"Were there any consequences to those two assaults?"

"Consequences?" I frowned, and my hand unconsciously went to my rounded stomach. "You mean like an STD or something?"

"Or a pregnancy." His voice was flat.

"No, no." At the back of my mind, a memory niggled, threatened to snap back to the surface. "I would have known if I was pregnant." I pointed to my stomach. "I mean, you can't exactly ignore it." God knows I'd tried.

From his folder, he pulled out a white sheet and stared at it for a moment before sliding it across. "You went to a clinic just outside Nashville with your mother. Do you remember that?"

"I had ovarian cysts." I couldn't look at the sheet, refused to lower my gaze. Tears pooled in my eyes, blurring my vision. "My mom said I had ovarian cysts."

"You didn't go there for ovarian cysts." He pursed his lips. "That's not the procedure you had done." He inclined his head toward the document in front of me. "Is that your signature?"

Through my tears, I scanned the document. "No, it's not. That's my name. That's not my signature." My mother sometimes signed things as if she was me, but she never quite got the M right. "Dilation and curettage—that's what it says here. What's...what is that?"

"It's often called a D and C and is used in abortions."

"An abortion?" I dropped the page as though it burned my fingertips. When I'd woken up groggy from the sedative, my mother had brought up Kenny. For the first time, I had told her the truth—too out of it to care what was said. Or I'd told her some of it, anyway. How had Laura known? I hadn't even realized I was pregnant. "I didn't sign this. How...how could this have happened to me without my consent?"

"There is mounting evidence that Kenny Connors might have orchestrated abortions when he impregnated the young girls he was producing."

"But I didn't even know I was pregnant."

"A week before the abortion, you went to the clinic with your mother and had bloodwork done." He removed another paper from the folder and slid it across the desk.

"Sure, for the cysts." Except it wasn't about cysts. I'd probably never had any cysts. I groaned and cradled my head in my hands. "To confirm I was pregnant."

"Yes."

"Oh, my God." I repeated the phrase over and over, trying to wrap my head around what he was saying. "I don't understand how this is possible."

"It's not legal. What happened to you isn't legal. The clinic has been shut down. Charges have been laid against the people working during these procedures." A heavy silence sat between us. "If you didn't sign your name, who did?"

"I wasn't the only one?"

"I don't have all the details. The prosecution tomorrow will decide what you need to know."

"I need to know it all." I stood up, the chair tipping with the force of rising. My body, still sore from giving birth, protested. "Are we done here? Because if you can't give me answers, I know someone who can." Rage coursed through me, so violent, so unexpected I feared I might murder someone.

"Maybe you should stay here—"

"Are we done?"

"We can be, yes. I just didn't want you blindsided tomorrow."

"Today. Tomorrow. What's the fucking difference?" I grabbed my purse from the seat and stormed out the door. Pasha, standing next to the conference room, fell into step beside me. "Not a word, Pasha or I might literally rip your head off."

He grunted in response.

In my head, I did the calculations, tried to remember when Pasha had started working for us. He hadn't been around. The first tour was when he started, but I couldn't be completely sure. He wouldn't know what happened.

"I want my mother in the car. I don't care how you get her there." We stormed into the lobby, and I locked gazes with Pasha.

He swept Laura off her feet like a linebacker, barreling through the lobby and out the doors ahead of me. She let out one noise of protest and then took his treatment without further comment.

Opening the rear door, he tossed Laura inside and slammed it shut. With his finger, he pointed to the front passenger seat for me and opened the door. He was probably right. The amount of anger racing through might cause me to do something rash like strangle her. I wasn't sure Pasha would stop me if I did.

As soon as I was in the front seat, I turned on Laura. "Why? Why would you do that to me?"

"Don't act like you didn't know. You signed the paperwork." Laura crossed her arms and eased into the seat as though I was being irrational.

"You forged my signature. You lied to me about what was happening that day." My voice shook.

"And you had no clue? Never suspected? Never looked up the procedure online and thought, 'Mmm...that's not what happened to me.'

Never?" Laura scoffed. "You knew. It's why you didn't tell me about *this* baby."

Sarah and I had spent a drunken night looking up ovarian cyst procedures when it turned out Sarah was prone to them and might need surgery. After several pages of the search engine, I'd realized my procedure probably hadn't been for cysts. I'd been too afraid to look any further.

"You're blaming me for this?"

"I didn't know *how* you'd gotten pregnant, but I knew you were." Laura's shoulders collapsed, and she sighed. She pulled her elbows closer to her chest and gazed out the window. "Okay? I was managing every aspect of your career so we didn't screw up. We'd had that massive advance, and I'd bought us a house. Our first house. A place that was really ours. If we defaulted on our contract in any way, we had to pay back that advance. The housing market had soured."

"What does that have to do with you drugging me and forcing me to have an abortion?"

"There was a morality clause in your contract. One of the things you weren't allowed to be was a teenage mom. Right there in bold black and white." She swallowed. "When I realized you were pregnant, I went to see Kenny."

I stiffened.

"I needed some advice, and he'd always been easy to talk to. I thought...I thought he'd help us. I didn't know he was the reason we needed help." She shrugged. "He suggested the clinic, told me how to get it done if you were resistant, said the label would drop us and insist on getting their money back if you had the baby."

"The house was more important to you than my health? Than my well-being?"

"No! No." Laura glared. "With the market soured, we'd have lost money on the sale of the house, assuming we could even sell it in a decent amount of time. We would have been homeless, in debt, so much debt."

"You should have told me." My voice vibrated with rage. "If we were in that much trouble, you should have told me."

"Would you have gotten an abortion?"

"I don't know!" I cried. "I was fifteen. I probably would have done whatever you told me to do."

"Telling you was too risky." Laura shook her head. "You would have wanted to keep it. You're softer than me. You wouldn't have been able to do what needed to be done."

Bile climbed my throat. For twenty-one years, I'd been chasing her love, but I'd been outrun even before I was born. "You never wanted me."

"You're so melodramatic." She pinched the bridge of her nose.

My anger dissipated quicker than I expected. A deep sense of loss rushed into its place. The one thing I'd have done almost anything to earn, and I'd never stood a chance. "Pasha, I want you to remove my mother from this vehicle. I'm going to work on removing her from my life."

"Mia, honey, don't be rash." Laura sat forward and reached for my hand, but I tugged it away, out of sight. "We can work through this."

Turning my back on her, I dialed Taryn's number. Pasha veered to the side of the road.

Taryn answered while Pasha dragged my mother out of the backseat, and I said, "I've fired Laura as my manager, and I'm firing her from being my mother. I need your help to cut her out of my life for good."

"That might be tough, but I'll help in any way I can. If she has access to bank accounts, phone numbers..." Taryn droned on while my mind spiraled out of control at the impossibility of the task. By the time we got home, Laura would be ten steps ahead of us. I didn't know how anything worked.

When Pasha's door opened again and he slid into the driver's seat, Laura's enraged screams followed him. He passed my mother's purse to me. "I have phone, too."

"You got her phone and her purse?" I glanced over my shoulder at Laura's livid expression outside the rear window.

"Cut her out," Pasha said. "Then you be happy."

That seemed so simple. Was it really that easy?

Chapter Twenty-Eight
Tyler

One week. She'd been gone for one week, and my heart was ragged, worn out, in desperate need of mending. If I didn't have Victoria, I'd have dipped into the alcohol, succumbed to the haze. As it was, I was getting less and less sleep.

Each time I sank into unconsciousness, she visited, the sweetest torture. Sometimes, she was flirting, at the edge of the stage, a show just for me. Other times, we were lounging in bed, highlights of our pillow talk playing on a loop long enough to make me believe the dream might be real. Eventually, something would tip me off—an action, a word she wouldn't use—and I'd be yanked out, woken up. I'd lay in bed, staring at the ceiling, so full of wishes I expected a genie or the devil to materialize so I could make a bargain for my heart to return.

When I fed Victoria and rocked her back to sleep, I saw Mia in every expression, every movement. Never before had I been this fulfilled and empty at the same time.

In some ways, her absence was an echo of something I experienced before. Unlike with Katie, I understood Mia's conflict. Mia asked me not to call, not to text, not to reach out while the Kenny Connors trial stormed around her. She didn't want me dragged into the turmoil.

I didn't need to be dragged; I would have walked into the eye of the storm with her hand cradled in mine.

As it was, I'd lumbered through the week in a fog of sleepless nights and long days trying to figure out how to tend to a newborn. YouTube videos and frequent calls to my mother and Emily had gotten me by, but it was draining to juggle the baby, my shop, and my fraying feelings for Mia.

I'd thought I'd see her splashed across social media the day of her deposition, but somehow her team managed to keep her out of the press. Their ability to shelter her wasn't that surprising. I knew from the tour how her core group circled her in times of need with Laura cracking the whip. Trust almost no one, and leaks of information were nearly impossible.

During the long nights, I often played Mia's music or watched old interviews and tried to convince myself it was so Victoria would know her mother's voice if she ever came back. I hated that her return was an "if" and not "when."

The doorbell rang, and I had to readjust Victoria so I could keep the bottle propped in her mouth while I answered the door. She wailed if I removed it before she was done. Since Mia had given the warning about the paparazzi coming for me and Victoria, I never answered the door blind. On the other side, Katie had her medical bag slung over her shoulder, her scrubs fluttering in the light breeze.

I closed my eyes. It was Monday. How had I forgotten it was Monday? My gaze darted around the house, taking in the clear signs I wasn't coping. Dishes in the sink. Clothes strewn over chairs. Burp cloths on almost every surface. The sour stench of soiled diapers from the garbage was a reminder that I wasn't dumping the can frequently enough.

Most people might not notice the disorganization or put it down to the newborn learning curve, and maybe that was part of what was happening. My instinct was to run around hiding all the signs. But I suspected Katie still knew enough to see through any façade I tried to present. Even if I had the energy to pretend this week, I might not next time. Might as well face the music today.

Swinging open the door, I plastered a smile on my face. "Gotta be honest. I forgot you were coming."

"It's fine." Katie waved me off. "I'm just coming to see how you're getting along and to make sure Victoria is progressing. First babies are hard." She slipped past into the house and stopped in the foyer. "Oh," she said.

"Yeah. Like I said, I forgot." I gave a nervous chuckle.

"Is Mia here?" She peered around me to the hallway, her long brown ponytail swaying. "Or any of the people she hired to cook and clean for you?"

So, she'd heard about that. As soon as Mia had started to show, she'd fired all of them, but for those first few weeks after Mia arrived, I'd appreciated the good food and clean house accomplished by someone else's hard work. Although, I was perfectly capable of doing both...normally. "Uh, no. Um...she's not here."

"Oh, okay. That's fine. You said you forgot, so perhaps she did as well. I can wait or come back." Katie clenched her hands in front of her, and I was sure she was appalled by the mess. I was tidy, but Katie had been almost militant about order in the house. "I could...I could help you get a little more organized while we wait."

"No." I shook my head. "No." I could picture how pissed off Mia would be to know Katie had offered, had felt I wasn't capable. "I have to finish feeding her or she'll scream bloody murder, but we don't need to wait for Mia."

Besides, we'd be waiting a hell of a long time.

"Right," Katie said, setting down her bag and digging through it. "Have you been having any problems with feeding? Diaper rash? Questions about bowel movements?"

"No, everything has been great." My voice was too bright, false.

She eyed the state of the house again but didn't contradict me. "What about Mia? How is she coping?" After the briefest hesitation, she said, "Because I know you, Tyler, and this doesn't look like you're doing well. New baby and all, but your house is a disaster."

"Yeah, the house is a disaster, but Victoria is fine. I'll call that a win."

"And Mia?"

"She's fine, too."

"She's left town already?" With a sigh, Katie sank into the closest chair. "Why don't you want to tell me?"

I hadn't told anyone. Every time I called someone for help, I insisted I could handle things with a bit of direction over the phone. They assumed Mia and Pasha were still in the house, and we were learning to be a family. I hadn't been able to correct them. Just the thought of uttering the words made the deadness inside spread. At some point, the sucking wound of her absence would be sewn up.

Perseverance. That was what this situation called for. Endurance.

"I'm sorry," Katie said. "I know you really cared about her."

I stared at her and thought about how inadequate her words were for the feelings eating at me. "I'm capable of coming out the other side. I know that already."

"Yeah." She picked at the strap of her bag. "I guess you do. For what it's worth, I've had a lot of regrets about what happened between us."

"I haven't had nearly enough sleep to have this conversation." The last of the formula squeezed out of the bottle, and I pulled the nipple out of Victoria's mouth before she could start sucking air. "I'm not in a very diplomatic mood."

"I can take your blunt honesty, Tyler."

"I would have liked some of that from you eight years ago."

"Understandable. I was...I was too young to—I don't know—comprehend what I was doing, what I was giving up." Her hands twisted in her lap.

"For just over seven years, I probably would have been content to hear an explanation, something that made sense. But I don't need one anymore." I burped Victoria. A surge of triumph stormed through me that I'd made the task look so easy with Katie here. See? I was fine.

"I know you'll need some time to adjust to a new normal. But I was hoping we could hang out a bit, get to know each other again."

I stared at her, baffled. She still thought there was a chance for us?

"All right. Fuck it. Turns out I *do* need to know." I set Victoria in the living room playpen. "You can't disappear for eight years, and now that I've finally moved on, show up expecting things to go back to, quite frankly, what you left in the first place."

"We were good together," Katie whispered. She didn't meet my gaze and was instead focused on Victoria through the mesh.

"You're fucking right we were. But you left. You decided we weren't something you wanted."

"That's not exactly what happened."

"Clue me in."

"My parents don't even know why I left…not really." She twisted her ponytail around her finger and released it. "I was free-falling, and looking back, I don't even know why. Well, I *know* why, but my feelings got out of control."

Instead of sitting down, I paced the room, running my hands through my hair. "Spit it out, Katie. For months, you've been telling me you wanted to give me the truth. I'm listening, but I'm not going to be listening for long. I'm not even sure I care." My thoughts had been so consumed by Mia that it was nice to care about something else for a change, even if it was only for a moment.

I didn't know if Katie and I could find our way back to each other. Right now, I couldn't imagine I'd even want that. With the way I felt about Mia, being with her was unthinkable. Mia's name was scrawled across my life as though she'd autographed everything she touched while she was here, including my heart. Katie didn't own even a tiny piece of my emotional landscape anymore. Mia had claimed it all.

"While you were gone on tour with that musical, I found out I wouldn't ever be able to carry children."

The admission stopped me in my tracks, and I slid down into the couch. "What? But—" That made no sense. "Why?"

"Apparently, I was born with a tiny uterus. The name of the medical condition is big and long and not particularly exciting. Being a mom meant a lot to me, so much to me." Tears filled her eyes. She gestured toward Victoria. "I wanted a baby—your baby."

I rubbed my index fingers along my eyebrows and tried to think through what she was saying. We'd been together long enough that kids, marriage, all of it had come up at some point. She'd wanted to be a nurse and a mother. For her, there'd been no question of whether we'd have kids, just when. "You can't have kids?"

"It's not quite that simple." She scooped up her tears. "I mean, nowadays I could get a surrogate, probably, if I could afford it." She took a deep, shaky breath. "We could have gotten a surrogate back then if we could have afforded it."

Both our fathers had been doctors. My mother had worked part-time as a lawyer. "We could have found a way to afford it."

"Probably, yeah." Katie sniffed. "But the news, well, it put me in a tailspin. We'd always talked about having kids. The thought of never having that, of denying you that, I just...I couldn't get my head wrapped around it." She made a winding motion with her finger at her temple. "The more I thought about it, the more determined I was to give you a chance at finding that with someone else."

All of her words were landing, but I couldn't get any of them to stick. I wouldn't have been able to leave the way she did. There was too much fight in me. If she'd said something, I'd have argued with her, tried to make her see sense, told her none of it mattered if we were together. The time for that was long gone.

My conversation with Emily months ago resurfaced. She'd said she hadn't loved her high school boyfriend enough to make it work. And Katie hadn't loved me enough to make our relationship work.

Maybe Mia didn't either. But she'd been honest and up front about her issues. I'd never questioned her honesty, even when it hadn't been what I'd wanted to hear.

"You hid your diagnosis from me."

"I hid it from everyone." She wiped her eyes. "Well, I hid it from everyone *here*. Every boyfriend after you got the 'I don't want kids' speech. I convinced myself I didn't want them. Can't have them. Don't want them." A bitter chuckle escaped her lips.

She'd always been stubborn. That quality was the one thing I'd seen and believed about her departure. Once she decided she was leaving, there hadn't been anything I could do to persuade her to stay.

"Then I got drunk with a friend back in October and told her the whole story of us. She convinced me to look you up on social media. Everything said you were single, and Mom said she had heard you weren't seeing anyone. So, I applied for a job back here. A lateral step, not even a promotion. On a whim. Just like that. I got here and you were seeing Danai, but then you asked Dad to help with the Mia situation. My return, your baby—the family we once planned together. It felt like fate."

Wow. The word bounced around my head, and I rubbed my face. "Fate?" I asked, squinting at her. Exhaustion and annoyance went to war for dominance. "You thought you'd show up and snatch me back like a lost toy? I don't know what happened to you eight years ago. I know what you're telling me now, but something doesn't quite add up for me. You know what I think it is? Eight years ago, you didn't know how good we had it. We were young. Our relationship was all we'd ever really known. You go out and see other things and then you decide, *oh hey, that guy back home wasn't so bad after all.*"

"I always knew how good we had it."

"But you left. You threw us away. For a long time, I let myself be lost. I chose relationships I knew weren't quite right for me. I see that now."

"We can get back what we had. All the pieces are here."

"We can't. We really can't. Maybe a year ago we could have tried, even nine months ago. But now? I...I can't go back. I want something else now. A different life."

"With her? But she left, Tyler. She did the same thing as me. Except she's left a baby behind. A baby. I'd never leave my child."

Mia left because she *needed* to go. Katie *chose* to leave. Mia *had* to go. "There's a lot you don't know."

"You'd give her a second chance, but not me?"

"If she stays away for eight years, her window might be closed too." I rose from my seat. "But I know for sure yours is sealed shut. Too much has happened." I shoved my hands into my pockets. "I'm sorry you can't have kids. I'm sorry you didn't tell me eight years ago or any of the years in between. It's too late for us."

In my pocket, my phone started to chime with email notifications. More online orders for the thrift store, probably. "You can either ask your dad to assign another nurse to me, or I can. But I don't want to make this harder on you than it needs to be." Without Mia as a barrier, I didn't want more of these conversations either. Whatever had been between us years ago had died off—love untended.

"I'll talk to him." She wiped at more tears as they slid down her cheeks.

Strange that Mia's tears made my heart clench and my chest ache, but I felt almost nothing at the sight of Katie's. I crossed to the door, and she eased her bag back onto her shoulder. When I opened the front entrance, Katie's hand rested on my shoulder, and then, on her toes, she kissed my cheek.

A cacophony of slamming car doors and scattered conversation hit me at the same moment the flashbulbs went off. Outside, news vans lined the street. Seemed impossible, but I'd missed their arrival. All week, I'd been so careful. The noise of the press echoed into the house, and Victoria put the lungs she'd inherited from her mother to work, screaming in rage at the disturbance.

Katie's hand stayed on my arm; her body positioned too close.

Far, far too close.

My heart pounded. For a moment, I didn't move, stunned by the booming chaos.

Well, rock bottom, here I come.

Chapter Twenty-Nine
Mia

For months, I hadn't worried about the flash of a camera or the roar of the press. In Little Falls, I wasn't doing anything interesting enough for the paparazzi to care at first, and then I'd stayed housebound once my pregnancy was obvious.

As soon as my leg emerged from the back of the car, my gut clenched in anticipation. Pasha's hand reached down to help me exit with something resembling grace. The baby weight was still heavy on my frame, but I didn't look as pregnant as I had a week ago.

Keeping my head down, I rushed toward the side entrance of the DA's office. My lawyer had gotten my deposition delayed in an effort to shield me from the press's attention. Apparently, someone at the office had leaked my new deposition date. There was always someone making a buck off my back.

Led by Pasha, my cluster of bodyguards kept the press at bay. The exclamations of shock and surprise over my appearance would have normally had me smiling. But the questions that followed hit like bullets.

Mia, are you pregnant? When are you due? Mia, is Tyler Sullivan the father? Mia, did you know Kenny Connors was assaulting other girls and women? Mia, why didn't you come forward earlier? Mia, have you reached out to the other victims? Mia, was the abortion you had a few years ago related to Kenny Connors?

Before getting out of the car, I'd put on my emotional armor, but the last question, just as I squeezed in the rear entrance, was like shrapnel wedging into my side, an infection waiting to happen.

Once inside the office, I took a deep breath and gave Pasha a wry smile. If only that interaction was the worst of it, this whole situation would be a breeze. Instead, I knew from the conversation with my lawyer last week that the deposition would be painful, eye-opening, and perhaps devastating. Would they tell me how many other women? I'd tried to research it online, but the case was closely guarded, and I couldn't find much. A few names, ones almost as big as mine, had been dropped like pebbles across the speculative blog posts and news articles. The tentacles of his reach slithered underneath too many deals, so many albums.

I'd thought the week I found out I was pregnant was long, but this week, since my mother had been banished from my inner circle, had beaten it by a thousand miles. Taryn and Rebecca had worked tirelessly alongside me to put the right people in place to manage the collapse. We'd cut Laura off from everything but her own personal bank accounts.

Judging by the funds in my accounts, Laura paid herself extremely well, especially in the weeks after the subpoena was issued. In the moments that weren't consumed with sorting out the mess left in the wake of firing my mother, I pored over the photos of Tyler on my phone and the few I'd managed to snap of our daughter. Calling Victoria my daughter still felt surreal. I'd spent nine months thinking of the baby as Tyler's alone. But I was trying out this new thought process, determining whether it should stick.

As soon as my thoughts drifted to him, I remembered I'd forgotten to tell him the deposition had been moved to today. My fingers had hovered over the keyboard of my phone so many times in the last week, determined to text him, determined not to crack open the window in case the breeze of my feelings swept us both away.

I couldn't go back unless I was sure I could be a good parent, the right parent for Victoria. While it felt as though Tyler was the only person capable of stitching my heart together, I couldn't let my emotions overrule my head. A good mom. The best mom. Anything less than that wasn't enough.

In the DA's office, I insisted on having Pasha in the room for the deposition. The prosecutor had grimaced and then said, "I understand. You probably don't go in many rooms without a witness or protection, right?"

"Sure...well...price of fame." I grabbed my hair and laid it across my shoulder.

"The common thread in all these depositions has been, not necessarily fame, but the need to have someone close." He eased into one of the chairs on the other side of the table and looked to her lawyer, to Pasha. "For a lot of the girls, it's their mom or their dad. For others, like you, it's a bodyguard or a boyfriend, or the like."

"Are there a lot of us?" I whispered.

"He started working at the company when he was twenty-two. He's fifty-one now. Twenty-nine years of having some form of influence in the entertainment industry."

"Will you need me to testify?" I braided the tips of my hair, my fingers working furiously. Tyler. Lollipops. His hand gripping mine. I wanted it all. Why hadn't I at least grabbed one of his favorite jasmine ones? I could breathe in the scent right now and gather my strength.

"Well," he said, drawing his lined paper close, "we'll see what you have to say. We haven't charged him with anything yet. We're gathering evidence, talking to victims and witnesses, figuring out the best course of action."

"How did this...how did you know to investigate?"

He seemed to weigh his words before speaking. "The mother of his latest victim came forward."

"The mother?"

"Yes."

"The mom went to the police and reported him? Did the...did the daughter know?"

"Yes. Her daughter was afraid of what would happen, but her mother has been really supportive of her story."

Supportive. "That sounds nice."

"Are you ready to tell me your version of events?" A ghost of a smile flickered across his face.

"Yeah," I said, letting my hands fall into my lap. "I am."

On the way out of the office, I turned on my phone, which then exploded with notifications. I silenced everything without looking at them. Whatever the world thought of how I acted or what I looked like wasn't important right now. There was one person I desperately wanted to talk to, but I couldn't reach out to him. If I asked, he'd come. A bigger complication.

Turning to Pasha as we got closer to exiting the office, I said, "It was a mom that blew the whistle. Can you believe it?"

"Yes." Pasha's body was tense and alert as we neared the rear door.

"You can believe that?"

"Good parents put daughter first. Not career. Not money." His hand rested on the small of my back as we paused at the door. "Child not always know what they need. This mother know her daughter need protected. So, she protect. Shield daughter, not make daughter shield." The curving motion of his shoulders made it look as though he was encircling some absent person.

Tears sprung to my eyes at the simplicity of his words. If I went back to Victoria and Tyler, that was the kind of mother I wanted to be—one who put her daughter's well-being above everything else. I would testify against Kenny if it came to that, so no one else had to worry about protecting their daughter from him.

I was beginning to realize what had bothered me about our silence all these years. He'd gotten away with it, yes. But if we'd come forward, if every woman who suffered such an incredible violation came forward, maybe there'd be less and less of them. You had to hope, right? Throw open the doors and let the light in. Don't let the monsters skulk around under the cover of darkness.

Taking a deep breath, I gave Pasha the nod to throw open the exit door, hurling us back into the barrage of press. Through the sea of lenses, shouted questions, and microphones nudging me to say something, we arrived at the car. I collapsed into the back and breathed a sigh of relief. Then, a few of the questions sank in.

Had I heard them right? Digging around in my purse, I found my phone. From the front, Pasha tried to catch my eye.

"Okay?" he asked.

"Mmm..." I responded as I scrolled through the notifications and the car lurched forward. So many stupid people commenting on things they didn't understand.

The video of Tyler outside his house was the worst bit. I hadn't seen him in a week. So long. An eternity. After the third time I played it, the reality of the scene hit me. Victoria's cry in the background, the smugness splashed across Katie as she came down from kissing his cheek, the shock on Tyler's face. Apparently, I should have sent him a warning text after all. Sometimes I forgot how naïve he was about the press.

One week. It had taken Katie one week to wedge herself into Tyler's life. I'd expected it, but seeing it with my own eyes still stung. My hand shook, and I wanted to scream at my phone. He was mine. Other people could look at him, envy me, but they weren't supposed to touch. No touching.

Except, he wasn't mine anymore. I forfeited that right when I left. It wasn't reasonable to ask him to wait forever, even if I wanted him to.

A cold sweat broke out across my back. Pasha navigated Nashville's streets, headed toward my house, and my brain spun with the reality of what I'd done. Just like Katie, I'd left him. Would I turn up on his doorstep eight years from now trying to reclaim my place? Victoria would be eight. I'd have missed *eight years*. All those firsts. I was probably missing some already. The progression of a baby from bundle to walker would be lost.

As I came through the front door, Taryn peered around the island. "God, you're so pale. It was that bad? I told you I'd come with you."

Rebecca appeared at Taryn's shoulder. "Mia, you look like you're going to puke."

"Have you been following the news? My mentions are out of control." My hand rested on my stomach, and if I was being honest, I felt a bit like I might lose the little I'd eaten today all over the floor.

"We saw a few things." Taryn hedged as she exchanged a silent look with Rebecca.

"Was one of those things Tyler being assaulted by his ex-girlfriend?"

"Assaulted?" Rebecca raised her eyebrows.

"Sure. There's no way he *wanted* her to do that. Tyler doesn't have a mean bone in his body. He would *never* have wanted me to see that, probably didn't even want her to do that."

But someday, he'd want someone to touch him like Katie had, would want more than a chaste kiss on the cheek in front of his house. My stomach clenched. Tyler had warned me that regret was desperate and ugly.

"You know him best," Rebecca said. "I don't want to be an asshole, Mia, but if you want to be with him, you gotta keep in mind he's not going to wait around forever."

"It's been a week." My voice was tight. "That's hardly forever." My mind swung back to the other comments I'd seen as I'd scrolled through. "I need to send him some bodyguards. He's got my baby, and there are so many nutjobs out there." I snatched the remote off the island and pointed it at the TV over the fireplace. "Do you think the press is still camped out at his house?"

Taryn and Rebecca were quiet behind me as I searched all the gossip channels.

Then he was there, almost as large as life on the screen. My heart thumped in response, and a rush of love followed. Was there a better sight in all of the world? All of the times he'd made my heart ache played on repeat in my mind—in the hospital, cradling our baby, knowing he'd protect me.

Katie slithered off him, demurring *no comment* like she had something to say. Even through the screen, Tyler's annoyance was clear.

The vultures with cameras and microphones closed in on Tyler, obscuring the view of Katie as she left. I needed to send protection to him, maybe a PR person. The press would tear into him relentlessly, and the more anyone fed them, the hungrier they became.

For a moment, he looked overwhelmed and seemed to be searching the crowd for something or someone. Then he took a deep breath, and I could see him gearing up, preparing himself. I'd told him if the press came, he could say whatever he wanted. But I hadn't thought he'd bother and that he knew better. No words would ever be enough to fill their hunger.

"Look," he said. "If you'll quiet down for a second, I'll make a statement, but I'm not taking questions. You get what you get, and then I'm done talking about all this." He held up a hand, and the crowd quieted. "Mia's not here. I'm guessing you all know where she is since *you're* here. You're not going to get anything negative or salacious. That doesn't exist in this situation. When you're lucky enough to love someone and to have that love returned, you protect them, you protect that relationship. You protect it with everything in you. I completely and totally support what Mia is doing in Nashville. She's incredibly brave for speaking the truth and for bringing all the awfulness into the light. I believe her. I believe all of them. That's all I have to say." He gave a wave and turned toward the closed door behind him.

When he opened it, Victoria started up another cry. Without a backward glance, he closed the door tight, sealing them off.

At the entrance, the reporters burst into another round of questions.

Is that Mia's baby? Tyler, is Mia pregnant, or is that your baby in there? Are you two still together? Why aren't you and the baby in Nashville?

The feed cut out.

"Oh, my God," Taryn and Rebecca breathed in unison behind me.

"I know, all of those reporters are hounding him." My heart beat a drum solo in my chest.

"But what he said..." Taryn murmured. "I think I'm swooning over a guy. Rebecca, is this what swooning feels like?"

"If I wasn't swooning myself, I'd be insulted right now."

"I shouldn't have left him, right? That's what you're telling me." I put my head in my hands and sank into the closest recliner. "God, I miss him. Seeing him on the screen, it's like getting a taste of a drug you thought you might be able to kick and realizing you can't do it."

"Why did you leave him?" Rebecca asked.

I was surprised Taryn hadn't told her. We'd had a long talk about it the other night when we'd been up late trying to sort out my finances. "I don't know how to be a mother."

"Oh, honey." Rebecca came around the chairs and sank into the one opposite me. "No one knows how to be a mother. Everyone is a novice with their first child. Everyone."

"That's not good enough." I shook my head and stared at Rebecca. "You know what my mother has been like. What if I turn out to be just like her?"

With a sigh, Rebecca took my hands in hers. "Close your eyes."

"Close my eyes?" I gave her a wary glance.

"Yes. Trust me." Rebecca smiled.

Once my eyes were closed, I took a deep, centering breath. The breathing was a coping mechanism my mother had taught me when I'd first gotten famous. Remembering my mother hadn't been all bad wasn't what I needed right now. Maybe she hadn't been all bad, but she'd been bad enough.

"Five years from now, if you could have anything you wanted, anything—what would it be?"

"Anything?" My voice cracked.

"What do *you* want, Mia?"

Tears slipped down my cheeks, and I wasn't sure I could speak the words out loud around the lump in my throat.

"You *can* be happy, Mia." Rebecca cupped my face and drew me close. "But you have to know what you want, and then we need to take the steps to get you there. Taryn and I will help you get there."

"I want Tyler. I want my baby. I want to know I can be a good mom." A sob escaped, and Rebecca pulled me close. Taryn's arms wrapped around us both, and her soothing sounds circled us all.

"Will you go to therapy, Mia? I think we can get you there, but we're gonna need help," Taryn said.

"I don't want to turn out like Katie or like my mother. I don't want to regret her or him or any of this." I sobbed.

"I know a person," Pasha said from the door.

I hadn't realized Pasha had come into the house. Someone else must be at the gate to the property. We were expecting an onslaught of press now that I'd inadvertently revealed my condition at the deposition, and since Tyler was harboring a baby, I was sure the crush of curiosity would be worse.

"You went to therapy?" I sniffed, taking a tissue from Taryn's outstretched hand.

"Yes. Someone I love die. I need help. I go. Very good. You like her." Pasha tugged his wallet out of his pants and removed a card.

"The choice is yours, Mia." Rebecca took it and flipped it between her fingers. "But I think if what you want is Tyler, Victoria, and to know if you're capable of being a good mother, then I think this is the first step."

Tears flooded my vision as I looked between Taryn, Rebecca, and Pasha. "Make the call," I whispered. "I don't want to live like this anymore."

Chapter Thirty

Tyler

When the knock sounded on the door, I froze for a second, waiting to see whether the noise would wake Victoria from her nap. She liked her sleep. I shut her bedroom door tight and then checked the peephole. Gerald, one of two bodyguards Mia had sent, was out there, so whoever was knocking had to be approved.

She'd been gone almost four months. Four months since I'd seen her in person. Four months since I'd heard her whisper in my ear just before sleep took over. Four months since she'd held our daughter.

I had to be careful about answering the door even with a bodyguard, about navigating around town with our daughter. Whenever Mia came to New York State for anything, the press assumed she'd be coming here as well. They'd camp out on my doorstep, and I'd either be housebound, or I'd be stuck at a family member's place until it was clear she wouldn't appear. The reports in the press were a mixture of vitriol toward Mia for abandoning me and Victoria, understanding over the stress of the trial, and sprawling narratives about secret meetings between the three of us. There'd been no meetings.

But I wouldn't call us out of touch either.

"Grady," I said, swinging the door back. Gerald kept his gaze focused on the street, scanning for trouble, ignoring our exchange. I'd thought Pasha was a man of few words, but Gerald had him beat.

I peered around Grady, trying to determine if he'd come alone or if Maggie was somewhere behind him. Although Grady had been re-assigned to New York, he'd been spending a lot of time traveling to Nashville to meet artists, executives and so forth. He'd told me once that the traveling was a waste of money. The label could do so much virtually, but they were in a PR nightmare with Kenny Connors and needed to soothe old wounds in person. Mia trusted Grady, and he'd been in the right place at the right time. It meant a lot of responsibility was being loaded onto his broad shoulders.

"Mind if I come in for a moment?" he asked, an envelope in his hands.

"No, yeah, of course. Victoria's sleeping, so we'll have to keep it down." I moved back to let him in the house. "Everything okay?"

"Yeah," Grady said with a smile. "Just playing the middleman again." He waved the envelope and slid it onto the island.

"That's from Mia?" I snatched it off the granite surface and ripped it open. Inside was a USB stick. I frowned and turned it over.

"Files. From her new album. She wanted you to hear them before anyone else." Grady took one of the stools at the island and straddled it. "She's written some fucking brilliant stuff."

"Yeah?" I clutched the stick in my hand and wished Victoria was awake so I could play them right now.

"You two haven't talked in person? Email? Text messages? Nothing?" Grady raised his eyebrows. "You're still the person she talks about the most. That and music. But the two are so closely linked right now, what with the album and all."

We hadn't spoken in person, not once since she left. I had social media accounts set up under an alias. The privacy settings were tight, and there was only one follower, who called herself theoriginalpretty-boylover. Mia's alias account she'd made up while she was living with me was alive and well. She never posted, but she watched everything I uploaded, sometimes multiple times.

Mostly, I stuck to Victoria's milestones and things I thought Mia might wish she'd seen. Occasionally, I'd film myself, and I'd fill the video with inside jokes and rambling stories to make her laugh. Maybe she needed some lightness with all the darkness she faced.

When I'd given her the link to the account, I'd done it through a letter I'd sent with Grady. I'd written the letter about five times before I thought I'd struck the right note. Having her return to us had to be because she wanted to, because we were the life she was choosing, but I struggled not to present a case, to argue, to persuade. In the end, all my note had said was, *In case it might help to know*, and I'd signed it with love.

To my surprise, the next time Grady had come to town, he'd had a letter from her for me. She'd written about her mother, about going to therapy, about missing me but not feeling ready yet, about her plans for the future, about the album. Pages and pages of feelings scrawled in her handwriting that must have made her hand ache. My heart had ached reading it. I'd almost memorized it now.

Every time missing her got to be too much to bear, prodded me to do something rash or stupid, I read it. She was taking control of her life, and I clung onto the pride that swept over every time I read her words. Staying with me, having me step into Laura's shoes, sticking Band-Aids on all her feelings would have been the easier thing to do. Instead, she was taking the hardest, most difficult path.

I was praying that path led her back to us. But I couldn't be sure until she either showed up or didn't. The wait was excruciating, but I didn't resent her for it.

"Are these songs about..." I cleared my throat. I wasn't sure what I wanted to say. Me? Victoria? Her mother? The life she wanted? How much was I meant to read into the lyrics if she needed me to hear them first?

Panic squeezed my chest that she might be saying goodbye in these songs. Her last and only letter had been two months ago. A lot could happen in two months. She'd never made any promises.

When she'd lived with me, I'd spent countless hours listening to her dissect lyrics from her favorite songwriters and artists, her voice breathless with excitement and enthusiasm. To her, every phrase, every word meant something. She loved putting Easter eggs in her own lyrics and videos for super fans to find. There was no doubt I'd ponder what she'd written for days, weeks, but I prayed it wouldn't be years.

"She didn't want me to tell you anything—she wanted you to listen."

"How's she doing? Really? I've been following the trial on the news, and it's..." *Horrific.*

"Rumors swirled about Kenny for years. Whispers. People implying things. Never anything definite." Grady rubbed his face and leaned on the island. "No one ever said it had happened to them. It was a friend of a friend of a friend. But it sounds like most of the women didn't say anything at all. Did Mia ever talk to you about him?"

I'd read or watched everything I could find on the trial. Those women were being crucified for their silence. Mia's sweeping speech at a women's rights march had played on my laptop for days after she made it. How could women win in a system where they were vilified for coming forward and equally so for staying silent? Give women the space to speak their truth and then believe them.

Her voice had cracked and broken at the end, and I'd yearned to be there for her, to be standing behind her, helping to keep her up. But I supposed the point of all this was about her learning to stand on her own feet, keep herself afloat. She'd let other people both hold her up and keep her down for too long.

"No. Not really." I sighed, grabbed a beer from the fridge, and passed one to Grady. "I knew something happened, but any time I tried to prod, she shut me down."

"The whole thing is just..."

The word *awful* hung between us.

"Yeah, it is," I agreed.

"She's reached out to a bunch of the other women and started a support group with her therapist." Grady picked at the label on his beer bottle.

My heart expanded in response. I remembered when she'd come to my trailer after seeing the producer in Nashville, how confused and vulnerable she'd been. Look at her now—support groups, therapy, and lifting those other girls and women up to the surface so they could all take a deep, healing breath. I was so fucking *proud* of her.

"You know," Grady said. "Laura always made Mia seem like she was unstable. And in the industry, Mia had a reputation for being difficult. When she asked to work with me, people warned me off—said she was too much. I think it was Laura who was too much. Mia just let her run her life."

"Mia's not difficult," I said with a shake of my head. "But I can't imagine what would have happened to her if she'd stayed in that toxic partnership with her mother."

We both sat in silence, drinking our beers. I glanced at the clock. Victoria probably wouldn't wake up for another half an hour. Could I play the songs low and risk her angry scream, or should I wait until she was awake, but my attention was divided?

"I'll have to come back tomorrow and get that USB from you." Tipping back the rest of his beer, Grady rose from the island. "Press sniffing around here all the time, so we can't be too careful. Oh, and listen to the whole thing from start to finish. No jumping around. The album has a great narrative through-line. One of the best, if you ask me." He grinned and gave a wave as he let himself out.

I wondered when the press would fade away. If she never came back, would they lose interest, or would Victoria always be dogged by people hoping to catch a taste of Mia?

I turned the USB over and over. Headphones. I needed headphones. Would she have left some here? After going to the master bedroom in the basement, I searched the closet and all the drawers. I'd almost given up when a stray pair of bright-pink earbuds peeked out from the cupboard in the en suite. Sweet relief.

Snatching them from the wooden surface, I raced up the stairs. With the video baby monitor perched in front of me, I slipped the USB into the computer and wedged the earbuds in tight enough to block out everything else. If Victoria cried, I could see her on the monitor.

Before I pressed play, I stared at the track list. Eighteen in total. None of them were named. I had no idea what waited for me on the other side of this album. Would it be a clear sign she was working her way back, or was she ready to let me go instead? There was no note with the USB stick, so it was up to me to take what I knew about her, what I'd learned about writing songs, and to come up with the right answer. My heart hammered.

What would it be?

With a deep breath, I tapped the mouse to play the first song.

Chapter Thirty-One

Mia

I had written him an album. Well, that wasn't completely true. The first few songs were more about my childhood, or lack of it, and my relationship with my mother. Grady had called the album an awakening. By the end, the songs were filled with so much hope and love and joy, I'd wanted to scream the lyrics from the rooftops. I'd never felt so sure of what I wanted and needed.

When I'd asked Grady to deliver the files to Tyler, I'd considered penning another epic letter to accompany it. But I didn't think I could have expressed myself more clearly than I had in my music. I laid my true self bare to him, and when the album released in a couple of months, I'd be exposed to the world.

Maybe not wise. People were mean. Honesty wasn't easy. For the first time, my fans would be getting me unfiltered, without my mother leaning over my shoulder whispering, *what will people think?* as though other peoples' opinions were the most important to consider. I'd let the weight of those words sink my conviction, my gut feeling about what was right, and those words had almost cost me Tyler and Victoria.

Tyler.

The beauty of Tyler, as I'd come to realize the last few months without him, was his ability to adapt. From the minute I'd walked into his shop almost a year ago, he'd steered through every intersection and curve in my mood as though he'd been given a map to my soul. The video he posted after listening to the album only solidified my feelings, not that I needed confirmation.

My love for him was a steel rod through my body, unbreakable, unbendable, propping me up during my toughest moments. The power of unconditional love had surprised me. Even though we hadn't been together, at every turn, I'd known he was out in the world cheering for me. I never doubted his commitment, even as I'd been trying to figure out if I was capable of returning it.

In the video he posted about the album, he'd taken notes—*notes on my songs*—and he understood all the nuances, things I never thought anyone would get, about the songs, about me. As much as writing the lyrics had been cathartic, listening to him pull them apart and realizing he *saw me and still loved me* was a gift I never anticipated. At the end of his video, he held Victoria up to his camera and said they'd be waiting when I was ready to come home.

Home.

I owned a lot of houses, but I'd never had a home until him, until *them*. Each therapy session had gotten me closer and closer to feeling capable, worthy, of what he was offering. Five months of tearing myself apart and stitching myself together had led me here—to Little Falls, to my family.

Pasha nudged my arm from the driver's seat, and I tore my gaze from the snowy front door of Tyler's store. I hadn't told Tyler I was coming, but it was four days before Christmas, and today was his birthday.

"Ready?" Pasha asked, his accent still thick, but his English had improved tenfold with all of the time he'd spent as my favorite bodyguard. Someday, I hoped I'd see him happy, instead of brooding and stoic.

"There's no such thing as perfect," I reminded myself as I twisted the rings on my fingers. Whenever I got anxious in therapy about being a good partner to Tyler or a good parent to Victoria, those words were my lifeline. "If I screw up, I own it, and we figure out how to move forward."

Beside me, Pasha said nothing. *Own it.* Laura had forgotten that step every time she'd screwed up. Who was to blame? Anyone and everyone but her.

We'd met in one therapy session to disastrous results. Among other things, my mother had said I needed to grow a thicker skin, and if I thought I was the only woman who'd ever been wronged by a man, Laura could fill me in on just how bad it could be. My head had spun at the lunacy, the self-centered importance. The trial, the women's march, my support group, even some of the songs on the album were rooted in too many women having gone through the things I had suffered.

I knew I wasn't special, but it had taken that moment to make me realize our mother-daughter bond lived in the dirt of conflict and competition. Nothing could grow there. That dirt was filled with toxins. Before Tyler, before therapy, deep down I would have thought my mother knew best, and I'd have grown a thicker skin, sealed my emotions tighter. Not anymore.

I didn't want to wilt. I wanted to bloom.

"Do you think anyone else is in there?" I slid a ring off my index finger and pushed it back on. Anxiety zipped through at the realization I hadn't talked to Tyler for months. *Months.* What had he told me about love? Untended, it withered and died.

"We here fifteen minutes. No customers." He glanced at his phone. "Gerald says they alone."

"I should just go in, right? He'll be happy to see me, right?" I heaped my hair onto my shoulder and toyed with the ends. "What if he's not happy to see me?"

"Only question right now. Are *you* ready?"

Before we'd arrived in the parking lot, I'd been sure surprising him was the best idea. Happy Birthday! Merry Christmas! We could be each other's presents.

Faced with entering the building, I was second-guessing my impulsiveness. I'd left him and his love untended, and while leaving had felt as necessary as returning did now, I couldn't open my door.

"I'm ready," I said. "But what if he's angry with me for being gone this long?" He hadn't given me any indication he felt that way, but I couldn't imagine not being angry if our roles were reversed.

"Own it. Move forward." His lips twitched, and he patted my leg. "You need space. He give you. You think he angry." He placed his hand over his heart. "I think he heartbroken, and you," he tried to catch my gaze, "coming back can mend together."

"You think he'll forgive me?"

"It me? Nothing to forgive. Confused. Need time. Come back. All's well."

All's well. I wanted to believe it could be that simple. If I never went in, I'd never know, and I'd spent all these months yearning to be here. I took a deep breath and released it slowly. "I'm going in."

"Want me to come?"

"No." A chuckle escaped. "If you could get Gerald to make himself disappear, that'd be awesome too. No need for anyone else to witness this potential disaster."

Once I was out of the car, I brushed my hands down my skirt, and it swished around my thighs. Maybe I should have worn something warmer, but it was too late now. I opened the door, and the doorbell above signaled my arrival. From the racks of clothes near the back, I could just spot the top of Tyler's head. Normally when he wasn't busy, he'd be in the back stitching together some masterpiece. Not today.

My heart thumped, and my palms became slick with sweat.

"Be with you in a minute," his deep tenor called out.

His voice, in person. Oh, God, I loved that sound. my stomach dipped. I was really here. I took another deep, steadying breath, but I didn't call back to him. In my head, we would have locked eyes from the moment I entered, but of course, reality never went quite as expected.

When he rounded the rack of clothes, an ugly checkered shirt clutched in his hand, he glanced in my direction and did a double take before stumbling slightly. His hand went to the back of his neck as he righted himself, and he stared.

"Oh, wow. Mia." My name was a rough almost whisper. "You're here." The reverence with which he said it made my stomach clench, and the way his shoulders rose as though I'd lifted a weight off him made my heart ache.

"Surprise," I said, afraid I looked as stunned as him. He'd missed me, and I breathed a sigh of relief he wasn't hiding his feelings.

The glib videos he'd posted had been a front. Maybe he'd been as miserable as me. The videos had been a blessing and a curse. I'd missed him as though I'd cut off a limb, but seeing him happy and joking had sliced into my sadness, causing it to ooze everywhere. Sometimes, I'd wondered if he was happier without me.

A few times my fingers had hovered over the comment icon. Did I dare ask?

I didn't have to wonder anymore. The old familiar tension hummed in the air, a shock to my system. The air was alive. To love someone and to have it so clearly returned was a revelation.

"Happy birthday, Pretty Boy."

He closed the distance between us until there were only a couple of feet separating us. "Are you..." He scanned me from head to toe, longing settling over his face. "Are you my present?" His voice was hoarse.

"Would you like that?" Goose bumps rose on my arms, and I clenched my thighs at the lick of desire.

A deep chuckle emerged from his chest, and his hand smoothed my hair before drawing me closer. "For the first time in my life, I don't mind if my birthday and Christmas present are the same. You're the...best..." He kissed my forehead. "Present." He pressed his lips to my temple. "Ever." He buried his head in my neck and breathed me in. "I can't believe you're here."

"Where's Victoria?" I whispered, clutching onto his broad back.

"My mom has her." He kept his head buried in my neck, his hands running along my body as though he was trying to remember every curve. "Gerald knew you were coming to New York State, so we keep Victoria under lock and key in case the press swarms." A chuckle rumbled through him. "I guess they've given up."

"But you didn't?" I toyed with the tips of his hair, and the scent of jasmine surrounded us. No matter how many jasmine-scented things I bought, none of them quite smelled like him.

"You gave me enough to keep hope alive—the letter, the album, your speech at the women's march where you said meeting me had changed your life." His lips brushed against my shoulder.

"You're not mad at me?"

His shoulders tensed under my fingers, and he emerged from my neck to press his forehead to mine.

"Never to each other," I whispered, afraid he wouldn't tell me the truth. We had a lot to talk about, but this question was the one weighing heaviest on my mind.

"Mad isn't the right word." He sighed and pressed his lips to my forehead. "I knew you needed to figure everything out. Was it hard? Yeah. Incredibly hard sometimes to not be part of the process. Did I wish you could have done it differently? Yep." He gave me a small smile. "But I knew if you came back, you'd be here to stay. I was never mad, Mia. You never lied to me. There was work to be done for you to be sure about what you wanted, and you did the work. Quite frankly, watching you give that speech at the march, reading your testimony at the trial. It was—I don't think I've ever been prouder of anyone. You've turned yourself into a beacon of hope for other women. You're incredible."

"Really?"

"I wish you could see yourself like I see you. The girl I met last October doesn't exist anymore. You've become a force in the world, and not just for your music, but for your principles and conviction and your desire to help other women. Victoria is going to see the things you've done, and she'll be in awe of what a strong mom she has."

His words settled, and they meant more than I'd ever be able to tell him. My moments of pride in my mother were few and far between. In that final meeting with Kenny, maybe. But then I'd discovered she'd worked alongside Kenny to rob me of choices. Any pride I felt had been squashed.

To realize my daughter might examine something I'd done and think with pride, *That's my mom*, was almost more than I could comprehend.

"I don't have all the answers yet," I admitted. "But I want to work on the rest of them with you and her as a family." The word was foreign on my lips. Before Tyler, the closest I'd come was my grandmother, but our connection had been complicated by my mother's resentment and my father's abandonment. "Can we go get her and go home?"

He pressed his lips to mine, and I relaxed into him, tugging him closer, threading my fingers through his short strands. When we broke apart, he slipped his hand into mine, leading me toward the door.

"Last time I talked to Grady, he said you were still deciding on an album title. Did you pick one yet?"

"Yeah, we did." A smile broke out across my face. We'd settled on the name of the last song on the album, the one I'd written about Tyler. "Mending Hearts. We've called the album Mending Hearts."

His eyes softened, and it was clear he understood I'd named it after him, after his ability to stitch together things that seemed beyond repair.

"I love it," he said and kissed my temple. "We touring?"

I bit my lip and walked through the front door he held open. Pasha stood outside the car, a smile on his face. "A tour has to be scheduled so far in advance," I said. "And I wasn't sure how you'd feel...but I went ahead and booked a few venues. Are you up for it? I can cancel."

"All I need is you and Victoria." He squeezed my hand. "Wherever that is, that's where I'll be. On a tour bus, in a hotel, in a house, it doesn't matter. If I've got the two of you, I've got everything I need. You want to tour? We'll figure it out."

My heart swelled and threatened to burst from my chest. How had I ever thought I'd be able to resist him? Why had I even bothered to try? "I won the life partner lottery."

"They have one of those? I'll have to sign up next time." His lips twitched in amusement.

"Next time?" I smacked his arm and laughed.

He stopped a few feet from Pasha and framed my face. "Nah," he said. "You're it for me. This time, next time, every time." His lips grazed mine in the sweetest, tenderest kiss that made my insides turn to goo.

Pasha cleared his throat and opened the rear door. "I tell Gerald I drive you both home. He meet us there with car and baby."

On impulse, I released Tyler and latched onto Pasha's waist to hug him. Logistics weren't always my strong point, and he never let me down. "Thank you."

"Happy?" Pasha murmured.

"The happiest," I sighed. "Take me home, Pasha. I finally understand what that means."

Not ready to say goodbye to Mia and Tyler? Download the bonus chapters here: https://bookhip.com/QDAXMZG

Trent and Emily are next – read Healing Hearts here: https://mybook.to/HealingHearts2025

What else have I written?

Bellerive Royals Series – Interconnected standalones

Fake Crown

Scarred Crown

Heavy Crown

Fallen Crown

Tucker Billionaires – Interconnected standalones

Temporary Love

New Adult Sports

Saving Us

Fake Crown

Donaghey Brothers Series – Romantic suspense

Retribution

Resurrection

Redemption

Little Falls Series – Small Town Romance

Rival Hearts

Mending Hearts

Healing Hearts

Guarded Hearts

First Date Challenge – loosely linked to the same world – for maximum enjoyment, read after Book 2

Adult Contemporary Romance

When Stars Fall

Miss Matched

Acknowledgements
My Personal Love Notes

As with any book, I'm thankful for such a supportive partner and my understanding children. Sometimes I'm lost in a book idea or writing a chapter when I'm sure they'd like my attention elsewhere. Hopefully, seeing my pursue my dreams has a net positive impact.

I'm really grateful to my proofreaders, Isabella Bauer, Angela at Proof Positive, and Kristina at Red Adept whose keen eyes caught a lot of my mistakes.

Thank you to the Bookish Girls who gave me a lot of content ideas for this book for social media, and to Pretty Little Images that made some wonderful teasers for this series.

Thanks to my cover designer, Shannon Passmore, who is always really patient with me. Covers are probably one of the most stressful parts of this job for me and she makes it much easier!

About Wendy Million/W. Million

Wendy Million is a high school teacher whose award winning contemporary romances about strong women and troubled men have captivated her loyal readers.

Writing as Wendy Million, she is the author of the romantic suspense series *The Donaghey Brothers,* as well as the contemporary second chance romances, *When Stars Fall*, and *Miss Matched*.

Writing as W. Million, she's the author of the *Bellerive Royals* series, the *Little Falls* series, and the *Tucker Billionaires* series.

When not writing, Wendy enjoys spending time in or around the water. She lives in Ontario, Canada with two beautiful daughters, two cute pooches, and one handsome husband (who is grateful she doesn't need two of those).